Dead on Dartmoor

By Stephanie Austin

Dead in Devon
Dead on Dartmoor

Dead on Dartmoor

STEPHANIE AUSTIN

Allison & Busby Limited
11 Wardour Mews
London W1F 8AN
allisonandbusby.com

First published in Great Britain by Allison & Busby in 2019.

A CIP catalogue record for this book is available from
the British Library.

First Edition

ISBN 978-0-7490-2442-0

Typeset in 11/16 pt Sabon LT Pro by
Allison & Busby Ltd.

The paper used for this Allison & Busby publication
has been produced from trees that have been legally sourced
from well-managed and credibly certified forests.

Printed and bound by
CPI Group (UK) Ltd, Croydon, CR0 4YY

For Dad, who would have loved this

AUTHOR'S NOTE

The town of Ashburton is real, and people living there will recognise streets, shops, pubs, cafes and other places of good cheer mentioned in this book, but there are a few foggy areas around the town where fact and my imagination merge, places that will not be found on any map. For taking these liberties, I apologise.

CHAPTER ONE

A week before the murder, my van went up in flames.

It seemed fine in the morning, when I took the dogs out. I only had three to walk that day and I collected them in the van as usual, before their owners left for work, and drove them to the woods beyond the edge of town where they could romp around unfettered.

They raced ahead of me in the cool shade beneath the trees, sniffing at trails left by night-time creatures, snuffling at prints in the soft, dark mud. As I followed, they dashed off through the undergrowth, bursting from beneath the shadows onto sunlit grass and sending strutting black crows flapping into the air. Here, in open pasture, I could launch balls for them to chase. I could see up the valley, fields sweeping upward to the moor, green grass fading to tawny yellow and the granite knuckle of a distant tor. It was going to be another fine day.

Later I deposited two of the dogs back at their homes, using spare keys to let myself in.

I don't have a spare key for EB, because his mum is always waiting for him at home. But as we approached her front door, I could see a scrawled note taped to the wood. *Juno*, it read, *Alan taken to hospital with chest pain. I've gone with him in ambulance. Can you hang on to EB until I get back? I will ring you. Sorry. Elaine x*

EB waited patiently by my feet as I read the message, his overarching eyebrows twitching in confusion. He didn't seem to mind getting back into the van. I let him sit on the front seat with me instead of putting him in the back behind the wire grille where the dogs normally ride. He leant the weight of his warm little body against mine and I turned back to Ashburton, meandering between hedgerows in full green flourish.

It had been a long, hot summer that seemed as if it would never end, sunshine and blue skies lasting through September. But the swallows had flown, and although the sunny weather continued, the green treetops were brushed with bronze and gold; the leaves were on the turn.

I was forced to brake suddenly. A woman was in the road, standing perfectly still, a few inches of floral nightdress hanging down beneath her long blue dressing gown. Her hair was a silver halo but flattened at the back of her skull, as if it had not been brushed since her head left the pillow that morning. I pulled on the handbrake and climbed out, shutting the door on the muzzle of a curious EB. Despite the noise of the van's approach she seemed oblivious of my presence, staring up at the flickering light through the trees above her, at the shifting shadows, and murmuring quietly to herself.

'Hello,' I called out. 'Are you all right?' She turned at the sound of my voice, not by twisting her head, but by a series of tiny, rocking steps, until she had manoeuvred herself around to face me. Her eyes were blue, her skin rose petals crushed into a thousand tiny wrinkles. She would have been pretty once.

'Can I help you?' I asked.

She scowled at me, didn't answer. A few hundred yards further along the road was Oakdene, a care home for patients with dementia, and I reckoned I was looking at an escapee. 'Only, if you're going for a walk,' I went on reasonably, 'I think you'll need your slippers.'

She gazed down at feet wrapped in woolly bedsocks and wriggled her toes experimentally before returning her gaze to my face. It was an untroubled gaze, full of childlike innocence, as if all care, all stress, had been gently washed away. She reached out. For a moment I thought she was going to slap me, but instead she grabbed a handful of my curls, squeezing lightly with her fingers. 'All curly,' she breathed in delight, 'all red.'

All curly, all red – she'd just about summed up my hair.

'You're not Samantha,' she told me, although she didn't sound sure.

'No, I'm Juno. What's your name?'

'Marianne,' she declared after a moment's thought. 'Are we going in the little bus?'

I glanced back at the van. It was yellow with black writing on the sides. I suppose it didn't look unlike a small bus, except for EB frowning at us from behind the steering wheel.

'Why don't we?'

She allowed me to lead her to the passenger door and sit her in the seat, despite being hampered by EB,

11

who'd decided that any friend of mine must be a friend of his. Fortunately, Marianne didn't seem to mind an enthusiastic face licking, and responded with cries of rapture and much patting. In spite of the two of them, I managed to get her seat belt done up and headed for Oakdene, hoping to God that was where Marianne had come from. If she hadn't, I didn't have a clue where to take her next, and somehow I had the feeling that she wouldn't know either.

Thankfully, the next bend revealed two ladies in blue uniforms peering anxiously into the hedgerows as they scurried along, as if hoping to find something hidden amongst the brambles and blackberries. I stopped, flashed my lights and tooted at them. At the sight of my passenger one cried out in relief. 'Oh, thank God! Judith!'

Judith? What happened to Marianne?

The woman approaching on my side began talking as I wound the window down. The name badge pinned to her ample bosom identified her as Barbara. She was a comfy, little body and was slightly out of breath. 'Thank you so much! Where did you find her?'

'Not far,' I answered as Judith-Marianne climbed out with the help of her colleague, who was younger and taller, her hair scraped back to reveal a large, pale forehead. 'Has she gone walkabout before?'

'All the time, bless her! She keeps trying to find her way to her old home . . . Oxford,' she added in a whisper.

I'm not sure how many miles away Oxford is, but it's a long way from Ashburton.

I watched her depart without a backward glance to me or EB, her arm linked companionably with that of the care assistant, the two of them chatting amiably. 'She seems happy enough.'

'Oh, she's a sweetheart,' Barbara informed me. 'Anyway, thank you so much . . . um . . .'

'Juno.'

'Juno,' she repeated. She hesitated a moment, brows drawn together in a worried frown, her lips compressed in a line. 'I wonder . . . our boss doesn't know she's got out again. We don't want to see her locked in her room. I wonder if . . .'

'Your secret's safe with me.' I didn't know the boss of Oakdene and I certainly wasn't about to go round there causing trouble.

'Thank you,' she breathed and then hurried off after Judith-Marianne and her colleague.

'Life is full of strange little happenings,' I informed a mystified EB, watching them go, and we set off once again towards the town.

I was half an hour late arriving at *Old Nick's* because I'd driven home on the way to check my answering machine for any message from Elaine. She might not have been able to contact me on my mobile: the signal is dodgy on Dartmoor, to say the least.

There was no message. I wondered if EB had been fed before we went walkies this morning, or whether he was still awaiting his breakfast, so I stopped at the baker's in West Street and bought him a jumbo sausage roll.

Old Nick's has only been open for two months. The shop belonged to an elderly client of mine, Mr Nikolai, who lived in the flat above. He was an antiques dealer. Unfortunately,

Nick was a bit criminal around the edges and got himself murdered as a consequence. Why he decided to leave the entire property to me is still a mystery. I suppose he felt I'd earned it; a feeling not shared by members of his family.

Whatever, it is no longer the shabby, run-down old junk shop it once was, but is now freshly painted in pale green, its windows glossy, and *Old Nick's*, picked out in gold, swinging on the sign above the door. Each time I draw up outside it I cannot resist a tiny stab of pride and offer up a silent prayer of gratitude to cousin Brian, my one remaining relative, who'd come up with the cash for the makeover.

Unfortunately, no amount of cash could magically transport *Old Nick's* from Shadow Lane to North Street or East Street, where it needed to be to bring in the required customers. The little town of Ashburton is one of the four stannary towns on Dartmoor, where locally mined tin used to be stamped and assayed, and the townspeople are proud of its history. It also had a reputation for drunkenness. Nowadays it's a real tourist trap, with more antique shops than taverns; but *Old Nick's* is obstinately stuck around the corner from the scene of all the action. The only other businesses in Shadow Lane are a launderette and an undertaker, so there's not a lot of footfall. Generally, people who don't own washing machines are not in the market for the art, crafts and antiques which we sell, and those who need the services of an undertaker have lost interest in buying things altogether. I've placed a hopeful cafe board at the corner of the lane, pointing the way for customers. *Old Nick's: Art, Crafts, Books, Antiques and Collectibles.*

Another problem is that when Nick died and left me the shop, I already had a business of my own. Not exactly thriving, but it kept body and soul together. *Juno Browne, Domestic Goddess – Housework, Gardening, Home Help, Domestic Care, House-sitting, Pet-sitting, Dog walking. No job too small.* The legend is still proudly proclaimed on the sides of my van. I don't want, and can't afford, to give my business up: I'm too attached to some of my clients, and until there's sufficient income from the shop I can't even consider it – and that day, I fear, is a long way off. The stuff I sell is mostly bric-a-brac and the profits so far amount to pocket money, whilst the overheads for the shop are draining money I rely on to live.

One sensible move I could make, apart from just selling the property and pocketing the cash, would be to give up the flat I currently rent from Adam and Kate and move myself into the empty rooms above the shop. But I can't bring myself to do that. I'm not of a nervous disposition, but I just don't fancy living in the room where Nick was murdered. Not yet, anyway, not unless I have to.

The lights were on inside the shop when I arrived, and I could see Pat arranging her display of craft items on one of the wide windowsills. She gave me a little wave. I let EB trot into the shop ahead of me. He pattered over to her and began an exhaustive inspection of her trainers. She and her sister and brother-in-law run a sanctuary for abandoned pets and farm animals and her shoes are covered in information of great interest to the canine mind.

I was surprised to see her, though. 'I thought Sophie was opening up today.'

'It was her turn,' Pat stooped to stroke EB as he snuffled around her shoelaces, 'but she got offered a shift at The Dartmoor Lodge so I said I'd swop with her. I don't mind.'

Sophie and Pat man the shop on alternate days, instead of paying me rent. They get free space to sell the lovely things they make, and I get the time to keep my business going. The downside is that I don't get any money.

I've divided the shop into several rental units, hoping to attract a variety of sellers under one roof. Sophie and Pat take up the front of the shop, with two other units behind theirs. My own unit is at the back, in what was once the old storeroom. A sign in the corridor points to it: *This way for bric-a-brac, antiques and collectibles* – an optimistic way of describing a few sticks of junk furniture and an assortment of cheap knick-knacks.

As yet, the only other unit that is taken, and the only one paying me rent, belongs to Gavin, who sailed past the window on his bike at that moment, clad in pointy helmet and full racing gear, like a Lycra-covered stick insect on wheels. I don't know why he dresses up as if he's riding in the Tour de France, he only lives five minutes' ride away. What, I ask, is wrong with cycle clips?

Pat rolled her eyes at the sight of him. 'He's driving Sophie up the wall,' she whispered.

Gavin would be chaining up his bike in the alleyway at the side of the building and would not appear for at least five minutes; even so, I whispered. 'Is he?'

'He's got . . . you know . . . a *thing* about her,' she mouthed. 'He won't leave her alone, always hovering, looking over her shoulder when she's working.'

Sophie didn't really like painting in the shop as customers tended to watch her working, which she found unsettling. She was prepared to put up with it if it might lead to a sale, but wasn't keen on people who hung around too long, stood

16

too close, or chattered too much. She got all three with Gavin.

I could understand why she attracted him. Sophie was twenty-five but could pass for seventeen without make-up – and carried an air of childlike vulnerability. An orphaned seal pup abandoned on an ice floe could not melt your heart more easily than Sophie Child when she turned her big brown eyes on you. They even worked on me, for God's sake, so what chance did a poor sap like Gavin stand? Gavin, nineteen, but with all the emotional maturity of a twelve-year-old, was no match for her at all.

I looked down at the artwork that currently occupied Sophie's desk, the thick watercolour paper pinned at the corners. It was one of her hedgerow paintings: a drystone wall, its rough, mossy stones seen through a delicate tracery of wild flowers, some, as yet, white and unpainted.

Gavin appeared in the doorway, tall and bespectacled, carrying his silly helmet. EB let out a little yip and he scowled. I don't think Gavin liked dogs. 'Where's Sophie?' was his first question.

'Good morning, Gavin, and how are you?' I asked pleasantly.

'Isn't she coming in today?' Poor boy, his disappointment was obvious.

'She'll be in later. She's waitressing on breakfasts at The Dartmoor Lodge.'

'I don't know why she wants to bother with that,' he sneered loftily, 'wasting her talent.'

'She's gotta live, Gavin,' Pat told him flatly. 'We can't all go to the bank of Mum and Dad.'

He grunted, colouring slightly, and hurried through the door at the back of the shop and up the stairs, to change.

There was a bathroom on the landing, once part of Nick's flat, and we used his old kitchen for making refreshments.

'Now he'll be half an hour changing,' Pat complained, 'and then he'll come down with a cup of coffee, you'll see. Never offers to make one for anyone else.'

I couldn't hang around to find out; I had clients to get to. 'Look, Pat, I don't want to leave EB in the van, can I dump him with you? I can put him up in the kitchen if you'd rather.' But EB had already settled down by her chair and I handed her the slightly greasy paper bag containing his breakfast.

The Brownlows were a husband and wife team of GPs with three teenage children and a breezy, devil-may-care attitude to safety and hygiene in the home that I fervently hoped did not extend into their professional lives. I spent half of my allotted two hours washing dishes – the dishwasher was already full – before I could reach the kitchen surfaces I was paid to clean. But after I'd scraped brown gloop out of a gravy boat and cleared up spattered globules of pink icing after someone who'd made a cake, I attacked the waiting worktops and the floor, and left the kitchen looking sparkling; temporarily, at least. I just had time to call in on Maisie, check her agency carer had arrived to help her bathe and dress, change her bedclothes and stuff them in the laundry basket, before I headed out again. I did an hour's ironing for Simon the accountant who likes the collars of his shirts *just so*, and made it back to *Old Nick's* a little before midday.

Sophie had obviously arrived, her jacket and bag hanging on her chair; but there was no sign of her. Gavin was sitting at the table of his unit, hidden behind one of his graphic novels, and Pat was concentrating ferociously on counting stitches on her knitting needle. Neither of them spoke. There was, to say the least of it, an atmosphere.

EB skipped over to greet me, his claws clicking on the wooden floor.

'Where's Sophie?' I asked.

'Upstairs.' Pat directed a fierce glance at Gavin. 'Trying to rescue her painting.'

I flicked another look at Gavin, whose ears were suspiciously pink, and climbed the stairs to the kitchen. Sophie was by the sink, her painting laid out on one of the worktops, dabbing at it carefully with a sponge.

'What happened?'

'Bloody Gavin,' she responded, not looking up. 'He would bring me a cup of coffee. I told him I didn't want one. Then he put it down on my table and knocked it over with his sleeve.'

'Has he ruined it?'

'I'd already covered these with masking fluid,' she said, pointing at the white, unpainted stalks of cow parsley, 'so they were protected. But some of this background will need repainting.'

'Oh, Soph, it's taken you ages! What did you say to him?'

'Not much. I didn't need to.' She chuckled. 'Pat gave him a real ear-bashing.' She pushed her big red-framed specs up the bridge of her tiny nose. 'Well, you know what she's like.'

Pat was one of most generous and kind people I knew, but she seemed to have it in for Gavin. 'I hope she doesn't piss him off too much, I don't want him to leave. I need his rent money.'

'It's one of those days, I suppose.' Sophie blotted a tiny flower with a corner of paper towel. 'I was supposed to be taking some stuff to that new arts centre near Dartmeet. I got it all packed up, ready to go.' She turned her dark eyes on me mournfully. 'But I'll have to cancel, I can't get there now.'

'Why not?'

'Mum's had to work and has taken the car.'

'I'll take you.' I heard the words come out of my mouth before I'd even thought about it.

Sophie continued to gaze at me soulfully. 'Don't you have to work this afternoon?'

'I said I'd help Ricky and Morris, but they won't mind. I can put some time in for them later. I'll give them a call.'

I'd kept Nick's old phone in his living room, sitting on the floor. Like the bedroom, it was empty, cleared of his furniture, walls painted, floorboards sanded down and varnished, new spotlights in the ceiling: just waiting to be rented by traders or to be moved into by me. Pat was of the opinion that the rooms were haunted; at least that's what she told Gavin to wind him up. I'm not sure I believe in ghosts, but I still couldn't walk into those rooms without thinking of Nick, hearing his chuckle, seeing his wicked blue eyes. My call made, I went back down into the shop.

'Gavin,' Pat called out when I appeared, 'what have you got to remember to tell Juno?'

He looked up from his reading, returning to the real world after a definite pause. 'What?'

'What happened yesterday?' Pat insisted.

'Oh . . . yes,' he responded, peering vaguely through his specs as if struggling to remember. 'Some woman came in, enquiring about a unit.'

'Great!' I was instantly cheered at the possibility of more rent. 'What does she do?'

He shrugged. 'I don't know. I told her she'd have to come back when you were here.'

'Well, did you take her number?'

'No . . . sorry,' he added, in the voice of someone who really couldn't give a shit and tried to return to his reading.

'Well, if she comes in again, or if anyone else comes in enquiring, will you be sure to take their details, please? I need to fill these units.'

'Oh? Yes, of course.'

'And by the way,' I added, addressing the room in general, 'I had eighteen pounds extra in my cash box last night. Someone must have taken a sale for me yesterday. Does anyone know what it was?'

'That was me.' Gavin was beginning to look sheepish. 'You sold a silver thing . . . a rounded knife, bone handle . . . um . . . bit like an apple corer.'

'That would have been the stilton scoop,' I told him, 'it would have been written on the label.' I was trying not to lecture him but failing miserably. 'That's why we all label everything, Gavin, so we can keep track of sales. Next time, please write the details in the book on the counter. That's what it's for.' It was a simple enough system if we all followed it. Poor Gavin; if I'd had any idea what terrible things were about to happen, I like to think I'd have been more patient with him, more understanding of his complete lack of interest, his callow lack of charm – but probably not.

Once we'd loaded Sophie's paintings, we put EB in the back of the van. He wanted to ride in the front, but dogs tend to make Sophie wheeze, although EB's mum would have pointed out indignantly that Miniature Schnauzers' coats never shed hair. But I made Sophie check she had her inhaler with her before we left, I know what she's like. We weren't taking any of her big hedgerow pictures, but some of her miniatures: charming studies of birds, bees, dragonflies and amphibians. We took boxes of these together with a portfolio containing prints of her larger works. She had, after a great deal of nagging from me, begun to paint pet portraits, but so far EB was her sole commission.

We took the road to Buckland. No sooner had we climbed the wooded hill towards the church and farmland opened out beneath a wide blue sky, than an irritating ping from my bag announced my mobile phone had returned to the land of the living, and a fuzzy buzzing noise told me that a call was coming in. 'I bet that's Elaine. Have a look, will you?'

By the time Sophie had dug the phone out of my bag, it had switched to voicemail. She listened as I pulled into a gateway to let a farm vehicle pass in the narrow road, a huge machine with spiky arms folded up in front of the cab like the claws of a praying mantis, something to do with hay cutting, probably: the long, dry spell meant that many farmers locally had managed a second cut.

'Alan's fine,' she reported, phone to her ear, as the deeply cut treads of the machine's giant tyres rolled past my window, bending my wing mirror out of position. 'He's had a stent fitted and he's staying in hospital for a couple of nights. Elaine's home and you can take EB back whenever you like.'

'Would you text her and say I'll be an hour or two?'

She nodded and got busy with her thumbs.

* * *

22

After we'd left Sophie at the collection of old stone farm buildings, which had been converted into the new gallery and arts centre, I took EB for another walk. At the end of the lane we sat on a drystone wall and gazed over fields of stubble scattered with golden rolls of hay. A second crop had been harvested here. In the distance, a machine was lifting the rolled bales into a pile, wrapping them in black plastic ready for silage, an activity we didn't usually see in September.

Back to the arts centre, where we waited for Sophie in the shiny new cafe and tested their crumbly apple cake. She appeared after another twenty minutes, grinning broadly and empty-handed except for her portfolio.

'They're taking all my paintings,' she announced happily, 'sale or return.'

I offered tea and cake in celebration but she declined, and we decided to get going. I put EB into the back of the van, but Sophie decided to hang on to her portfolio and we started off for home.

'This is going to deplete your stock at the shop,' I said, after we'd rattled over a cattle grid and turned onto the road that led home across the moor. The rough grass on either side was parched after the drying winds of summer, the leaves of stunted hawthorn bushes already withering and yellow. 'You're going to have to get busy with that paintbrush.'

'Actually,' she admitted after a sly, sideways glance at me, 'they asked for some local scenes.'

I groaned. 'Isn't that what I'm always telling you?' I took my hand off the wheel to wave an arm at the rolling grandeur of the moor around us, a ragged granite tor like a ruined castle snagging the horizon. 'Local scenes sell!'

She ignored this completely and switched on the radio.

'Honestly, Soph, what's wrong with painting Buckland Church or Hound Tor?'

'Everybody does it!' she said dismissively. This was an argument we'd had before. 'Can you smell burning?'

'Don't change the subject. What about some paintings of Ashburton? I've got lovely photos of St Andrew's churchyard in the snow . . . Yes I can!' There was a definite whiff of burning and a blue haze was rapidly filling the cab. 'I'm going to pull over.' I'd barely made it to the verge before tiny bright flames began licking their way up from under the dashboard. Sophie dabbed at them ineffectually with her fingers.

'Out!' I ordered her, switching off the engine. 'Get out now!' She already had the passenger door open, her portfolio clutched to her chest. Smoke was pouring from under the dashboard, hot and black. I had just the time to rescue my bag from the footwell. I held my breath and grabbed the vehicle's paperwork from the glove compartment. 'Ring the fire brigade!' I yelled, coughing. 'I'll get EB out of the back.'

CHAPTER TWO

I count that moment when I tried the handle on the back door of the van and it refused to turn as one of the worst of my life so far. It had never stuck before. I jiggled it. It wouldn't budge. I pressed down hard. Inside the van EB was barking, trying to tell me how wrong things were.

'It's OK, EB!' I called. But it wasn't. I yanked on the handle, bracing one foot on the adjoining door to give myself extra pulling power. The smoke from the engine was blowing back towards me, rolling over the roof of the van, stinging my eyes, making me cough. It must be filling up inside. I looked around me desperately for a stick, anything I could use for leverage. Behind me I could hear Sophie screaming down the phone.

There was a fist-sized lump of granite lying in the ditch and I picked it up, raised it in both hands and clobbered the handle with it. No good. I could hear EB scrabbling at the door with his claws, whimpering to be let out. I rushed to the front of the van. Could I get back inside and rip out the grille behind the driver's seat, get him out that way? But I couldn't get near it. Choking black smoke belched from the open doors; it would be impossible to see, let alone breathe. Orange flames were shooting up from under the bonnet, the air above quivering with heat, with a suffocating smell of boiling oil and melting plastic, of engine fluids sizzling, getting way too hot. How long before the fire brigade could get here? There was a retained service at Ashburton, but by the time they were mustered it would be too late for poor EB. There was a bang from the engine, the bonnet burst open, flames and sparks spiralling into the sky. Those sparks could set the dry countryside alight. I didn't care. All I cared about was EB.

I tried the stone again, raising it above my head. I could hear the terrible sounds of EB choking. *Don't let him burn*, I whispered to whatever god might be listening, *please, don't let him burn*. I brought the stone crashing down, feeling the shockwave up my arms. Sophie was running about in the road, screeching. I tried the rock again. Dimly I heard a voice ordering me to stand back. It barely registered before I was thrust aside and a fist with a lump hammer in it struck a mighty blow at the lock. The door burst open and smoke poured from inside as EB's inert little body was hauled out and carried to the side of the road. I followed, dazed.

A Cherokee Jeep was parked a few yards behind us, its doors wide open. Sophie must have flagged it down. Its driver was laying EB down on the grassy verge. An older man, in baggy tweed jacket and a flat cap, was approaching my blazing van with a car fire extinguisher.

'He's not dead?' I knelt down next to EB.

His rescuer was rubbing EB's furry chest. 'Come on, little fella,' he kept saying encouragingly. 'Come on.' But EB didn't move.

'EB, please!' I begged stupidly.

Sirens in the distance announced the fact that the fire brigade was coming. A few moments later it arrived, blue lights flashing, air brakes hissing as the engine drew to a halt. Suddenly the road was full of men in yellow helmets and big boots, and hoses unreeling; all too late for my van.

'Got a casualty, have we?' A young fireman squatted down by the roadside and then yelled over his shoulder. 'Ed! Bring out the MARS, will you?'

The MARS turned out to be a resuscitation machine about the size of a diver's air tank. The fireman fitted a plastic mask over EB's muzzle and turned on the oxygen. After a few heart-stopping moments, EB's head jerked, and he snuffled and coughed his way back to life.

'Oh, thank God!' I cried, as he raised his head. The fireman gave EB a few more deep breaths of oxygen before he removed the mask, by which time his patient was already trying to scrabble it off his nose with his front paws.

'He'll be fine,' he assured me, picking up his machine. I drew EB onto my lap and cuddled him hard, rubbing my face into his smoky-smelling fur.

'And the next!' the fireman called out cheerfully. It was only then I looked around for Sophie. She was sitting in a heap on the grass verge, white-faced and in serious danger of overdosing on her inhaler.

'Oh, Soph!' I hurried over, clutching EB in my arms like a baby. 'Are you all right?'

'The petrol tank won't explode, will it?' she gasped

nervously as the van gave vent to a belch of black smoke.

'Contrary to what they'd have you believe in films,' the fireman replied a little severely, as he fitted the mask over her face, 'petrol tanks rarely explode.'

I looked around for our rescuer, but he was standing by his jeep, barking orders into his mobile phone. His companion, the old guy with the flat cap and fire extinguisher, hovered deferentially at his elbow, an air of subservience about him; the younger man was obviously the boss.

So I sat by the roadside, and watched the fire brigade's finest having a wonderful time hosing down the smoking, blackened hulk that had once been my van. Steam rose hissing and fizzing, and shiny rivulets of water ran off the tarmac into the grass.

'I hope you're insured!' one of the fire crew called to me jovially.

Of course I was insured: third party, fire and theft. Trouble was, my insurance company was not going to pay out megabucks for a clapped-out old Astra. It was worth next to nothing. The paint job on the sides had cost more than the vehicle; the paint job that was now just a leprous rash of blisters on scorched and buckled metal.

The fireman with the MARS machine, whose name, he told us, was Andy, had finished with Sophie.

'Will she need to go to hospital?'

'I'm all right,' she assured me wheezily. 'And I'm not going to sit around in casualty for hours just to be told to go home and rest.'

Andy gestured with his mask towards me.

'I don't need it.'

'I'll be the judge of that,' he insisted.

28

'Juno, you do look dreadful,' Sophie added solemnly.

It was only as I breathed in cool, clear oxygen that I realised how sore my chest and throat felt from inhaling scorching smoke. I began to cough. Andy told me to relax and breathe deeply. Whilst I sat there, breathing obediently, he went away and came back with a can with which he sprayed the pads of EB's feet. 'Floor of that van would have been hot,' he remarked in a mastery of understatement. 'This will cool his paws down.'

Sophie put an arm around my shoulders and gave me a hug. 'I'm so sorry about your van. What are you going to do?'

I couldn't answer. I didn't know. I didn't even know how I was going to get us home. The firemen had obviously done all they could. They were rolling up their hoses.

'Well, it could have been worse,' I coughed. 'If this had happened on the way there instead of on the way back, we might have lost all your lovely paintings as well.'

'We got EB out.' Sophie smiled, rubbing his head. 'That's the main thing.'

'Well, someone did.' EB was huddled in my lap, very subdued, very frightened. He licked my hand.

'Ah, ladies!' cried a cheerful voice and we all looked up. The tall figure of EB's saviour was standing in the road in front of us. 'Is everyone OK?'

'Thanks to you,' I told him. 'I can't thank you enough. I—'

He dismissed my thanks with a wave of his hand. 'Not at all,' he said, 'damsels in distress and all that!'

He squatted by us and stroked EB's head. 'How is the little fellow?' This was the first time I had looked at him properly. He was younger than I'd thought, about my

29

age. Beneath short blonde hair he had lively blue eyes and an engaging smile. He was pretty bloody gorgeous, as a matter of fact.

'Now, what's going to happen is this,' he began, as if he were an army officer addressing chaps about to go on a mission, 'I've phoned a break-down firm and they're sending out a lorry to haul away your van. Well, what's left of it,' he added, grinning. 'It can stay at your local garage until your insurance assessor arrives. Moss,' he indicated the old chap in the flat cap, 'will stand by here until the break-down lorry arrives.'

Moss did not look thrilled, but he was obviously under orders. 'Sir,' he muttered.

'Meantime,' our hero continued, 'I will drive you ladies home.'

'We live in Ashburton.'

'No trouble at all,' he assured me.

'Well, thank you, Mr . . .'

'Jamie.' He held out a large hand. 'Jamie Westershall.'

We shook hands and introduced ourselves. We all stood up. I was still carrying EB, who whimpered when I tried to put him down.

'I'm afraid I shall have to call in at home on the way,' Jamie warned us, as we clambered into the back of the jeep. 'I hope that's not inconvenient.'

The fire brigade were climbing back into their engine and slamming doors. As we pulled away, we left Moss standing gloomily in the road, next to the smouldering, blackened hulk that had once been my pride and joy.

'Um, how will Moss get home?' Sophie asked, turning back to look at him.

'Oh, I don't know,' Jamie responded breezily. 'He'll think of something.' He pulled out his phone as he drove along, obviously unconcerned about the rule of law. 'Danny!' he called loudly after a few seconds. 'James here. You still at Home Farm? About to pack up? Excellent! How did we do? All clear! No reactors at all? Well, that's fantastic news. Listen, you couldn't come up to the house when you're done, could you? I've got a little casualty I'd like you to run your eye over. You can? Splendid!' He disconnected. 'My vet,' he explained, thrusting his phone back into his pocket, 'he's just been checking the herd for TB.'

'You're a farmer?' Sophie asked.

'Well, we have several farms on the estate. I'm more of a farm manager, really.'

We were travelling with the woods of Holne Chase on our left. On the other side, the short grass and granite outcrops of open moorland spread to the horizon, black-faced sheep grazing amongst clumps of gorse still yellow with flowers. We passed a muddy track leading to a farm, and from then on were driving alongside a high stone wall enclosing cultivated woodland, majestic green crowns of mature oaks, beech and hornbeam rising above it. Suddenly the jeep swung between tall stone gateposts. I just glimpsed the legend carved into the stonework as we flashed by, a name I can't remember now without a shudder: Moorworthy House.

CHAPTER THREE

The vast Victorian mansion, at which we arrived after driving through acres of rolling parkland, loomed above us like the setting for a Gothic horror movie: tall chimneys, steeply pitching roofs, gargoyles glaring down from high parapets, balconies with stone balustrades – all haphazard somehow and confusing to the eye.

'Ghastly old pile, isn't it?' Jamie said cheerfully, as we gazed open-mouthed.

'Is this house yours?' Sophie breathed.

'Afraid so.' He grinned. 'I ought to pay someone to set fire to it. Anyway, come in, ladies!' We followed him through an arched doorway into a lofty hall. Oak-panelled walls bristled with antlers and the mounted heads of creatures with tusks and bared teeth. It wasn't exactly welcoming.

'Mrs Johnson!' Jamie called out, striding on ahead of us, his voice echoing around the hall. 'Mrs Johnson? Hello! Anyone at home?'

We trailed behind him, gawping around like tourists in a stately home as portraits of ancient ancestors stared down at us with obvious disapproval. A wide staircase with heavily carved bannisters swept up to a landing overlooked by a tall stained glass window letting in patterns of light in rose, green and gold. A brass candelabrum as wide as a wagon wheel hung down from above and a suit of armour lurked on the turn of the stairs.

'Is this place haunted, d'you think?' Sophie murmured.

'Well, if it isn't, it ought to be.'

Just like a ghost a woman materialised quietly from somewhere: dark-haired, smart but workmanlike in a navy skirt and cream blouse.

'Ah, Johnnie,' Jamie called to her affectionately, 'is my uncle or my sister at home?'

'Miss Emma is down at the stables, sir,' she responded quietly, 'but I believe Mr Sandy is in the library.'

'Ah, I'll go and roust the old devil out! These poor ladies,' he went on, indicating Sophie and me, 'have been in an accident. Van caught fire. I wonder if you could come up with some tea in the drawing room?'

'Of course, sir.' She turned to us with raised brows and a smile that didn't reach her eyes. 'Come with me.' I assumed she was a housekeeper or perhaps a secretary. I couldn't quite place her. 'Perhaps you'd like to visit the guest cloakroom first.' She spoke in a tone that didn't brook any argument. 'And when you've finished, the drawing room is over there.' She pointed down the hall, opening the door of the guest cloakroom for us and leaving us no option but to go inside.

I think the guest cloakroom was larger than my flat. Dark panelling gave way to rose-coloured marble, covering the floor and walls and surrounding the washbasins that stood side by side, complete with oversized gold taps and heavily framed gilt mirrors.

I often feel like shrieking at my reflection, but this time it wasn't the mane of untameable red curls that was distressing. My face was black with sooty smudges except for two white tracks where tears had flowed from my red-rimmed eyes. It was no wonder Mrs Johnson didn't want me in the drawing room.

I passed EB over to Sophie whilst I filled the basin and washed my face with the fragrantly expensive hand soap provided. 'My God, I smell like a kipper!' I moaned as I splashed repeatedly.

'You did get well smoked.' Sophie was filling up the adjacent basin. I picked up a snowy-white towel from a pile folded in a basket and rubbed my face with it. It wasn't snowy any longer. Meanwhile EB was enjoying a long, gulping drink from the basin Sophie had filled.

'Poor little boy!' I took him back when he'd finished, his whiskery chops dripping, his eyebrows twitching anxiously.

I gazed at our reflections. Sophie and I are such contrasts. She, small and delicately boned with her neat, dark head: me, tall and – well, 'statuesque' is a word I have heard applied to myself. Standing next to Sophie always makes me feel like a bloody great Valkyrie. 'Am I fit for the drawing room?' I asked.

She made a face. 'Have you got a comb?'

'I can only get a comb through this lot when it's wet.'

She sighed. 'You'll have to do, then.'

We found our way back to the drawing room after first opening the wrong door which revealed a long empty room with gilded mirrors and an acre of shiny floor: it could only have been a ballroom. 'Bloody hell!' Sophie squeaked in amazement.

The drawing room was large and chintzy with three sofas grouped around a carved marble fireplace wide enough to drive a horse and cart through, a scattering of occasional chairs, a grand piano and long windows opening out onto a wide terrace. Flower arrangements and silver photo frames stood on various tables, porcelain figurines adorned the mantelpiece, oil paintings depicting classical subjects hung on the walls and there was no sign of a television anywhere.

'Do you think we've fallen through a time warp?' Sophie asked. 'What decade are we in?'

'I think we're back in the Agatha Christies.'

I wandered out onto the terrace. A balustrade separated it from the garden, marked every few feet by a heavy stone urn filled with trailing flowers. In front of me a wide lawn stretched away into the distance. Beyond it I could make out the rocky outline of a distant tor, but I couldn't work out which one. We'd taken too many turns since leaving the main road; I had lost my bearings. I turned back to look at the house.

It didn't look so ugly from the back. Much of its granite walls were covered by an ancient wisteria, twisting stems as thick as ships' cables testament to its extreme age. It reached almost to the third-storey windows and must have been a hundred years old. I wished I could have seen it back in May, hanging with clusters of flowers, with dripping waterfalls of blue.

The soft click of the drawing-room door and the faint tinkle of teacups announced the arrival of Mrs Johnson with the tea. She set the tray down on a table by the fireplace.

'Mr Jamie asks you to excuse him for the present,' she said, as she straightened up, 'but he'll be with you before long.'

I put EB down gently on the hearthrug, where he seemed happy to lie. I was afraid Mrs Johnson might feel it necessary to hang around but, to my relief, she headed for the door.

'I think you have everything you need, ladies,' she pointed to the laden tray, 'but if there's anything else you require, just ring.' She indicated a bell push in the corner and went out.

'Do you find her slightly scary?' Sophie whispered when she'd gone.

'Definitely,' I nodded, surveying the silver teapot, dainty china cups and saucers, plate of biscuits and buttered tea-loaf that filled the tray. 'She's got a touch of the Mrs Danvers.'

I turned over a delicate tea plate to look at the maker's marks. 'This is Spode,' I told Sophie as I poured tea and passed her a cup, 'for God's sake don't break anything.' I slipped EB a biscuit. I'd already ruined his figure that morning with the flaky sausage roll, but I can testify to the reviving effect of a biscuit and, sure enough, he showed signs of perking up.

Sophie and I fell on the buttered tea-loaf like a pair of starving gannets. Left to ourselves, we would have demolished the lot, but we were forced to restrain our uncouth behaviour when the door opened again and a jocular voice drifted in from the hall.

'Now, now,' it said, 'I hear we have visitors, two lovely ladies.'

The man who came in, dressed in a dark blazer and yellow cravat, was in his sixties, his purple veined nose and raddled complexion evidence of considerable debauch. He sported a silver comb-over that ended in a tiny little flick above his left ear. He stopped and surveyed us from heavy-lidded eyes. 'How delightful!' He came forward to shake our hands, his own extended. 'No, please don't get up. I'm Jamie's wicked Uncle Sandy,' he informed us proudly, 'how do you do?' His hand was smooth and pale with manicured nails; not a farmer's hand, obviously. He dutifully patted EB, who disgraced himself by growling.

I was shocked, it was so unlike him. 'EB! Mind your manners!' But I didn't blame him: he sensed something about the man I couldn't put a name to, something vaguely unpleasant like the very faint odour of corruption.

He sat down on a sofa. 'Ebee?' he repeated, brows raised faintly.

'EB,' I corrected, 'his initials.'

'What do they stand for?'

'It's a secret, you have to guess.'

'Juno won't tell,' Sophie complained bitterly. 'I've been trying to guess it for the last two years.'

I changed the subject. 'This is a most interesting house.'

'Not mine, my dear,' he answered, puffing out his cheeks. 'It was my elder brother who was the squire. Jamie is the heir – not that I envy him – a crumbling pile of death duties and dry rot, that's what this place is.' He chuckled. 'I used to tell his father he should have sold the lot to the National Trust years ago, but he wouldn't listen. But Jamie's a sensible lad,' he added, laying a finger against his nose, 'he's marrying the money!'

I exchanged a glance with Sophie. Neither of us knew if this was a joke. Meanwhile, Uncle Sandy had begun leafing through the portfolio that Sophie had dropped onto the sofa. 'I say,' he remarked, studying the reproductions of her paintings, 'this is lovely work.' He glanced at me. 'Is this yours?'

I pointed at Sophie. 'Really?' He looked surprised. 'Did you do all these by yourself?'

I have to say that Sophie replied with admirable composure, used, as she is, to being taken for a minor.

'Well, well!' he exclaimed at the portrait of EB and pointed to him on the hearthrug. 'It's this little fella to the life!'

Just then, a young woman strode in from the terrace. For a moment I wondered if she might be the 'money' Jamie was marrying, but the resemblance to her brother was too strong.

'Emma!' Uncle Sandy hailed her breezily. 'How went the dressage?'

'Foul!' she flung back without looking at him, tossing a riding hat onto a chair as she passed. She headed for a table on which stood decanters and began to pour herself what I guessed was gin. A little early in the day, I thought. 'Digby behaved like a fucking brute!'

Ah! Perhaps we weren't in the Agatha Christies, after all.

Emma was stunning: slim with straight, gleaming blonde hair drawn back into an elegant chignon. She wore thigh-hugging breeches, a fitting black coat, and a white stock tight around her swan-like neck. She turned, glass in hand, and for the first time registered our presence. She stared at Sophie and me as if we'd come in on the sole of her riding boot. Her uncle hastily introduced us and explained why we were there. She neither spoke nor smiled, clearly resenting our presence. 'Look, Em, look at this,' he went on, showing her the photo of EB's portrait. 'It's that little fella there. Hasn't little Sophie captured him to the life?'

She glanced at it over his shoulder. 'It's quite a good likeness, I suppose,' she admitted grudgingly, then turned her back on all of us and stood, gin in hand, pacing in front of the windows, staring moodily out onto the terrace, as edgy and highly strung as a thoroughbred racehorse.

'Well, I wish Old Thunderer was still alive,' Sandy prattled on, oblivious of her bad manners. 'I'd have loved to have had his portrait.'

Before we could ask who 'Old Thunderer' was, Jamie came into the room accompanied by the vet, who got down on the hearthrug next to EB, listened to his heartbeat and pronounced him perfectly fit. 'He's got a few blisters on his paws,' he said to me, 'best not to walk him for a day or two.' No danger of that, I thought miserably, wondering how I was going to exercise the Tribe next morning with no van to pick them up in.

Shortly after this, we left, Uncle Sandy expressing the hope that he'd see us again, Emma ignoring us, pouring another gin and striding out onto the terrace. 'We've got a garden fete on next week,' he told us, 'why don't you girls come along? Bit of fun, eh?'

We lied through our teeth and promised him we'd think about it. As we followed Jamie back out to the waiting Cherokee, Sophie whispered, 'He's gorgeous isn't he, Jamie?'

'Yes, but it's no good looking at him,' I murmured, 'he's "marrying the money".'

'I wonder who she is.'

'And does the poor girl know she's the money?'

'She may not be *only* the money,' Sophie pointed out, in an effort to be generous. 'Anyway, it makes no difference,' she sighed. 'The only men who are interested in me are perverts.'

'There's Gavin,' I reminded her, and she gave me a dark look.

On the ride home I suggested that she sit in the front with Jamie so that EB and I had more room in the back. 'Your garden goes on for ever,' she observed as we drove through the grounds. 'That lawn must be a mile long.'

He grinned. 'It's a trick of perspective. You have to watch out for the ha-ha.'

'Ha-ha?'

'It's a sunken wall,' he explained. 'You can't see it until you're on the edge of it. By then it's too late. The Victorians were fond of putting them in gardens to help open up their views. They called them "ha-has" because they thought it was so bloody funny when people fell off 'em. Odd what some people find amusing.'

'They didn't have television in those days,' I pointed out.

Jamie laughed. He chatted on, happy to regale us with how extensive the Westershall estate was, how many hectares of land, how many farms it contained, mostly, it seemed, worked by tenants. The grounds of the house were edged on one side by thick woodland, the mature oaks and beeches that we had glimpsed earlier, a long ribbon of woodland walled off from the road. 'This will be a beautiful walk in a week or so,' I said, 'when the leaves have properly turned.'

'There is a footpath through a small section, but most of the woods are fenced off, I'm afraid. Site of Special Scientific Interest,' Jamie explained. 'Rare bats – we can't have the public wandering about, disturbing them. I don't know much about bats, myself.' He gave a slight shudder. 'I stay well away. But the woods are full of old mine workings, disused shafts. That's another reason we can't have people wandering about – it's dangerous.'

We had driven through the gates by now and were back on the road, although still, Jamie assured us, surrounded by Westershall land. We hadn't gone far when he suddenly brought the jeep to an abrupt halt, cursing. 'Will you look at that!' he cried out in disgust. 'Will you bloody look at that?'

What we were being asked to bloody look at was a narrow track leading off into a farmer's field. The earthen trackway was strewn with rubbish – plastic packing material spilling out of broken cardboard boxes, scraps of paper flung into the hedge and scattered on the ground like dirty confetti. Further off, a torn sofa bursting with foam stuffing lay on its side amongst piles of shattered timber and oil drums. 'These damn fly-tippers!' Jamie slammed out of the car, ordering us to stay put while he went for a closer look. He came back, shaking his head. 'Does it happen a lot round here?' I asked. Things were often dumped on the tiny patch of waste ground at the end of my lane, usually just an old microwave or a shopping trolley, nothing on this scale.

'It's gets worse every year,' Jamie started up the car again. 'Bastards! They'd get what for if I caught them.'

'Don't the police do anything?'

41

He gave a grim laugh. 'We'll report it, of course. But there's so much of it going on. The police don't have the resources.' He was clearly angry and for a few minutes we travelled in silence.

'I wish they wouldn't wrap hay bales in black plastic,' Sophie remarked idly as we passed a pile of them stacked on the edge of a field. 'They look awful.'

'They're silage.' Jamie still sounded on edge. 'I suppose you're one of those people who want the countryside to look romantic.'

'People who buy my paintings do,' she answered honestly. 'They don't want rolls of black plastic. They want old-fashioned haystacks and wooden wagons piled high with rosy-cheeked children riding on top.'

'Tell me, would a combine harvester be allowed in one of your paintings?'

'Certainly not!'

'What about an old tractor,' he asked, 'a vintage John Deere, for example?'

Sophie considered for a moment. 'Only if it's rusty,' she decided.

Jamie threw his head back and laughed. They were getting on well, these two, I thought. And he was marrying the money; shame.

CHAPTER FOUR

'What sort of bleedin' time do you call this to turn up?' Ricky demanded acidly. 'You're a day and a half late.'

'My van caught fire and nearly cooked a dog.'

Just for a moment he hesitated, blue eyes narrowed, not sure if I was serious, then he grabbed my arm, pulled me inside, propelling me across the patterned marble floor of the hallway, past piles of cardboard boxes, towards the breakfast room.

'Maurice!' he bellowed up the stairs. 'Get your arse down here! You'll want to hear this! I'm putting the kettle on. Sit,' he pushed me down into a chair at the breakfast table, 'and don't say another word until Morris gets here!'

I did as I was told, sitting mutely, lusting after Morris's teapot collection proudly displayed on the Welsh dresser and wishing I had at least one of them for sale in my shop.

Ricky and Morris live in a lovely Georgian house, not on the scale of Moorworthy, but large enough to house them both and their stock of several thousand theatrical costumes. They run a costume hire business. The cardboard boxes in the hallway were stuffed with World War I uniforms, which they were selling to a film company. They were always moaning about retiring, reducing their vast stock of costumes. At least in selling the uniforms they were making a start, and that was why I was supposed to have been with them the day before: I was meant to be helping with the packing.

Morris arrived, looking slightly flustered after hurrying down the stairs. He and Ricky are as much of a contrast as Sophie and me. Ricky is tall, with iron-grey curls and completely wasted, rugged good looks. Morris is short, fat and bald with little gold specs perched on his nose. They've been together since they met in the theatre as chorus boys.

'What's up?' he puffed.

I recounted my adventures whilst they fussed about making tea and Morris produced a chocolate cake he'd baked the day before.

'Moorworthy House? We've been there!' Ricky told me. 'We did a concert there a few years ago, didn't we, Maurice?' He and Morris performed as Sauce and Slander, a musical double act, usually to raise money for charity. 'We're going there again in a few weeks.'

Morris nodded. 'We are. But you should have phoned us, Juno,' he stared at me reproachfully over his specs, 'we could have popped down and picked you up. You needn't have walked all the way up this hill.'

I had meant to phone them the night before, just hadn't got around to it. Jamie had been wonderful, driving us first to Elaine's house, so that I could deliver EB, and waiting

44

while I explained what had happened and made necessary enquiries about her brother. He was quite prepared to take me and Sophie to our respective homes, but we felt we'd troubled him enough and got him to drop us both back at the shop.

The lights were still on in *Old Nick's* and Pat was on her own, tidying up.

'Has Gavin gone?' I asked, although the answer was obvious.

She gave a grunt of disgust. 'He went half an hour ago.'

We told her about our exciting afternoon. She gasped and looked horrified in all the right places. 'What about you?' I asked her eventually. 'Any customers?'

She shook her head. 'None that bought anything, but that creepy bloke came in again.'

'What creepy bloke?' I asked.

'I don't think Juno will have come across him,' Sophie told Pat. 'I don't think he's been in here when she's been here.'

'What bloke?' I repeated. 'In what way creepy?'

'He only comes in when Gavin's here,' she went on. 'He never buys anything, just sort of hangs about, around Gavin.'

'Lurks,' Pat confirmed, nodding mysteriously. 'And he walks ever so quietly. You never know he's there until he's right behind you.'

'Is he some friend of Gavin's, then?'

'We're not sure,' Sophie went on. 'Gavin's really awkward when he's around. They talk in whispers. You can tell, whenever this man comes in, that Gavin wishes we weren't here.'

'He tried to get rid of me this afternoon,' Pat told us, voice hushed with drama. 'He said to me, "Why don't you go upstairs and have a tea break, Pat? I can look after the shop." Well, I wasn't falling for that, I stayed right here. I wouldn't leave that pair alone down here. God knows what they might get up to!'

'But this creepy bloke has never tried to steal anything?'

Pat's eyes narrowed. 'No, but I don't trust him.'

'Haven't you asked Gavin who he is?'

'That's just it, he won't say,' Sophie explained. 'If you ask him, he changes the subject.'

'What does this man look like?'

She wrinkled her brow in a frown. 'Small and sort of ferrety.'

'Shifty,' Pat added.

I wasn't sure I'd be able to identify him from that description, but I was certain that he hadn't come into the shop when I'd been around. And it wasn't really any surprise to me that Gavin had weird friends. 'Oh, let's go home, girls,' I begged, 'it's been a long day.' And Pat dropped the pair of us off at home.

My flat occupies the upper half of a decrepit Victorian house and the bathroom lacks the facility of a proper shower, so I soaked for a long time in the old enamel bath, repeatedly washing the smell of smoke out of my hair. Then, wrapped in my dressing gown, I flopped down in my chair with a mug of tea. I knew I ought to concoct some kind of supper from whatever scraps were in the fridge, but after apple cake and tea-bread I wasn't that bothered. This was unusual for me as I have an appetite so healthy it glows. I'm not a great cook. My dietary needs are mostly taken care of by my landlords, Adam and Kate, who run a vegetarian cafe, *Sunflowers*, and are very generous with leftovers. Little plastic boxes and parcels wrapped in foil are often left on the table on the landing outside my door, like offerings for some gluttonous god, and I am rarely at a loss for a vegetable samosa or a helping of bean casserole. As I like a balanced diet, and Kate and Adam provide the healthy stuff, I get the unhealthy stuff from Ricky and Morris who are always stuffing me with cake. I don't put weight on. Ricky says this is because I have hollow legs, but really it's because I work too bloody hard. But that night I couldn't be bothered with food: I had more urgent things to think about.

The following morning, as every morning, I had to walk the Tribe. On a Friday, there were usually five of them. I wouldn't be taking EB; he'd be staying at home for a few days, resting his paws. Of the remaining four, two would be easy to fetch because they lived in Ashburton, within walking distance of the town; the other dogs I always collected in the van because they lived further off. I rang their owners and explained I couldn't pick them up in the morning and why. Then I sat with my diary and worked out what I could and couldn't do next day without transport. Thank God the weekend was coming up, but I needed a new vehicle by Monday. I couldn't afford to wait around for the insurers.

I spent a couple of dispiriting hours comparing prices of second-hand vans on the Internet and got so depressed I weakened and ate a banana. I knew I could always ask my cousin Brian out in South Korea for money, but he had already been so generous with funds for the shop, money I intended to repay, that I cringed at the idea of approaching him for more.

By the time I'd slogged up the hill to Ricky and Morris's place that afternoon, I'd already spent most of the morning with Maisie, unclogging the drain of the sink she swore she wasn't responsible for clogging. I went into town to do her shopping, her beastly terrier, Jacko, on the lead. I refuse to walk him with the Tribe because he's so badly behaved. As usual, he growled filthy language at any other dog we saw, lurching at anything within snapping distance.

I took him on a detour along a path that sweeps in a curve behind St Andrew's churchyard. On one side, ivy clings to ancient gravestones leaning at odd angles, their carved epitaphs worn smooth by age; on the other side of the path brightly painted play equipment stands in the recreation ground, together with the sweeping concrete lines of the new skateboard park. It's as if Ashburton's past is on one side of the path, its future on the other.

The lane led me to a small commercial estate where I was sure, a few days before, I'd noticed a van with a 'for sale' sign in its window. It was still parked there, a little white Peugeot Partner, with '£500 ono' written on a notice on the windscreen. It was an older model, but big enough for me to get the Tribe in the back, or carry stock about. It also had windows in the back doors, which the old van hadn't, and would give me a decent rearward view as well as allowing the dogs to see out. I scribbled down the seller's number so that I could phone him later.

'So is little EB all right?' Morris asked, cutting me a slice of chocolate cake.

'He's fine.' I'd rung Elaine that morning to enquire after both the invalids.

'What about you, Juno?' He blinked at me anxiously. 'Are you fine too?'

I'd had to trim off a few frazzled ends of singed hair but otherwise I was unscathed.

Ricky lit up a cigarette and strolled to the open door to aim his smoke into the garden. 'You know we'll run you anywhere, Princess, if you need a lift.'

'Thanks, but I've arranged to meet the man selling the Peugeot tomorrow morning so I'm hoping I'll be mobile again by Sunday.'

Morris flicked a sly glance at Ricky. 'You know, Juno, we've had an idea.'

'We have.' Ricky came back to the table and drummed his fingers on it in excitement. 'It's brilliant!'

I groaned. I'd heard their brilliant ideas before.

'We're going to rent a unit in your shop.' They were both grinning at me broadly, waiting for my reaction.

'No, you're not.'

Their faces fell.

'This is just an excuse to help me out,' I went on. 'It's very kind of you, but I'm not letting you do it.'

'But we've got lots of stock we want to get rid of,' Morris argued, 'vintage sixties and seventies stuff that we don't get much call for theatrically.'

'Its lovely stuff,' Ricky put in, 'all very saleable.'

'Then sell it on the Internet. You'll get more money.'

'Can't be arsed!' he said flatly. 'And let's face it, you've got sod all to sell at the moment, your bit of the shop is half-empty!'

This was true; the back room I occupied was practically bare. What little stuff I had was spread out to make it look less empty. I didn't have much spare cash and didn't get time to go hunting for stock. As a result, I was spending far too many evenings in front of the laptop, trawling through auctions, hunting for stuff I could afford to buy online.

'You're not paying me rent,' I insisted.

'No, and nobody else is either,' Ricky retorted. 'You've let Beatrix Potter have her unit for nothing.'

'Sophie needs a chance to establish herself without all her money going out in rent,' I argued. 'She can barely afford to buy paintbrushes, as it is. And we've agreed to review the situation at Christmas. As for Pat, she sells her stuff to raise money for the animals. If I took money from her, I'd just be taking it from them.'

'Juno, love, it's not your responsibility to solve other people's problems,' Morris told me. Ricky nodded frantically.

This was rich, coming from them. They were always trying to solve my problems. Ricky pointed his fag-hand at me, his cigarette trailing smoke. 'You're always doing it, you silly cow, and it's what gets you into trouble.' He took a long drag as if to underline his point.

It was time to divert their minds from my failings. After all, selling the vintage clothes was a good idea and would help to fill some empty space. 'How about this?' I suggested. 'I'll put the clothes on my unit and sell them for you, just take a commission.'

It was a compromise that seemed to mollify them. After a few moments of slightly sulkily tossing the idea back and forth, they agreed. 'But you'll have to price everything,' I warned them, 'because I won't have a clue.'

Morris clapped his hands together like an excited child. 'We'll sort out the clothes this afternoon.'

'No,' I said firmly. 'I'm here to help you pack up those uniforms.'

'Well start packing, then.' Ricky rose and stubbed out his cigarette in the sink. 'The sooner we've got 'em finished, the sooner we can have some fun.'

CHAPTER FIVE

If Thursday was a weird day, what with Judith-Marianne and the van catching fire, Saturday contained elements of the surreal. It started off well. In the morning I took the white van for a test run. It had new tyres and a year's MOT, but it also had a few miles on the clock and I managed to buy it for £450. I was to become a White Van Woman. Perhaps an anonymous-looking vehicle wouldn't be such a bad thing. In the past, the advertising on my yellow van had made it easy for the wrong people to find me and nearly got me murdered. Anyway, I shook hands with the vendor and agreed to bring the money around to his house first thing next morning. White Van would be mine.

When I got to *Old Nick's*, I found a more expensive vehicle parked outside: a brand-new soft-top Mazda MX5, in powder blue with beige leather interior, was blocking most of the pavement. I squeezed past it, barely able to get in through the door. Inside, who should be in conversation with Sophie but Jamie's sister, the lovely Emma. I suppose her brother must have told her where to find us. She was wearing a summery dress, her pale gold hair loose about her smoothly tanned shoulders. She'd dazzled Gavin into an awed, slack-jawed stare.

'So can you do it?' she was demanding of Sophie, as I came in. 'You can work from photographs, I take it?'

Sophie was leafing through a thick sheaf of photos. 'Oh yes,' she replied, nodding, 'no problem at all.' She smiled and held out a photo for me to see. 'The Old Thunderer,' she explained. 'He's a Highland bull. Isn't he wonderful?'

'Hello, Emma.' I took the photo from Sophie. The Old Thunderer was certainly impressive, his massive head crowned with thick, curling brown hair and wide, wicked-looking horns. Beneath a long fringe one baleful eye glared at the camera.

'Does Jamie have a herd of these?' I asked. Highland cattle were often to be seen grazing on the moor, imported from Scotland because they were hardy enough to stand up to Dartmoor weather. I'd have preferred to see Ruby Reds or South Devon cattle, but I can hardly complain about imports when I'm a bit of an import myself.

'No, Thunderer was Sandy's, really just a pet.' Emma spoke the last word almost with contempt. 'He sired a lot of champions of course,' she added by way of compensation.

'It's Sandy's birthday on 29th October,' she went on. 'Jamie and I thought it would make a wonderful surprise present. You can get it done by then, I suppose?'

'Of course.' Sophie answered brightly, determined to ignore her haughty tone. 'How big do you want this portrait?'

I prayed Sophie wouldn't undersell herself and

wandered away. Pat was putting up pictures of her own, papering the wall behind her with printed sheets showing the latest waifs and strays at Honeysuckle Farm looking for a home. I snapped my fingers under Gavin's nose, breaking Emma's spell and whatever fantasy he was weaving in his head.

'Don't drool,' I whispered. He blushed and went back to the newspaper he was reading.

I glimpsed a headline over his shoulder: *Batman Dies*. I should have known he wouldn't be reading anything sensible.

I was disappointed with Gavin; perhaps that was why I found him so irritating. When he'd rented his unit, or I should say when his parents, Mr and Mrs Hall, had rented it for him, the understanding was that he would be selling their collection of second-hand books. I'd been delighted at first. We currently have only one bookshop in Ashburton, a specialist dealing almost exclusively in classic comics and graphic novels. It's a wonderful place, full of beautifully crafted illustrated volumes. I'd bought a lovely book in there for Sophie's birthday. Gavin haunts the place, not because he appreciates graphic art, but because he's obsessed by superheroes and spends most of his time reading the adventures of mythical kingdoms and warrior queens, and not doing what he's supposed to be doing: setting up his own bookstall. Ashburton has a library but it's small and can't provide for everyone's needs. I was convinced that second-hand books would have really helped to drag the locals into *Old Nick's*. But I was hoping for books with general appeal. Trouble was, Gavin wasn't interested in mainstream and frankly, I doubt if his own collection of cheap and tawdry comics, mostly obtained from dubious sources on the internet, would be of much interest to anyone.

I'm sure his parents had only forced him into renting space in the shop to prise him away from his computer, drag him from the darkened tomb of his bedroom into the daylight.

To an extent I couldn't blame him for his lack of enthusiasm. The Halls' book collection consisted of the kind of stock that charity shops end up throwing away: old and unfashionable cookery books, yellowing paperbacks, mostly turgid hospital romances, a few dry academic tomes from the days when Mr Hall was a student, out-of-date atlases and little else. Basically, they had cleared out the contents of their loft. I'd offered to take Gavin to the market in Newton Abbot, where he could see how some really thriving bookstalls had set up their businesses, but he wasn't interested. I looked at his shelves, only half-filled, most of the stock still in boxes, and sighed.

'Is there a toilet I can use here?' Emma's voice cut in suddenly. She and Sophie had finished striking their deal and judging by the grin on Sophie's face she was happy with her end of it. I was going upstairs myself and pointed her in the direction of the bathroom on the landing. I went on up to the kitchen. I'd replaced Nick's old cooker with a microwave and toaster, which was all we needed. Gavin had tried to persuade me into investing in an expensive coffee machine, but I told him if he wanted posh coffee he could buy it himself. As I extracted the milk from Nick's ancient fridge, I heard the bathroom door slam and looked out of the kitchen, down the stairs, calling out a goodbye to the descending Emma. She didn't answer. She was sniffing heavily, her hand up to her nose. Summer cold or hay fever, I wondered naively, or was she upset? I went to the bathroom myself.

I'd locked the door and was just about to flip up the lid of the loo when something glistening on its surface caught my eye. I bent down and peered at a line of very fine white crystals. It was the straightness of that line that riveted my attention. I switched on the bathroom light and hunkered down, peering. I wanted to be absolutely certain about what I suspected I was looking at. I could see a pattern of tiny cut marks on the lid's plastic surface. I flipped open the pedal bin under the basin. Sure enough, there was a razor blade and a little scroll of paper in there; it looked like one of Sophie's business cards, rolled up. And one end of it, I was now perfectly sure, had been stuffed up Emma's horrible little nose. No wonder she was sniffing.

The hot wave of anger that came up from the soles of my feet was so intense I found myself gripping the edge of the basin for support. How dare she? How dare that posh little cow bring her stash into my shop and snort her evil drug on my premises? And be so contemptuous of others that she didn't even bother to conceal the evidence; she didn't care who found out. I felt faint with anger and sat down on the edge of the bath. My mother had died of a drug overdose when she was twenty-three. It was one of the few things I knew about her. I was already older than she would ever be. I suppose that's why I was so angry, because of my mother, because of the waste. I wondered if Jamie knew about Emma's habit. Not my business, I warned myself resolutely, don't get involved. She would now be driving her little sports car through the streets of Ashburton under the influence of a dangerous drug. I ought to call the police and report her. But in the end I calmed down, swept the tiny remnants of her guilty secret away with a cloth, binned it, and decided not to say anything to anyone; certainly not to those downstairs. Sophie would be celebrating getting her commission. I didn't want to ruin her moment.

But when I got down there, no one was celebrating. Something else entirely was going on.

'I tell you, it must have been her!' Sophie was saying loudly. 'It was right there on my desk, and now it's gone!' Gavin was on his hands and knees, searching for something under her desk.

'What's up?'

'Sophie's lost her inhaler,' Pat told me.

'I have not lost it,' she insisted. 'It was there, on the desk. No one else has been in here.' She rolled her eyes. 'It's not like we've had any customers.'

'Well, I did see Miss Hoity-Toity put her hand in her pocket,' Pat admitted, 'just before she went out.'

'But who would do that?' Gavin objected, standing up and dusting his hands. 'Who would steal an inhaler from an asthmatic?'

I could think of someone. I had no doubt that gin-guzzling, cocaine-snorting, horse-riding, sports-car-driving, thrill-seeking Emma could get high on just about anything.

Barely two hours after Emma had departed, during which time one customer had come in, wandered around and left without buying anything, Jamie himself arrived. Unlike his sister he was charm itself, asking after our welfare and EB's, introducing himself to Pat and Gavin, admiring Pat's wares and asking her questions about the animal sanctuary. We mentioned Emma's earlier visit, but I didn't say anything about the drugs. No one said anything about the inhaler.

Sophie's mum had been phoned and had already popped in with a spare one from home.

'The portrait was her idea,' Jamie admitted. 'But that's not why I'm here. I'll come straight to the point,' he added briskly, perching his rear on the edge of Sophie's desk and folding his arms. 'I'm hoping you might be able to dig me out of a hole.'

'We'll try,' I assured him. We could refuse nothing to the handsome saviour of EB.

'We've got this fete up at the house a week from today,' he went on. 'I heard Sandy mention it to you. Well, it's more of an autumn country fair, really. We do it every year, to raise money for the lifeboats or some charity. Always brings in the crowds. This year it's for the air ambulance. Usual thing, you know, gymkhana, dog show, beer tent, all that. Well, we always have a tent for art and crafts. Dartmoor Guild of Arts come every year, put on a great display. Unfortunately, this year there's been some mix up over dates and they're not coming. They're already booked for somewhere else—'

'—leaving you with an empty art and craft tent,' I said.

'Exactly, bit awkward. So Sandy and I wondered if you ladies might be able to come along and bring your wares – and you, too, of course,' he added, turning around to include Pat and Gavin.

'Well, I don't do crafts, as such,' I warned him. 'I sell antiques and collectibles.'

'That would be fine. In fact, Sandy's got a few mates in the antiques trade. We can invite them along too. And if you know of anyone else who . . .'

He saw Sophie and me exchanging glances. 'We'd waive

the normal stallholder charges, of course,' he went on. 'You'd be doing us a favour. Perhaps, if you do well on the day, you might consider making a small donation to the charity?'

'Well, in that case—'

'Good, so you'll come?' he asked, turning round to include all of us.

'I'll come,' Gavin said instantly.

'That's fixed, then. Can't tell you how grateful I am. Any news on your van, Juno?' he asked. 'Has the insurance chap turned up?'

I explained I was still waiting for the insurance assessor to come, my local garage playing host to the burnt-out wreck, but that I was getting new wheels in the meantime.

He raised his brows. 'Oh yes?'

'Peugeot Partner,' I told him.

'Excellent.' He left, well pleased with the success of his mission, as suddenly as he'd come.

There followed a brief argument with Gavin, who was intent on bringing his collection of comics to sell at the fete, about the unsuitability of his stock for such an occasion, but he remained obstinate; he was determined to come along.

'I don't see why my comics shouldn't sell as well as Pat's knitted sheep or Juno's old tat,' he argued.

'This is a country fair, not a fantasy convention, Gavin,' I pointed out. 'Perhaps some mainstream books would be more suitable, you know, appeal to a wider range of interests? You'll probably sell more that way.'

'Gavin has got a point,' Sophie said reluctantly. 'There will be families there, and lots of kids read comics.'

'These aren't for kids!' Pat snatched up the fantasy novel that Gavin had been reading.

'*The Sword of Virangha*,' she read out loud. 'Look at this female on the front. She's got nothing on except a metal bikini.'

'She's a warrior queen,' Gavin said hastily, a telltale blush beginning to tinge his cheeks,'she's wearing armour.'

'I don't fancy her chances going into battle in that,' Pat went on remorselessly, 'it only covers up her rude bits.'

Gavin snatched the book out of her hands. 'Mr Westershall extended the invitation to include me, so I'm coming. And anyway,' he added childishly, 'you can't stop me.'

'I think we're missing the point,' I said before hostilities could escalate. 'If we all go next Saturday, who's going to look after the shop?'

There was a moment's gloomy silence. It was obvious that no one was going to volunteer to stay behind. It was equally obvious that it wasn't a good idea to close the shop on a Saturday. Whilst the fine autumn weather continued, Ashburton would be full of visitors.

The silence was broken by the mad jangling of the bell above the shop door. Ricky and Morris struggled in through the doorway, each carrying what looked like the severed halves of a naked female corpse but turned out to be a dress-shop mannequin. 'This is Mavis,' they chorused, grinning. 'Where do you want her?'

I pointed them in the direction of my unit in the stockroom. Then I turned to grin at the others. 'We *will* go to the ball, Cinderella,' I promised, and then followed, to talk nicely to my Fairy Godmothers.

Sunday morning I finally became the owner of White Van and took it for a spin up the A38 to Newton Abbot. A large market town, it has in abundance things that Ashburton doesn't have, like supermarkets, charity shops and takeaways. It is the kind of town that guidebooks describe as 'bustling'. Holidaymakers in their thousands pass through its railway station every year: change at Newton Abbot for Totnes and Plymouth – or for Dawlish, Teignmouth and the delights of the English Riviera. Famously, it boasts a racecourse, which on occasional weekends when the horses aren't running hosts a giant car boot sale.

As my ignorance about antiques is profound, the only chance I stand of making any profit is to buy cheap from people who know even less about them than I do. Boot sales can be quite good in this regard. I picked up half a 1960s coffee set, a Torquay pottery milk jug, a few pieces of nasty but collectable Goss ware, a sandalwood writing slope with a broken hinge, some strings of coloured glass beads that Pat could break down into earrings, and a cast-iron boot scraper: the sort of original feature that rich people doing up old houses will pay silly money for. I also invested in a box of paperback books in reasonably pristine condition, in the hope I could talk some sense into Gavin about putting them on his shelves.

As I was about to leave, I found a cardboard box full of electric light switches. The man who sold them to me was surprised I wanted them. After all, he said, they were just rubbish he'd found in his garage. It was true, many were plastic and broken and would be thrown away, but as I gleefully handed over my five pounds and gaily lied that my partner was an electrician and collected old switches, it occurred to him, judging by his slight frown, that he should have inspected the contents of the box more carefully. But it was too late then.

Three of the switches were made of Bakelite – always collectable no matter what the object – and four were Edwardian switches with brass covers in a decorative shell pattern. I knew that all of these would be of interest to the architectural salvage merchant in Ashburton, the same merchant who had removed the Victorian fireplace from Nick's old living room. I remembered his surprise at my wanting to dispose of such an original feature, but it was no longer a living room and a saleroom doesn't need a fireplace; and for me, it was too vivid a reminder of Nick's murder.

The day ended with another strange little incident. I was thinking about going to bed when I realised that I'd been carrying around in the depths of my bag a birthday card Maisie had given to me to post through the letter box of her friend, whose birthday was yesterday. Conscience pricked, I got in the van and drove to the little sheltered housing development where she lived. I parked in the council car park behind the town hall. Even the car park in Ashburton is picturesque by most standards, surrounded by old stone walls and overlooked by trees, sheep grazing on the steep field that rises up behind it.

Card delivered, I walked back to the van. It must have been nearing midnight. All was quiet, all was dark. A car was parked in the corner that I hadn't noticed on my way in. The tailgate was up, lighting up the interior, and a woman was standing behind it, fiddling with something. A small pale form sidled towards me across the tarmac: a cat, one of those thin, leggy, oriental breeds. It was wearing a harness on the end of an extendable lead. It yowled in a friendly fashion as I bent to stroke it. Oriental breeds of cat are very vocal, they like to chat. 'Hello,' I said, 'who are you?'

The woman shut the tailgate of her car and wandered over, the lead in her grasp. She was tall and slim, dressed in cords and a padded body warmer, her hair – in the dim light I couldn't tell if it was blonde or grey – worn in a French pleat. I judged her to be in her late sixties. 'He's Toby,' she informed me in a pleasant, cultured voice, 'just giving him a walk.'

I asked if he was Siamese, a breed I knew was easily trained to walk on a lead.

'Yes. He's a lilac point,' she confirmed, bending to scoop him up. 'Time to be on our way.'

I was close enough to her car to see that the back was piled high with bedding. I wondered if she and her cat were sleeping in it. 'Going far?' I asked.

'Yes. Goodnight,' she answered, pleasantly, but as a definite end to the conversation.

'Well, goodnight,' I said, and returned to my van.

She also went to her car, put the cat in the back on the pile of bedding, and sat in the driving seat. But the car hadn't moved when I turned out of the car park, its driver sitting motionless, and I had the feeling she was waiting for me to go, to be out of sight before she moved on.

Running away, I thought to myself, she and her cat are running away, and for the rest of the night, until sleep claimed me, I couldn't get them out of my mind.

I was alone in the shop with Gavin. It was the afternoon before the Moorworthy fete and I was in the storeroom sorting out what stock I was going to take with me. Was it worth taking a fluted carnival glass bowl with amber

63

lustre, I wondered, and risking it getting broken en route? I decided it was and was carefully wrapping it in bubble wrap when I heard the bell jingle on the shop door as someone came in.

I didn't rush because I knew Gavin was sitting at his post, although as he was deep into one of his fantasy comics it was debatable whether the sound would have penetrated his consciousness. Then I heard his voice. 'I want you to leave me alone,' he was saying loudly. 'I've told you to stop coming in here.'

The reply, whatever it was, was spoken too quietly for me to hear. Curious, I crept into the corridor and peered into the shop. The man muttering inaudibly to Gavin was exactly as Sophie and Pat had described: ferrety-looking, a skinny man in jeans and an old denim jacket, thinning brown hair brushed across his head failing to conceal the red scabbiness of his scalp. His neck and hands were peppered with scabs too, as if he was suffering from some unfortunate skin condition. He was older than Gavin and, despite his general seediness, had an air of menace about him, like a small-time crook. I couldn't hear what he was saying, but I realised he wasn't purposely whispering. His voice was just very soft; a collection of breathy, sibilant sounds came from his lips, the sounds a snake might make if it could speak.

'I've told you, no,' Gavin's voice was edgy with panic.

'Anything wrong?' I asked, strolling into the shop. I stopped and smiled innocently at his companion. 'Did this gentleman come in to buy something?'

He slid a glance at me, hissed something inaudible and slipped out, not bothering to close the door behind him.

I walked over and shut it, turning to study Gavin, who looked paler than usual and slightly unwell. 'Who was he?'

'No one,' he mumbled, averting his gaze, 'just a creep.'

'Does this creep have a name?'

'Croaker, that's what he calls himself.'

I folded my arms. 'Do you want to tell me what that was about?'

He shook his head. 'Nothing – it's nothing.' He blushed deeply. 'He's just a pervert.' Flustered, he began to tidy his table in an effort to cover his discomfort, hastily sliding comics into a box.

'If he's bothering you, we could call the police. You don't have to put up with—'

'No! No, I'll sort him out,' he cried hastily. 'Honestly, Juno. I'll make sure he doesn't come in here again.'

'Gav, if you're in any kind of trouble—'

'I'm not!' He gave me a steady stare, lifting his chin in defiance. 'It's fine, really.'

'OK.' I held up my hands in a gesture of surrender. 'But you can tell him from me that if he comes in here again upsetting anyone, I will call the police.'

'I've told you, I'll deal with him.'

I let it go at that, but I was dubious about Gavin's powers to deal with the creepy Mr Croaker and resigned myself to the fact that I might not have seen the last of him.

CHAPTER SIX

The wisdom of letting Ricky and Morris look after *Old Nick's* whilst we were at the fete was something I pondered more than once on our drive to Moorworthy House. It wasn't that they couldn't be trusted with handling customers, or cash; it was their fondness for putting their own stamp on things that had me worried. They could rearrange my stuff as much as they liked, had already done so in the intervening week as they produced a clothes rail with more and more vintage garments to fill it. But if they started tinkering with Sophie's or Pat's stock it would not go down well. I needn't have been concerned. Sophie had almost none left after her visit to the arts centre, and during the week she'd been busy dashing off quick watercolour sketches of Dartmoor and comical cartoons of farm animals to sell at the fete. There wasn't time to get them framed, just mounted and cellophane-wrapped.

She rode with me in White Van. Pat had nobly volunteered to take Gavin and his boxes of comics in her old station wagon. We arrived before them – quite a long time before them, as it turned out; Gavin wasn't ready to be picked up at the promised hour and had to be rousted out of bed whilst Pat sat drumming her fingers on the steering wheel.

The fete was taking place on the vast lawn at the back of the house, with a central arena for the gymkhana, dog shows and livestock competitions. A beer tent and pavilions housing flower and vegetable shows and cake competitions vied for attention alongside tents selling locally produced cheese, cider, honey and even Dartmoor gin and chocolate. In a marked-off area stood a Punch and Judy show for children and a bouncy castle, while a colourful bunch of helium balloons bobbed like a big bouquet over the face-painting stall.

The Craft and Antiques tent was situated nearest to the house, which was a bonus as far as I was concerned as the ballroom had been set up for lunches and teas. The long windows were thrown open, the terrace scattered with garden tables and chairs. Admittedly the Portaloos were way over the other side of the fair, but you can't have it all.

As Jamie had asked, I'd contacted some other traders to see if they could help fill the empty stalls. Tom and Vicky Smithson from Exeter had readily agreed, and when Sophie and I arrived in the tent, they were already busily dressing their table. Their stock was infinitely superior to mine, mostly delicate pieces of china and small items of highly polished silver. I gazed enviously at an arrangement of dainty vinaigrettes and snuffboxes. Tom and Vicky had been in the antiques trade a long time, they knew their stuff. I only wished the same could have been said of me. I had begun to educate myself when I started working with Nick; I just hadn't got very far.

Once Sophie and I had unloaded our boxes, I parked the van in an adjoining field and trudged back to the marquee. The sky was clear blue overhead, the air already warm, a perfect day for a garden fete. Further down the lawn a painted sign warned visitors to *Beware of the Ha-Ha*. The trees in the woodland had turned a deeper gold, a reminder that summer was over. In a few short weeks we would be turning back the clocks; there were not many of these long, golden afternoons left.

I lingered by a stall selling locally pressed apple juice, sipped the proffered samples and chatted to the young couple running it. Devon used to be famous for its orchards and they owned one just outside of Lustleigh. They talked passionately about the revival of old varieties of apple; varieties with lovely names like Sweet Coppin and Fair Maid of Devon, or Pig's Nose and Hangy Down. They were also selling pork and apple sausages, jars of apple chutney, and slices of apple pie served with thick clotted cream. I resisted. It was too early in the day to start being naughty and I had to get back. I contented myself with a sample of sausage speared on a cocktail stick and moved on.

The marquee had begun to fill up in my absence. I'd barely begun to lay out my own wares when Uncle Sandy came in, accompanied by one of his antique dealer chums and I heard a soft groan from Vicky Smithson, whose table was on my right. 'Oh no, not Barty!' she muttered to herself. I craned my neck to see Sandy's companion, a florid

68

individual in a natty sports jacket. Sandy was introducing him to other traders and there was a lot of loud guffawing going on. I turned to Vicky. 'Friend of yours?'

'Not exactly friend, no,' she answered softly. 'Oh God, he's coming this way! Has he got this table next to mine?' She groaned again and clasped my arm. 'Whatever you do, don't let him get you in a confined space.'

Vicky, a slim and attractive sixty-something, favoured the approaching Barty with an engaging smile and submitted herself graciously to his embrace. She then introduced him to me. 'Eddie Bartholomew,' he said, pumping my hand with enthusiasm, 'but everyone calls me Barty.'

'Juno,' I responded, as coolly as I could.

'Juno, eh?' He rolled a lascivious eye over my body. 'How apt!'

Fortunately, Sandy, after enquiring if we were happy with the tables we'd been given, bore Barty off to meet his other comrades and I was able to get on with setting out my stock.

I took my jacket off. It was already warm inside the canvas tent, and stuffy; a sickly smell of fudge was wafting in from the tent where it was being made. The public address system whined and coughed as it spluttered into life, a hearty voice announcing the day's events. Later, we were promised, there would be a display by the Dartmoor Majorettes and a performance by Bovey Brass Band. Inside my skull a faint headache began to beat a warning tattoo. It was going to be a long, hot day.

If Gavin's fantasy magazines and graphic novels didn't strike me as suitable for a country fair, I have to say that Barty's stock struck me as even less appropriate: arms and militaria.

I know some people are fascinated by medals and wartime memorabilia, but there were far too many nasty-looking knives and weapons on his table for me to feel comfortable with all the children around. One of these children was Gavin who, having plonked his magazines down on his table in two untidy piles, more or less abandoned his stall for the day, assuming that Pat would look after it. He spent ages poring over Barty's weapons and came back brandishing a short, curved sword with a wicked-looking blade and even more lethal point.

'You haven't bought that?' I asked, horrified.

'Of course I have!' He unsheathed it with a slither of metal and brandished it aloft. 'The Sword of Virangha!' he cried proudly.

'Don't wave that thing about in here,' Pat told him crossly, 'you'll have someone's eye out!' The tent had become far too crowded for him to be messing about with a lethal weapon.

'Put it away somewhere safe, Gavin!' I hissed at him. 'Why don't you go and lock it in the station wagon?'

'Good idea!' he agreed readily. He swaggered off, the scabbard stuck through the belt of his jeans, and that was the last I saw of him.

Pat sold two of his comics for him in his absence. Better still, she had a good day herself, selling several pairs of handmade earrings as well as knitted toys and animal doorstops. She has a real talent for creating animals with comic expressions and she'd sold a frowning pug and three particularly bonkers-looking sheep before I made my first sale of the day. Meanwhile, Sophie was doing well with her watercolour sketches and greetings cards. Her hedgerow paintings attracted great admiration, although they're a bit expensive for an impulse purchase. She didn't sell one, but four people walked away with her business card.

I just wished I was doing half as well. I did sell a brass shell case – to Barty, of all people – a few glass brooches and the boot scraper. Unfortunately, I couldn't resist a mother-of-pearl hatpin from one of Sandy's chums, which wiped out most of my meagre profit.

It became oppressively hot in the tent during the afternoon, and we took it in turns to make our escape and walk around the fete in the fresh air. Not being interested in small girls jumping fat ponies over bales of straw, and teenagers in short skirts twirling batons even less, I turned my back on the arena and headed for the house. Here I found Vicky, who had somehow escaped before me, enjoying tea on the terrace. I joined her in a pot of Earl Grey and a plate of dainty sandwiches.

'Any trouble with the abominable Barty?' I asked.

'Not really. Thank God, I've got Tom between us to act as a buffer!'

Whilst we sat watching the crowds of people milling about in the sunshine, thankful for a while to be separate from them, Jamie came up with a young woman on his arm who he introduced as his fiancée.

Jessica was a pleasant young woman with soft brown hair and infinitely better manners than her future sister-in-law. She seemed a little shy and clung to Jamie's arm with obvious adoration. I couldn't believe he could be marrying such a sweet girl for money. I tried to imagine this English rose when she was older: the mistress of Moorworthy House, the gracious hostess in twinset and pearls. But there was something about her that didn't quite fit. Her pretty floral dress was appropriate for a garden party, but I couldn't see her mixing with the country landowners set, couldn't quite see her in jodhpurs and waxed jacket, like Emma.

'Emma not here?' I enquired, after we'd engaged in a little polite conversation.

Jamie shrugged. 'Oh, she'll be around somewhere.'

Stuffing something nasty up her nose, no doubt. Jamie was concerned that we were having a good day, that we thought coming to the fete had been worthwhile. We assured him that it had, and he went off to attend to something, leaving Jessica to sit and drink a cup of tea with us.

I was right about her as it turned out. She wasn't a country girl at all. She lived in London where she worked as a PA. I asked how she and Jamie had met. They'd been introduced at some company event, apparently. Sandy had once worked with her father who owned a pharmaceutical firm. 'I don't expect you've heard of it,' she said shyly. 'Dravizax.'

She was right, I hadn't. It sounded like the name of a villain from one of Gavin's graphic novels.

Jamie came back to claim Jessica as they were due to judge the Scruffiest Dog in Show together, and Vicky strolled back to the marquee. Before I went back in, I popped to the loo, a trip that took me to the other end of the garden. It was when I was returning from there that I spotted Emma, holding on to the bridle of a fidgeting bay horse whilst she stood in earnest conversation with a man I recognised as Moss. I didn't particularly want to say hello to her, and they seemed to be talking intently, so I just passed them by unnoticed and returned to the stifling canvas cave of the tent for the rest of the afternoon.

The final judging had taken place, the brass band had trumpeted its last, the crowds had dispersed and we were packing up to go home. Barty and his chums had already left, Vicky had almost packed her stock and Tom had gone off to fetch their car.

'Where's Gavin?' Sophie asked suddenly.

I realised I hadn't seen him for hours. His table was unoccupied, as it had been for most of the day. He'd shown no interest in it and I really don't know why he'd been so insistent about coming. Pat shook her head. 'He'd better come back and start packing up soon or I shall go home without him.'

'I haven't seen him since he went to put that stupid sword in the car.'

'He couldn't have done that. He'd have needed my car keys and he didn't ask for 'em. Not,' she added, 'that I'd have trusted that ninny with my keys. He'd probably drop them in the field and lose 'em.'

'He must come back soon.' Sophie was carefully stacking bubble-wrapped paintings in a box. 'Even he must realise it's all over. We could try his phone.'

I should have thought of that straight away but, unused as I am to the luxury of a signal, it's not always the first thing that occurs. After a few moments, Gavin's phone began to ring, loudly, inside the tent. Pat bent down behind his table, where his jacket had slipped off the back of his chair, and produced the ringing phone from his pocket.

'Moron,' I pronounced, as I terminated the call.

'Are you girls OK?' Tom had returned to the tent, ready to load up.

'We seem to have lost Gavin. He went off for a look around but that was hours ago.'

'Do you want me to have a scout about?'

'Oh, please don't trouble, he can't have got far.' As I said it, I realised that this wasn't true. Gavin could have gone anywhere. He might have decided to explore the house, although apart from the tea room it was strictly off limits to the public, or he could have gone for a walk and got lost. He could be anywhere.

'Let me check out the beer tent, make sure he's not passed out drunk,' Tom offered with a grin, 'and I'll check out the gents' loos, while I'm about it.'

'That's kind, Tom, thank you.'

As Vicky had packed up and could do nothing until Tom returned, she volunteered to box up Gavin's comics for him. Pat and I went off to retrieve our respective vehicles, leaving Sophie on guard in case he turned up whilst we were gone. We didn't want him wandering off again.

As we crossed the field where cars were parked, I saw a now familiar figure walking towards us. Not Gavin, but Moss. I had never spoken to the man, and other than just briefly with Emma, hadn't seen him since we'd left him standing in the road after my van caught fire. I thought I ought to thank him for waiting for the break-down lorry to arrive and overseeing its removal to the garage. 'Mr Moss!' I called out.

He saw me, halted in his stride and stared at me from pale-blue eyes. He looked horrified.

'Mr Moss,' I began, 'I just wanted to thank you—'

He turned his back and headed off in the opposite direction. As I called his name again, he quickened his pace. It was obvious from the rigid set of his shoulders and his lengthening stride that he didn't want to talk me. 'Well, I won't thank you, then, you miserable, rude old bugger!' I muttered. Takes all sorts.

There was still no sign of Gavin. Tom had had no luck in tracking him down. He and Vicky were loading up. Pat had stowed her stuff and was leaning against her station wagon looking fed up.

'It's pointless you hanging around,' I told her. 'I've got room in the van for Gavin's boxes; he can come home with Sophie and me.'

'I'll hang on a bit longer,' she insisted, but after a few more minutes of standing uselessly fiddling with her keys, she allowed herself to be persuaded and we decanted his boxes into White Van. 'You'd better take his rucksack,' she said, handing it to me. 'I don't know why he brought it. It's been sitting in the car all day.'

Pat's car trundled away across the grass, and Sophie and I began loading White Van. By now, the tent was almost deserted, the tables bare, the odd plastic carrier bag and sandwich wrapper left behind, littering the grass. 'That boy is a bloody nuisance,' I muttered, slamming the van doors shut.

'I don't like leaving you girls like this.' Tom came up, looking at his watch. It was close on seven o'clock. It would be light for a while yet, but the sun was sinking lower, the sky over the moor blushing pink. 'Something is obviously amiss.'

'Not necessarily. If Gavin got fed up, I wouldn't put it past him to have hitch-hiked home.' But I was getting worried, and cross that the wretched boy was inconveniencing so many people.

'Let's see if we can find the organisers,' Tom suggested. 'They must be around somewhere.'

We split up, Sophie and I to go up to the house in search of Jamie, Tom to check the other tents and talk to some volunteers gathering litter into bin bags, to ask if anyone had seen Gavin. Vicky was to stay with the cars and phone us if he arrived.

We found Mrs Johnson and a team of ladies in the ballroom. Every scone had been scoffed and they were clearing up after tea. We described Gavin and our predicament. She hadn't seen him and assured us, her face as starched as her apron, that no member of the public would have got past her and her team into the rest of the house. She suggested that we speak to Mr Jamie, who she believed was in the drawing room. Our quickest way, she added pointedly, was to go back outside and along the terrace.

We passed the balustrade, an evening scent drifting from the flower-filled urns. But before we reached the drawing room's open windows, we heard Jamie's voice, loud and furious. 'In broad daylight?' he was yelling at someone. 'With all these people about? Are you out of your mind?' I wondered if he'd caught Emma snorting cocaine from some horse's nosebag. Whatever, this was not a good moment to approach. We veered off, across the lawn.

'I don't suppose he went into the wood.' The trees were ahead of us, a dark tracery of branches with the sun melting gold behind them.

Sophie frowned. 'It's fenced off, isn't it?'

'Didn't Jamie say there was a path, that part of it is open to walkers?' There was certainly a gate in the fence that separated the trees from the lawn. As we approached, we could see a sign hung on it: *Please keep to the path*. I swung it open.

Sophie hung back. 'Do you think we should?'

'Yes, I do. He might have gone in there and sprained an ankle or something.'

The gate shut with a little click behind us. It was quiet under the trees, and growing dim. I yelled Gavin's name. There was no reply, just a frantic rustle amongst the leaf litter from some tiny creature I'd frightened. The path was directly ahead, wide enough for us to walk side by side: bare earth scattered with bark chippings, a pale strip against the surrounding undergrowth. It was well maintained, with no ruts or stones to trip on. The setting sun sent shafts of gold into the surrounding shadows and gilded gnats danced a ballet in the dying light. We walked, stopping twice to call out Gavin's name.

The path veered around a high fence that blocked the way ahead. Signs on the wire warned trespassers they would be prosecuted. We followed the path for a hundred yards or so, before it ended abruptly, the wire fence cutting it off. We couldn't go any further. Sophie sighed. 'He's not here.'

I peered through the fence into the dusky woods beyond. The ground sloped away sharply, tree trunks jutting at odd angles from steep, rocky banks.

'You don't think he climbed over the fence, do you?' she asked.

I looked up. It was topped with vicious razor wire. 'I don't think he could have.'

'We might as well go back.' The gathering gloom was getting to Sophie. She sounded nervous. Something dark fluttered between the trees above us, but whether it was bird or bat I couldn't tell, its darting, flickering movement was so swift.

We began to retrace our steps. The shadows were thickening, reducing the green vegetation to a tangled mass of darkness. Something white caught my eye, about fifty yards from the path; it snagged my attention and held it. An oak had fallen long ago, a tree of great age and girth, its gnarled roots left exposed, its branching crown holding the stricken trunk at an angle, not allowing it to sink to the ground in rest. Tiny ferns grew along its mossy branches and something white, some object, was hooked over the slanting trunk. 'Stay there, Soph.'

As I made off through the undergrowth, she began to follow. 'Where are you going?'

'Stay there,' I repeated. There was no point in both of us crashing about amongst the vegetation. I picked my way between saplings and ferns that swished against my thighs as I brushed past. Even in the twilight I could see where someone had been before me. I followed a trail of snapped off branches and broken twigs. A terrible feeling of misgiving was growing with every step. A few yards further and I knew what I was looking at: the sole of a trainer, white, like the ones Gavin wore.

'Gavin?'

There was no answer, no moans or groans from the other side of the tree. No movement from the shoe, or the

78

jean-clad leg I could see as I drew close: all perfectly still. I leant over the stricken tree trunk. Gavin was lying face down. My first thought was that he'd broken his neck; he'd tried to leap over the trunk, caught his foot and fallen. 'Sophie!' I yelled. 'Ring for an ambulance. Then you'd better run back to the house, bring Jamie.'

'Have you found him?'

I clambered over the stricken trunk, clutching at twisting stems of ivy clinging to the bark and heaved myself over. I could hear the rustling of Sophie's steps as she hurried up behind me. 'Stay back, Soph!' I knelt down by Gavin's side and touched his neck gently, feeling for a pulse.

Sophie was on tiptoe, peering over the tree trunk, her voice tremulous. 'Is he dead?'

'I think so, yes.' I could smell blood; the leafy ground beneath his body was sticky with it. I gently turned him over and heard Sophie gasp. Gavin was dead, his eyes staring, a fallen oak leaf clinging to his pale cheek, and the Sword of Virangha sticking out of his chest, the handle between his clutching hands.

CHAPTER SEVEN

Call it a run of bad luck, but Gavin's was the third dead body I'd discovered in less than a year. Perhaps that's why Detective Inspector Ford favoured me with such a long and thoughtful stare before he spoke. 'We always seem to meet under distressing circumstances, Miss Browne.'

'We do,' I agreed foolishly. We were sitting in the study at Moorworthy House, facing each other across the polished surface of a wide mahogany desk. It was dark outside, and the room was lit by lamps, heavy brocade curtains pulled across the windows, the only sound the measured ticking of a clock. In the next room, the inspector's sidekick, Det. Constable DeVille, was talking to Sophie.

'So, Juno, tell me in your own words what happened. Begin with how you know the deceased.'

I explained that Gavin rented space in *Old Nick's*, that we'd all come to the fete, how keen Gavin had seemed to come with us, and how he'd bought the sword and then disappeared.

'I thought he'd gone to put the thing away in the car.'

'And you say he bought this weapon here, at the fete?' The inspector raised a sandy eyebrow. 'Who from?'

'His name is Eddie Bartholomew. I've never met him before. He's a friend of Uncle . . . of Mr Sandy Westershall.'

The inspector was scribbling down names. 'Do you know if Mr Bartholomew is still here?'

'Everyone had gone except for Tom and Vicky . . . Mr and Mrs Smithson. They stayed to try and help us find Gavin. They're not still waiting, are they?'

'We've taken brief statements and let them go home. Someone will be interviewing them more fully tomorrow.' The inspector smiled. 'Juno, tell me a bit more about Gavin. Have you any idea how he . . . how this terrible thing happened?'

'In the shop he was quiet, reading most of the time. He was really into all this fantasy stuff . . . superheroes and . . . I don't want to make him sound stupid,' I said awkwardly. 'Actually, he was very intelligent, but . . . impressionable – immature, I suppose. I can imagine him running about in the woods, brandishing that dreadful weapon, stabbing himself.' I found I was fiddling with the lid of a silver inkwell and stopped. 'Sorry, but he was accident-prone.'

'That's all right.' The inspector smiled. 'I wanted your honest assessment. So, as far as you're aware, he didn't quarrel with anyone during the day?'

'Well, as I say, I didn't really see much—' I stopped and stared. 'You don't think someone else stabbed him?'

The inspector spread his hands in an almost defensive gesture. 'I would be very surprised if this turns out to be anything other than a bizarre and horrible accident,' he responded gently, 'but I have to keep an open mind. At this stage I can't rule out foul play.'

I suddenly felt sick. I must have looked a bit green because the inspector paused to ask me if I was feeling all right. I assured him I was, and he carried on.

'It's a pity that so many people had already left the fete before this poor young man's body was discovered. Mr Westershall will be supplying us with a list of stallholders, and we shall be speaking to them all. Other than that, all we can do is broadcast an appeal to anyone attending the fete to come forward. There were hundreds of people here today. Someone may remember Gavin, may remember seeing him go into the woods.'

I thought of him lying there alone, bleeding, frightened, unable to call for help. 'Do you think if we'd found him earlier—'

The inspector was shaking his head. 'We'll have to wait for the pathologist's report but I'm certain that death would have been instantaneous.'

Instantaneous? Did that mean that there wasn't even a moment, however fleeting, that Gavin knew he was dying? Tears stung my eyes and I blinked them away. 'His poor parents, they don't know yet, do they? Who will tell them?'

'Don't worry about that, Juno,' the inspector reassured me. 'You can safely leave that to us.' He stood up, clearly my signal to go. 'And if you think of anything else—'

'Actually, there is something – something that happened yesterday.' I went on to tell him about Gavin being visited by the man who called himself Croaker, and what Gavin had said about him.

'Croaker?' he repeated, his sandy brows raised in surprise. 'Creeping Ted Croaker?'

I wasn't familiar with the sobriquet, but I described him as well as I could. The inspector was nodding. 'You know him?' I asked.

'He's a particularly unpleasant species of low life. Not violent, though. We put him away a couple of years ago for trying to sell Ecstasy tablets at the school gates.' He paused for a moment. 'Tell me, was Gavin on drugs?'

'No!' I was shocked at the idea. He often seemed like he was away with the fairies but that was a different matter. I'd certainly never seen him high on anything. As far as I knew he didn't even drink.

'Well, thank you. That's useful information,' he told me as he walked me to the door.

'We shall talk to Mr Croaker.'

Jamie was pacing in the hallway outside and as I left the study he came towards me and enfolded me in a hug. 'God, Juno, this is so bloody awful! You poor girl, it must have been a terrible shock finding him like that.'

'Mr Westershall.' The inspector's voice called to him from the study door.

'Yes, one moment, Inspector,' he called back. 'Juno, Sophie's in the drawing room with Jess, waiting for you. Please go in, let Jess give you a drink.'

Sophie had obviously been sobbing; she was white as a wraith, her dark eyes huge in her little face. She clung to me and sobbed some more. I could have enjoyed a good sob myself, but somehow, like a big sister, I felt I had to keep it together. Jessica, wide-eyed and obviously horrified at the afternoon's events, was doing a great job with the tea and sympathy. There was no sign of Emma.

'Unless you'd like something stronger?' she offered.

'Better not, I've got to drive home.'

I accepted tea with gratitude but neither Sophie nor I wanted to linger. Moorworthy House had lost its curious charm. We drove in silence. For hours our attention had been focussed on police and ambulances and answering a thousand questions. Now the shock was sinking in we were too numb to speak.

'It's horrible,' was all Sophie would say. 'Poor Gavin.'

White Van juddered over a cattle grid as the woods on either side gave way to open moor. The night was black around us, tiny pinpricks of gold from some isolated dwellings the only lights that showed. Our headlights probed the road ahead, picked up the white backside of a ewe sitting on black tarmac. I slowed to a stop. She got slowly to her feet and ambled across in front of us to join a knot of others, scruffy pale shapes huddled in the shelter of granite boulders on the verge.

I kept thinking of Gavin's face, of that moment when I'd turned him over. He'd looked so childlike, that oak leaf clinging to his pale cheek, his blue eyes staring at the sky. I'd never really noticed that his eyes were blue before.

'Sophie,' I began thoughtfully, as we turned onto the Ashburton road, 'do you remember seeing Gavin without his glasses? Ever remember him not wearing them?'

She thought about it. 'He was very short-sighted,' she responded slowly. 'He told me once that he'd tried contact lenses but didn't like them. No, I've never seen him without his specs.'

'No,' I agreed, thinking about it some more, 'neither have I.'

* * *

The last thing we wanted to do when we got back was to unload all our stuff. It was already late and we both longed to get home. But we didn't want to leave our worldly goods in White Van overnight either, so I parked outside the shop. The first things that confronted us when we opened the van doors were Gavin's rucksack and jacket and his boxes of stock. We placed all his things on his table. We didn't know what else to do with them. As I put the jacket down, I felt the hard lump of Gavin's phone in the pocket. 'The police might want this,' I said, drawing it out. 'I'll ring Inspector Ford in the morning and let him know I've got it.'

'Sunday tomorrow,' I yawned when we had unloaded everything. 'I'll come in and sort this stuff out.'

Sophie said she would come in too. 'Will you ring Pat?' she asked anxiously. 'She doesn't know what's happened yet.'

'Yes, but in the morning.' I rubbed my hand over my face. I was so tired suddenly. 'Why stop her getting a good night's sleep?'

When I got home, the house was in darkness. Adam and Kate were already in bed. They opened *Sunflowers* for breakfast, and except in the winter months that meant on Sundays too. I tiptoed up the stairs and let myself into an empty flat, silent and dark. It must be good, at times like these, to belong to someone, to have someone to come home to.

I could see a red eye blinking in the darkness before I switched on the lamp in the living room. I pressed the button on the answering machine, but I already knew who the message would be from. Ricky and Morris were bursting to tell me about their day in the shop, curious to know how I'd got on at the fete and worried that it was so late and I hadn't rung.

I knew I could ring them anytime, but they'd want to know every tiny detail of what had happened, and I wasn't sure I could face a barrage of questions right now. Perhaps it was better not to have anyone to talk to, after all. It occurred to me that in South Korea, where my cousin Brian served as a diplomat, it would be breakfast time and he would certainly be up and about. But he had enough on his plate; I didn't want him worrying about me.

I dropped down on the sofa and slumped there, too tired to get up and go to bed. I felt empty, as if someone had drained all the blood out of me. A soft chirruping noise and a thump from the bedroom told me that Bill had been on my bed and was obviously fed up of waiting for me to join him. His black shape slid sinuously around the open door and in one long leap he landed on my lap.

'You'll get me in trouble,' I told him softly, 'being up here all the time.' He wasn't my cat. He belonged to Adam and Kate but preferred to spend his time with me. Cats are like that, they choose their own people. He gazed at me from his one green eye and pushed his head against my hand, rubbing me with his cheek, marking me as his own. It seemed I belonged to someone after all.

CHAPTER EIGHT

Feeling ragged after a rotten night's sleep, I rang Inspector Ford and told him I had Gavin's phone.

'We've been looking for that.' His voice betrayed the weariness of a man who'd been up all night too. 'Gavin's father seemed to think he should have had his mobile on him.'

'It was in his jacket. Sorry. We'd packed up all his things before we knew what had happened to him. How are Gavin's parents?'

The inspector sighed. 'As you might expect. His father did the formal identification late last night.'

'It must be dreadful for them.'

'Yes,' he agreed sadly. 'I'll send someone over for the phone.'

'Can I ask you something?'

'Of course you can. I can't promise I'll be able to answer it.'

'When I found him, Gavin wasn't wearing his glasses. They must have come off when he fell. Have you found them?'

'No. They can't have fallen far. But looking for a pair of specs on a woodland floor is a bit like looking for—'

'—a needle in a haystack.'

'Precisely.' He thanked me for calling him about Gavin's phone and rang off.

Next, I phoned Pat, who listened to me in growing horror. She became very agitated, her voice turning to a low-pitched moan, convinced the whole thing was her fault because she hadn't given Gavin the car keys so that he could put the sword away.

'Please don't think that,' I begged her. 'I don't believe he had any intention of putting that sword in the car. He went off into the woods by himself so he could swagger about and pretend he was Robin Hood or someone.' Pat didn't sound convinced, but she calmed down. She'd brought her remaining stock home with her after the fete and planned to come into the shop to put it all back. I said I'd see her there.

I didn't need to ring Ricky and Morris because no sooner had I put the phone down than it rang, and Ricky's commanding voice was blasting down the line, demanding to know how the previous day had gone. I began to tell him, forced to stop so that he could put the phone on loudspeaker and Morris could hear it all. They listened pretty much as Pat had done but without the self-recrimination, constantly stopping me to ask questions, and declared their intention of coming down to the shop that morning to see me. I put the phone down. It seemed the whole world was coming to *Old Nick's* that morning.

Pat got there before me. Her pale eyes were watery and her nose was red. She's not the huggy-kissy sort, but she let me fold her in a big hug. She's thin and strong, all bone and sinew, no softness in her body at all. I could feel her heart beating in her flat chest. 'If only I'd . . .' she began, voice trembling with emotion.

'Stop it. It wasn't your fault. Gavin should never have bought that sword. Bloody Barty,' I went on in disgust, 'should never have bloody sold it to him. Weapons like that shouldn't be on sale, especially to impressionable young twerps like Gavin.'

Unconvinced, Pat blew her nose. 'What are we going to do with all his stuff?'

'Give it to his family I suppose, at some point.' I patted her arm. 'C'mon. Let's get it stowed out of the way for the moment.' We put the boxes and rucksack out of sight on the floor behind Gavin's table. I placed his jacket over the back of his chair, which made it look as if he had just popped out for something and would be coming back.

We began to sort out our own stuff, working in subdued silence. It was difficult to think of anything to say. Trying to cheer each other up seemed wrong when Gavin was lying dead in a hospital mortuary. But in spite of myself, a laugh escaped me before I could stop it. I clapped a guilty hand over my mouth. 'What's she doing there?'

I couldn't believe that I had been so wrapped in woe that I hadn't noticed her, and hadn't seen her the night before either, when Sophie and I dropped off our things. Mavis, the shop mannequin, had moved from my unit in the storeroom into the doorway at the back of the shop, half-blocking the corridor. In her arms she carried the sign that pointed the way to *Antiques and Collectibles*. The words *Vintage Clothes* had been added to the sign in felt pen. Mavis now wore a 1960s yellow mini-dress which zipped up the front, a long, straight black wig and a hippy hat. A macramé bag dangled from one shoulder and she sported huge pink sunglasses.

'That looks good,' Pat said, after we'd stared at Mavis for a moment.

'Yes, it does,' I agreed, wondering what else Ricky and Morris had been up to while we were away.

Sophie came in, pale and heavy-eyed and we exchanged hugs and sorrowful greetings. Her huge dark eyes shone with tears, but she smiled at the sight of Mavis. 'Can you believe we didn't notice her last night?' I asked. 'C'mon, let's have a look,' and we all trooped into the storeroom.

My unit had been transformed. A Spanish shawl, black, deeply fringed and dramatically embroidered with roses, had been pinned at an angle across one white wall, and as well as the hanging clothes rail, which was now stuffed with clothes, a hatstand and a folding wicker screen had made their appearance.

'This is great!' Sophie exclaimed. 'People can try things on now.' She grabbed a white, baker's boy cap from the hatstand, jauntily placing it on her dark head, and admired her reflection in a full-length mirror that Ricky and Morris had brought in. On the folding screen hung a plastic mac in swirling, psychedelic colours, a pair of white knee-length boots placed neatly beneath it. A dressmaker's dummy wore a feather boa and a starched net petticoat.

'My mum used to have one of them,' Pat cried, fingering its stiff frills. 'I've got an old photo of her going out to a dance with a beehive hairdo and a big taffeta skirt.'

Sophie had grabbed the white boots and was sitting on a

little chair, rolling up the legs of her jeans. I was still looking around me. My shaded lamps had been draped with gauzy scarves and a drop-leaf table pulled to the centre of the room and opened out. Several pairs of long kid gloves lay on its dark glossy surface, together with a top hat, a pair of opera glasses, and an open biscuit tin full of buttons. A garden trug was filled with ribbons, braids and lengths of fringe, the sort that Morris used in making theatrical costumes, and a vase was stuffed with curling ostrich feathers.

'What do you think?' Ricky's voice demanded suddenly from the doorway. He and Morris were standing there, laden with carrier bags.

'It's a bit over the top quite frankly,' I told him.

'The style is Early Tarts' Boudoir.' He dropped the bags and advanced on me, arms outstretched. 'Are you all right, darlin'?' He enveloped me in a cashmere hug and a miasma of menthol cigarettes, mints and citrus aftershave. 'What a horrible, terrible thing to happen.' He released me and descended on Sophie. Morris, I noticed, had laid a consoling hand on Pat's arm and was whispering to her solicitously.

For a while the talk was all of Gavin and whether he could have stabbed himself accidentally. 'If anyone could do it, he could,' Ricky said frankly. 'D'you remember, Maurice, when he was a kid, we had him in the pantomime?'

Morris nodded mournfully. Every few years, he and Ricky wrote and directed the Ashburton panto. '*Dick Whittington*, it was,' he confirmed. 'He was one of the rats. He went wrong in the middle of a dance routine and sent all the others tumbling over like dominoes.'

'God, he was hopeless!' Ricky shuddered. 'Always two steps behind everyone else.'

'Poor boy.' Morris began blinking a lot and took off his round, gold spectacles, polishing them on his jersey.

Sophie threatened to start crying again so we changed the subject, forcing ourselves to behave as if everything was normal. Morris volunteered to go upstairs and make us all a cup of tea. He extracted a brick wrapped in foil from one of the carrier bags. 'Banana bread,' he explained, 'just baked.'

I love that man. 'So, what's in all these bags, then?'

'More stuff for sale.' Ricky pulled out a black dress, its layers heavily beaded.

'This isn't from the sixties.' I took it from him and held it up. 'This is earlier – forties, I would think – and it's an original.'

'That's the point,' he said. 'It is an antique. We can't send it out on hire, the fabric is too fragile – rips if you so much as look at it. And everyone was smaller back then,' he added. 'This won't fit anyone now – well, not the strapping great tarts you see these days – might just as well sell it.'

'If you're sure . . .' I said, doubtfully, holding it up for a closer look.

'Same with those white boots,' Ricky went on. 'No one can fit into them these days.'

'What size are they?'

'It's not the shoe size, it's the calves. Skinny legs those dolly birds had . . . Oh, hello! I stand corrected,' he said as Sophie stood triumphantly in the boots and began parading about in them. 'Sparrow's Ankles has got 'em zipped up. Mind you, look at them calves,' he went on, nodding at her legs, 'no fatter than a pair of sauce bottles . . .'

We were all laughing as Morris appeared with a loaded tray of tea and buttered banana bread. And it was in that

92

moment that a voice cut through our merriment like an arctic wind and froze it on our lips.

'Enjoying ourselves, are we?'

Detective Constable DeVille, Inspector Ford's sidekick, known to all who loathe her as Cruella, had come in through the shop and was standing in the storeroom doorway. She's a striking-looking young woman with ebony hair in a sleek bob, an almost unnaturally pale face, and huge, violet-blue eyes. But her bid for beauty is ruined by a small, downturned mouth that gives her a permanent look of disapproval. Today, it seemed, she had a sidekick of her own. He was a broad-shouldered individual with brown hair shaved to stubble and the solid, stocky build that should make criminals think twice about grappling with him; he looked like a rugby player. She introduced him as Detective Constable Dean Collins. He gave a silent nod of greeting.

'You've left the door of your shop unlocked,' Constable DeVille went on, in the voice of a headmistress addressing naughty schoolchildren, 'and there are three handbags in plain sight.' She might as well have added it would serve us right if they got nicked.

No one said anything. We all felt chastened, not by leaving our bags unguarded but by our laughter, by being caught out in behaviour that seemed inappropriate in the tragic circumstances. She should have arrived half an hour before when we were weeping like drains.

'We've come for Gavin Hall's phone.'

'It's in the shop, I'll get it.'

The two detectives trailed after me, and as I took the phone from Gavin's jacket pocket, DeVille was ready with a plastic evidence bag open in her hand and I dropped it in. Collins had picked up one of Gavin's magazines and was leafing through it. Cruella scowled over his shoulder. 'Is this the sort of stuff he sold?' she asked, picking up another.

'Is there any more news,' I asked, 'about what happened to Gavin?'

'We're keeping an open mind at present.' Her voice told me to mind my own business.

I persevered. 'Have you found his spectacles yet?'

DC Collins glanced up from his comic. 'Forensics found them this morning, on the path. He must have dropped them.'

Ricky appeared from the storeroom at that moment carrying a short, white fake-fur jacket freckled with black spots. 'You know, Constable DeVille, you'd look sensational in this!'

Cruella's black brows arched upward and her little mouth quivered. For a moment she struggled, not sure if she was being mocked. I caught a twinkle in her colleague's eye. He folded his lips to hide a smile. If only she had laughed, treated the whole thing as a joke; instead she flung the comic back on the table and glared. 'Come on, Collins. We've got what we came for,' and she marched out. Collins, who looked as if he would have liked to peruse his comic for a bit longer, put it back and followed her. He nodded a goodbye to me and, as he passed the shop window, I could see he was grinning.

I turned the key in the lock after him so that we could enjoy our tea in peace.

'You're evil,' I told Ricky as we trooped back into the storeroom.

'S'not my fault she can't take a joke.' He looked at the fur jacket and sighed. 'The sad thing is, she *would* look sensational in this.'

'Can I try it?' Sophie mumbled through a mouthful of banana bread. She was still wearing the cap and boots.

'Too big for you,' he told her frankly. 'You stick with the cap and boots.'

'I can't afford them,' she sighed soulfully, turning tragic dark eyes upon him. She caught a warning frown from me. 'I'll have to save up,' she added quickly, unzipping the boots and wriggling her feet out.

'Yes, you will,' Ricky told her flatly. 'But you can keep the cap,' he added, winking at her.

'You look fab.'

'Oh, thank you!' She spun around to take another look at herself in the mirror.

'Did you see we'd sold a painting for you yesterday, Sophie?' Morris asked coyly.

'No!' she squeaked. 'Which one?'

'You'd better go and look in the book,' Ricky recommended, and she rushed out into the shop. Pat, during all this, had seated herself at the table, and was carefully selecting lengths of ribbon from the trug, laying each strip out methodically.

'Aren't these trimmings precious?' I asked Morris, watching her. 'Don't you need all these for costumes?'

'I've got miles and miles of the stuff,' he assured me, 'and these are just odd bits.'

'I want a word with you, anyway, Pat,' Ricky began ominously, making her stop and look up. 'Your country panoramas—'

'What's wrong with 'em?' she demanded, immediately suspicious.

'You're not charging enough for them.'

I cheered. I'd been telling Pat this for ages. Her country panoramas are created from felt and wool, delightful scenes of fields and cottages, with knitted trees and woolly sheep, little dressed figures of shepherds and farmers, each scene contained in a deep box frame behind glass. 'They must take you hours and hours,' Morris said.

'If I make 'em too expensive, I won't sell them,' Pat told him.

'And you won't sell 'em if you make them too cheap,' Ricky argued, mimicking her local accent. 'People equate cheap with tat. They won't value your work if you don't.'

Pat was shaking her head. 'Look, I sold one yesterday,' Ricky went on, 'and I whacked another fifteen quid on the price. The customer walked off with it, perfectly happy.'

Pat, who suspected Ricky of winding her up whenever he opened his mouth, scurried off into the shop to check the veracity of this in the ledger.

'Sell anything for me?' I asked, ever hopeful.

'Nah, sorry!'

'Take no notice of him, Juno.' Morris bustled up to me. 'We sold a pair of brass candlesticks and a very pretty ribbon plate.'

Sophie rushed back in, pink with pleasure: one of her most expensive paintings had been sold, an autumn hedgerow scene. 'Who bought it?' she demanded.

Ricky shrugged. 'Oh, some pair of old tarts.'

'They said they had the perfect place for it,' Morris added.

There was something about Ricky's shrug, Morris's coy

smile. A little cat's tail of suspicion twitched in my mind. I leant in close to him and murmured, 'Would that perfect place be in your breakfast room or over the mantelpiece in your lounge?'

Morris placed a finger against his lips. 'Don't spoil it for her,' he whispered, as Sophie went rushing back into the shop to choose a replacement to hang on the wall. 'It's in the music room,' he confessed, when she'd gone out.

'I'm not going to find that ribbon plate hanging in there as well, am I?'

'Don't be silly,' he admonished me, patting my hand, 'that's in the downstairs loo.'

Later, much later, when I was back in the flat on my own, feet up on the sofa, radio playing softly, my diary open on my lap, I found myself thinking about spectacles. I was supposed to be going through the diary, reworking the shop rota for next week. With no Gavin, I had spaces to fill. Fortunately, Sophie would be starting work on the bull portrait for Sandy Westershall's birthday and so would have to be in the shop most of the time. At least, I hoped she'd be starting work on it. She'd announced during the afternoon that she didn't want to do it any more, after what had happened to Gavin, and it took a stern talking-to from me and Ricky to persuade her that she couldn't afford to pass up the opportunity. I understood how she felt. I didn't want to go back to Moorworthy House again either, or even think about the place, but she would have to toughen up, put her feelings to one side. Business was business.

Pat had already done more than her fair share in *Old Nick's* last week and I knew she was needed at Honeysuckle

Farm. But I had a full week's work ahead of me and didn't know how I was going to manage extra hours in the shop. My attempts to wrestle with the diary weren't helped by the sudden appearance of Bill, who leapt on the sofa and settled down on top of the pages, obliterating them from view. I gave him a brief summary of how helpful this was, and he responded by purring like a buzz saw, tucking his paws under and closing his one eye.

I gave up on the diary and lay back, eyes closed, listening to the rasping rhythm of Bill's purr. My mind kept drifting back to spectacles. Morris wore his all the time, but peered over the top of them mostly, only really using them for sewing or reading. Sophie was supposed to wear hers, but was too vain, so coped without them unless she really needed them. Nick used to wear his, but only when he was working on the fine details of some restoration work. But Gavin wore his all the time. When he was in the shop, when he was cycling, I had never seen his face without them, never seen him put them down on a table, or fold them and tuck them away in a pocket. He was very short-sighted. Without them his world must have been a blur. So if they had fallen off when he was larking around in the woods, waving that silly sword about, and his whole world turned fuzzy, surely he would have stopped to find them, there and then? He depended on them totally. He couldn't have carried on through the wood for another fifty yards to the place where I had found his body. He would have been forced to stop; unless of course, he was running away from something, or from someone – running for his life.

CHAPTER NINE

I didn't get to *Old Nick's* until closing time. Monday was a busy day, with five dogs to walk now that EB had fully recovered, Maisie to clean and shop for, a towering pile of shirts to iron for Simon the accountant, and a full afternoon's tidy-up of Mrs Berkeley-Smythe's garden. It was a large garden and she liked it kept tidy even though she was away on the high seas most of the time and rarely home to appreciate it. This meant that I fell in through the shop door just as Sophie was putting on her coat to go home. She'd had a quiet day: no customers, but she'd made a start on preliminary sketches for her portrait of the Old Thunderer. There'd been a phone call from Vicky Smithson, to ask how we all were, but otherwise she'd had no human contact and was looking forward to going to the pub that evening with friends. She invited me to join them, but I declined and offered to lock up the shop. I wanted to do some rearranging of my stock after the hostile takeover of my unit by the vintage clothes mafia.

I spent an hour in the stockroom, mooching about without achieving much, moving things around and then putting them back again, before I decided I might as well give up, go home and spend another thrilling evening watching auction lots on eBay. I had my eye on some pretty 1920s evening bags; unfortunately, so did a lot of other people. Staying up until the early hours, trying to slip in the final bid before the auction closed, only to be pipped at the post at the very last second, was a frustrating experience. But as well as the bags there was a job lot of hatpins for sale, complete with two pretty porcelain hatpin holders that I was determined to get my hands on, so I reckoned it was worth another night at the screen-face.

It was only as I went to switch the lights off in the shop that I realised someone was lurking in the lane outside the door. A hunched figure, a hand shading his eyes, was staring in through the glass. For a moment I thought it was Creeping Ted Croaker but realised the figure was too tall. The closed sign was on the door, but as he saw me, whoever it was, he began to rattle the handle.

'I'm sorry, we're closed,' I said, loudly enough for him to hear me from the other side of the door, but he started banging on the glass. Surely he realised it was too late for the shop to be open? But there was a grim purposefulness to his banging, and I knew I would have to open the door. Then I recognised him, although he seemed to have aged a hundred years since I last saw him, his features gaunt, his eyes sunken and wretched: the face of a man who had lost his only child.

'Mr Hall,' I breathed, when I had got the door open. 'Please, come in.'

'I'm sorry,' he began brokenly,' I didn't really expect anyone to be here . . . then I saw the lights . . . I just wondered if I could talk to you . . .'

I stood staring at him, unprepared for this moment.

'It was you, wasn't it, who found my poor son?'

'Yes,' I said, recovering my wits. 'I'm so very sorry . . . Look, please . . . would you like to come upstairs? We could sit down . . . I could make some tea . . .'

He didn't answer, just stared around him, his gaze finally resting on Gavin's jacket hanging on the back of his chair. 'How is your wife?' I asked him in the silence.

He dragged his eyes away from the jacket and stared at me, his gaze almost unfocussed. He spoke slowly, as if his thoughts were happening in slow motion, as if he were sleepwalking. 'She . . . her sister has come to stay. She's with her now.'

I wasn't sure what to say next. Mr Hall had picked up one of the comics from Gavin's table and was staring at it, turning the pages over slowly as he spoke.

'He was supposed to go to university, you know. He got top grades in his A levels. But Gavin didn't always get on with his peers. His mother and I thought perhaps, it might be wise, give him a little experience of the world before he went . . . but now, I wonder, if Gavin might not have—' His voice broke and he stood with the magazine shaking in his hands.

'Please, Mr Hall,' I begged, touching his arm tentatively, 'I think it might be best if you sat down. Here,' I brought a chair up behind him and he sank down into it, the magazine dropping to the floor. I picked it up as Gavin's father sat with his head in his hands and wept, his shoulders shaking piteously.

'Would you like a drink of water?' I asked, after I had let him sob a while.

He looked up, wiping his streaming eyes with the heels of his hands. 'No, thank you.' He took a deep breath, steadying himself. 'I'd just like you to tell me what happened.'

I told him, as gently as I could, about our day at the fair, about the last time I had seen Gavin, heading, as I thought, for the car, and how Sophie and I had found his body in the woods.

'And the man who sold him this dreadful weapon . . .' He leant forward, gripped my wrist with a sudden force that made me wince, and stared intently into my face. '. . . does he know what happened to my son as a consequence?'

'I'm sure he does,' I answered. Cautiously, I put my hand over his gripping one and he released me, muttering an apology. 'But I think if you wanted to know more about that,' I went on, 'the correct person to speak to would be Inspector Ford.'

He stood suddenly, as if by some inner prompting, and then looked around him, lost, as if he didn't know why he'd got up, as if he wasn't sure where he was.

'Mr Hall, if there is anything I can do . . .' I left the rest hanging, as we all do, when we know that there is nothing we can do, nothing that will make the loved one live again.

He touched the cover of one of the graphic novels on Gavin's table. 'He was so into all this stuff,' he said bitterly. 'I'll come and get rid of it all . . . sometime.'

'There's no rush.' I picked up Gavin's jacket and held it out to him. 'You'll want to take this.'

For a moment I thought he would hug it to him, bury his face in it, breathe in his dead child's smell. Perhaps if I had not been standing there, he would have done. 'And there's his rucksack,' I said, producing it from under the table.

He shook his head. 'That's not his.'

'Are you sure? He took it to the fete with him. It was in the car.'

'That's not Gavin's,' he said emphatically. 'His backpack is blue, not black, and it's up in his room. I saw it this . . .' His voice cracked again. 'Thank you, Juno, for talking to me . . .' and he rushed out of the shop, leaving the door open, the bell jangling. He was away, down Shadow Lane before I could call out to him, poor man.

I looked down at the rucksack in my hands and put it back on the table, unclipping the plastic cover. On the inside of the flap a name and address had been carefully painted in block capitals: OLIVER KNOLLYS, 4 DAISON COTTAGES, ASHBURTON. I frowned, fingering the white-painted letters. Who was Oliver Knollys and why did Gavin have his rucksack?

Judging by the weight, there was something inside. I decided to have a look, undoing the drawstring and peering in. Whatever was in there was cushioned, enclosed in a cloud of bubble wrap. I took off the top covering. I could see white metal, hinged and folded legs, tiny rotor blades: a toy helicopter, perhaps? I lifted it out to get a better look.

It wasn't a helicopter. It might be a toy, but if it was, it was a very expensive one. I returned it carefully to its bubble-wrap nest. I knew Daison Cottages, passed them every week on my way to the Brownlows. I didn't know what Gavin was doing with the contents of Mr Knollys' rucksack but I intended to find out, and the only way to do that was to return it to its owner.

CHAPTER TEN

Daison Cottages are not really cottages at all. They are council houses, built after the war for agricultural workers. Like all council houses constructed back then, they are solid, well built, and have large garden plots. These stand in an isolated group of four on the road towards Owlacombe Cross, separated from the roadway by a low stone wall and surrounded on all sides by fields. At some time during the Thatcher era they must have been sold by the council and acquired by their owners. Since then, some have been resold and various degrees of gentrification have taken place. Of the four identical houses, originally painted cream, one is now pistachio green, and one pink, giving the whole row the appearance of a block of Neapolitan ice cream. The third cottage, still vanilla flavour, has sprouted an unconvincing Grecian portico and has a front door painted blue, with flowering baskets hung on either side. It matches the blue-painted wheelbarrow sitting on the front lawn, filled with pink petunias. Pretty, but undeniably naff. It's the last house, number four, which seems to have undergone no change at all, the cream-painted walls grubby and slightly sad, the front door a dull brown and the wire fence separating the garden from the adjacent field set in concrete posts that look original. This is Chez Knollys.

The garden gate was rusty and squeaked when I opened it, a cracked concrete path leading to the front door. The strips of lawn on either side could have done with a trim and the scruffy rosebushes were overgrown. There was no sound when I pressed the doorbell, so I rapped the brass pixie knocker for backup. As neither of these attempts produced any answer from within, I wandered around the side to the rear of the house.

The back garden was long, a washing line strung down its entire length, a solitary floral nightdress billowing gently in the breeze. There was a large vegetable plot on one side with some old cold frames, a water butt and a wizened apple tree. I picked up a fallen apple, hard as a conker and bright green – a cooking apple, probably. Apart from a few dishevelled dahlias, the rest of the garden was grass, except at the far end, where a small patch of wildflower meadow had been sown. I wandered down to take a look. Earlier in the summer, poppies and cornflowers would have glowed amongst tall, rustling grasses ticking and buzzing with insects. Now it was mostly gone, just a tangle of brown stems and rattling seed pods. Beyond the garden fence was a paddock, three ponies watching me from the far end, swishing their tails.

The neighbour with the blue wheelbarrow out front had constructed an imposing length of fence separating the two back gardens, the panels topped with sections of trellis, the whole lot stained a fashionable shade of green. It made the divide between the two neighbours abundantly clear: *We are not like that shabby lot next door*, it seemed to be saying. As I walked back up the path towards the house, it spoke to me.

'Can I help you?'

I had to draw close to the trellis and peer through a diamond-shaped hole to see who had spoken. I could see part of a woman's face through the lattice work, her brown hair wavy and short. 'Are you from social services?' she asked.

Well, I didn't say I was and I didn't say I wasn't. She just made her own assumptions and went plunging on. 'Only, I've phoned your department more than once.'

'Oh?'

'Well, I worry about the old lady.'

'Mrs Knollys?' I ventured.

'There's only that young lad to look after her, and he's still at school. He's away all day and that poor old soul is bedridden. In fact, I've never laid eyes on her.' She stopped, apparently expecting some response.

'Ah!' I said. 'So there is no Mr Knollys?'

She shook her head, 'Only young Oliver.'

So Oliver Knollys was a schoolboy. 'I'm afraid these days it's not unusual for a child to be the sole carer in their family,' I told her, shaking my head sadly.

'I'm sure he does his best, bless him,' the neighbour went on, 'but I've never seen a doctor, or a district nurse go in . . . or a carer . . . or anyone.'

'Have you lived here long?'

'About eighteen months now.'

'Well, I'm here to have a chat with Oliver,' I told her, with the voice of one who has arrived to take control of all problems.

'He won't be back from school yet.' She seemed slightly ruffled, as if she thought I should already know this.

'Do you know what time he gets home?'

'About half past four.'

'You've been most helpful, Mrs . . .'

'Hardiman,' she told me, 'April Hardiman.'

'You've been most helpful, Mrs Hardiman. I'll come back.'

'And what did you say your name was?' she asked.

I didn't. Damn. 'Juno,' I said, turning to smile at her. 'Juno Browne.'

As I reached the front gate and turned to close it, I could see Mrs Hardiman watching me from her living-room window. She must have run back through the house to get a proper look at me. Obviously the diamond-shaped view was not sufficient. I gave her a cheery wave. I don't know whether I make a convincing social worker. I generally look a bit scruffy so I'm sure I fit the bill.

I had an hour before Oliver was due home, time to drive down to *Old Nick's* and check on the takings, possibly pick up a few groceries whilst I was in town. For the first time I switched on White Van's radio, something I'd been reluctant to do because of what happened when Sophie did it in my last vehicle. This time there was no conflagration, just the local news. There had been a double murder at Dartmoor Prison, so the newscaster told me, and a riot during which prisoners had set fire to their cells. But police were not looking for anyone else in connection with the tragic death of nineteen-year-old Gavin Hall, she went on, who died in a stabbing at the weekend, and whose death was being treated as unexplained but not suspicious. She started blathering about the weather, but I switched her off.

I drove back to the shop, and after the briefest of hellos to Sophie and Pat, ran upstairs, sat on the bare floorboards in the living room and picked up Nick's phone.

Unfortunately, it wasn't picked up on the other end by the person I wanted to speak to, but by Det. Constable DeVille. Inspector Ford was at the prison, she informed me, investigating a double murder, what did I want? I didn't want to speak to her. I asked if the inspector could phone me back. There was a weary sigh at the end of the line. She would leave a message – she was obviously doing me an immense favour – but I shouldn't anticipate a response any time soon. The inspector was busy. She hung up.

But I was barely halfway down the stairs before the phone rang and I doubled back on myself to pick up the receiver. 'Juno Browne?' It was a man's voice, but not the inspector's. 'This is Detective Constable Collins. You phoned the station just now.'

It took me a moment to realise who was speaking: Detective Constable Collins, he of the burly, no-nonsense physique and twinkly eyes, the sidekick's sidekick. He must have been earwigging on my conversation with Cruella. 'The inspector won't be free for hours,' he went on. He definitely wasn't a Devon man. His flattened vowels suggested a northerner to me – well, north of Bristol, anyway. 'I wondered if there was anything I could help you with, Ms Browne?' Meaning: he was curious to know why I'd phoned. Whatever, it was nicer talking to him than Cruella. I asked him if what I'd heard on the radio was correct, that they thought Gavin's death was an accident.

'Well, there are no prints on the weapon except for Gavin's and those of Mr Bartholomew who sold it to him,' he explained patiently. 'There's no sign of pursuit, no evidence that anyone had been fighting with Gavin, or chasing him. There's a clear mark on the trunk of the tree where his foot had slipped. And . . .' He hesitated.

'Go on.'

'The pathologist confirms that the weapon's angle of thrust—'

'Dear God,' I moaned.

'Sorry, but you did ask. Shall I go on?'

'Yes, please.'

'The weapon's angle of thrust is consistent with the wound being self-inflicted. When he hit the ground, the blade was forced into his body.' Constable Collins allowed me a few moments to ruminate over this before he spoke again. 'You found him, Juno. Don't you think it was an accident?'

'It's his specs that bother me. They were found so far from his body.' I told him I couldn't believe that anyone as blind as Gavin could have carried on running after he'd dropped his spectacles, not unless all the fiends in hell were on his tail.

Constable Collins did a bit of silent ruminating himself. Then he said, 'I'll make sure your concerns are passed on to the detective inspector.'

It was the best I was going to get and a damn sight more than I'd have got from Cruella DeVille. At least he'd listened. I thanked him and put the phone down. Then I headed off down the stairs. If I didn't get a move on, I was going to miss the bus from school.

* * *

110

Most kids in Ashburton attend South Dartmoor College. I passed clusters of them in their uniforms dawdling home in the way that only adolescents can dawdle, as I drove up to Owlacombe Cross. I climbed the hill, following a road twisting between overgrown hedgerows until I was forced to brake sharply, the way ahead blocked by a twisted knot of kicking feet and flailing fists. I couldn't see the target at the centre of this affray, but whoever it was, he was outnumbered. I blasted my horn and the group scattered. Four lads, about fourteen years old, shot off in different directions, two of them scrambling through the nearest hedge. I opened the van door and yelled after them.

'Olly Nolly!' they chanted as they escaped, laughing. 'Olly Nolly!'

A small skinny figure was curled up in the road, lying on his side in a foetal position, knees drawn up protectively, elbows tucked in. I couldn't see his face because he had sensibly buried it in the schoolbag that he was clutching to his chest. I could only see short, spiky fair hair and one pink ear.

I leant over him. 'It's all right, they've gone now.'

He moved cautiously, uncurling like a little hedgehog, and one blue eye stared at me apprehensively. I had expected the owner of the rucksack to be older, a sixth-former perhaps, but I had no doubt that this skinny little lad was the one I was looking for. I held out my hand to help him up. 'Oliver Knollys, I presume.'

CHAPTER ELEVEN

Oliver Knollys had a split lip, torn trousers, a bloodied knee and probably a black eye brewing, but it still took a lot of persuasion to get him into my van and let me drive him the short distance home. It was only when I showed him his rucksack caged in the back he agreed to slide into the passenger seat next to me.

'So, what was all that about?' I asked.

'Nothing,' he hunched a shoulder, feigning unconcern. 'They're just smegheads.'

'Do they bother you a lot?'

He dabbed at his bleeding lip. 'Sometimes.'

'Have you told anyone you're being bullied?'

He didn't answer, didn't look at me.

'A teacher?' I prompted.

He gave a little snort of laughter. 'That'd make it worse.'

'Your grandmother, then?'

He looked taken aback. 'How do you know about my grandmother?'

I told him how I'd tried to return the rucksack to him earlier and had talked to his neighbour.

'Nosy cow, she is!' He turned to look at me suddenly, blue eyes wide with alarm. 'You aren't going to tell no one, are you? I don't want people coming round the house. I don't want anyone upsetting my nan.'

'I won't tell anyone if you don't want me to.'

Oliver stared unconvinced.

'I promise.'

He frowned. 'Who are you, anyway?' By now we were pulling up outside his house.

'Juno. I was a friend of Gavin's . . .'

He lowered his head. 'I know what happened to him,' he told me, fiddling uncomfortably with the strap of his schoolbag. 'They told us in assembly at school.'

'He used to be a pupil at South Dartmoor, didn't he?'

'Then they gave us a lecture about carrying knives.' He swung the van door open. 'Can I have my bag now?'

'Not just yet. We're going to patch you up first.'

He froze like a startled rabbit. 'You're not coming in?'

'We won't disturb your nan,' I assured him. 'She needn't even know I'm in the house.'

I pointed to his reflection in the rear-view mirror. 'You don't want her to see you like that, do you?'

'Well, all right,' he muttered, and led me reluctantly up the front path and around the side of the house, his schoolbag thumping on his shoulder. I held on to his rucksack. He dug a key from his pocket and let us through the back door into a large, square kitchen. A scrubbed pine table took up the middle of the room, an original oil-fired range set against the wall with clean washing hanging around it on an old wooden clothes horse.

'D'you want to sit down, Oliver? We need to get that dirt and gravel out of your knee.'

'Call me Olly,' he said, rolling up the leg of his trousers. 'Only teachers call me Oliver.'

I swung open the door of a fridge almost as old as Nick's. 'Any ice?' I pulled a tray of ice cubes from the tiny freezing compartment, bashed some out into the sink, grabbed a handkerchief from the clothes horse, wrapped some cubes in it and handed it to Olly. 'Hold that against your lip.' It had stopped bleeding but was puffing up ominously. I asked if there was a first-aid kit in the house.

'There's some stuff up in the bathroom cabinet,' he mumbled. 'I'll get it.'

'Sit!' I commanded. 'I can find it.'

'Nan will be having her nap,' he said anxiously.

'I'll be quiet as a mouse, I promise.'

'I'll make her tea in a minute,' he said, then added pointedly, 'when you've gone.'

I was getting curious about Olly's nan. He seemed terrified of disturbing her. Or was it Nan herself he was terrified of? Was he being overprotective or was she some kind of gorgon?

I crept up the stairs. The door of his bedroom stood open, the bed tidily made. It looked like the room of a much younger boy; the Thunderbird wallpaper was probably an embarrassment to him now, much of it covered up by film posters. I listened outside Nan's door, which was shut: no sound from inside, no muffled television or radio, no enquiring voice. She must have been sleeping. The bathroom

114

was pink-tiled, with a frilly curtain at the little window and a crocheted loo roll cover sitting on the windowsill, a medicine cabinet with a speckled mirror over the sink. I came downstairs armed with scissors, cotton wool, plasters and a bottle of TCP.

In my absence Olly had grabbed the rucksack and was checking out the contents. On the table lay a cloud of bubble wrap, and a few inches above it, four little motor blades whirring softly, the drone hovered like a giant dragonfly.

'It's working all right, then?' I don't like drones. I think they're a bloody nuisance. But I'd never seen one working at close quarters before and it was fascinating. Olly's fingers were busy on the controls as he sent it higher, circling the kitchen, before bringing it back to the table for a controlled landing.

'That must have cost a lot,' I said.

He shook his head. 'I made it.'

'You made it?' I cleared a little space amongst the bubble wrap to put down the things I carried.

'It's not difficult,' he informed me nonchalantly, 'I got the parts off the Internet.'

'In a kit?' I knelt before him and began dabbing gingerly at his bloodied knee. 'Sorry, this might hurt a bit.'

'Yeh, but some of the parts were a bit crap, I had to modify 'em.'

'Do you want to do this kind of thing when you leave school? Electronics?'

'Nah! I'm going to be a chef.' He watched me picking grit out of the wound. My teeth were on edge, but he was remarkably stoical about the process. 'You got a boyfriend?'

115

I don't currently have a man in my life. Men tend to want to murder me. 'Actually, there's a vacancy in that department at the moment. Did you want to apply?'

He shook his head and grinned, his face flushing faintly pink. 'I'm too young for girls.'

'How old are you?'

'Fourteen. But I look younger, don't I? People are always telling me.'

He was certainly still a child, no sign of the volcanic eruption which must shortly take place in his hormones. His skin was clear, cheek soft as a girl's, his voice a childish pipe; a skinny pixie of a boy, with spiky hair and sticky-out ears. There was something old-fashioned, almost quaint about him. Perhaps it came from living alone with his nan, being her sole carer. I looked around me. The kitchen was clean, the washing aired. When I'd opened the fridge I'd noticed the remains of a shepherd's pie in an enamel dish. He put me to shame. I felt quite moved at the idea of this little lad coping on his own. 'Do you get any help with your nan? You're entitled to support, you know, from the council.'

'We don't need any help,' he answered defiantly. 'Besides, Nan doesn't like anyone coming here. Look, thanks and all that, but you'll have to go now. I need to give Nan her tea.'

'I wanted to ask you a few things about Gavin. Look, now you don't look quite so scary, why don't you go and check on your nan, see she's OK? She might like a cup of tea.'

He agreed reluctantly and limped upstairs. I heard him knock on the door, calling softly.

It opened and then closed as I binned the bloodied cotton wool. He came down a few moments later.

'She's all right, for a few minutes. She sleeps most of the time,' he went on, 'or watches telly. I leave her sandwiches for lunch before I go to school, and a flask of tea. We have our proper meal in the evening.'

'What's wrong with her?' I asked.

'She's old.'

Old age isn't a disease, but I decided not to pursue it. I reckoned if her grandson was only fourteen, she couldn't be very old, anyway. 'I won't keep you long,' I promised. 'You knew Gavin from school?'

'Not really. I mean, I knew him to look at, he was a prefect. But he was years above me, he left last year.'

'But you were friends?'

'He was all right.' His eyes became shiny suddenly and he looked away. 'It was horrible what happened to him. Was he really just messing about with a knife?'

'That's what the police think. Actually, it was a sword. He was carrying it when he jumped up on a fallen tree and slipped.'

He was silent a moment, taking this in. 'I was out in the field one day, flying the drone. Gav was going by on his bike and stopped to have a look. Course, he wanted to have a go with it.' He grinned suddenly. 'He was hopeless with the controls. Anyway, he wanted me to go up Moorworthy with him, fly it around up there.'

'You mean where the big house is?'

'That's right.'

'When was this?'

He rubbed his nose reflectively. 'Weeks ago, the school holidays had just started. I told him we couldn't fly it over private property, it's against the law. But he said he just wanted to look in the woods.'

117

'Did he say why?'

Olly's gaze slid away, eyes hidden by pale pink lids and fair lashes. 'No.'

He was holding out on me, but I knew I mustn't press him too hard, I didn't want him to clam up altogether. 'How did you get there? Gavin didn't drive.'

'We cycled up to Buckfast, picked up the path to Holne Chase. We walked the last bit, Gav wanted us to hide our bikes in the woods. When we got to the gates, we flew the drone up over that long wall, and over them woods, but there were too many trees for us to see much. We couldn't see the entrance to the mine—'

'That's what he wanted to see, the entrance to the mine?'

He nodded.

'Where were you when you were doing this?'

'On that bit of common, across the road,' he said.

'Sorry, Olly, I don't know anything about drones. I can see there's a camera on it.' It was mounted in the centre, a shiny black eye at the junction of the four legs. 'But how do you see what the camera is seeing?'

'It sends pictures to my smartphone. We watched on that.'

'Right. But you couldn't see what Gavin wanted to see?'

'The trees grow too thick. He wanted me to bring it down low, fly it amongst 'em, but it's too risky. So I brought it round, over a field and then we saw the bloke with the gun so—'

'Whoa!' I stopped him. 'What bloke with a gun?'

'When we flew the drone over this field – still on Moorworthy land, like – he was standing there with a shotgun, pointed right at us. He must have been watching it flying above the trees. He was going to shoot it out of the sky. D'you want to see?'

118

'You've still got the film on your phone?'

'I downloaded it onto the laptop. Come on.' Suddenly fired with enthusiasm, he hopped across the kitchen and into the living room. I followed him and sat at the table as he woke up the laptop and began keying in passwords and other mysterious stuff. The living room had the chilly feel of a room that is not used much, the wallpaper and curtains dating back to the sixties. Apart from a few china ornaments on the windowsill, the only objects of interest were an upright piano and a music stand. After a few moments Olly angled the screen of the laptop so I could see.

At first I was looking through blades of grass, an insect-eye view, and then as the drone rose higher, it gradually revealed the scruffy turf of the moor, boulder-strewn, with Gavin in his specs, grinning, waving up at it. He looked as if he was really enjoying himself. I felt a tug in my chest at the sight of him; I had never seen him looking so happy. The drone crossed the grey ribbon of road and the wall, going higher again, almost brushing the treetops. Then I was looking down over the impenetrable green mass of trees in full leaf. 'The entrance to the mine is under there somewhere,' Olly told me, 'but we couldn't see . . . so I brought the drone back over and . . . there he is!'

I found myself looking down into the face of a man in a sagging tweed jacket and flat cap, his shotgun raised, aiming straight at the drone. 'That's Moss!'

'D'you know him?'

'I suppose you could say I've met him.'

'I pressed *home*.' It seemed as if the film speeded up, going backwards over the trees, back over the wall, over the road, until the drone landed amongst the grass. 'It's a control that brings it straight back to the launch point,' Olly explained proudly. 'I reckon that bloke would have shot us right out of the sky.'

'Some people will go to any lengths to protect their privacy,' I pointed out.

'I told Gav, you're not supposed to fly it within fifty metres of private property. But you're not supposed to shoot at people either, even if they are trespassing.'

'I don't know if the law applies to drones.'

'I didn't mean the drone.'

I stared. 'You don't mean he shot at *you*?'

Olly's face was deadly serious. 'We was just packing up, had got the drone back in the bag, and we heard a shout, and there was that bloke coming towards us with the shotgun, yelling and waving. So we legged it. He fired over our heads.'

My very brief acquaintance with Moss had given me the impression he was a bit odd, certainly uncommunicative, but he must be an absolute nutter to fire a shotgun in the direction of two young boys, even if he was aiming high to frighten them off. 'What did you do?'

'We kept running. Then we hid in the woods. We had to wait ages till we were sure it was safe to come out, that he'd gone.' He gave a grim little smile. 'Then we had to cycle back home. We were knackered.'

'Did you tell anyone what had happened?'

'You mean, like the police?' He shook his head. 'I didn't want anyone round here, asking questions. My nan—'

'Yes, I understand, but, after all this, you were happy to loan the drone to Gavin on the day of the fete?'

'Didn't loan it to him, did I?' he responded bitterly. 'He was dead keen to go back to this place, wanted me to go with him. But I've got Youth Band on a Saturday morning. I told him, I'm not missing band practice just to go to some crappy garden fete.'

I pointed to the music stand. 'So, you're the musician?'

He shrugged. 'Not really. I wanted to play the clarinet, but when I tried to join the band, they said they had enough clarinets. They couldn't get anyone to play the bassoon. No one wanted to play it, so I said I'd have a go. And I like it, it's sort of sad-sounding.'

'Yes, it is.' I'd have liked to have heard him play. 'But getting back to Gavin—'

'He pinched it, didn't he?' Olly said in disgust. 'I come home from school on Friday night, he'd got in here, must've found where I keep the spare key. He's left me a note. He said he was sorry, but promised he'd take care of it and bring it back on Sunday. I thought, he'll wreck it if he tries to fly it in them woods, he'll crash it into a tree.'

'Didn't you try and get it back?'

'I don't know where he lives, do I? I mean, I know his parents live in one of them posh places up on Druid somewhere, but I've never been to his house, don't know his address. When he didn't bring it back on Sunday I tried his phone. I was going to try again, when I got back from school, but then they told us he was dead, so . . .' He tailed off.

'He didn't fly the drone on Saturday,' I told him. 'It was locked in the car all day. Perhaps he thought better of trying it once he'd been in the woods himself . . . Olly,' I began tentatively, 'you really don't know why he was so keen to go back to Moorworthy House? He didn't tell you?'

He looked down and picked silently at a scab on his finger.

'This is really important, Olly.'

He wouldn't look at me. 'I don't want to get in any trouble.'

'You won't, honestly. Only I'm not sure that Gavin's death was really an accident—'

'I've told you I don't know.' He looked straight at me then, his little pointed chin lifted obstinately. 'I want you to go now.'

'Olly—'

'I want you to go,' he repeated firmly, closing the lid of the laptop. 'I've got to give my nan her tea.'

I know what I should have done. I should have called Inspector Ford straight away and reported the incident of Moss firing the shotgun. I should have betrayed Olly's confidence and told him everything he had told me. The police have to investigate any incident involving a firearm. But somehow, I didn't; somehow I didn't think Olly's nan would like her house filled with policemen. Besides, I needed to gain Olly's trust. He knew why Gavin was so keen to go back into the woods, to find the entrance to the Moorworthy mine. So, even when I had the perfect opportunity, when the inspector phoned me that evening, I held back.

I'd got out a map of Dartmoor when I got home and spread it on the kitchen table, much to the delight of Bill, who immediately sat in the middle of it. I'd locked him out of the flat that morning, but as always, he found his way back in. I think he has a network of secret tunnels behind the wainscot like one of Beatrix Potter's mice. Anyway, his entry into the flat is made easy for him at the moment because my bathroom window has been stuck open about six inches for months, letting in considerably more fresh air than I want, particularly when I'm naked and wet. I keep complaining to Adam, who promises he will get round to fixing it, but as the sash cords are broken and he's probably not capable of dealing with them himself, I doubt if this will be any time soon.

Despite Bill parking his furry body amongst the contour lines, I managed to locate the road to Moorworthy, tracing it with my finger until I found the house. The woods were marked as a green-coloured wedge. The thin end of the wedge must have been where Sophie and I had entered, through the little gate in the grounds. The footpath was just visible, if I squinted until my eyes hurt, as a tiny broken line. It was fenced off now, but originally it would have gone right through the woods, disappeared under Bill's tummy for a bit, and emerged close to a farm building close by. The words 'Moorworthy Mineshaft, disused' were written within the green shape of the woods. The farm building was marked as 'Applecote Farm, abandoned'. The footpath led away from the farm, across open fields to 'Applecote Pit, mineshaft, disused'. I reckoned the distance between the two disused mineshafts could not have been more than a mile.

The phone rang. It was Inspector Ford, to warn me that the coroner would be contacting me to ask me some questions about Gavin.

'Will I have to give evidence at the inquest?'

'Not necessarily,' he said. 'But she will want to ask you questions about how you found Gavin's body.' It was good of him to call me himself. Other police officers might have left such a call to one of his underlings. 'Collins tells me you were concerned about Gavin's glasses.'

He listened politely as I explained my theory about Gavin being chased. 'There's no evidence of any pursuit,' he told me. 'Of course, from a forensic point of view, it doesn't help that so many visitors to the fete decided to explore the little woodland during the course of the afternoon. We've been contacted by some, but no one saw Gavin or noticed anything untoward.'

This was understandable. I wouldn't have found him myself if I hadn't been looking for him.

'Oh . . . excuse me a moment.' The inspector must have turned his face away from the receiver. I heard his voice, slightly muffled, calling to someone. 'Dale! Where is Collins?'

'On paternity leave, sir,' a cheery voice replied.

'Has that started already?'

'Last night, sir – a little girl – mother and baby doing well.'

'Excellent. Are we sending any—'

'Flowers for the new mother, sir, present for the baby – all in hand.'

'Thank you, Constable . . . Sorry about that.' He returned his attention to me.

No need to apologise, I was fascinated. So Detective Constable Collins was a new daddy. How sweet. I just hoped the baby looked like her mother.

'Forensics were able to trace the route that Gavin had taken,' the inspector went on, 'when he departed from the main path. It was evident from ferns and other plants that had been cut with something sharp, some sort of blade, rather than just broken off. This rather supports your theory that he had gone into the woods to play with the sword.'

'He'd been swiping at the undergrowth with it?'

'It seems so.'

'Just messing about?'

'Well, he didn't need to clear a path,' the inspector pointed out dryly. 'He was walking in lightly covered woodland, not hacking through tropical rainforest.'

So Gavin had just been fooling around. I could imagine him swaggering and swiping the heads off innocent plants. I began to feel vaguely idiotic.

'And let's just suppose this was murder,' the inspector went on, 'what was the motive? Why would anyone want to kill Gavin Hall?'

I'd asked myself the same question over and over. 'Did his phone reveal anything?'

'We've found nothing suspicious so far,' he answered, 'just some rather strange conversations about Batman.'

Inwardly I groaned. 'Gavin was obsessed with superheroes . . . What about that strange man who came into my shop . . . creeping someone or other?'

'Creeping Ted Croaker? Yes, we still intend to interview him, find out what his connection to Gavin was, but he seems to have gone to ground. We can't find him for the moment.'

'Well, if he comes to the shop again—'

'Please get in touch. Well, good luck with the coroner, Juno.'

This was my moment, before the inspector rang off, to tell him about the incident with Moss and the shotgun. But I didn't, I let him go. I left the phone, moved Bill and folded up the map. I still didn't know why Gavin had been so keen to go to the Moorworthy fete, or why he had wanted to search for the entrance to the mine with Olly's drone weeks before I was even aware that it existed. But I was convinced Olly knew, and the little sod was damn well going to tell me.

CHAPTER TWELVE

I arrived at Maisie's next morning, too late to prevent a flood. The smell of hot, wet washing hit me as soon as I opened her cottage door.

'It's the machine!' she wailed at me, standing in the kitchen, a shallow puddle of hot soapy water spreading towards her furry slippers. Jacko lapped at it experimentally then thought better of it.

'You've forced the door again, haven't you?' The washing machine was wide open, water dribbling from its rubber seal, sodden washing in a steaming heap on the floor. I moved Maisie firmly out of the path of the encroaching flood. 'Why don't you sit down? I'll deal with this.'

'It wouldn't let me have me washing,' she moaned dramatically, tottering towards her chair. 'I thought it had finished but the door wouldn't open.'

I sloshed through the puddle and switched the machine off. The red light stopped flashing.

'You changed the programme again,' I told her, pointing to the dial. 'Now, you know we don't use that one. I've painted the only button you need to use with your red nail varnish, remember? You don't need to touch anything else.'

Her face flushed with indignant innocence. 'I never touched anything!' At ninety-four, Maisie can lie with the mendacity of someone ninety years younger.

'It must have been Jacko, then.' I scooped her wet washing into a bucket and reached for a mop.

'I told our Janet I didn't want that washing machine,' Maisie said petulantly.

'Our Janet' was her daughter, who lives up north. She had bought her mother the new machine after the old one collapsed from exhaustion. 'I wanted one just like the old one.'

'I know,' I sympathised as I finished mopping, 'but they don't make that sort any more, Maisie. You've broken the lock again. We'll have to get that fella to come and fix it. Give him a call.' I picked up the bucket of laundry. 'I'll wring this lot out and hang it on the line. And don't come onto this wet floor,' I warned her, 'in case you slip.'

I lugged the bucket into the garden. Wet washing weighs a lot. As I wrung out each garment and pegged it on the line, I thought suddenly of Olly's garden, of the single floral nightdress blowing in the breeze.

'You ever know a family called Knollys, Maisie?' I asked when I came back inside. 'They lived up Owlacombe way?'

'I went to school with a Fred Knollys.' She was sitting safely on the sofa by now, her feet up on a stool, making a big production number of behaving herself. 'He's dead, years ago. Now, he married . . . what was her name?'

127

'I've met a little boy called Knollys,' I told her, sitting down. 'Oliver.' I smiled. 'Olly Knolly, they call him.'

Maisie suddenly laughed, bringing her hands together in a single clap of delight. 'That's it!' she cried, remembering. 'Dolly Knolly we used to call her! Dorothy was her real name.' She frowned. 'She still alive? She must be my age.'

'Olly only has his grandmother, but I think she must be younger than you.'

Maisie was shaking her head with the certainty of one who can remember years ago, even if she can't remember yesterday. 'No. There was no grandson. There was a granddaughter, and she was no better than she should be.' She rolled her eyes in disapproval. 'Now, she had a babby . . . now let me think. Course, he killed himself.'

'Who did? Fred?'

'No. Not Fred!' she snorted, as if she was talking to an idiot. 'The son! I'll think of his name in a minute. Suicide. Ever such a fuss, there was. Vicar only let him be buried in the corner of the churchyard. Mind you, this was years ago, be different now.'

'Are we talking about Oliver's father?'

Maisie looked blank. 'Who's Oliver?'

I began to wish I hadn't started this conversation. 'The grandson.'

'No! I told you, there wasn't any grandson, just the girl.'

I gave up after a couple more minutes, still unable to sort out the Knollys' family tree.

Fortunately, there were other people I could ask, and I'd be seeing them that afternoon.

* * *

128

Jamie Westershall was waiting in *Old Nick's* when I popped in at lunchtime, standing behind Sophie, admiring the progress of her portrait of the Old Thunderer, whose magnificent head was emerging from the white background of the thick watercolour paper like a ghost through the mist: his staring dark eye, the moist pinkness of his nose. His horns and curls were as yet unpainted, just faint strokes of Sophie's pencil, the background of field and woods a hazy wash of green.

There was something almost proprietorial about the way he was leaning over Sophie's shoulder, as she sat smiling up at him. But Sophie brings out the protective instinct in men.

I don't seem to have the same effect, possibly because I'm tall enough to look most of 'em in the eye and spit in it if necessary. They both looked up as I came in, spell broken.

'Ah, the gorgeous Juno!' Jamie came swiftly forward to give me a hug. 'Just wanted to see how you girls were after that terrible business the other day.' He sighed. 'Of course, I blame myself,' he added sadly.

'Why on earth should you?' It was looking more and more as if the only person to blame for what had happened was Gavin himself.

'I wanted to get the whole wood fenced off years ago, when we first discovered there were rare bats in the old mineshaft, but there was a lot of fuss from local ramblers about the right of way through the woods being kept open. In the end we came to a compromise, just fenced off part of it, but now I wish I'd stuck to my guns.'

'It's not your fault, Jamie,' Sophie assured him solemnly. She gave him a long-lashed blink, her dark eyes turned on him, full beam.

'No, it's not,' I added. 'Gavin shouldn't have been messing about with a lethal weapon. The police seem convinced it was an accident.'

'Of course it was an accident!' Jamie's eyes widened in surprise. 'What else could it have been? But listen, that's only part of the reason I came. I'm hoping that you haven't been put off Moorworthy House altogether. As you know, this portrait is a present for Sandy's birthday. Quite a big birthday, the old devil is seventy this year and we're throwing a party. I was hoping that you, Sophie, as the artist, would come along. And you too, Juno, of course.'

Sophie glanced at me, taken aback and uncertain. 'That's wonderful, thank you,' I put in hastily, before her little mouth had a chance to open. I knew she was reluctant to go back there again, but I didn't want her to blow my chances of taking another look around.

'We'll both be delighted. This could be very good for business, Soph,' I added. 'You might pick up another commission.'

'Just what I thought,' Jamie agreed. 'So you'll come? It's the 29th of October.'

'We'll be there,' I promised.

'Excellent.' He strode to the shop door.

'By the way,' I called out to him, 'I saw Mr Moss at the fete. I tried to thank him for getting my van taken to the garage, but he didn't give me the chance.'

'Moss?' he laughed. 'He's a bit of an oddball. He's worked on the estate for years. Believe me, he wouldn't bother about being thanked, especially by a young lady. He'd be covered in embarrassment, I expect. He barely ever speaks. Anyway,' he looked at his watch, 'must dash. Oh,' he paused as he opened the door, 'nearly forgot to say, this party is fancy dress.'

'Any particular theme?'

'Oh, hell, now, what is it? Emma thought it up.' Jamie frowned, drumming his fingers on the edge of the door. 'I know!' He snapped them, remembering. 'Legends of the Silver Screen. That won't cause any problems, will it?'

'None at all,' I told him, as Sophie grinned at me. 'That's absolutely perfect.'

Autumn had really arrived. In the distant woods bronze had mellowed to gold, acorns were dropping, rusty flakes of leaves falling on pavements; there was smell of woodsmoke, and any gust of wind was likely to bring down a painful shower of conkers, still in their spiky green jackets. But mostly what alerted me to the changing season was the increasingly chilly air blasting through my bathroom window. I called in at *Sunflowers*, when I came away from *Old Nick's*, to speak to Adam, my landlord. I could see his bearded figure through the window as I crossed the road. He spotted me and tried to hide behind the counter.

As the cafe was empty, I felt I could be direct. 'I've got just two words to say to you, Adam,' I told him as he lurked beardily behind the cake cabinet. 'Bathroom window.'

He held up his hands in apology. 'I know, Juno, I'm sorry. I'll get round to it.'

I reminded him that I'd heard this before. 'There's a bloke who advertises repairing sash windows in the Ashburton magazine. Shall I just call him in and send you the bill?'

'No, I'll do it,' he insisted. 'I promise.'

'This week?'

He sighed, rubbing his face with weariness. 'This week,' he promised reluctantly.

'Thank you.' I turned to go but he stopped me.

'Do me a favour,' he said, lowering his voice, 'only Kate's not here.' He pointed to an empty table, where a copy of *The Times* lay open at the crossword page, a woman's padded jacket slung over the back of the chair. 'That customer went into the ladies' loo a good half-hour ago. You wouldn't pop in there, check she's not been taken ill or something?'

'Perhaps she's wriggled out the back window,' I told him, grinning. 'Done a bunk, left you her jacket in lieu of payment.'

'Well, brilliant! She only had a coffee.'

I marched up to the ladies', opening the door a little cautiously. Standing in the tiny space occupied by the basin was someone I recognised immediately. I'd only seen her once, at night in a dimly lit car park, but she'd been difficult to forget. In the light of day her face was even more striking, with large, shrewd grey eyes, high cheekbones and a thin, slightly prominent nose. Her hair turned out to be more blonde than grey, and she seemed to be in the process of putting it up, arms raised, a hairpin pressed between her lips. On the edge of the basin was a washbag with a toothbrush sticking out of it, a pink towel, and a smaller zipped bag that I guessed contained make-up. There was a smell of expensive perfume.

'Excuse me.' I pretended I wanted the toilet and wriggled past her. She smiled pleasantly as I closed the door, but if she recognised me, she didn't reveal it. As I slid the bolt, I could hear her hastily zipping up her washbag, gathering up her things. I decided I might as well use the loo after all, and by the time I came out, the mystery lady had gone. Back in the cafe, I found the padded jacket had been taken from the chair and Adam was picking up three pound coins that she had flung on the counter in payment for her coffee as she left.

'She was all right, then?' he asked me. 'She certainly left in a hurry.'

'She was just having a wash and brush-up.' I frowned. I was willing to bet she'd left in a hurry because she had recognised me; she obviously didn't wish to be engaged in conversation. Who cleans their teeth and does their hair and their make-up in the cramped space of a cafe toilet except someone who has no access to better facilities? Like someone sleeping in a car? The good leather handbag and the expensive perfume suggested someone with money. Was this elegant, respectable-looking woman really living rough? And why was she hanging around Ashburton? Curiouser and curiouser. I was intrigued.

'I suppose you want a coffee now?' Adam offered ungraciously.

'Only if it's free,' I answered sunnily, 'and there's a raisin flapjack with it.'

He muttered something inaudible as he turned to the coffee machine.

CHAPTER THIRTEEN

'So, we'll be all right for costumes, then, me and Sophie, for this party?'

'I expect we can find you a couple of old rags,' Ricky muttered, his fag pursed between his lips as he sat at the breakfast-room table.

'After the last hour I've spent up that rickety ladder, scouring your loft for a box of spats you were so convinced was up there, and turned out to be down in your spare bedroom, you'd better come up with something fabulous.'

'Don't you worry, Juno,' Morris passed me a cup of tea, 'you leave it to us. You'll be the belles of the ball.'

'Damn right,' I told him, helping myself to a biscuit.

'No news on poor Gavin?' he asked.

I shook my head, mouth too busy with biscuit to respond.

'The police must be satisfied it was an accident,' Ricky said.

'Well, there's still the formality of the inquest, but yes, I suppose they are.'

There were a few moments of thoughtful silence as we all sipped our tea and munched. Ricky's fag lay untouched in the ashtray.

'You don't know someone called Creeping Ted Croaker, I suppose?' I asked.

They had never heard of him but there are circles not even Ricky and Morris mix in. Then, of course, I had to explain who he was.

'You don't think he was involved in Gavin's death somehow?'

'Difficult to see how,' I admitted, 'unless he knew Gavin was going to the fete and followed him into the woods. But Inspector Ford says Croaker is just a small-time drugs pusher, not a violent character.'

Morris shook his head solemnly. 'You can never tell, not when drugs are involved.'

'It's funny you going up to Moorworthy House again,' Ricky said, 'for this party. Maurice and I have been asked to do another concert there in a few weeks.'

'You mentioned you'd done one there before.'

'We've been there a couple of times,' Morris put in, 'fundraising events.'

Ricky laughed mirthlessly. 'They could do with a few funds themselves. That place is falling apart. It's got dry rot, needs a new roof. I remember the old man telling me.'

'Jamie's uncle?' I asked.

He nodded. 'Very strapped for cash, they are.'

'They don't behave like it.'

'That's your landed gentry for you,' he said, picking up his cigarette, 'fur coat and no knickers. They gave us a grand tour of the house once, didn't they, Maurice? It's all very lovely on the ground floor, but the further up you go, the shabbier it gets.'

Morris was nodding. 'They've got a real damp problem, the ceiling in one bedroom was grey with mould.'

'Don't talk to me about mouldy ceilings, you should see the state of my kitchen.' Another thing I had to tackle Adam about. Stoically I resisted taking a second biscuit from the packet Morris was waving about under my nose. 'I wanted to ask you something. I've met a young friend of Gavin's, Olly Knollys. Did you ever know anyone called Knollys?'

Morris took off his specs and began cleaning them on a corner of the tablecloth, frowning thoughtfully. 'The name rings a bell.'

'Course it does!' Ricky poked him with his fag fingers as if to wake him up. I suddenly felt like Alice at the tea party: Ricky was the Mad Hatter and Morris was the Dormouse. 'Abigail! Our Princess Jasmine!'

'Princess Jasmine?'

'We were putting on *Aladdin*,' Ricky explained. 'Abigail Knollys was playing the princess. Only seventeen, she was—'

'Pretty girl,' Morris interrupted, shaking his head sadly, 'pretty girl.'

'There was a lot of fuss when we cast her. Some people felt she was a bad example. She'd got herself knocked up the year before, had a baby boy. She was still at school, in the sixth form, wouldn't say who the father was.'

'When was this?'

Ricky shrugged. 'Ten years ago?' He glanced at Morris for confirmation. 'Twelve? Anyway, poor maid never got to play the part because she and her mum went out

Christmas shopping in Exeter and got wiped out in some pile-up on the A38.'

'Shortly afterwards, her father killed himself,' Morris added sadly. 'Couldn't cope with the loss of his wife and daughter, I suppose.'

'Right,' I said. 'So, in a short time, this baby boy, who I assume must be Olly, had lost his mother and both grandparents. His father is absent, unknown. So, who was left to look after him?'

'His great-grandma,' he answered. 'Dorothy.'

'Dolly Knolly?'

Morris chuckled. 'That's what they used to call her.'

Ricky frowned. 'Is she still alive? She must be over ninety.'

So, Olly's nan was really his great-grandmother, ninety-something years old, bedridden and left alone all day whilst he was at school. His neighbour was right to be concerned.

I glanced at my watch. Olly wouldn't be home yet. But if Gavin could find out where he kept his spare key, I was damn sure I could.

It was underneath a small stone tortoise in the back garden. Not the most original of hiding places. Fortunately, Gavin had replaced the key there after he'd borrowed the drone. I'd parked the van way down the road, where I was sure no one would see it, and managed to creep up the path without being observed by Olly's neighbour. There was washing blowing on the line, a different nightdress this time, pink, and a pair of large floral knickers, plus two school shirts and grey socks. Olly had been busy with the laundry. I fitted the key into the lock and it turned with a satisfying click.

I let myself into the kitchen and looked around. An upturned cereal bowl and a spoon lay on the draining board, otherwise the room looked exactly as I had last seen it. The house was quiet as a grave, no sound, not even the ticking of a clock. It felt strange. I softly opened the door into the hall and then into the living room. The curtains were pulled back, but grubby nets filtered the light from outside, turning it grey. There was sheet music on the music stand, and an instrument case, lined in red plush, lay open on the floor, the bassoon, disassembled into its various parts, placed inside in tidy compartments. The drone must have been put away somewhere, and the laptop. On the mantelpiece I noticed some family photographs and went in for a closer look. A pretty blonde teenager smiled back at me, a baby in her arms, a man and woman, her parents I assumed, on either side. There was also a photo of a woman wrapped in a floral pinafore, a basket of washing on her hip: a woman with strong, tanned arms and thick, iron-grey hair that looked as if she'd chopped it short with shears, the front held back by a single hairgrip. She faced the camera boldly, an indomitable face but not without humour. Could this be Dolly Knolly, I wondered, Olly's nan? Well, it was time I met the lady. Feeling a little as if I might be in the Bates Motel, I quietly climbed the stairs. I hesitated for a moment outside the closed bedroom door, before I called out Mrs Knollys' name, and knocked.

Fifteen minutes later, Olly came home. He stopped in the doorway at the sight of me sitting at the kitchen table and his face blanched white.

'What are you doing here?' His voice rose in panic. 'You can't just . . .' His eyes flicked beyond me to the stairs. 'My nan—'

'You haven't got a nan, Olly,' I told him flatly. 'Putting her washing on the line is a clever touch, but no one has slept in that bedroom for a long time.' Her bed was stripped, blankets folded, the room cold, unlived in. But I'd known before I'd knocked on the bedroom door, as I'd climbed the stairs, felt that sense of nothing alive in the house, nothing breathing under that roof at that moment but me.

He stood transfixed, staring, blue eyes wide with terror, mouth hanging open in shock.

'There's no one in this house but you, Olly,' I carried on remorselessly. 'Your nan is dead. And I want to know what you've done with her body.'

CHAPTER FOURTEEN

I didn't expect him to faint. I thought he might start yelling, attack me, or panic and run away, but I did not expect the kid to pass out in a dead faint, flat on the kitchen floor.

It was only momentary. He started to come round almost immediately and I was able to help him up onto a kitchen chair. I felt dreadful. My stupid remark about where his nan's body was buried had only been a joke. I'd assumed she was safely tucked up in a care home somewhere. 'Take some deep breaths,' I told him as I fetched him a glass of water and placed it in front of him. He glared at me across the table, his face white, his body shaking.

'I'm not going into a children's home,' he vowed, his eyes brimming. 'I won't. I'll run away!'

'It's all right,' I told him softly. 'There's no need to be afraid.'

'What are you doing here, anyway? I never asked you to come.'

'Olly, you shouldn't be living here alone. You're not old enough.' I was wondering how on earth he'd managed to slip through the net. When his great-grandmother had been taken into care surely someone in social services would have picked up on the fact that there was no one at home to take care of him.

'You got no right,' he went on, 'breaking into my house—'

'Listen, Olly. My mum died when I was a baby, just like yours. I don't remember her at all. For a while, I was in care—'

'Was it bad?'

'I don't remember much about it,' I admitted. 'I'm sure nothing terrible happened to me. But I'm also sure that once I'd left it behind, I wouldn't have wanted to go back again. All I'm trying to say is, I understand how you feel. You can trust me.'

He gazed at me silently, eyes wide, like a frightened animal. At any moment I felt he might bolt, make a run for it. 'So, what happened to you?' he asked.

'My mother died of a drugs overdose. I must have been two or three at the time. I was taken into care. Like I said, I don't remember much about it. Then my cousin found me and sent me to boarding school.'

'Boarding school?' he repeated, horrified.

'He was a diplomat in the Far East – still is. He couldn't care for me. But in the holidays I'd come down to Devon and stay with another cousin, Cordelia . . . But Olly, we're not talking about me. Now, why don't you tell me what happened?'

He swallowed nervously. It took him a few moments to get his thoughts together. 'When Grandpa died . . . killed himself . . . there was just Nan and me living here. We were all right. We looked after each other. We didn't need anyone. Then Nan got ill . . .' He stopped, looked down at the table.

'Is she in a home?' I spoke in a quiet voice, gently. I didn't want to scare him.

He wouldn't look up at me. I was staring at the top of his head, his pink scalp visible through his spiky blonde hair.

'Is she dead?'

He nodded, his eyes still fixed on the tabletop.

'When did she die?'

'Last year.' His voice had sunk almost to a whisper.

'And you've been living here on your own since then?'

He sniffed.

'Did she die in hospital?'

He shook his head. 'Here.'

'When the doctor came,' I began, still trying to work out when things had gone wrong, 'didn't he realise that you were here on your own?'

Olly muttered something.

'What did you say?'

He looked up at me, dashing away glistening drops of tears with the back of one hand. 'She's buried in the garden.' He began sobbing helplessly. I foraged a tissue from my jeans pocket and gave it to him, waited for the sobs to subside, but he went on weeping unashamedly, an outpouring of suppressed anguish that continued for several minutes. I kept handing him sheets of kitchen paper from the roll by the sink, but every time the poor kid tried to stop crying and draw breath he started over again. 'She didn't want to be buried in the churchyard,' he gulped

142

eventually, 'not after what happened to Grandpa . . . she wanted to be buried in her own garden . . . she wanted to be near to the paddock and the ponies . . . she used to give 'em carrots . . .'

'Olly,' I breathed, finally catching on. 'Are you telling me *you* buried her, that no one knows she's dead?'

He nodded, swallowing back another sob. 'Please don't tell! They'll put me in care. I don't want to go in a home!'

I sat back in my chair, gaping at him. 'But how on earth did you manage it . . . you could only have been . . . what, twelve or thirteen. Did anyone help you?'

'She was away, that nosy woman next door, on holiday, so I could dig the hole without being seen. All day it took me. I did it proper, you know, deep.'

'Is she *in* anything?' I asked, aghast.

'I wrapped her in her eiderdown, took her down the path in the wheelbarrow. I gave her a pillow and put her gold necklace round her neck and a bunch of flowers in her hands and her prayer book. And I put in things she'd like . . . you know, like you see in graves on those history programmes on telly. They put in swords and pots and stuff. I put in photos of Grandma and Grandpa, and an old teddy that used to be Mum's. Then I covered her up with a coverlet, and earth and I sowed wild flowers over the top of her. I thought she'd like that . . . wild flowers. They're good for the bees. She was so worried about the bees . . .' He stopped, staring at me, waiting for me to speak. But I was speechless. 'I've done a crime, haven't I?' he asked, his voice rising pathetically. 'Burying her in the garden?'

143

'Well . . .' I breathed at last. 'I don't think there's any reason why someone can't be buried in their garden if they wish, but . . . you see, every death has to be registered, officially. The doctor has to sign a death certificate, to say what a person died of. And if you're saying that no one else knows . . .' I puffed out my cheeks in a sigh. 'So, how did she die?'

'I went up with her tea one morning and she wouldn't wake up. Course, she'd been in bed for weeks. Just too tired to get up, she said. She wouldn't have the doctor, dared me to ring him.'

'And you're absolutely certain she was dead?'

'Course she was!' he cried indignantly. 'She was lying stone cold in her bed for two days whilst I waited for that old cow next door to get off on her holiday!'

'And ever since,' I said slowly, just to be sure, 'you've lived here alone and kept up the pretence that she's still alive. And no one knows?'

'I don't want them to take me into care. Her next door, she'd bring in the social services if she knew.'

'But you can't keep this up for ever!'

'Just until I'm eighteen,' he told me innocently. 'They can't put me in care then.'

'I don't know how you've managed it,' I admitted, shaking my head. I couldn't believe he'd kept this secret for over a year without something going wrong. He'd been incredibly lucky.

'I stay out of trouble. I never bunk off school, I do all my homework,' he told me solemnly. 'I don't give no one a reason to come round here, asking questions. I feed myself proper, like Nan taught me—'

'But how do you manage for money? What about the bills?'

'Oh, I started forging Nan's signature years ago,' he said nonchalantly, a touch of pride in his voice. 'She wanted me to do it,' he added hastily, 'her eyes were bad. She couldn't see to write. Course, she'd never go to the optician. I used to write all the cheques and sign forms for school and everything. Then we put all the bills, electric and council tax and that, online. Dead easy. I set it all up for her, on the laptop.'

'What about cash?' I asked.

'Grandpa left me his money. I get it from the post office, I've got my own account.'

'What about your nan's pension?'

He blushed, red, to the tips of his ears. 'Well, I couldn't stop it, could I? Not without telling them she was dead . . . I don't spend it on rubbish. I'm ever so careful. Just on food . . .'

'And the bassoon?'

'That's not mine,' he responded defensively, 'it belongs to the band.'

'And the laptop and the drone?'

'I am allowed Christmas presents!' he answered indignantly.

'You're committing fraud, Olly.'

He bit his lip. 'I'll be in trouble, won't I?'

'Perhaps, a bit,' I responded evasively. 'And you've got no other family?'

He shook his head. 'Nan left this house to me in her will. There was no one else to leave it to.'

'Have you got a copy of that will kept safe somewhere?'

'Yes, this house is mine.'

'Well, not quite.'

His pale eyes narrowed. 'What do you mean?'

'Your nan can't leave you anything if she's not legally dead. When a person dies their will has to be sorted out by lawyers, go through a process called probate. But she can't be legally dead without a death certificate. D'you see?'

'What am I going to do?'

'I don't know,' I admitted hopelessly.

'They won't want to dig Nan up, will they?' he asked anxiously. 'If anyone finds out?'

'Well, of course they will! There will have to be an autopsy, to make sure she died of natural causes.'

'You gonna tell?'

'No. No I'm not,' I promised after a moment. 'I give you my word.'

He let out a breath. 'Thanks.'

'But,' I added, leaning across the table towards him, 'there is a price for my silence.'

His eyes grew round in horror. 'That's blackmail, that is.'

'It most certainly is,' I assured him. 'You can tell me everything you know about Gavin, for a start. Why did he want to look in that mine on the Moorworthy estate? And don't try telling me that you don't know because I don't believe you.'

Olly bit his lip, hesitating. 'He said that a friend of his had been killed there . . . about a year back. Fell off a cliff or something.'

'In the woods?'

'He got over the fence one night, he was trespassing.'

'Did he tell you this friend's name?'

'Gavin just called him Ben,' he replied, shrugging. 'I don't

146

know how he knew him, but it wasn't from our school.'

'And he didn't say why Ben had gone there?'

'No, he didn't. But he didn't believe he'd fallen off a cliff. He thought someone had pushed him.'

I considered this for a moment. Olly suddenly got up and opened a kitchen drawer, took something out and threw it on the table in front of me. 'And these aren't mine.'

I picked up a pair of wire cutters.

'I found them in a pocket of the rucksack,' he said. 'They must be Gav's.'

I squeezed the handles of the wire cutters experimentally. If Gavin intended to cut through the wire fence in the woods, he would have needed something more powerful, heavier. I doubted if these were man enough for the job. I considered them for a moment, then pulled Olly's spare key from my back pocket.

'I'm holding on to this.'

'Why?' he demanded indignantly.

'Because you need me. Your next-door neighbour is very concerned about you and your nan. She was ready to phone social services when I talked to her. Don't panic!' I added, seeing the alarm flare up in his eyes. 'She took me for a social worker. We'll let her go on thinking that's what I am. If she sees me coming in and out whilst you're away at school, she'll believe that I'm looking after your nan and there's nothing to worry about.' I sighed. 'Somehow, I'll find the time to pop in here a couple of times this week, and I'll make sure she sees me going in and out. That should set her mind at rest.'

Olly gave me a long, considering stare. 'Why are you helping me?'

147

'Because you're going to help me, Olly. What's the flying time of that drone of yours?'

'Half an hour if the batteries are fully charged.'

'Then get 'em powered up, ready for the weekend. You and I are going back to Moorworthy. We're going to take a second look.'

CHAPTER FIFTEEN

Some people think Dartmoor is unspoilt wilderness, untouched by man. But tin has been mined here since the Bronze Age, and copper and silver; and granite quarried. Over the centuries great oak forests have been cleared. The land has been ripped open, patched and pitted and scored with scars. Mining has created wrinkles in the landscape, long deep gullies, which, once the ore has been exhausted, are abandoned to gorse and scrub, to thorns, ferns and nettles, so that it becomes difficult to see them from above: from a drone, for example, especially when, as with the Moorworthy mine, there are also surrounding trees.

It's not that I'm interested in mines. Dark holes in the ground, natural or man-made, do not fill me with enthusiasm. I went caving with a boyfriend once, in Pridhamsleigh Cavern nearby. It was easy going, though horribly muddy, as far as the main cave, but I wasn't mad enough to go deeper in. And no attempts of his to persuade me how wonderful it would be to squeeze my body through narrow fissures in the rock or dive under pools of icy black water could convince me otherwise. And I *know* that the screeching and wailing heard down there is caused by the wind and not the ghosts of lost cavers, but I was still scared shitless.

No, my only interest in the mines of Moorworthy lay in finding out what Gavin was up to.

I'd have liked to have phoned his parents and ask if they knew anything about the death of his friend Ben, but I didn't want to intrude on their grief; and if they'd asked why I wanted to know I wouldn't have been able to tell them.

On Thursday I managed to find time to drop in at Olly's house, parking on the verge outside his neighbour's and waving to her cheerily when she saw me. I didn't see the owner of the property; he was at school. I let myself in through the back door, and as I went through the garden my eyes strayed instinctively to the far end, where Dolly Knolly was sleeping peacefully, surrounded by her ceremonial grave goods, beneath her coverlet of flowers.

I wandered down to where she lay and stood looking over the hedge into the field behind. It was a peaceful spot, surrounded by fields that swept upward to a copse of birch trees on the hill. I could hear rooks calling, the occasional bleat of sheep from distant pastures. I could understand her wanting to be buried here, where she had lived so long, rather than in the town churchyard. The ponies came down the field, pushing their heads over the hedge, gazing at me expectantly beneath long forelocks. I fed them fallen apples from Dolly's garden, the soft hair around their muzzles brushing my open palm.

I stayed in the house half an hour and had a good snoop around. Olly must have suspected I would do this because he'd locked his bedroom, and his nan's. There was a third bedroom with a double bed and a dressing table in it, but the drawers had been emptied.

As I was in the house anyway, I took down the grubby nets in the living room and put them in the washing machine, with a note to Olly to hang them straight back up, damp, when he got home.

He was a remarkable boy. Most fourteen-year-olds, given money and complete freedom from adult control, would be living in squalor by now, surrounded by coke cans and pizza boxes, bunking off school, money all spent on computer games, getting into trouble and high on drugs. But not Olly. I looked around his neat and tidy home, his school shirts carefully hung on hangers on the old clothes horse, and I could have wept for him, for his neat and lonely little life.

His terror of social services seemed to have come from the indomitable Dolly, who'd threatened to put him in a home if he misbehaved, and been fed by television reports of the terrible abuse suffered by children in some of these places. His whole life was now dominated by the fear of being found out, the danger of putting a foot wrong. He had no friends at school. He dared not invite anyone home, in case they discovered his secret. He dared not visit them, in case parents asked questions. The only time he seemed to interact with others was when he attended his youth band rehearsals once a month. He spent his evenings, weekends and school holidays completely on his own. And he was entirely without self-pity. He just got on with it. But it wasn't good for him. He was learning to lie and to be a loner. What Olly needed in his life right now was a responsible adult, and I had no idea where I was going to get one of those.

The coroner phoned me next morning, a softly spoken lady, Mrs Drew. She asked me if I could see her in her office, which meant a trip down to Plymouth. Fortunately, she had a window of opportunity that afternoon, which suited me because I wanted to get it over with. This was partly because I wasn't looking forward to the interview, but also because the city of Plymouth is just too big, noisy and too full of concrete and traffic for my taste. The sooner I was in and out the better.

Mrs Drew was very sweet and sympathetic, treading carefully with someone who had been through, as she put it, a traumatic experience. She asked me to tell how I discovered Gavin's body in my own words and listened without interrupting; then she asked me to go over several points again. She was armed with photographs and little diagrams of the scene showing the exact position of Gavin's body, provided by the police. She asked if I felt these were an accurate reflection of how I remembered things. I said that I did. I said nothing about drones or wire cutters. She told me that she would call me to give evidence at the inquest, but that this may not happen for several months. All I would be required to do was tell the court exactly what I had told her.

'All the evidence so far points to this tragic death being an accident,' she told me. 'Of course, the presence of the weapon is disturbing, but again, the evidence points to the wound being self-inflicted. However, I may direct the jury to record an open verdict.'

'I see.'

'No death certificate may be signed until after the inquest has taken place,' she told me apologetically. 'However, I am satisfied that no further evidence can be gathered from Gavin's body, so I will be issuing an order of release so that his parents can bury their son.'

'I'm sure that will be a comfort to them,' I told her, and she smiled.

And that will be it, I thought unhappily, as I made my way down the stairs from her office. Accidental death, open verdict, what does it matter? It will be finished with, tied up neatly, no further investigation deemed necessary. It will be done. Case closed.

CHAPTER SIXTEEN

I collected Olly after his band practice on Saturday morning, dropping his bassoon back at Daison Cottages and picking up the drone. It was a fine day, with a clear blue sky that would offer it uninterrupted views. It was almost lunchtime by then, so we stopped off in Holne and I treated him to egg and chips in the community cafe which, like the only shop in the tiny village, is run by local volunteers.

When we came to the gates of Moorworthy House, I drove on past. I wanted to tuck White Van out of sight of the road. But before I could find a likely spot, we were forced to slow down to a crawl behind a rumbling beast of a lorry piled high with black, plastic-wrapped bales of silage. Its swaying tailgate bore the legend 'Moss and Pike', its green paintwork thickly coated in dust. Some wag had written 'clean me' underneath the name with a finger. We trundled along behind it for about a mile.

'It stinks!' Olly complained, his hands over his nose.

'It's silage,' I told him. 'It's fermenting. If you were fermenting, you'd stink.'

He shook his head. 'Silage doesn't stink like that!'

I had to admit the fumes wafting our way from the back of the truck were particularly noxious. In addition to the fermenting silage, periodic belches of grey smoke from the exhaust pipe added to the unpleasant ambience. I dropped back, away from the fumes, veering off the road when a muddy track into the woods opened suddenly on our right, bringing White Van to a squelchy halt in the golden shade of some beech trees. 'This'll do.'

We clambered out and walked through the woods onto open ground. The moor stretched away into the distance, the purple flowers of heather gone with the end of summer, the green bracken ferns turning to rust. Ollie knelt on the grass and set up the drone, fixing his phone into the control unit so that we would be able to see what the camera was seeing. He switched the drone on and red lights flashed on its four rotors. A central light turned green. 'Ready!' he called out. It rose into the air, a giant insect, buzzing faintly.

I had the map out and pointed in the direction I wanted Olly to fly it. 'Over the road,' I told him, 'down towards the farm.'

He sent it soaring into the blue until it hung above us no bigger than a sparrow, its tiny red lights winking. I crouched behind him, watching the screen over his shoulder as the drone flew over the road and across the fields opposite, the hedgerow appearing beneath it as a crooked line of dark green.

'Look!' Olly cried. 'There's that stinky old lorry we were following just now!'

We were looking directly down on the lumbering beast, on its piles of black plastic bales.

It had turned off down the track to Applecote Farm. 'What's it gone down there for?'

He brought the drone down for a closer look. 'I thought you said it wasn't a farm no more.'

'It's not operating as a farm. No reason why it shouldn't be used for storing silage, though.'

He giggled. 'Let's buzz it!' And before I could stop him the drone shot forward, dropped in front of the truck and hovered before the windscreen. The driver and his passenger, both thickset individuals, the driver wearing a green knitted hat, gaped, astonished.

This was not what we'd come to see. 'That's not a good idea, Olly.'

He sent the drone rocketing off at an angle, soaring higher, his fingers working the twin controls with practised ease. It whizzed away over the chimneys and slate roof of the old farmhouse. A motorbike was parked in the farmyard, a small knot of people gathered near the doors of a cowshed. Without any prompting from me, Olly sent the drone swooping down for a closer look.

Three men were talking, one wearing a trilby and a sheepskin jacket, one in a flat cap, and the third, the owner of the motorbike, clad in leathers and black helmet. The truck jerked to a stop beside them, the driver leaning out of his cab, yelling, jabbing his arm skyward. They looked up, saw the drone, and began pointing. The driver shook his fist. Clearly, they were not pleased at being observed.

'Time we weren't here,' I warned Olly.

He sent the drone around in a curve. As we passed over

156

the farmyard again, we saw the biker racing for his bike, sitting astride it. Olly pressed *home* on his controls and the drone came swooping back across the road like a returning falcon and landed neatly in the grass.

He picked it up and we jogged smartly back to the safety of the trees and climbed, a little breathlessly, into White Van. I decided we'd better abandon our search for Moorworthy Mine and beat a hasty retreat. Olly struggled to fit the drone into the rucksack as I backed down the muddy track, and hid it beneath his seat. I turned the van and sped off down the road.

'What if they catch us?' he asked, eyes wide.

I shrugged. 'We're just driving along. There's no reason for them to think the drone is anything to do with us.'

It turned out I was being just a smidgen overconfident. Suddenly the motorbike roared into sight in the rear-view mirror, a gleaming black predator racing up behind us, only slowing when it was close on our back bumper. Then it swung out into the road, riding alongside so that the biker was able to turn his helmeted head and get a good look at us. We couldn't see his face at all, masked behind his mirrored visor.

'It's a Harley Davidson!' Olly breathed, awestruck at the sleek, powerful machine riding beside us.

I speeded up. The bike overtook, swerving in front of us, slowing and settling there, forcing us to slow again, hogging the centre of the road, making it impossible to overtake. The road ahead was narrow, hugged on either side by high green hedgerows. All we could do was carry on, stuck behind the bike for another half-mile.

I heard the thundering of the truck before I saw it,

looming up behind, filling up the rear-view mirror, massive and menacing. For a moment I glimpsed the driver, his beefy red face, green woolly hat pulled down over his head like a tea cosy; then all I could see was the chrome bulwark of his bumper, the teeth of his radiator grille blocking the entire back window as it closed up behind us, growling. We were trapped, the bike maintaining a slow and steady speed just in front of us, the green walls of the hedgerow rising on either side. The truck nudged us, gently, bumping us forward.

'What are they doing?' Olly cried in alarm.

'They're just trying to intimidate us, that's all. Frighten us.' Or very possibly kill us, I added silently. This was a lonely road, a good place to stage an accident. The truck bumped us again, harder this time, jolting us forward, making us rock in our seats like crash dummies. Olly stared at me, white-faced in fright. 'Hold tight!' I yelled. There was an unhealthy crunching sound from the rear of White Van as they bumped us again.

'Bastards! I've only had this van five minutes!' I tried to pull out around the bike, but the biker weaved across the road, preventing us from getting past, cutting off our escape.

The truck dropped back in preparation for a more powerful, more violent shunt. 'To hell with this!' I gritted my teeth and put my foot down hard. We hit the rear wheel of the Harley Davidson and sent it slewing onto its side, sparks flying as the mudguard scraped along the tarmac, the driver skidding on his back before flailing to a halt in the hedgerow. The truck behind was forced to swerve to avoid hitting him, its giant tyres bouncing over the back wheel of the bike as it lay on the ground. As we sped away it jammed to a halt, blocking the road slantwise, the driver's cab crashing into the bushes.

Olly gave a yelp of delight and punched the air in triumph. I swung the van off the road at the next turning, a lane so narrow that the hedges brushed the van on either side. It would be impossible for the truck to follow. Judging by the bumps and ruts, and the grass growing up the middle, it was a track not much used and I had no idea where it was going to come out.

'You don't think we've killed him, do you?' Olly asked, as a blackberry briar thwacked against the windscreen. 'The biker, I mean?'

'I wouldn't think so. He wasn't doing any speed for one thing.' For another, when he came to rest, the bushes must have cushioned the impact. If he'd slammed against a drystone wall it might have been a different story. 'But you know what?' I asked him as poor White Van bumped and rattled down the rutted lane. 'Right now, I really don't give a shit.'

Back in the safety of Olly's kitchen we reviewed the film from the drone, watching the group of men talking in the farmyard. We couldn't make out the face of the individual in the trilby hat but the tall, loose-limbed figure in the sagging tweeds and flat cap was definitely Moss. Besides, his was one of the names painted on the truck, which was unlikely to be coincidence. So what were Moss and friends up to? They disliked being spied upon by the drone so much they were prepared to play lethal games to warn us off. They could have killed us. They had to be up to something. And whatever they were up to, Applecote Farm was on Jamie Westershall's land. Was he a part of it? Was he the masked rider on the bike?

I didn't like to think that might be true; but whoever that was, he'd got a good look at me and Olly.

'Tell me something,' I asked, as he placed a steaming mug of hot chocolate by my elbow and slid back into his seat at the kitchen table. 'The first time you went out with the drone, with Gavin, did Moss – you know, the old guy with the shotgun – get close enough to get a good look at you? When he was chasing you, did he get close enough to Gavin to see his face?'

Olly thought about it, silent for a moment. 'Perhaps,' he said eventually. 'Gav kept turning around to see if he was still behind us. Why?'

'I'm just wondering if Moss would have recognised Gavin if he'd seen him again at the Moorworthy fete.' And if he had, would he have followed him into the woods and killed him?

'Are we going back there again?' he asked excitedly. Now that time and distance had recovered him from his fright, he was talking about the whole incident as if it was a great adventure.

'*We* are not going anywhere.' It was too dangerous. Even I wasn't irresponsible enough to involve a fourteen-year-old boy with thugs who were prepared to run us off the road. As it was, the bumper of White Van was buckled and the back doors dented. I didn't want Olly getting buckled and dented too. 'Look, I may have to call the police and you've got to stay out of trouble, remember?'

'Oh, yeah, right.' He looked disappointed but didn't argue.

'Look, we'll take the drone out again,' I added, trying to cheer him up, 'somewhere safer next time.'

'Tomorrow?' he asked hopefully.

'Sorry, I can't tomorrow. I'm working.'

'But tomorrow's Sunday,' he objected.

'Yeah, well, no rest for the wicked. So, what do you do with yourself on Sundays?'

He shrugged. 'Homework,' he answered miserably. 'But I've only got history and I don't have to hand that in till Tuesday.' He stared down at his finger and began picking at a cuticle. 'I might weed the veg patch. I'm growing kale. It's good for you. Nan always grew cabbage. She didn't hold with kale.'

'You must miss her.'

'We used to have a laugh. I go down the end of the garden and talk to her sometimes. You know, just tell her what I'm doing, tell her what's going on.' He flicked a sheepish glance at me. 'Stupid, aren't I?'

'Not at all. I think you should talk to her any time you feel like it. But don't you get lonely, living on your own?'

'Not really. I don't like other people much . . . Oh, you're all right,' he added graciously.

'Thanks.' I tried not to feel overwhelmed by the compliment. 'Tell you what, I'll pick you up in the morning, take you to Honeysuckle Farm, to the animal sanctuary. They can always use a volunteer up there. You like animals, don't you?'

'Yeah!' His sharp little face brightened. 'Are you hungry? I picked some blackberries out of the hedge yesterday, made a crumble. There's loads of it left. Do you want some?'

Silly question. He got a dish out of the fridge and put it in an oven in the Rayburn. 'It'll take a few minutes to warm up. I haven't got a microwave.'

'Let me guess. Your nan didn't hold with microwaves?'

He nodded, grinning.

'Was it your nan who taught you to cook?'

'We always used to cook meals together, right from when I was small. Then, for the last year, it was just me doing the cooking. But she didn't like anything fancy. I couldn't get her to eat anything foreign, not even pasta.'

'A bit frustrating when you want to be a chef.'

'Well, I think I do.' He rubbed the side of his nose thoughtfully. 'I can't make my mind up. I might play the bassoon. It's hard, isn't it, working out what you want to do with your life?'

Certainly is. So far, I haven't managed it.

'Or I might just do science. I can do anything I want,' he added, giving a smug little grin. 'I'm a genius, me. I got the same birthday as Albert Einstein.'

And just for a moment I understood what made other boys want to kick him.

Albert Einstein, in case you're wondering, was born on 14th March. This makes him a Pisces, like Olly. Like Sophie, like Morris, like Cordelia. I am always surrounded by them, these romantic, imaginative, sensitive, dreamy, muddled, vulnerable, hopeless, bloody irritating people: me, an organised, practical, down-to-earth, sane and sensible Capricorn.

As a Capricorn, of course, I am not remotely interested in astrology. The only reason I know anything about it is because I absorbed it by some kind of weird osmosis as I was growing up. My cousin Cordelia, whose life was tragically cut short, was a real wise woman. She practised astrology in a little shop in Totnes, giving consultations on horoscopes.

162

And in the wee small hours, when any sensible Capricorn should have been asleep, I lay awake thinking about Gavin. I bet he was a Pisces. I was still trying to work out what had happened to him that day. Suppose he'd gone to Pat's car, intending to put the sword away, to get out the rucksack containing the drone and wire cutters so that he could get through the fence, then discovered the car was locked. What did he do? He didn't come back to ask Pat for the keys so perhaps he decided to go for a walk in the woods, reconnoitre, find another way in? Or just mess about with the sword? And at some time during all this, did he and Moss encounter one another? Did Moss challenge him, chase him, cause him to fall on his sword, or did Gavin panic and run?

Bill leapt onto my pillow suddenly and began to tread about in my hair, purring seductively. I don't know how he got in because Adam had finally got around to fixing my bathroom window and it was shut. I put up with Bill's rasping lullaby for a bit before yanking my hair out from underneath him so that I could turn over. I drifted off to sleep with no questions answered and dreamt of Dolly Knolly at peace in her bed of earth, beneath the borage and the honeywort, the field poppies and corn cockle, the meadowsweet and the butterflies.

CHAPTER SEVENTEEN

On Sunday I promised to help with the fat fairies. Ricky and Morris had spotted me in the week doing errands when they were sunning themselves at a table outside The Old Library Cafe and had begun yelling embarrassing things like 'yoo-hoo!' and 'cooee!' to attract my attention. Attempting to ignore them was useless so I'd sat down and let them buy me a coffee and recruit me to help them on Sunday with a sudden demand for costumes.

First of all, I dropped Olly off at Honeysuckle Farm. It's not as pretty as it sounds. Years ago, some idiot thought it would be a good idea to demolish the seventeenth-century farmhouse and replace it with a concrete bungalow. A barn and other old farm buildings remain, but it's hardly picturesque. Visitors arriving at the gate have been known to turn away in disappointment. Because, although the animals are fed and well-cared for, their pens and enclosures scrupulously clean, what visitors to an animal sanctuary expect is a cafe and a gift shop, easy parking and civilised loos. All that requires investment: money. And money is what Pat, her sister Sue and brother-in-law Ken, who devote their lives to caring for injured wildlife, unwanted pets and abandoned farm animals, do not have, and are never likely to have. So, although they were surprised, they didn't question the arrival of an enthusiastic little helper who wasn't looking for payment. My last sight of Olly, after I'd made the introductions and was driving away, was of him crossing the yard in a pair of oversized wellingtons, running to keep up with Ken. I'd promised to pick him up later, when I'd finished with the fairies.

But first I made a slight detour. I backtracked, turning the van up over the hill to Buckland, past the lovely thatched cottages and church, on to Holne Chase and the Moorworthy estate. The early morning cloud had fled, leaving an open sky, the moon a chalk sketch against the clear blue.

I'd packed my rucksack and put it in the van along with walking boots, maps, compass and binoculars. I wasn't planning on any serious hiking, but I never went walking on the moor without the essentials. I drove past the impressive gates of Moorworthy House and pulled in half a mile further on, by the track that led to Applecote Farm.

The gate was closed, a five-bar steel gate, rails twined with barbed wire, a heavy chain wound about its locking bar, finishing with a weighty padlock; and a sign, 'Private. Keep Out', just in case you didn't get the message. The track was wide enough to take a tractor or a lorry, a simple earthen road that would have been muddy most of the year but had dried to dust after the long hot summer. It led straight down to the farm. I could see the stone chimneys of the farmhouse, its roof and upstairs windows. Strangely, for a farm that was abandoned, there was a whisper of grey smoke coming from the chimney.

I could have climbed over the gate, with extreme caution, but anyone on the track could be seen from those upstairs windows and I didn't want to risk being spotted. I contented myself with placing my hands carefully on the gate and rocking it with my weight, just to feel it move, just to hear the metal clang, a tiny act of rebellion. Then I got back into the van and drove on.

I pulled in again a few miles further on, on a small gravelled space by the verge. I put on thick socks and laced on my leather walking boots, enjoying their chunkiness, their weight, as I crunched gravel underfoot. A wooden signpost pointed across the moor to stone circles and distant tors, but I was heading back the way I'd come, towards Moorworthy.

I left the road, heading across the short grass, picking my way between granite boulders scattered like dinosaur bones, following pony tracks between gorse bushes and twisted hawthorns, and jumped a tiny stream. I was heading for a steep rise, a tumble of rocks on its summit. The air was fresh and I was breathing harder than I should have been by the time I'd climbed to the top.

But it was a great viewpoint, rising above the stunted rowan trees that grew all around it, their clusters of berries red as lipstick, and vicious blackthorns heavy with sloes, and showing me a far-reaching sweep of open moorland and rocky tors, of distant blue hills. I sat my bum down on a rock and looked through my field glasses. They were powerful, but small and neat, easy to slip in a pocket, an expensive gift from cousin Brian. I began sweeping from left to right until I found what I was looking for.

You couldn't spot it from the road, but from here it stood out as a dark irregular line crossing the landscape: a steep bank, topped with hedgerow, the border between the pastures of Applecote Farm and the open heath. It would have been built a hundred years ago or more, to prevent valuable dairy or beef cattle from wandering onto the moor.

The hedge bank enclosed the farmland as solidly as a wall. But walls have weaknesses, points of entry. It might offer me a back way in, a chance to get into the Moorworthy estate unobserved, to take a proper look at Applecote Farm, and Moorworthy Mine, and what might be going on there.

But it would have to wait for another day now. I'd promised this day to Ricky and Morris and I was already late. I turned and began to jog back the way I had come, towards the roadside where I had parked the van.

As my parking spot came into view, I could see a jeep had drawn in behind it. Someone was walking around my van, taking a lot of interest in it. Someone was surveying the damage, trying the doors. I'd already packed my damn binoculars back in the rucksack, thinking that I'd finished with them and I could only just about make out a figure in a flat cap before he climbed in the jeep and drove away. But I was sure it was Moss.

I waited a few minutes before I set off down the road. I didn't want to catch up with him. I slowed down as I came to the turn off for Applecote Farm. The gate was open, and I just glimpsed the back of a silage lorry as it trundled down the track.

* * *

'The DOs are doing *Iolanthe*,' Ricky explained as I arrived.

Dartmoor Operatic Society, known hereabouts as The DOs, are generally held in great affection because of the enthusiasm with which they tackle the works of Gilbert and Sullivan. Their voices still sound lovely, but most of them are far too old to be gondoliers, pirates or little maids from school. Ricky says they really ought to be known as the DON'Ts, but that's typical of him.

'They don't usually hire costumes from you, do they?' I asked. For years they'd got their togs from a G and S specialist in London.

'No, but they're not happy with what they've been sent.'

'Well, the men's costumes are all right,' Morris interrupted, coming into the workroom carrying a plastic skip full of rolled-up ribbons. 'It's the ladies that are the problem.'

'Specifically, the fairies,' Ricky went on, eyes twinkling with mischief as he held up an example of the costumes sent.

'Oh!' I exclaimed. 'They sent costumes for *real* fairies!' Obviously, the costume company in London didn't appreciate that there was not a fairy in The DOs under the age of fifty. The dainty little outfit held up by Ricky, flimsy and transparent in places, would have suited a slender young sylph but was not suitable for the bingo wings, sausage-meat arms and cellulite-dimpled thighs of the ladies of The DOs chorus.

'They are not happy,' Ricky said. 'They've asked us to help 'em out.'

'How many fairies are there?'

'Twenty.'

'We can't possibly make them all new costumes in the time,' Morris sat down, taking the lid off the skip. 'So we asked ourselves, what have we already got a lot of? We had a look at the ball dresses from *Cinderella* but . . .' He shook his head, pulling down the corners of his mouth. This idea was obviously a no-no.

'Then we thought of those Victorian nightdresses we've got dozens of,' Ricky went on, 'we thought we'd put wings on them. Well, they looked more like angels from some bleedin' school nativity than fairies—'

'So, then we thought—'

'So *then* we thought,' Ricky carried on, 'about long petticoats. We've got hundreds of them. We could team each one with a pretty white blouse, and make sashes to go round the waist . . .'

'Coloured sashes—' Morris put in.

'Coloured sashes. With wings. And trim the petticoats and blouses with flowers and ribbons.'

'We might even have time to make them little bonnets,' Morris added. 'They'll look very pretty and demure.'

'Course, half of them will keep their specs on, which will ruin the effect,' Ricky finished, 'but at least they won't look like something in a geriatric porn video.'

'So, where do I come in?'

Morris shoved the skip of ribbons in my direction. 'You're making flowers from ribbon, please, Juno. We'll need a couple of hundred.' He peered at me over his half-moon specs. 'You remember how to make them?'

I did. So all day, between cups of tea and pieces of cake, I sewed pink ribbon, blue ribbon, lilac ribbon, lemon ribbon, red ribbon – if a colour came in ribbon, I made flowers from it, whilst Ricky cut twenty pairs of wings from very stiffly starched net and Morris rattled away on the sewing machine, creating sashes.

They didn't talk much – well, comparatively. I didn't want to be drawn into discussion about Olly and fortunately they'd forgotten our talk about his family and didn't ask. I didn't mention what had happened the day before with Messrs Moss and Pike. I had a story ready about how the van came to grief, but I'd parked it up the drive a bit and, so far, they hadn't noticed it. Mostly I kept quiet, working away at my ribbon flowers until my fingers were sore.

They did ask how things were going at the shop, specifically if I was selling any of their vintage clothes. I had to admit I didn't know. I'd hardly been near *Old Nick's* all week. Sophie had been holding the fort. But now she'd finished the portrait of the Old Thunderer, she wanted a day off. It would be my turn tomorrow.

At the end of the day, Morris offered me supper, but I declined. I had to go and fetch Olly.

He was full of it, sliding into the van beside me, bursting to tell me about ferrets and hedgehogs, ducks, baby owls, donkeys and all the other critters he'd dealt with.

'D'you know, they've got a llama?' he asked me excitedly. 'They just found it one morning, tied to the gate. They don't know where it came from. Anyway, it's a lady llama, so they could put it in the paddock with Bam-a-lam and he doesn't mind it. Bam-a-lam's a ram,' he explained. 'Ken says he's an old bugger, butts anything that moves.'

'Oh, I know Bam-a-lam.' He was a black-faced ram sporting particularly impressive headgear. He'd been useful to me more than once. Any dog who took it into its head to start chasing sheep needed only half an hour in a pen with Bam-a-lam to seriously go off the idea.

Olly pulled a rumpled paper bag from his pocket and began chewing a rather limp sandwich.

'Didn't you have those for lunch?'

'We all had roast dinner,' he told me happily. 'Chicken and peas and carrots and roast potatoes and cabbage. Pat cooked it. And apple pie and ice cream.'

I tried not to think of the Moroccan tagine, whose spicy aromas I had been savouring all day as it cooked slowly in Morris's oven, and which I had turned down so that I could pick Olly up; not to mention the glass of red wine. 'Would you like to go there again?' I asked.

'Ken says I can go anytime. So I'm going to go at half-term, every day.' He chuckled. 'That'll be better than going to bloody Lanzarote.'

I could only assume that was where one of his classmates had boasted of going. I let him out at Daison Cottages and he waved to me cheerily as he bounded up the garden path. I was glad he'd enjoyed himself. As I turned White Van towards home, I tried to remember what food I had in the fridge for my supper; or if I had any at all.

My luck was in. When I got back home there were several offerings on the table on the landing outside my door – two promising plastic boxes and three interesting-looking objects wrapped in foil. There was also a ladder leading up into the loft. I could hear voices coming from the roof space and footsteps thumping about, so I stood at the foot of the ladder and hallooed upward.

Kate's little face appeared framed in the hatch, her black plait swinging down towards me like Rapunzel. I thanked her for her offerings.

'Veggie curry and homity pie,' she informed me, 'and a couple of cheese scones.'

'Fantastic. What are you doing up there?'

'Adam's worried about your kitchen ceiling, about where the damp's coming in. He thinks we might have dry rot. So he called in Roy the roofer. Hang on.' She climbed down the ladder. 'Go up and have a look whilst I make him a coffee.'

Well, if I must. I climbed the ladder obediently and stuck my head and shoulders through the hatch. There was no sign of Adam, just a thin man in overalls who must be Roy the roofer.

He beamed when he saw me, showing large front teeth, like a beaver. 'Hello! You must be the lady in the upstairs flat.'

'Yes, I am.' I climbed into the loft.

'Well, as I explained to Kate, there is nothing much to worry about. No dry rot, I could tell that immediately, just a few slipped slates where the rain is getting in.'

'Well, good, I suppose.' I frowned. 'But I don't know anything about these things. Why would damp give you dry rot?'

'Ah, well, there has to be a certain amount of moisture present,' he informed me, 'because dry rot is, in fact, a fungus.'

'I see.' For the first couple of minutes I was genuinely interested. But Roy's high-pitched nasal monotone could render the most fascinating subject boring. After a minute or two my eyes glazed over, quickly followed by my brain.

'I could tell at once there was no dry rot in here because there was no dust,' he intoned. 'Well, I don't mean your usual dust. To the uninitiated it looks like a brown powder, but it is, in fact, the fungal spores . . .'

I wondered where the hell Kate was with his coffee. I suspected her of deliberately taking her time. I endured at least twenty minutes as Roy aired his knowledge. 'The fungus draws all the moisture out of the wood, you see, in fact, eats it from the inside . . .'

I was convinced by the time that Kate finally appeared with his coffee that there wasn't a thing about dry rot I didn't know.

'I have seen rafters disintegrate with a single hammer blow . . .' he was saying as her head finally appeared through the loft hatch. It was too late. I had lost the will to live by then.

I glared at her and she gave me a guilty look as she handed Roy his coffee.

'They call him Boring Roy,' she admitted when he had finally taken his leave.

'Well, you might have warned me before you encouraged me to go up there with him.'

'Sorry, but I knew if he had no one to talk to, he'd follow me down to the kitchen.'

'How on earth did you manage to get him to call on a Sunday evening?'

'Oh, he offered. I think he's lonely.'

'I'm not surprised.'

'Sorry.'

'I forgive you,' I told her magnanimously as I gathered up the offerings from her kitchen, 'but only because of these.'

CHAPTER EIGHTEEN

I was late opening *Old Nick's* next morning, didn't get there until ten o'clock.

At least there was no queue of customers waiting outside: fat chance of that, frankly. I didn't like being forced to waste the entire day waiting to serve non-existent customers when I had more urgent things I could be doing. But it was my turn. Not for the first time I cursed Nick for leaving me the shop.

Then I stepped inside, let the door close behind me, experienced a moment of total quiet, absolute calm, and realised that a day in the empty shop was just what I needed: a day without rushing around, a day when all I could do was sit and literally take stock. I looked around me and let out a breath I didn't realise I'd been holding in.

For a start, the shop looked fantastic. The portrait of Old Thunderer stood on an easel in Sophie's window. She'd done a magnificent job. You could almost touch his matted hair, feel his hot breath, almost smell him. Pat's window looked great too. Soft, knitted shawls in rich autumn colours lay in undulating folds on the wide windowsill, whilst suspended above them on fishing line hung stuffed felt pumpkins and cute, funny little witches on broomsticks, which she'd obviously crafted herself. It was a good job she was more awake to the sales opportunities of approaching Hallowe'en than I was. Even Mavis the mannequin was sporting a witch's hat. It was just a pity all this talent and enterprise would go largely unnoticed in the quiet of Shadow Lane.

I locked the door behind me whilst I nipped up to the kitchen and made myself a coffee. Then I brought it down, turned the sign on the shop door to *Open* and sat at the counter for an overdue look at the ledger to see if I'd taken any money that week.

My day had not started well. I'd overslept, gone rushing out of the house without breakfast and walked the dogs through the woods. Schnitzel the sausage dog had run off amongst the undergrowth and I'd lost him for half an hour. When the smug little *Schweinehund* deigned to return he'd obviously been rolling in badger shit and I had to clean him off before I could take him home. This made me late returning the dogs, which pissed off one owner, who was waiting to leave for a dental appointment and gave me a right earful.

I had dumped the last of my doggy charges and was driving back towards town, trying to make up time, when I was forced to screech to a halt. Amongst the shaggy heads of old man's beard that twines itself amongst the yellowing leaves, the clusters of blackberries and tight clumps of green ivy flowers buzzing with wasps, and all the other things one expects to see in an autumn hedgerow, there was something big and blue that definitely shouldn't have been there: Judith-Marianne in her dressing gown, attempting another escape from Oakdene Nursing Home, was stuck in the bushes.

As I climbed out of the van, she began trying to attract my attention, waving ineffectually with one hand, the only part of her that wasn't completely hitched up on surrounding thorns. 'Help! Oh, help!' she was mewing softly. I surveyed her for a moment, wondering whether it would be easier to pull her forward into the lane or push her back the way she'd come, into Oakdene's gardens. I decided on the former. I reached cautiously through the cat's cradle of branches, trying not to snag myself on the surrounding armoury of thorns.

'Silly me!' she kept repeating. 'Silly me!'

'Well, you've got that bit right.' A long bramble, vicious with thorns and laden with juicy berries was tangled in her woolly blue sleeve. I unhooked it cautiously, leaving a purple smear. She began singing softly to herself, rocking backwards and forwards, her blue eyes staring into a place and time that had nothing to do with here and now. It would have been much easier if she'd kept still. As soon as I'd unhitched her from one lot of thorns, she was getting caught up on others.

I was beginning to think my attempt to rescue her was hopeless and I'd have to call the cavalry, when it arrived in the short, curvaceous form of Barbara the care assistant and her colleague with the ponytail, whose name turned out to be Camille. They'd bustled along the lane in the hope of catching Judith-Marianne before anyone had realised she was missing. Between the three of us we managed to ease her free of enclosing brambles and pull her gently through the hedge onto the road.

'Sleeping Beauty,' she told us solemnly as we were standing on the road, picking off bits of twig and flakes of leaves that crowned her silver hair and clung to her dressing gown.

'Yes,' I agreed, as we checked her over for scratches, 'you were just like Sleeping Beauty, imprisoned by thorns.' She frowned at me, picking at some thread of her unravelling memory, trying to place who I was.

'This is Juno,' Barbara told her. 'Remember? She found you the last time.'

'Are we going back to the hotel?' Judith-Marianne asked suddenly.

Camille took her arm. 'That's right, back to hotel.' She spoke with a Polish accent.

'Do we have to dress for dinner?'

'Yes. We must get you dressed. But we have breakfast before dinner,' Camille told her. 'There's lovely breakfast waiting for you.'

Barbara turned to smile at me as they began walking their docile prisoner back to Oakdene. 'You've changed your van.'

'Yes, I have,' I sighed at its bent doors and buckled bumper. 'I'm not having much luck with vans, lately.'

I sat behind the shop counter, going through the sales ledger, copying out my sales and adding up my takings, which did not take long, and then counting up sales of

177

vintage clothes for Ricky and Morris, which took a bit longer. I found that the money in the cash box was all mine, Pat and Sophie having already sensibly removed anything owing to them, so I counted out Ricky and Morris's money and pocketed the rest.

It was only as I picked up my shoulder bag and wondered why it weighed so much, that I remembered the package I'd grabbed off the hall table that morning before I'd rushed out of the front door. It seemed like I'd been waiting ages for it to arrive. Feeling like a kid at Christmas, I tore open the padded envelope and unwrapped my job lot of hatpins and their two porcelain holders. I'd been successful in my bid for them on eBay, although I'd lost out on the 1920s handbags. I inspected each pin carefully. Some were small and dainty, some were long with wicked points and weighty, knobby ends. None of them was very expensive, but sold individually they'd fetch far more than I'd paid for them, and they'd look pretty displayed in their holders, once I'd given each of them a jolly good scrub with a child's toothbrush, followed by a buffing up with some silver polish: that was my evening sorted.

I remembered I was supposed to have phoned my mechanic. Dave is a proper, old-fashioned mechanic, who'll have a go at anything. He'd managed to smuggle my van through its MOT on the last two occasions. I don't mean White Van, the bent and battered one, I mean the previous one, the burnt-out hulk. I explained White Van had been in an accident.

'You're not having a lot of luck, are you?' he commented.

No, I'm not, Dave, funny you should mention that. Apart from the fact that Green Bastard Hat in the truck had smashed one of my rear lights and buckled my bumper, the newly dented back doors didn't line up as they had before. They were sticking slightly when I tried to open them and as there was no way I was going through another experience like the one I'd had with EB, I wanted them fixed.

'I'll have to pay you,' I told him. 'This isn't an insurance job.'

That reminded Dave that the assessor had finally turned up at the garage and declared my burnt-out hulk a write-off. I'd had to wait nearly three weeks for that assessment. Still, now at least the cheque would be in the post.

A thought occurred to me. 'Dave, when my van was brought in, the day it caught fire, you don't remember the name on the break-down truck?'

'Yeh, it was Moss and Pike.'

'Are they a local firm?'

Dave thought a moment. In the background I could hear the ring of metal beating on metal, a radio playing, someone whistling along to the music as he worked. 'Well, they've got a depot in Moretonhampstead,' he shouted a little above the noise, 'but they've got depots all over, I think. Anyway, I can't do your van today,' he went on, 'I've got a rush job on a beaten-up Harley Davidson.' He chuckled grimly. 'Not as beaten up as its rider, though.'

'Really? A friend of mine rides one of those,' I lied blithely, 'you can't tell me the name of the bike's owner?'

'Westershall.'

A cold, hollow feeling settled inside my stomach.

'Look, Juno, we're busy, I gotta go. Bring your van in in a day or two and I'll see what I can do.'

'Thanks, Dave,' I said as I disconnected. 'Cheers.'

Westershall. My feeble brain was grappling with the horrible idea that Jamie really was the bike rider who'd tried to run me off the road when it received another confusing blow. Standing outside in Shadow Lane, studying the portrait of the bull in the window, was Jamie himself. I tried to gather my scattered wits as he walked into the shop.

'Hi, Juno,' he began, and stopped, frowning. 'Are you all right?'

'Er . . . yes, fine.'

'You look a bit flustered.'

'No, I'm fine, thanks.' I rummaged for a smile. 'How are you?'

'I'm good.' He certainly didn't look like someone who'd recently been thrown into a hedgerow or had any kind of close encounter with a hard surface. He was staring at my head.

'Do you know you've got stuff in your hair?'

'Stuff?' I hadn't bothered to check the mirror since I'd come in the shop. I put up a hand to my hair and pulled out a little twig with two leaves attached. Well, I had been dragging an old lady through a hedge backwards. I checked with my fingers for any other detritus. 'Anyway, what can I do for you?'

He jerked a thumb in the direction of the window. 'The portrait is fantastic. Old Sandy is going to be over the moon. As a matter of fact, I was hoping to see Sophie. Is she about?'

'Day off. Can I help?'

'I was hoping she might be able to get it framed for us. Emma was going to arrange it but she's a bit *hors de combat* at the moment.'

'Not well?'

'She got a bit smashed up,' he explained, with a rather fixed smile, 'got thrown from her steed.'

Enlightenment dawned. 'Nothing serious, I hope?'

'Scrapes and bruises mostly. She jarred her neck rather badly, but nothing broken.'

'She'll be all right for the party, will she?' I did my best to sound solicitous. I was feeling a whole lot better, myself. That cold, hollow feeling in my stomach had melted away, realising that Jamie had not been the rider of the motorbike, and that the steed that had thrown Emma was not a horse, but a hog.

'Oh, God yes!' he answered cheerfully. 'Take more than a fall to make her miss Sandy's birthday bash. But she can't drive for a day or two. So I was hoping that Sophie could get the portrait framed. I'm afraid I haven't got much of an eye for that sort of thing.'

'Of course, she'll be delighted to do it. I'll give her a call.'

'Would you mind, Juno? Only, I've got to dash.'

'Leave it to me.'

He thanked me and made to leave, but as he reached the shop door, he suddenly turned as if he'd thought of something. 'That is your new van parked down the road, isn't it? The white Peugeot—'

'—with the missing rear light and buckled bumper? That's mine.'

He nodded, as if confirming something to himself, his lower lip caught between his white teeth in a strange smile. 'What happened?'

That cold feeling settled in my stomach again. There was an intensity in his gaze that told me his question wasn't

181

a casual one; this was what he'd wanted to know all along. 'Some fool rear-ended me,' I said after a moment.

'Did you get his number?' His blue eyes held mine.

'No,' I answered steadily. 'It was parked at the time.'

He raised his eyebrows. 'So, no witnesses?' he asked lightly.

'No,' I assured him. 'No witnesses.'

His smile as he left was enigmatic. I couldn't read it at all.

I phoned Sophie as soon as he had gone and gave her the news about the framing. She asked if Jamie had left any money and when I told her he hadn't, she moaned down the phone. 'It's going to be so expensive. Something that size will want double-mounting, and they'll need a wide moulding on the frame to do it justice, something heavy and gilt.'

'Well, they'll pay you for it.'

'Eventually, but I'll have to shell out for it upfront. My usual framing guy is away on holiday and I'll have to go to Newton Abbot to get the job done.'

Excellent, I thought, and offered to drive her there. Newton Abbot has as many charity shops as Ashburton has antique shops. Whilst Sophie was taking ages choosing mounting board and mouldings, I could give them all a quick tour. Not only could I hunt for stock for my unit, I might find some jeans. I refuse to pay silly money for denims I'm going to scrub floors and walk dogs in. And needing ones with extra-long legs only adds to the expense, so pre-loved ones are fine. I told her I would take her the following afternoon and resigned myself to rearranging my timetable all over again.

Three ladies came into the shop then, all together, probably the biggest crowd of customers the shop has ever experienced, and for the next half-hour they happily exclaimed over this and that before they went out with two of Pat's little witches, a watercolour sketch of Haytor, three of Sophie's greetings cards and a pair of handmade earrings.

I must confess to a slight stab of envy as I wrapped the earrings in tissue paper. I had taught Pat how to make them and now she sold quite a lot. I could have done with some small and steady sales myself. I thrust such ignominious feelings aside. Her profits went to the animal sanctuary; she gained nothing from her hard work, except the pleasure of doing it. I told myself off in no uncertain terms.

Whilst the three ladies had been looking round, I had noticed a fourth person gazing in Pat's window. It was the mystery lady. This time she didn't look quite as well groomed as when I'd last seen her. Perhaps she hadn't been able to make use of a cafe toilet. Her hair was not arranged in a French pleat but hanging down over one shoulder in a plait, wispy ends making it untidy. Perhaps because there was a wind blowing that was the raw side of fresh, she huddled in her padded jacket, her hands thrust into her pockets. She looked a bit more bag lady than mystery lady, to be honest. I really wanted to go out and talk to her, but I was trapped by my chattering customers, and when I glanced at the window a second time, she had gone.

I realised I was bloody starving, what with no breakfast and lunchtime approaching. Ricky and Morris always brought cake – where were they when I needed them? I popped upstairs to the kitchen, in the hope that there might be some crumbs of comfort somewhere. I found half a packet of Hobnob biscuits in the cupboard and some cheese triangles in the fridge. Perfect. I took the lot downstairs and hid them under the counter so that I could ditch them quickly if a customer came in.

I tore the fiddly silver paper off the cheese triangle and made myself a Hobnob sandwich.

The customers had distracted me from thoughts about my conversation with Jamie. I still wasn't sure what to make of it. Did he know that it was my van that had caused Emma to come off her bike or was he merely suspicious? I wondered what she'd told him about the accident. When he asked about witnesses, was he just trying to protect his sister or was that a warning to me to keep quiet? And whatever she, Moss and the other man had been doing at Applecote Farm, was Jamie any part of it? I'd prefer to think he wasn't, but I was far from sure.

I sat at the counter, munching, gazing distractedly at Gavin's bookshelves and thinking how empty and dismal they looked. I would have to do something about them.

I brushed myself off for crumbs, fetched the box of books I'd bought at the boot sale and placed them on an empty shelf. They looked good but only filled about a quarter of it. I would go through Gavin's boxes of stock, I decided, pick out anything remotely saleable, and fill the shelves up. I picked up the first box, opened it and began taking the books out. There was a newspaper, a copy of the *Dartmoor Gazette*, folded on the top. *Batman Dies* – I remembered the headline. Gavin had been reading the article that day when Jamie had invited us all to the fete. I tossed it to one side.

Then, for some reason, I picked it up again and opened out the folded page. *Batman Dies in Bat Cave* was the full headline. It turned out to be more sensational than accurate. I read the article twice.

An open verdict was recorded today at the inquest into the death of Ben Luscombe of Buckfast, whose body was found on the Moorworthy estate last November. Mr Luscombe, who was twenty-one, was found at the foot of rocks near a disused mineshaft known locally as Moorworthy Pit. A keen member of the Devon Bat Society, it is believed that Mr Luscombe entered the estate without permission to monitor a colony of rare greater horseshoe bats in woods nearby. It is believed he lost his way in the darkness and fell to his death. The post-mortem revealed that he had recently taken cocaine.

Estate owner, James Westershall, made the following statement. 'The woods are fenced off to protect roosts of rare bats and Mr Luscombe was trespassing on a site of special scientific interest. We are only too happy to assist members of the local bat society with the National Bat Monitoring Programme, but visits are strictly by appointment. The old mine workings are dangerous and, sadly, Mr Luscombe paid the price for entering the woods unaccompanied. We are very sorry for his death and our thoughts are with his family at this time.'

Mr Alec Pedrick, local secretary of the Devon Bat Society paid tribute to Mr Luscombe. 'Ben was a passionate conservationist and did important work for the British Bat Survey and National Bat Monitoring Programme. He will be sadly missed.'

The newspaper was dated the previous June, which meant the inquest referred to an incident that was now almost a year old. As I looked up from the article, I just caught sight of the mystery lady hurrying past the window, carrying a large laundry bag, and I realised she had probably spent the last hour in the launderette two doors down. I had missed my opportunity to speak to her. But that didn't matter now. There was someone I wanted to speak to more urgently. I grabbed a copy of the local phone book from under the counter and began looking for the number of Mr Alec Pedrick.

CHAPTER NINETEEN

Alec Pedrick was a bearded man in his fifties, who welcomed me warmly into his cottage. I'd found his address on the Widecombe road, just up the hill towards Buckland.

'It's kind of you to see me at such short notice, Mr Pedrick.' I'd driven straight there as soon as I'd closed up the shop. It was good to get inside, into the warm. It was dark under the trees and growing misty.

'Call me Alec.' He offered me tea and I followed him into his kitchen, passing two young children sitting on the floor in the living room, engrossed in the television. 'I'm only looking after the grandkids till their mother picks them up after work,' he told me, 'so it's no trouble, no trouble at all.' He smiled, waiting for the kettle to boil. 'So, you were a friend of Gavin's? Terrible tragedy, that was,' he added, shaking his head. 'Terrible.'

I sat in the chair that he indicated, next to the orange

glow of a wood-burning stove. The kitchen was cosy, book-filled, as if it also served as a study. 'I didn't realise Gavin was interested in bats.'

'Well, to be honest, I'm not sure that he was,' he admitted, taking the seat opposite me. 'He never joined the society as a member, but he did come along with Ben two or three times. Nice lad, but a bit of a dreamer, I thought.' He laughed. 'I mean, he seemed more excited about being out in the woods at night than interested in the bats. We go out to monitor bat numbers, but he was always chatting on about Dracula and werewolves and stuff like that.'

'That sounds like Gavin.'

Alec stretched out his legs towards the glow of the wood-burning stove and crossed his ankles, making himself comfortable. 'Do you know that there are eighteen different species of bat in this country and sixteen of those are found in Devon? And,' he went on, warming to his theme, 'Devon has the largest population of rare greater horseshoe bats in western Europe.'

'And some of those are on the Moorworthy estate?'

He nodded. 'There's a large roost in Moorworthy Pit.'

'Is that what Ben was interested in, monitoring the numbers of greater horseshoes there?'

'Well, not quite,' he admitted. 'We've known about the greater horseshoe bats for years. Course, we still monitor their numbers. But a couple of years back there had been sightings of barbastelles. Now they are very rare,' he told me, holding up a finger, 'threatened as a species. And they don't roost in caves or mines, they roost in hollow trees.' He stood up, searched his shelves for a book and began leafing through it until he found a picture. 'There!' he showed me. 'That's a barbastelle. See?'

I've always thought bats were ugly little buggers and the barbastelle was no exception. It had a squashed-in, leathery face like a tiny gorilla's. 'And these have been seen in Moorworthy woods?'

Alec nodded enthusiastically, taking back the book. 'They like mature trees, broad-leaved woodland. Ben was very keen to carry out a transect of the area . . .'

'Transect?' I repeated.

'It's just a walk, really,' he explained. 'You walk for an hour, traversing a specified area, carrying a recording device. You can analyse the recordings later and identify the bat species present. Well, the society had always had free access until then, no problem. But shortly after the discovery of the barbastelles, Mr Westershall had the woods fenced off.'

'Do you know why?'

Alec shrugged. 'He said it was dangerous, said some old shaft had opened up that no one knew about and he had a duty to protect the public. Well, there was no argument, really, was there? I mean, you can't quarrel with public safety. Anyway, it's all on his property, so what could we do? But Ben was furious, he—' His mouth clamped shut suddenly as if he was afraid to say more, afraid his emotions would betray him. He stared into the flames of the wood-burner.

'He went back there, didn't he?' I prompted. 'The night he died?'

Alec nodded. 'What they didn't say in that newspaper report was that he'd been chased out of those woods before that night. He'd got through the fence under cover of darkness.' He chuckled in spite of himself. 'He took wire cutters with him. He was determined to carry out this transect. He said he saw lights coming from the old mineshaft, from Moorworthy Pit – before he was spotted and had to leg it.'

'Is that possible – the lights, I mean? The shaft is disused, isn't it?'

'Hasn't been worked in a hundred years,' he confirmed. 'But someone was there.'

We were both silent for a moment, thoughtful, the only sound the crackle of logs in the wood-burner and the distant tinkling of music from the television in the next room. Then Alec spoke again. 'My grandfather was a tin miner, you know, and his father before him. And *he* worked at Moorworthy. The old shaft in the woods, where the greater horseshoes roost now, was shutting down, even in his time, so then he worked at Applecote Pit.'

'On the farmland next door?'

'That's right.' He shot me a keen glance. 'Do you know how it's done, tin mining? A lot of it is open work, you know, open-cast. Been going on for centuries on the moor, like that. But sometimes they sink a shaft, deep, maybe fifty feet, like Moorworthy. Applecote was open-cast for a century or more,' he went on, 'then they sunk shafts from the bottom of it – that's what they used to do if they kept finding ore, and maybe dug an adit—'

I stopped him. 'Adit?'

'Sorry.' He smiled. 'An adit is just a tunnel – it gives a level access to the shaft for the workers. Sometimes they'd be forced to dig one to drain water off, if they were working down deep enough.'

'Where exactly was Ben's body found?'

'At the foot of some rocks.' Alec laughed softly, but it was a bitter, mirthless sound. 'He was determined to go back to that shaft in Moorworthy, find out what was going on. He was convinced the bats were being threatened. He'd have been nowhere near those rocks where they found his body. They were over half a mile away, surrounded by open ground, there are no bats there.'

'The inquest said he'd lost his way in the dark.'

'It was a full moon that night and Ben wasn't stupid. He'd have known where he was going.'

'The inquest said—'

'That he was high on cocaine?' Alec's lips pursed angrily. 'That boy never took drugs in his life. If there was cocaine in his system, it was because someone forced it on him.'

'You think he was murdered?'

'I do.' His voice shook. 'Someone killed that lad and threw his body off those rocks.'

'I'm sure that's what Gavin thought,' I said. 'He leapt at the invitation to go to the Moorworthy fete. I think he saw it as an opportunity to discover what happened to Ben, take a good look around in the woods, but . . . someone stopped him.'

Alec was nodding grimly.

'Did you ever talk to the police after Ben was killed? Tell them his suspicions, about the lights that he had seen coming from the old shaft?'

'I did. They said it was just all hallucinations, part of his drug-taking.' He snorted in disgust. 'It makes me sick to think about it.'

I hesitated before I asked the next question. 'So, who do you think killed him?'

'Westershall of course, it was his land he was on.'

'You mean Jamie?'

He nodded grimly.

I had gone over the circumstances of Gavin's death again and again, but I had never considered Jamie as a killer. Despite the warmth from the fire, I felt cold.

'But, let's just suppose that Jamie – or, anyway, one of the Westershalls – was responsible for Ben's death, why not drop his body down a mineshaft where no one would ever find him? Or leave him at the foot of Haytor? They could have dumped him anywhere on the moor. Why leave his body on their own doorstep?' I frowned. 'Who found him, anyway?'

'Jamie Westershall.'

'Now I'm confused.'

Alec leant forward intently. 'Listen, a lot of people knew what Ben was up to. He was a blogger, and in contact with Bat Conservation groups all around the country. He had family and friends, a girlfriend. He would soon have been reported missing and the police would have been given a pretty good idea of where to start looking. Now, whatever the Westershalls are up to, the last thing they would want is police searching all over their estate. Much better if Jamie Westershall contacts *them*, tells them there's been a tragic accident, he's found a body, and takes them straight to it.'

'It's still taking a risk.'

'Oh, I don't think Mr Westershall is averse to a risk.' Alec leant back in his chair. 'And another thing, he's been denying people access to his land, saying it's dangerous –

you read what he said at the inquest. Well, there was quite a lot of protest at the time, but finding Ben's body proved his point for him. No one was going to raise any objections after that. He can do what he likes—'

There was the sound of someone coming in, a footstep at the front door, a woman's voice calling out, and children scrambling, yelling, to greet her. Alec's daughter had come home. It was time I left. 'Well, thanks for seeing me, Alec. I'm sorry if talking about Ben's death upset you.'

As I rose to go, he stood and gripped my hand. 'You be careful,' he whispered urgently. 'Whatever's going on in that place, they've killed twice to keep it a secret. You be careful.'

I placed my hand over his. 'I will,' I promised him. And I left, not knowing what to think.

CHAPTER TWENTY

In Newton Abbot I bought two pairs of jeans, a silver caddy spoon I found in a box of old cutlery, an oak tea trolley with barley-twist legs, various pretty plates and a Moorcroft saucer; but when I went back to the framers where I had deposited Sophie an hour and a half before, she was still making up her mind about frame mouldings, so I dumped my haul in the van and went hunting again. This time my trawl of the charity shops brought me a willow pattern meat dish with a hairline crack in it and some decent paperback books, which would fill up another few inches on Gavin's empty shelves. Not as big a haul as I had been hoping for but at least it was something. And the caddy spoon and the Moorcroft were good finds.

At least Sophie had finished when I went back to the shop a second time. The framer promised to have the job done the day before Sandy's party.

Of course, she wanted to know what had happened

to White Van. I filled her in on some, but not all, of the details. I didn't tell her anything about Olly's domestic situation, but I told her the rest.

'You should have called the police!'

I knew she'd say that. 'What's the point? I can't prove anything. Even if I could prove that Moss and Pike's lorry went into the back of me, I can't prove they did it deliberately.'

'You could have been killed.'

'Jamie knows about it,' I went on. 'He knew my van had been involved in Emma's accident when he came into the shop yesterday.'

'Are you sure?' Like me, she didn't want to believe that the brave and handsome saviour of EB, the charming rescuer of damsels in distress, could be up to anything dodgy. 'Why didn't you ask him?'

'I don't know.' I had replayed that conversation over and over in my mind. Why hadn't I asked him what the hell his sister was up to, what was going on at Applecote Farm? Why hadn't he asked me why I was flying a drone over his property? Instead, we'd just stared at each other, like poker players trying to avoid a show of hands.

Sophie slanted me a dark look. 'This party's going to be interesting. Are you sure you still want to go?'

'Of course I want to go. I want to find out what's bloody going on!'

Perhaps, I realised, when I was thinking about it later, Jamie didn't say anything because, like me, like a poker player, he was considering his next move.

The following morning I saw the mystery lady again. I was up early, walking the dogs. The woods had turned to marmalade gold, sunlight pouring through translucent leaves like stained glass in a church window. The dogs raced through crunchy piles, paws scattering the leaves and sending them flying. I found her car parked by Cuddyford Cross, empty, tucked in by a farm gate. I peered in the back, at a folded sleeping bag, pillows, a shopping bag full of sachets of cat food. But no sign of the lady herself, or her cat.

I followed the lane down to Great Bridge and peered over the old stone wall. The River Ashburn, from which Ashburton takes its name, rises on Rippon Tor and flows down the valley, right through the centre of the town before it joins the Dart at Buckfastleigh. From the bridge I could look down onto the rushing water, fallen leaves like tiny boats swept along on the flood.

Then I took the dogs up steps to the Terrace Walk. It's a strange name for what is basically an earthen path traversing a sloping field. But the view from there is one of the most beautiful around Ashburton, across the wooded valley to the foothills of the moor. In summer the distant woods are just masses of green. But in autumn they become a tapestry of russet and brown. I could pick out the rusty gold of horse chestnuts, the lime glow of poplars and the bright firecracker red of maple against the deep, dark green of holly and spruce.

The view from this muddy path is so beautiful that over the years benches have been put there to allow people to sit and drink it in. Many of these have fallen into disrepair, their wooden seats entangled with bindweed and brambles, or rotted away. But there are one or two benches that are still useable, and seated alone on one of these, gazing across the valley, her cat sitting upright on her lap, was my mystery lady. Mist had filled the depths of the valley, and it lay in a milky layer so that the trees seemed to float above it. She was rapt in a view that was magical, quiet, until my tumbling, rushing dogs broke the spell by barking.

Schnitzel and EB made a beeline for her bench. They wanted to be friendly, to say hello.

I managed to grab Sally the Labrador by the collar before she could follow. As the dogs approached, her cat rose up on its legs, back arched, and became a spitting puffball of angry fur. Mystery Lady grabbed it and stood up, holding it clear of EB and Schnitzel, who were bouncing excitedly around her feet, trying to jump up.

'I'm so sorry!' I cried out to her, shouting at the two yapping hooligans to come back to me. She didn't turn around but began walking away up the path. 'Do you need help?' I called at her departing back, as I started fastening leads on collars. She walked on, ignoring me. 'You're sleeping in your car.'

That stopped her. She turned to look at me, stared hard. 'Am I?' she asked, arching her slim brows.

'Are you in some kind of trouble?' I asked. 'Can I do anything to help?'

'You can learn to mind your own business,' she responded in a controlled voice, turned and marched swiftly away down the field.

I didn't attempt to follow. 'We know when we're not wanted, don't we?' I said to my canine companions.

The last part of the Terrace Walk goes through a small wooded area until the path emerges at the top of Roborough Lane, which in turn leads back into town. As I walked the muddy path under the trees, I could tell I was approaching so-called civilisation by the number of nasty little doggie doo-doo bags littering the ground. It's as if people who have picked up their pet's poo can't bear to carry it as far as the nearest receptacle. But that's not the only kind of refuse lying there. Drink cans, broken bottles, chip papers and various other kinds of nasties littered the ground. I kept the dogs on short leads, didn't want one of them cutting a pad on something sharp.

After I'd taken the dogs back, I popped into Chloe Berkeley-Smythe's place, cleared a pile of junk mail from behind her front door and watered her house plants. The cross on her kitchen calendar showed she wouldn't be returning from her cruise for a few more weeks, so the pre-arrival clean of her house could wait. Chloe paid me a retainer to keep an eye on her place whilst she was away. As she spent most of her life cruising, this suited me very well.

She only stayed at her home in Ashburton for a few weeks, usually just enough time to unpack her cases, launder her clothes, and repack before she was off on her next adventure. She was the most indolent and pleasure-loving person I had ever met and great fun to be with.

Maisie, on the other hand, hardly ever left home, but she got her pleasure in other ways. As I let myself into her cottage, she was happily engaged in her favourite blood sport. 'But how can you tell there's something wrong with my computer,' she was asking someone on the phone, 'when I haven't got a computer?' There was a pause, a protest from the other end of the line. 'Well, you never asked me!' She slammed the receiver down with an evil chuckle.

'How long did you keep that one going, Maisie?' I asked,

fending off an imminent attack from Jacko with my boot.

'Ooh, a few minutes,' she responded happily. 'Few minutes they couldn't be pestering someone else. That'll teach 'em to ring me up, telling lies.'

She was slacking. I'd known Maisie torment call-centre employees for twenty minutes or more before they finally realised what the dear little old lady on the end of the line was up to.

She was resplendent in her black, beaver lamb coat with the fur collar, circa 1953, and a slightly dusty black velvet beret. These were her going-out clothes. I had rung her earlier and told her to be ready. I reckoned she could do with a change of scene and was taking her out for a little drive.

'Where would you like to go?' I asked, although I knew the answer already.

The parish church of St Pancras in Widecombe is often referred to as the Cathedral of the Moor, not just because of its perpendicular windows and tall tower, but because of the way it sits in the landscape, amongst a patchwork of fields that seem to be there just to show it off, to act as a green backcloth to its loveliness; and despite the Devil's attempts to smite it with a bolt of lightning, it has stood firm for five hundred years.

Widecombe Fair had been held earlier in the month, but the fame of Uncle Tom Cobley and his grey mare meant that the tiny village of Widecombe-in-the-Moor was full of visitors whatever the time of year. And it was one of Maisie's favourite places. After a little totter around the churchyard and the village green, Maisie's hand clinging tightly to my arm, and a wander around the National Trust shop, set in the old sexton's cottage, where she could draw in her breath in disgust at the price of the tea towels, we settled down for tea in the little cafe overlooking the green.

'We were talking about you the other day,' she informed me cheerfully as we sipped our tea, 'at my church coffee morning. There was a new woman there, turned out she's a neighbour of old Dolly Knollys'. Remember, we were talking about her? Up Daison Cottages?'

I was all ears, my attention dragged from our picturesque surroundings. I couldn't remember the woman's name, just her face peering through the diamond-shaped hole in her trellis. 'What did she have to say?'

'Oh, just that poor old Dolly was all alone except for that great-grandson of hers, and he was at school all day, and how worried she was,' Maisie rattled on. 'And then she said she'd met this great big tall girl with a mass of curly ginger hair, who'd come to call on her—'

Excuse me. *Ginger?*

'And Nelly Mole said that could only be Juno Browne cos there wasn't anyone else fitted that description round Ashburton . . . and we all said, yes, that's right. And then old Tom Hopkins said that you wasn't a great ginger girl, you was a flame-haired goddess, and Nelly Mole said to him, "You should be ashamed of yourself, Tom Hopkins, talking about goddesses, and you a Christian and a bell-ringer too." Well, poor old Tom, he blushed beetroot—'

'Maisie, can we just forget Tom for a moment, what did she actually say?'

'Who?' she asked blankly.

'Dolly Knollys' neighbour.'

'Oh, 'er! Nothing.'

'Nothing?'

'Well, only that you was calling in from time to time, but that she didn't think it was enough.'

Olly's neighbour had already stopped me on one of my visits, hailing me over the garden fence, asking how things were. I think the poor woman was only trying to be neighbourly; she offered to pop in on Dolly herself, keep the old dear company, and I had quite a job persuading her that this was not a good idea. She sleeps a lot, I'd said, and she gets very confused and distressed when she meets strangers. Best left alone. But I could tell she wasn't convinced. As I took Maisie back to the car, I made a mental note to try to call in at Daison Cottages more often.

We drove back through Holne Chase and Buckland, and stopped on the brow of the hill where we could get a clear view of Buckland's church tower and its clock, another of Maisie's favourites. The clock face has no numerals; in place of them, letters spell out the words 'My Dear Mother'. I have no idea why. You have to start at nine o'clock and read clockwise for 'My Dear', and then go back to nine and read anticlockwise for 'Mother'. I've no idea about that either.

'It's A past E,' Maisie chuckled, and we had to sit and wait until R past E so that we could hear the clock chime 'All Things Bright and Beautiful' on the quarter hour. We drove on down the hill, slowing down to gaze lustfully at the huddle of picture-perfect thatched cottages set in a little glade.

Maisie pointed out bare trees, the dark clumps of abandoned rooks' nests set high up amongst the mesh of branches.

'Rabbits' nests – that's what I used to tell our Janet when she was a little girl,' she said. 'I told her they were rabbits' nests.'

And I laughed, although she'd told me a hundred times before.

Next morning, I did her shopping in Ashburton and walked along the lane behind St Andrew's church, Jacko trotting jauntily on the lead, so that I could visit the garage and fix a date with Dave for the repair of White Van.

In the garage yard I nearly changed my mind at the sight of a massive flatbed truck, piled with black silage bales, 'Moss and Pike' written clearly on its tailgate, 'clean me' etched beneath it in the dust. I crept up the side of the vehicle and peeped cautiously around. Sure enough, Green Bastard Hat was standing talking to Dave. It was the first time I'd seen him outside of his cab and been treated to the sight of the considerable paunch bulging over the belt of the jeans he was struggling to keep hitched up.

I slipped back along the side of the truck and began to write on the dusty tailgate with one finger. I got so absorbed in what I was doing that I didn't spot him coming until it was almost too late. 'Here!' he shouted. 'What are you up to?'

I didn't know if he would recognise me as the driver of White Van. He hadn't got a good view of me, as Emma had, but he took a step towards me. Jacko gave a warning growl, his lip writhing back to show his teeth.

To give Green Bastard Hat credit, he wasn't a man to underestimate the crunching power of a terrier's jaws, even when the terrier in question is barely above ankle height. He hesitated, and in that moment Dave himself came around the truck, wiping his hands on an oily rag.

'Everything OK?' he asked, glancing from me to GBH.

'Hi, Dave!' I said brightly. 'Can I talk to you about my van?'

'Yes, let's book you in. Step inside the office.' He waved his hand in the direction of his workshop and I walked past Green Bastard Hat, Jacko still growling and muttering curses in his direction. GBH gave an impatient snort, got up into his cab and drove off with an angry grinding of gears and hissing of brakes. Through the grimy window of the office I watched him depart. He hadn't read what I had written on the back of his truck, wouldn't see it now until he reached the end of his journey. Then he could read two names: 'Gavin Hall' and 'Ben Luscombe', and a very large question mark, inscribed in the dust.

'You've got a customer,' Pat whispered excitedly as soon as I got in the shop door. She jerked her head in the direction of the storeroom. 'Back there,' she added, rolling her eyes.

'Well, who is it?' I asked, puzzled by the dramatics. 'Someone we know?'

She stifled a giggle with her hand. 'Go and see!' She tried pushing me in the direction of the storeroom.

'All right, I'm going!' I squeezed past Mavis in her witch's hat and down the corridor, peering around the door frame a bit cautiously. There, admiring her reflection in the full-length mirror stood Detective Constable Cruella DeVille, wearing the white fake-fur jacket with the black spots. I stopped in the doorway, watching her as she turned the collar up, then flipped it back down, turning her head

203

from side to side. She saw my reflection and a faint flush coloured her pale cheeks.

'It really does look good on you,' I told her honestly.

'Yes, it does,' she agreed, with a slight note of defiance, 'even though you and your friends were laughing at my expense the other day.'

'You mustn't mind Ricky,' I told her.

'Oh, I'm used to it,' she sighed, taking the jacket off and looking at the price tag.

'What is your name?' I ventured. 'Your first name?'

'Christine,' she told me flatly. 'And that doesn't help, having to sign myself C. DeVille.'

'I'd enjoy it. And I think you should too.'

She almost smiled, a tug of her tiny mouth. Was this a crack in the ice, the first hint of a thaw? I wondered.

'That's what Dean says.'

'Is Dean your boyfriend?'

'My colleague,' her little mouth twisted again. 'Detective Constable Collins.'

'Ah!' I wanted to ask how the paternity leave was going but thought perhaps I'd better not. I came up with a more serious question. 'Tell me, are the police aware that Gavin Hall and Ben Luscombe knew each other?'

'Ben Luscombe?' she repeated.

'He died at Moorworthy Pit a year ago, supposedly the victim of a fall.'

Her dark brows drew together. 'Supposedly?'

'Yes. He and Gavin were friends.'

'So?'

'Well, doesn't it strike anyone as odd that two young men should die in horrible accidents, both on the

204

Moorworthy estate, about half a mile from each other?'

'Accidents happen and these were over a year apart.'

'But I think Gavin tried to get into the woods because of what happened to Ben. They were both convinced that something was going on in the mines there. And they both ended up dead.'

DeVille stared at me impassively, her violet gaze icing over. No hint of a thaw now.

'So what did they think was going on?'

'Well, that's just it,' I admitted lamely, 'I don't know.'

The violet-eyed Medusa continued to stare. 'Then what exactly are you saying, Miss Browne?'

God, she was learning from her boss! I could hear him in her level voice, see him in the intensity of her stare. Yet, if Inspector Ford had been asking the questions, I wouldn't have felt quite so foolish. 'It just seems to me that their deaths have been too readily dismissed as accidents when there could be a connection between them.'

Cruella hunched a shoulder. 'Because they knew each other doesn't mean their deaths have to be connected. Ben Luscombe was wandering about in a dangerous place at night, and he was high on drugs . . .'

'His friends don't believe that.'

'And Gavin Hall,' she went on inexorably, 'was messing about with a dangerous weapon.'

'But . . .'

She silenced me with a shake of her head, pitying me. 'It's natural to want to find a reason when a death occurs, to make sense of a tragedy that seems senseless—'

I cut her off. 'Did that come out of some police training manual for dealing with the bereaved?'

I knew I was being rude, but her condescending tone irritated me.

Her little mouth twisted and she eyed me with hostility. 'Inspector Ford is a very busy man,' she told me, 'but I will pass on your concerns.'

'Thank you,' I responded, and gave her back a little smile, like hers, a tiny tug of the mouth.

She glanced at her watch as if to indicate she had wasted time enough on me already and I held out my hands for the jacket. 'If you're buying that, I'll find something to wrap it in.'

'No need, I can put it straight in the car.'

I charged her the full ticket price. I didn't feel like being generous.

Ricky and Morris had asked me to go and help fit the fat fairies. The whole fluttering flock was descending on them in the afternoon, and they could do with an extra pair of hands to make sure that each fairy got the right blouse and petticoat. Some of them looked very pretty in their frills and coloured sashes. Morris had looped lace and ribbon around each hemline, tying them up with little knots of silk flowers made by yours truly. They all had wings made from glittery net and tiny hats or headdresses to perch on their hair. It's true, there were a few sagging bosoms and unsightly bulges that weren't exactly fairy-like, and as Ricky had prophesied, some of them would be wearing their bifocals, but on the whole I thought they were a success, and I am sure when they all come tripping onto the stage in *Iolanthe*, the audience will be delighted.

But as I was down on my knees, pinning up a hem, I became aware of being stared at, and an increasingly hostile atmosphere. I looked up to see a lilac fairy fixing me with a baleful glare. It was Olly's next-door neighbour.

'Are you working here?' she asked, obviously upset. 'I thought you were a social worker.'

'I'm just helping out.' I felt at a disadvantage on my knees and scrambled to my feet, brushing cotton threads from my jeans. I tried a smile, but it got no response. 'I think there's been a misunderstanding. I work freelance. Some of my work involves care of the elderly, like Mrs Knollys. You met Maisie Biddle at the church coffee morning the other day,' I went on as she continued to glower at me, 'she's a client of mine.'

'Oh, yes, I did,' she admitted, her hackles lowering a little. 'But when we first met you gave me the distinct impression you were from social services.'

'I think you just assumed. I'd been asked to call in by one of the mothers at Olly's school,' I lied gaily. 'Now, have you got all the bits you need for your costume? Gloves, yes?' I caught her arm and steered her in the direction of Morris, who was trying to fit fairy bunions into dainty shoes and called, 'Next!' in a very determined voice.

He gave me an old-fashioned look over his little gold-rimmed specs. 'And what was all that about?' he asked me later, when we had sent the fairies home clutching their respective costumes.

'Nothing,' I assured him.

'She's up to something,' he said to Ricky.

'Yes,' he agreed, eyeing me narrowly, 'and what's worse, she's not telling us what it is.'

'I am not up to anything,' I assured them, trying to sound indignant. They weren't fooled.

'You're not getting into any trouble, are you, Juno?' Morris asked anxiously.

'Me?' I asked innocently. 'Noooo.'

Well, not yet anyway.

CHAPTER TWENTY-ONE

St Andrew's Church was packed for Gavin's funeral, local people turning out to support Gavin's parents who were well known in the town, and there were representatives from Gavin's old school. Sophie, Pat and I sat in a pew towards the back, and across the aisle, Jamie Westershall cut a lonely figure in black suit and tie. He nodded a greeting at me as he came in. I suppose he felt obliged to pay his respects. Emma obviously didn't feel such an obligation, or maybe she was still recovering after her accident. I saw him glance over his shoulder as new arrivals came in from the back of the church. As he turned to face the front again, I caught a glimpse of his expression for just a moment. He looked disconcerted, I thought, and began to flick through the pages of the order of service with unease.

I turned back to see who had entered and found myself staring at Detective Inspector Ford.

I must have been staring for a few seconds, because as

he inclined his head in a greeting, he gave me a slightly quizzical look. Embarrassed, I turned back to face the front. Was it routine for the police to attend a funeral when there had been a suspicious death? It was on the television. TV coppers are always turning up at the victim's funeral, convinced that the murderer will turn up to gloat. Except that, according to Cruella, they didn't believe Gavin's death was a case of murder.

The service was pitiful and mercifully short. Not the celebration of a life fulfilled but a lamentation for a life cut short. Poor Mrs Hall sobbed uncontrollably, and by the time we had struggled our way through 'The Day Thou Gavest, Lord, Is Ended', Pat was sniffing, surreptitiously wiping her eyes, and Sophie was in floods. I let the two of them go out ahead of me as the mourners filed out of the church. I wanted to talk to Inspector Ford.

'I'm surprised to see you here, Inspector,' I told him frankly.

'Just paying my respects, Miss Browne.' His manner was friendly but guarded, as always.

'So, the case of Gavin Hall is now closed, I take it?'

'Not officially, not until the coroner's ruling, but,' his shoulders lifted and fell in the slightest of shrugs, 'unofficially, yes. We are satisfied that we have pursued all lines of enquiry.'

'Detective Constable DeVille told me the same thing.'

I sensed he wasn't really listening to me. His concentration seemed fixed on someone else. Following the direction of his gaze I saw Jamie Westershall making his way out through the mourners. 'Excuse me, Miss Browne,' the inspector said politely, and walked swiftly after him.

I followed, watching Jamie climbing into a car that had drawn up outside the church gates. The inspector was also watching him go and I wondered whether the police were quite as uninterested in the death of Gavin Hall as they liked to pretend.

CHAPTER TWENTY-TWO

It took a long time to get ready for the Legends of the Silver Screen party. Ricky, who insisted on doing my hair, made me sit for hours with a head full of huge curlers, which frankly I thought was the last thing I needed. Meanwhile, Morris got Sophie ready. She emerged from his ministrations wearing a full-skirted black dress with white polka dots, a stiff petticoat underneath, and a bright-pink belt. She wore pink pumps and ankle socks, and tiny net gloves. A small pink hat perched on her dark head between two round black, cardboard ears. She was the prettiest, sexiest, most sophisticated Minnie Mouse you ever saw.

I was poured into plum-coloured velvet that fitted like a second skin from the very low neckline to the knee, where it suddenly flared out in a cascade of sparkling net, forming a train, which dragged on the floor behind me. Long black satin gloves completed the outfit, and my hair, released from the curlers, was brushed into glossy, rolling waves and swept over one shoulder. Then Ricky flung a pale mink stole around my shoulders.

'You look amazing!' Sophie breathed in awe. 'Who are you supposed to be? Jessica Rabbit?'

'Jessica Rabbit?' Ricky repeated, scandalised. 'Jessica fucking Rabbit!' he cried again, unable to believe his ears. 'She's Rita Hayworth!'

'I'm Rita Hayworth,' I repeated, just to be sure she knew.

'Now, listen, you!' Ricky pointed a warning finger in my face. 'You're not Miss Marple or Sherlock bleedin' Holmes, so don't get carried away up there this evening. No crawling about in the woods, understand? Not in that dress! Nor,' he added, waving his finger in Sophie's direction, 'you neither!'

'I'm not going near the woods,' Sophie protested with a shudder. 'I never want to go in them again, not after what happened to poor Gavin.'

'That's right,' Ricky nodded gravely. 'Just don't let Rita Hayworth lead you astray.'

'She was well known for that, was Rita,' Morris added.

The dress was tight about my knees and it was difficult not to step on the train. 'I'm not going crawling about anywhere. I can barely walk.'

'Take smaller steps!' Ricky cried. 'You can't stride about like a bloody Amazon! Oh my God! Shoes!' he exclaimed. 'What are you wearing?'

I raised the hem of the dress to reveal the flat leather pasties I find so comfortable. Ricky shuddered. Morris disappeared, giggling, and returned bearing high-heeled sandals in gold. 'The only thing in her size,' he told Ricky in a mournful whisper.

I tried them on and tottered about until I got the hang of them and my inelegant steps were pronounced passable by the two doyennes of Hollywood fashion.

'And don't get covered in dog hair!' Ricky ordered as a final caution.

I assured him that we weren't travelling in White Van but were borrowing Sophie's mum's car for the evening. And Sophie would be driving. She didn't really drink. Half a glass of Prosecco would be more than enough for her, whereas it certainly wouldn't be enough for me. Then, after hugs and kisses and more promises to behave ourselves, we were allowed to go.

'Have you got your inhaler?' I asked Sophie, before we set off.

She held up the dinky pink handbag that Morris had given her. 'In here.'

'Legends of the Silver Screen?' Ricky rapped on the car window, grinning. 'Just count the Marilyns!'

There were three, actually: three Marilyn Monroes in varying degrees of age and sadness. Emma was not one of them. She looked stunning, her hair drawn back in an elegant chignon, her dress a long sheath of ice-blue crystals. She looked very cool, very Grace Kelly, except that the surgical collar she was forced to wear rather spoilt the effect. Any momentary guilt I might have felt for her suffering evaporated when I thought of her riding her motorbike alongside White Van, looking in. She knew I was the driver, knew I had a child beside me on the front seat, but she'd still tried to trap us in a deadly game of cat and mouse. Remorse withered at the memory of Olly's terrified face.

214

'You've been in the wars, I hear.' I put on my best solicitous smile as I received her frosty greeting in the hall. She was on meet-and-greet duty with Uncle Sandy and other than dart me with an icy, cat-like glare, she couldn't really make a response. Besides, there were too many Legends of the Silver Screen trying to pile into the hall behind us for us to be able to linger. We were forced to grab a glass of something bubbly from a proffered tray and move on into the ballroom where a lot of Legends were standing about, glasses in hand, and we could take a really good look as we drifted around introducing ourselves.

There was a brunette, a friend of Emma's, with piled-up hair, lots of eye make-up and a long cigarette holder, who made a really good Audrey Hepburn, whilst Jess wore a white hospital smock and had somehow turned her hair into a stiff, upright column and sprayed one wriggly streak of it silver. She was, she told me giggling, the Bride of Frankenstein. I liked that about her, that she'd gone for something fun, rather than for glamour.

She wasn't the only one who'd come as a film character rather than the legend who might have portrayed it. An older lady had gamely painted her face green and come as the Wicked Witch of the West and there was a Snow White as well as a Cleopatra.

Most of the men just cheated. There were at least a dozen in dinner jackets, including Uncle Sandy, all claiming to be James Bond, and one in a white tuxedo who said he was Humphrey Bogart. Jamie wore a leather jacket and fedora and carried a whip, as Indiana Jones; there was an elderly Beau Geste, a rather rotund John Wayne, a Charlie Chaplin and a whippet of a fellow in white tie and tails who assured me, with a blast of truly appalling halitosis, that he was Fred Astaire. 'Are you Ginger Rogers?' he asked, grinning at me. 'We could dance cheek-to-cheek later.' Now there was something to look forward to.

'I thought she was Rita Hayworth,' Uncle Sandy approached, glass in hand. I dutifully gave him a birthday peck on the cheek. 'Well, whoever you are, you're absolutely magnificent,' he went on, looking me over. 'My word! But where's your little friend?'

I pointed out Sophie, who was chatting with a young man who could have been James Dean. 'Oh, look at that!' he exclaimed. 'Minnie Mouse! Isn't she cute? Mind you, with her looks, she could have come as Liza Minnelli.'

Well, she could if she had borrowed longer legs.

'And then,' Sandy went on incorrigibly, 'she could have worn the bowler hat and suspenders! Ah well!' he added, his voice laden with regret. Then he turned back to me, his eyes brightening. 'Now, you run a little antique shop.'

'Well, I wouldn't exactly describe it as—'

'We've got a few bits and pieces around the house you might find interesting. There's a fine collection of oriental ceramics upstairs, in one of the bedrooms. I'll show you later on, if you like,' he promised, patting me on my arm, and sailed forth to greet another of his guests, saving me the awkwardness of a reply. Whilst I would certainly have loved a tour around the house, visiting any of the bedrooms in Sandy's company was not on my agenda.

After a lot of preprandial mingling, Jamie tried to call the party to order by raising his voice. This had no effect at all and so he silenced the babbling horde by cracking his whip.

216

This had the desired result and caused Fred Astaire, who had been narrowly missed, to hop about a bit.

'Sorry! I've always wanted to do that,' Jamie admitted, grinning. I assume he meant cracking the whip, not flogging Fred Astaire. 'Anyway, we're here tonight to celebrate Sandy's birthday and . . . where is the old devil?' he asked, eyes searching the crowd. Sandy declared his presence, lurking rather closely behind Audrey Hepburn. 'Ah! There you are! Emma and I have got you a rather special present.'

A waiter, obviously ready for the signal, bore an easel into the room, the portrait covered by a cloth and Sandy, after a bit of prompting, performed the great reveal. The picture of the Old Thunderer was greeted by a genuine gasp of delight from Sandy and a burst of applause from the assembled throng. Sophie was dragged forward to receive her plaudits as artist and for several minutes she and the portrait became the centre of attention.

Then the dinner gong sounded. I had assumed that, as there were so many of us, any food would be in the form of a buffet, but I was wrong. The enormous dining room contained a table the length of a bowling alley, covered in white damask, and sparkling with cut glass and silverware. Sophie was dismayed to discover we weren't sitting together. She, the feted artist, was much nearer Sandy at the top of the table than I was. I waved to her as I sat down, bundling armfuls of sparkling net under the table. I wasn't seated anywhere near Emma, thankfully; she and her cronies were giggling together at the far end.

Sitting directly opposite me was Barty Bartholomew, looking truly awful in straining blue spandex as Superman, already crimson in the face and rather less than sober.

He boggled at me across the tablecloth. 'Are you Jessica Rabbit?' he asked, grinning.

He got a dig in the ribs from the Wicked Witch of the West on his right. 'Don't be ridiculous, Barty! She's Rita Hayworth.'

'And every bit as gorgeous!' Barty leered on, unabashed.

Next to me on the right was an empty chair, and I was just thinking I was condemned to spend the evening trying to drag conversation out of a po-faced and reticent Beau Geste on my left, when a bronzed hand grabbed the back of the chair and Jack Sparrow thrust himself into the seat. He must have been a late arrival because I hadn't noticed him in the ballroom. And I would have. I could tell he was Jack Sparrow, and not just any old pirate, because as well as the boots, baggy shirt, bandana and hat, he'd gone for the Johnny Depp eyeliner. I don't know if I should be worried about myself, but I find something rather attractive about a man in eyeliner. Well, this one anyway. He grinned at me as he sat down and proffered his hand. 'Jack Sparrow,' he said.

'Rita Hayworth.' We shook. I tried to see the printed place name, wondering what his real name was, but there were too many flowers and wine glasses in the way.

'Is that your real hair?' I asked, eyeing his dreadlocks.

'No, this comes off with the hat.'

'A gentleman should remove his hat at the dinner table,' Barty told him, a little sulky at his arrival.

'Couldn't possibly.' Jack nodded towards Beau Geste and John Wayne. 'And they're keeping theirs on.'

Making conversation as the chilled avocado soup was served, I learnt that the pirate on my right was a friend of Jamie's, had studied with him at agricultural college, lost contact, and bumped into him quite by accident a few weeks before.

'Are you a farmer too?' I asked.

'No, I'm just here temporarily. I'm based in London. I work for the Department of the Environment.'

I was barely halfway through my delicious pale-green soup, and had started to tell Mr Sparrow about how I'd met Jamie, when I became aware of a disturbance under the table. There was a lot of rustling amongst my net as if a mouse had got in there. Something slyly touched my ankle and began to slide up and down my calf. Bloody Barty was playing footsie. I glared at him, but he just continued to ogle me, grinning, and rub his foot up and down my leg. He was relying on the fact that a woman in company won't generally embarrass herself or others by making a fuss. He was about to learn he had mistaken his woman when I was saved the bother of retaliation. He suddenly let out a snort like a wounded buffalo and grabbed his shin.

'Sorry!' Jack Sparrow held up his hands helplessly. 'It's these swashbuckling boots, I do apologise.'

Barty muttered ungraciously, something about his being more careful, and sulked through the rest of the soup.

I smiled at Jack Sparrow. He smiled back but there was a slight wariness, a look of caution, almost, that lurked in his grey eyes, as if he was weighing me up carefully. 'You were saying . . .' he reminded me.

'Was I?'

'About the dog in the van . . .'

'Oh yes.' I don't remember too much about the rest of the meal. There were lots of courses and they were all delicious, and I have no idea how many times my wine glass was refilled, but by the time we got to the brandy posset with marrons glacé, Jack and I were definitely flirting. Perhaps he had decided to throw caution to the wind. Suddenly Beau Geste opened up. He leant across the table to Barty and asked a question that grabbed my attention.

'Barty, you didn't get any more trouble from the police, did you, over that unfortunate business of that young idiot with the sword?'

Barty had also had his wine glass filled several times and appeared to have difficulty remembering. 'Oh! Silly little ass who stabbed himself?' he cried at last. 'No, no.'

'His name was Gavin.' My voice cut into the conversation more loudly than I had intended. 'His name was Gavin Hall and he was nineteen.'

Beau Geste had the grace to look uncomfortable. 'Oh, knew him, did you?'

'I went to his funeral yesterday.'

The room had suddenly gone quiet. I decided to lob another pebble into the pool of silence and see if it caused any ripples. 'And he was a friend of Ben Luscombe, another young man who died on this estate.'

Jamie rose hastily. 'We've certainly had our fair share of tragic accidents. We're very sad, of course. But we're here to celebrate a happy occasion. So, if I could ask everyone to raise their glasses . . .'

There was an instant response, an exhalation of pent-up breath, the relief of people happily moving on from an awkward moment. They raised their glasses. We all toasted Sandy on his birthday and he made an amusing speech about how wonderful it was to have so many friends sharing his day with him, and how lovely all the ladies looked, and he finished by declaring that as it was his birthday he was jolly well going to drink brandy and smoke a cigar, inviting all the gentlemen at the table to join him, and promising the ladies they would find coffee and petits fours awaiting them in the drawing room.

We ladies dutifully withdrew, my exit made slightly less graceful by having to tug a bunch of sparkly net from under the leg of Beau Geste's chair as I got up to leave.

Sophie caught up with me on the way to the drawing room and we began to compare notes. 'I wish I'd been sitting near you,' she complained bitterly. 'I don't like the way Sandy keeps looking at me.'

'He's imagining you in a bowler hat and suspenders.'

'What?'

'Don't worry about it. I think he and Barty are about level-pegging in the dirty old man stakes. Barty was trying to play footsie under the table.'

'You seemed to be doing all right whenever I looked at you, heads together with that good-looking pirate.'

'He's nice, isn't he?' I was hoping we might get our heads together again later.

In the drawing room we found ourselves beckoned over by the Wicked Witch of the West, who patted the empty cushions of the sofa next to her. 'Come and sit with me, girls,' she called out, pouring coffee that had been left on a tray on the table in front of her.

'And you, my dear,' she added to Sophie, 'talk to me. I'm thinking of asking you to paint my bulldogs.'

I made my excuses, left the two of them chatting and headed for the guest cloakroom. Going to the loo was a more complicated process than usual: it involved stripping off long gloves and being very careful with an ocean of sparkly net. I put myself back together again and was heading back to the drawing room when I heard gales of girlish laughter coming from behind the library door, which was slightly ajar.

'I thought she was Jessica Rabbit!' a voice was shrieking loudly.

I lurked, ears straining.

'Who on earth invited her?'

'She's a friend of the artist woman.' Emma's voice was sour.

'So, I suppose I can understand inviting *her*,' chimed in someone else. 'But what does the other one do?'

'I like her!' I recognised the voice of the Bride of Frankenstein. Thank you, Jessica.

'She owns a shop, apparently.'

'So, I'd heard she was some kind of cleaner.'

'Well, I wish I had her figure.'

'It was Jamie who invited her,' Emma added. 'Sandy had told him to make sure there was some fuckable totty at his party.'

'Oh, charming!' cried the first voice.

'He meant someone not like us,' Emma assured her smugly. 'Anyway, come on girls, heads down, let's have a race!'

Intrigued, I pushed the library door a fraction wider. I was treated to the spectacle of two Marilyn Monroes, Audrey Hepburn, Snow White and, alas, the Bride of Frankenstein, each armed with a tube of paper, bending over the desk, racing to see who could snort white powder up her nasty little nose the fastest.

I slammed the door shut, which caused them all to shriek, first with terror and then with hysterical laughter. I stalked away, or rather minced, as swiftly as my tight skirt and trailing net would allow.

As I approached the drawing room I slowed down. The hall was deserted. I cast a quick look around me and headed for the door of the study, where I'd been interviewed on the day of Gavin's death by Inspector Ford. I didn't know what I expected to find, but a chance for a poke around seemed too good to miss.

The study was quiet and lamp-lit, heavy curtains drawn across the window. I stood still and looked around me. There were pictures on the wall, which I had not noticed when I was in the room before: engravings of mine workings on the Moorworthy estate, the earliest dated 1860. They showed the mineshaft in the woods, and the shaft at Applecote Farm and several underground passages connecting the two.

There was also a set of photographs, mostly featuring Sandy, who was obviously receiving an award of some kind, shaking hands with another man, the pair surrounded by self-satisfied men in dinner jackets and bow ties. The caption beneath mentioned Dravizax, the firm Jessica had said belonged to her father.

'Can I help you, miss?'

I nearly jumped out of my skin. Like Creeping Ted Croaker, Mrs Johnson seemed to possess the demonic power to materialise, silently, from nowhere. I hadn't heard her come in and she was standing right next to me.

'No, I'm . . . um . . . I was just interested in . . .' I blundered uselessly. 'This is a lovely room.'

223

'There's coffee in the drawing room.' She held the study door open, forcing me to leave.

'Yes, I know. Thank you,' I swept past her and carried on across the hall. I could feel her gaze drilling into me, right between the shoulder blades. She must have been satisfied I was going where she'd told me to because when I reached the living room door and turned around, hand on the handle, she had already disappeared.

The eyes of the ancestors stared from their portraits. But there was no one else about.

I gathered up my sparkly train and quickly nipped up the grand staircase. I came to the first landing, my hand resting on the oak bannister next to an impressively carved pineapple. For a moment the suit of armour and I stared at one another. I resisted the impulse to lift the visor of his helmet and check there was no one inside. I looked left and right. Which way to go? I turned right along a wide corridor, passing a series of doors separated by brass console tables and ornately framed mirrors. I stopped by a door that was open and poked my head inside.

I wondered if this was the bedroom that Sandy had mentioned earlier. It was certainly oriental in style, hung with Chinese wallpaper decorated with birds and flowers. A Japanese lacquer cabinet stood against one wall, whilst on the mantelpiece were placed two Canton vases and an Imari bowl. Whoever had put the collection together obviously didn't distinguish between Chinese and Japanese. There were several Nanking blue and white plates on the walls, but the pride of the collection was a chrysanthemum flower teapot, only a few inches high, and probably worth more than the rest put together. Very carefully, I picked it up for a closer look. Then I heard a man's cough in the corridor outside and hastily replaced it.

I needed a hiding place. I didn't want to be caught in here, especially not by Sandy. I tiptoed across the room to a closed door, which I hoped led to a lockable en suite, and opened it. It was a cupboard, but someone was coming into the room, so I had no choice but to duck inside. I waited in complete darkness, my breath held, trying to listen for muffled footsteps on the Chinese carpet.

The door opened and a light flipped on above my head. 'Well, this is cosy!' Jack Sparrow remarked pleasantly, his hand on the light switch. 'May I?' He stepped inside.

It was quite a tight fit, requiring an adjustment of feet, elbows, hips and hat before he could wedge himself in. The net did a lot of rustling.

'How did you know I was in here?' I was whispering for some stupid reason.

'I saw you come upstairs.'

'No, I mean, in *here*?'

He grinned. 'All that net sticking out from under the door is a bit of a giveaway. Anyway,' he shifted slightly to avoid the prong of a coat hook sticking into his shoulder, 'I'm impressed. There's nothing like causing a sensation at dinner.'

'Talking about Gavin as if his death was just an inconvenience—'

Mr Sparrow leant in even closer. 'Listen.' His face was just an inch from mine. There was no levity in his voice now, no laughter in his grey eyes. 'I want to hear what you know about Gavin and Ben.'

'They thought something—'

225

He laid a finger to his lips. 'Not now. We'll be missed if we're not careful. We're not exactly an inconspicuous couple—'

'Who are you?' I asked.

'Jack Sparrow.'

'No, what's your real name?'

He grinned. 'Nathan, Nathan Parr.'

I confessed that I wasn't really Rita Hayworth and we shook hands awkwardly in the confined space.

'And what are you doing here? You said you worked for the Environment Agency.'

'I do. Officially I'm down here as part of a survey into pollution along the River Dart.'

'And unofficially . . . ?'

He hesitated. 'Let's just say that I didn't bump into James Westershall by accident.'

'Is this about drugs?'

His dark brows drew together in a frown. 'Why should it be about drugs?'

'Because in this house they treat cocaine as if it's an after-dinner mint. Emma's a user and Ben Luscombe was found—'

The door swung open suddenly, making us both jump. 'Playing sardines?' Jamie asked, his brows raised quizzically.

'We're just getting acquainted,' Nathan told him coolly, sliding his arms around my waist. I gave a silly little laugh.

'I was just rounding up people for the fireworks,' Jamie responded. 'I thought I heard voices in here. So, if you two can bear to tear yourselves away . . .'

He stood back and we trailed past him, doing our best to look sheepish.

'You go on down,' Nathan murmured to me, 'I'll catch you up in a moment.'

The gentlemen had not lingered too long over their brandy and cigars and the sitting room had filled up in my absence. Sophie waved to me through the throng. 'Don't worry,' she whispered, patting her little pink handbag. 'I've saved you some petits fours.' Judging from the way the bag was bulging she must have slid an entire plateful in there.

The room was so warm now that someone had flung open the long windows onto the terrace and a few people had drifted out to look at the stars. I decided I could use some air and drifted out myself. After a few moments, Nathan Parr leant on the balustrade next to me.

'Can we meet?' he asked softly. 'Are you free on Tuesday evening?' He named an isolated pub on the moor. 'We can talk more freely there, less chance of being overheard.' He glanced at his watch. 'Look, I'd really love to stay and dance with you till dawn, but I have to go.' He raised my gloved hand to his lips and kissed it. 'Till Tuesday.'

'I'm not sure I'll know you without the hat and dreadlocks.'

'I'll wear a red carnation.'

'You might not know me either. I don't usually look like this.'

'You don't?' he asked in mock sadness.

'My hair is usually . . . um . . . wilder.'

'Wow!' he grinned. 'I'll look forward to that,' and walked away.

I felt mildly triumphant. At last there was someone interested in hearing about Gavin and Ben Luscombe, prepared to take their deaths seriously. He was also a very

227

attractive pirate and I was not at all unhappy at the thought of a little swashbuckling in his company. If things went well, we might even go as far as a jolly roger.

Jamie came out at that moment and announced that fireworks would be starting in five minutes, and that the place to view them from was the terrace, but if people wanted to wander down onto the lawn, he warned them, please beware of the ha-ha.

'We don't want any broken necks. Also, it's getting a bit chilly, so some of you might want to grab a coat or something before the fireworks start.'

I went inside and reached for the mink stole I'd left draped over the end of the sofa. I snatched it up just before Emma grabbed it. 'Mine, I think,' I told her, smiling sweetly. She glowered, her pupils mere pinpoints, then shrugged, a painful manoeuvre she obviously regretted, and stalked away.

'Well, I'm getting a coat,' Sandy announced loudly. 'I feel the cold these days. I blame it on these damned pills the doctor keeps giving me.'

'You're just getting old, you fool,' the Wicked Witch of the West informed him flatly.

'You're right, Margaret, m'dear, you're right,' he admitted, shaking his head.

A few minutes later I stood on the terrace with Sophie whilst rockets shot upward in golden, fizzing streaks and exploded in sparkling starbursts. I saw the figure of Sandy close by, suddenly silhouetted in a dazzling burst of brightness, wrapped up against the cold in a sheepskin coat and trilby hat, looking as he had when I had seen him standing outside the shed at Applecote Farm, just before Moss and Pike's lorry

228

had tried to run me off the road. I tried not to stare. Sophie was shivering. I wrapped one end of the mink stole around her shoulders and watched the dying glitter of the fireworks as they fell to earth over the dark masses of the woods, and the place where Gavin and Ben had died.

CHAPTER TWENTY-THREE

Never trust a pirate. The bastard stood me up. On Tuesday evening I drove all the way out to this damn pub in the dark and sat for two hours in a deserted and almost silent bar, nursing half a sour-tasting cider, waiting for him to show up, and receiving unwelcome glances from two fat blokes playing pool. At first, I thought I'd got the time wrong, then the place. And it was only then it got through to my dim brain that I didn't even have the man's phone number. I'd obviously got carried away on the bubbly at the party and the whole assignation was just a fantasy.

Sophie and I had not stayed long after the fireworks. James Dean wanted her to dance, so I sat down between the Wicked Witch of the West and the eldest Marilyn, and watched them join the jigging horde on the ballroom floor.

'Not dancing?' WWW asked me.

'Difficult to move at all in this dress,' I admitted.

'It is lovely. Did you get it from those two old reprobates up on Druid Lane? What do they call themselves, Sauce and something . . .'

'Sauce and Slander,' I told her. 'You know them?'

'They've done a couple of fundraisers for my charity. In fact, I've got a ticket for a concert they're doing soon.'

'They did say they were doing a concert here,' I remembered. We chatted on for a bit. She turned out to be neither Mrs Superman, nor Mrs Beau Geste, as I thought she might be, but a widowed aunt of Jamie's. 'Is Sophie going to paint your bulldogs?' I asked when we had exhausted the family connections.

'Florence has just produced a litter,' she answered with the beaming smile of a proud grandmother. 'I thought it might be fun, you know, a portrait of mother and babies. Sophie's coming to my house to make sketches and take photos. Come with her and have a cup of tea.'

'Well, thank you, Mrs . . . I will.'

'Call me Margaret.' She patted my arm. 'You're a good 'un. I like the way you spoke up about the death of your friend, put Barty and Geoffrey in their place—'

Fred Astaire came bounding up at this moment and tried to claim me for a dance he said I'd promised him and vowed he wouldn't take no for an answer.

'Oh, do fuck off, Robert!' Margaret commanded him, causing the eldest Marilyn to give a startled hiccup. 'We're trying to have a conversation.'

Poor Fred shrank visibly, mumbled an apology and left, muttering something about coming back later.

'Well really, Margaret!' Marilyn protested. 'Language!'

Margaret favoured her with a long stare. 'Why are you

231

got up like an old tart, Betty?' she demanded amiably. 'Who are you supposed to be?'

'Marilyn Monroe,' she responded, a red flush of embarrassment creeping up her neck.

Margaret gave a witch-like cackle and turned her attention back to me. 'No, you're a good 'un, I can tell. That one over there,' she nodded in the direction of Emma, who was dancing with Charlie Chaplin, 'she's a bad 'un, even though she is my god-daughter and I shouldn't say it.' She sighed. 'I don't know the half of what she gets up to and it's probably just as well.'

She was right about that. I doubt if she knew about the after-dinner cocaine. I was still angry about it, disappointed in the Bride of Frankenstein.

'Is Charlie Chaplin Emma's boyfriend?'

'Boyfriend?' Margaret's shoulders shook as she chuckled. 'She can't keep 'em, my dear. She's got the fiend's own temper. Men don't like it. I told you, she's a bad 'un.'

'And what about Jamie?' He was dancing with his whip twined around Audrey Hepburn's waist. 'Is he a good 'un, or a bad 'un?'

'That's a good question,' she answered me sadly. 'I've never been able to tell.'

Sophie flopped down into a nearby chair at this point. She was a bit wheezy and I judged it was time to be going home. Anyway, it seemed that Charlie Chaplin had now been abandoned and James Dean had been dragged away from her by an obviously possessive Emma. 'Eddie!' she'd hissed furiously, beckoning him to her. 'Eddie!' He'd scuttled obediently across the dance floor. I told Sophie to forget him. He was obviously a lap dog.

We made our excuses and left, carefully avoiding being spotted by Fred Astaire. When we got to the car, I asked Sophie if she felt well enough to drive.

'Well, I'm more sober than you,' she responded, dropping the pink handbag into my lap. So I let her steer our way down the darkened moorland road and tucked happily into the petits fours.

Next morning, Sunday, I took Rita Hayworth back to Ricky and Morris. She was carefully sheathed in plastic to avoid contact with any dog hair in the van, but actually, cat hair was more likely to be a problem. I had dutifully put the dress on a hanger before I went to bed, and hung it on the bedroom door, but the train was so long it reached the floor and lay in a big frothy cloud on the carpet. When I got up next morning, I found Bill, who'd been strangely absent from my bed all night, blissfully nesting in the middle of it. I didn't mention this to Morris and Ricky when I gave it back. In any case, they were more interested in who'd been at the party and what they'd worn than anything else. I gave them the details over coffee and croissants, adding good wishes sent from Margaret the WWW.

Then I drove to Olly's, making sure my arrival was clocked by his fairy neighbour, and offered him a trip up to the moor to fly the drone around. He said it was too windy for the drone, so I asked him what he'd like to do instead.

'Could we go to a supermarket?' he asked, eyes alight. 'A big one?'

Ashburton doesn't have a real supermarket. If he and his nan had wanted to shop in one they would have had to catch a bus; I suppose in Olly's mind a visit to a supermarket still represented a day out. So I took him to Newton Abbot, where there were several such cathedrals of consumerism, and told him to take his pick. He shopped like a thing demented, racing up and down the aisles with his trolley, buying new school trousers and stationery as well as stocking up on tins, cleaning materials and foodstuffs. 'It's all so cheap!' he squeaked ecstatically as he loaded up his trolley. It was true; the small independent shops of Ashburton could not compete in terms of price. Even I bought a few groceries and a T-shirt.

After a milkshake and sticky bun for Olly and a coffee and croissant for me we escaped the supermarket and I got my reward for taking him shopping: the racecourse was holding a boot sale. I wandered around, happily accruing an armful of paperback books, a box of china ornaments, a brass coal scuttle, a three-legged oak milking stool and a set of pretty pine shelves, which, even if they didn't sell, would look good on the wall in the shop and be useful for displaying other stuff. Olly helped me carry my spoils, along with a science annual he'd bought and a book about unexplained phenomena.

'I nearly bought a jigsaw,' he told me, as we were loading our booty into White Van.

'The man was trying to sell it to me, but I told him, I got lots of jigsaws. Nan used to like them. She'd got really old ones that were her mother's – you know, wooden ones with funny old pictures on – and he said if ever I wanted to sell them—'

'If ever you want to sell them,' I told him firmly, 'you sell them to me.'

'Why did you buy that box of stupid china animals? They can't be worth much.'

'No, most of them aren't,' I agreed, 'but if you turn them upside down, some have a magic word on the bottom.'

'What's that?'

'Wade. These little animal figures are collectors' items.'

'Are they worth a lot, then?'

'Just a few pounds each, but that's more than I paid for them.'

Olly digested this in thoughtful silence for a few moments and then stuck his head in unexplained phenomena for the rest of the journey home.

When we arrived back at Daison Cottages, his neighbour was weeding her front garden. As we drew up, I saw her sneak a look at her watch. We had abandoned Nan for hours.

'Just stocking up,' I called to her as I struggled up the front path laden with supermarket carriers and a giant pack of toilet rolls. And then I added to her in a low, conspiratorial voice. 'Some of the essentials were running low.'

'Such a good job you're here,' she answered, but her expression was sour. I got the feeling that the milk of human kindness had curdled.

I'd planned to suggest a walk up on the moor when we got back, but after cruelly abandoning Nan for such a long time, I thought we'd better stay indoors, so Olly and I sat and played Scrabble. I won. For a genius his spelling isn't very good.

Monday was Hallowe'en. Just an ordinary busy Monday: dogs, Maisie, Brownlows, shirts, shop. Pat did quite well with pumpkins and witches. I sold nothing at all. Late in the afternoon, Pat came in lugging a box from the orchard at Honeysuckle Farm. Showers of apples had been brought down by the wind, she told me, and there were basketfuls to be picked up before they rotted in the wet grass. Olly had started his half-term holiday and was helping out.

'So, who are this lot for?' I asked, as she dumped a second box on the shop floor.

'You and Sophie,' she answered breathlessly. 'Them's Lambournes, they're eaters,' she pointed at the apples in one box. 'The others are cookers. Can't you use 'em?'

'I know someone who can,' I assured her. And so I spent that evening seated at the big scrubbed table in Katie's kitchen, happily chatting as we cored and sliced until nearly midnight whilst the saucepans on the stove became steamy cauldrons of spice-scented stewed apple. She told me to drop into *Sunflowers* next day for a free lunch.

I took the Tribe for their usual walk in the morning and decided to take them home along the Terrace, where I had last seen the mystery lady enjoying a quiet moment with her cat. She wasn't there this time, but I still put the dogs back on their leads before we went through the little woodland that would take us down to Roborough Lane. I was trying to keep them away from any broken glass that might be littering the muddy path, so my eyes were fixed on the ground, rather than looking ahead.

Nookie the husky growled suddenly, stopping still, the silver fur around her neck bristling in a stiff ruff. She was staring off into to the trees, and as I peered between the ivy-covered trunks, I could see two figures standing. Lurking, you might say. Two men, one in a dark duffle coat, the other in a leather jacket. They were looking around furtively, casting anxious glances over their shoulders; but they didn't see me. Something passed between them. I couldn't see too clearly, but I'm sure money changed hands, and then something else.

The other dogs had picked up Nookie's alertness. EB began to bark, and then Schnitzel, Boog and Sally all joined in. I had to haul back hard on their leads to stop them rushing forward.

Startled by the raucous cacophony of noise, the men parted company, hastening away in opposite directions. Leather Jacket cast a glance over his shoulder, and I saw his face clearly. His hair had lost the quiff he'd worn when he'd danced with Sophie at the party, but it was James Dean, alias Eddie. The other man also risked a look behind him; none other than Creeping Ted Croaker. So, what was this unlikely pair up to that they had to move away sharpish at the sign of anyone's approach? The dogs were sniffing the ground inquisitively and I just snatched something that Eddie had dropped before Schnitzel's snout got to it. It was a clear, self-seal packet glistening with white crystals, like sugar. Except of course, it wasn't sugar and it wouldn't have done Schnitzel any good at all.

We dog walkers come prepared with pockets full of plastic bags. I fished one out, dropped the little bag of goodies into it and tied it up tightly. At the top of Roborough Lane I deposited the bag, along with a few others I had collected, into the evil-smelling red bin that stood there for the purpose. I shoved it down firmly, squishing it amongst the other parcels of dog poo. Let Eddie fish it out if he dared.

I tried phoning Inspector Ford to tell him I had seen Croaker, but as usual, he was unavailable. Even Cruella wasn't around to speak to. I left a message, without much hope that anyone would get back to me soon. So I was surprised later in the day when the inspector phoned back. They had found Creeping Ted and taken him to the police station for a little chat.

'Unfortunately, we had to let him go again,' the inspector told me. 'To begin with, he denied ever knowing Gavin Hall, but when we told him three different witnesses could swear to him speaking to Gavin in your shop, he admitted that he did. He said he'd come in because he was interested in the classic comics that Gavin was selling. That's rubbish, of course, but sadly, there's no law against it.'

'So we still don't know what he was up to?'

'He was almost certainly trying to sell Gavin drugs – or trying to recruit him.'

'Recruit him?'

'To sell drugs for him,' the inspector explained. 'Mr Croaker is desperately trying to claw his way up the supply chain.'

'I don't think Gavin would have got involved in selling drugs,' I said frankly. 'What about Eddie, do you think he's one of Croaker's recruits?'

'We've arrested Eddie Coates for possession on more than one occasion. But we have no evidence that he's supplying it to others.'

'Someone supplies it to Emma Westershall.' I told him

238

about the little cocaine-snorting party I'd witnessed on the night of Sandy's birthday. 'And Eddie was there that night.'

The inspector sighed in a way that told me this was not evidence. 'Well, we'll have words with Eddie, next time we catch hold of him,' he said wearily, and bid me goodbye.

I dropped into *Sunflowers* for my promised lunch and ate parsnip and apple soup so thick it was almost solid, followed by spiced apple cake with clotted cream. It was all delicious and I hoped there would be plenty of leftovers.

I spent the rest of Tuesday looking forward to meeting Nathan Parr in the evening and finished work early so that I could glam up. Alas, Rita Hayworth's glossy waves were long gone and the wild curls were back. I did the best I could with spritz and set out in nicely fitting jeans, ankle boots and a caramel silk shirt, to meet my pirate at the pub in the middle of the moor.

It was when one of the pool players came over and offered to buy me a drink that I decided it was time to leave. It was getting late by then and I still faced the drive home. I left a note with the girl behind the bar. Just in case a man came in and asked for me, I told her. It read: *Came. Waited. Went. Rita Hayworth.* And beneath my name I wrote my phone number.

During the evening the weather had finally broken. A gale had blown in from the west and rain was flinging itself in fitful gusts against the steamy windows of the pub. Outside, beyond the lighted haven of the car park, the night was black. Cursing, I turned up the collar of my jacket and ran across the uneven concrete to White Van, dodging puddles as I went. The wind was strafing through the trees, stripping the branches. Leaves clung wetly to the roof of the van and to my windscreen. I climbed in and got the windscreen wipers going, swishing them aside. The rain rattled on the roof, danced in the light of my headlamps and bounced up from the tarmac. I shivered. It would be a while before the van warmed up and as I turned out onto the moorland road, I cursed Nathan Parr alias Jack Sparrow several times over.

The headlights questioned the darkness ahead, picking out the road, the whiteness of granite boulders scattered on the grassy verge and the occasional shine of animal eyes, but beyond, the moor lay in darkness, sky black as molasses, no moon, stars blotted out. I drove slowly, as always on the moor at night, for fear of hitting wandering sheep or cattle. Now and again the golden lights of a lonely house glimmered in the distance, a welcome reminder that light, warmth and comfort existed out there somewhere.

The roaring wind stirred the gorse and heather into a shifting sea, buffeting the van as it crawled across the exposed moorland. I wasn't in any danger of getting lost; I was clinging to the only road I could, which would take me around the edge of Holne Moor, past the gates of the Moorworthy estate, and down the hill into Ashburton. My delicious apple-filled lunch seemed a long time ago now and I wondered if the Indian takeaway would still be open when I got back into town.

I was not far short of the gates of Moorworthy House when I hit something, or rather, something hit me. I felt it thump, bounce off my nearside wheel. I'd seen nothing in the headlights. Whatever it was must have come at me from the side, and it must have been small: a rabbit or a farm cat, perhaps a pheasant or a badger. I pulled up on the verge and got out, peering into the rainy dark. I couldn't bear the thought of leaving an animal injured. I fetched the torch from the glovebox and shone it back the way I'd come, peering through the slanting rain. There was nothing lying in the road, no sad little furry corpse. I crossed over, hunching my shoulders against the chill, against the fat wet drops rolling down inside my collar. I swept the torch beam up and down the verge, probing the bushes for any sign of an injured creature. Around me the moor was a wild thing, roaring wind thrashing the heaving gorse bushes, flailing and swishing the bracken, blowing my hair across my wet face so that I had to clutch at handfuls, drag it out of my vision.

I was caught suddenly in the headlights of an approaching vehicle. I ran to the verge out of its way and it pulled up behind me, quenching its tyres in wet gravel. For a moment I thought it might be Nathan, but the figure that climbed out of the driving seat was not him. It came towards me, silhouetted by the headlights behind. I could see only a stooping figure in a flat cap, but as he drew close and I pointed the torch in his direction, the glaring white light revealed the lugubrious features of Moss.

'What are you doing here?' he demanded loudly, eyes narrowed against my torch beam.

I had to raise my voice above the roar of the wind. 'I thought I'd hit something.'

He grabbed my arm. 'Put that torch out and dowse them headlights!'

I pulled away, wrenching my arm from his grip. 'Just a minute!'

'For the love of God, maid!' he cried, shaking me. 'They're coming! If you value your life, do as I say.' He pushed past me, opening the van door, switching off the engine and ripping out the keys. Then he slammed the door shut and thrust the keys into my hand.

'Down!' he told me. 'Get down in the ditch there, where they won't see you.' I stood goggling at him like an idiot. 'Quick!' he shouted, wresting the torch from my grasp. 'They mustn't see you.' He began to hustle me towards the ditch. 'There's too many dead already.'

The anguish in his voice, the desperation on his face, told me this was not a moment to argue. I did as I was told, hunkered in the ditch behind gorse bushes, out of sight of the road, seconds before the glaring lights of a large truck appeared around the bend. It thundered towards us, water spraying sideways beneath its heavy tyres and rumbled to a stop a few feet from Moss's Land Rover. I heard the cab door open and someone jump down onto the roadway on the passenger side.

'Something the matter, Moss?' It was Jamie's voice, but cold and authoritative, stripped of bonhomie. As I peered between the bushes, I saw the shadows of his legs scissoring across the road as he walked in front of the headlights. The driver in the cab was just a hunched shape slumped behind the steering wheel, but I was willing to bet he was wearing a green hat.

'I saw the van parked, sir,' Moss responded. 'Just thought I'd take a look around. But there's no one about.'

'Hang on, that's Juno Browne's van, isn't it? I recognise the number plate . . . and look at the back bumper! What the hell is that bloody woman doing up here?'

'If it is hers, she's long gone, sir.' Moss laid a hand on bonnet. 'Engine's stone cold,' he lied. 'And I think she's had a bit of a knock to this nearside wheel. Forced to abandon it, I reckon. She must've got a ride home.'

'Let's hope you're right. She's turning into a nuisance. We might have to do something about her. Look, just have another check around, will you, Moss? Make sure? There's too much at stake to leave any loose ends. We'll carry on.'

I saw his shadow cross the road in the glare of the truck's lights, heard the slam of the cab door. The truck growled into life again. As it roared past, tyres hissing on the wet road, I could see the back piled high with the rounded shapes of silage bales, light glimmering on black plastic.

'Stay down!' Moss yelled in my direction. After what seemed like an age cramped in the narrow wet ditch, scratched by the thorns of tossing gorse, he told me it was safe to stand up. 'They've turned off for the farm.'

'What the hell is going on?'

'Stop asking questions.' He handed me back the torch. 'Get home and stay away from here.'

'You said there'd been too many dead already.' I squinted into the rain, trying to read his face beneath his dripping cap. 'What did you mean?'

'You don't want to know.'

'Moss, what happened to Gavin?'

'I tried to warn him, all right?' His voice was broken, hoarse, shouting above the wind. 'I tried to scare 'em off, him and the other lad!' He headed back towards his car.

'The other lad?' I yelled after him. 'Do you mean Ben?'

'I'm not saying no more.' He pushed past me. 'My

243

family's been loyal to the Westershalls for years, but it never used to be like this. You don't want to let them catch you up here, maid.' He wrenched the car door open. 'Go home!' He climbed inside and drove off.

I watched his tail lights disappear. I was clutching the keys he had thrust into my hand so tightly they had dug an impression in my palm. I hurried to the van and got in. I was soaked, shaking with the cold, water running off the ends of my hair. My hands were icy and for a few moments they trembled too much for me to get the key in the ignition. I fished an old towel I used for wiping muddy paws from the back of the van and dried my face and hands with it. I breathed in deep; the doggy smell was comforting. I got going at last, headlights on, heater full blast, windscreen wipers swishing into action.

And as I passed the end of the lane that led to Applecote Farm, drove by the gates of Moorworthy House and trundled on down the hill towards the safety of Ashburton, I wondered why the hell anyone would be hauling trucks full of silage around empty farms at night. I wondered about Nathan Parr who just happened to have been placed next to me at dinner and who'd lured me to spend the evening alone in an isolated pub. And I wondered about Jamie. Was he a good 'un or a bad 'un? I think I had the answer to that now.

CHAPTER TWENTY-FOUR

Driving down the wooded hill towards Ashburton I had other things to worry about. The trees at the roadside shifted like restless giants. They came down in gales like this. I had to steer around branches wrenched off by the moaning wind, fearful that any moment a great trunk might fall across the road in front of me or come crashing through the roof of the van.

When I got home, I ran myself a hot bath. I was still shaking, from fear as well as cold, and I spent a long time soaking in the glistening bubbles, staring through clouds of steam, thinking of Jamie and what he'd said to Moss about having to do something about me. I didn't like the sound of that. And what about Nathan? Was he who he claimed to be, or had Jamie planted him next to me at dinner to find out what, if anything, I had said to the police about Gavin's death, or to discover what I'd been up to with the drone? But if Jamie had set Nathan on me to spy, why hadn't he

245

turned up at the pub? Was Nathan a good 'un or a bad 'un?

I slept badly. Even in my dreams I could hear the wind that had ripped and roared up on the moor. Down in the town it buffeted the houses like a drunken fist, smiting at chimneys and rooftops, rattling doors and windows, trying to get in.

I did not want to get out of bed next morning, leave its snuggly warmth, but there were five waggy creatures waiting expectantly for me to take them for a walk so I was forced to drag myself from under the duvet, despite Bill's best efforts to pin me down. Half of me wanted to drive them up onto Holne Moor, let them race around on the common land where I had stopped last night, just beyond Applecote Farm, and have a nose around. The other, more sensible half reminded me I had a full morning and not too much time. So we just followed the course of the river through the town and into the woods. Barely more than a stream for most of the year, after the storm it was swollen and muddy, choked in places by rafts of twigs and leaves.

The gale had blown itself out, but in the wood the trees still stirred. A few odd leaves clung like golden pennies to bare and dripping branches, but most lay on the ground in soggy heaps, their crunchy crispness lost. The dogs didn't care, snuffling amongst the sodden leaves. The wind stirred them up, ruffled their fur, excited them like kids in a playground, and the rain released fresh smells, wet smells, the earthy pungent tang of the forest floor and the creatures dwelling in it. For the dogs the world was new again.

Back in town, Tribe delivered, I checked in at *Old Nick's*, and had a brief chat with Pat.

'That Olly's a nice lad,' she told me approvingly, 'very eager. And you say he lives all alone with his nan?'

'Yes,' I said, hoping to turn the conversation in another direction.

'My mum knew old Dolly Knollys. I'd have thought she would have been dead long ago.'

'Mmm.' I nodded evasively. 'I'm glad Olly's being useful. I can't hang about, Pat. I've got errands to run for a few people. I'll be back here lunchtime to take over.'

I hurried out of the door before she could chat further. I threaded my way between the wheelie bins in the side alley, stepping over the puddles, emerged into Sun Street and bumped slap into Jamie Westershall.

'Hello!' he cried, grinning. 'Just the girl I was coming to see. Time for a coffee?'

For a moment I stared, unable to reconcile the smiling blue eyes, the easy charm, with the man standing in the road last night.

'Well . . .' I stumbled, 'I'm really short of time, I—'

'Oh, come on!' He grabbed my arm. 'Just a quick one, look, there's a place right here.' His grip on my arm was firm, almost tight. He steered me through the door of the coffee shop and we sat down. For a moment we stared across the table, considering each other. 'I've been worried about you, Juno.'

'Oh?' We paused, as the waitress came and took our order. 'Why?'

'I found your van abandoned on the moor last night. No sign of you. I wondered if you were all right.'

'Just a puncture,' I lied, with what I hoped was an airy shrug. 'Luckily, someone I knew came by and gave me a lift back into town.'

His brows lifted slightly. 'When I drove back a little later your van had gone.'

'We got the puncture fixed.'

'You came back to do it? Couldn't you and this friend have done it there and then?' His voice was light, but his blue eyes, narrow with suspicion, never left mine.

'We had to come back into town to fetch a toolbox.'

'Bit risky, I'd have thought, driving about the moor at night without proper tools. It makes me wonder what you were doing up there at all, Juno, on a terrible night like that.'

'Well, I'll tell you,' I volunteered, deciding to take the risk. 'I went to meet your old pal from agricultural college, Nathan Parr, alias Jack Sparrow.'

'Yes, I remember the two of you getting acquainted in a cupboard.'

'Well, Mr Nathan Parr invited me out for a drink in a pub up on the moor and then stood me up.' I waited to see his reaction, watched for any flicker in his blue eyes, but his gaze was unwavering. 'I don't suppose you would know anything about that?'

He laughed. 'Of course not, why would I?'

'I just wondered if it might have been someone's idea of a joke.'

'Certainly not mine. Nathan had to leave the party early for some reason and I haven't seen him since.' He took a sip of black coffee and sat back, studying me reflectively. 'So, he stood you up, eh? Poor old Juno!' His shoulders shook with silent laughter. 'And everything seemed so promising back in that cupboard.'

His smugness, his amusement, convinced me that he knew more about this than he was saying. He'd set me up with his friend, I was sure of it. But then for some reason, he'd called him off.

'It just seems a bit strange, you know, Juno,' he went on, all trace of humour vanishing, 'finding your van parked on my land like that, especially after the little stunt you pulled at Sandy's party. I'm wondering if you've got something on your mind.'

'I didn't bring up Gavin's name,' I pointed out.

'No, but you brought up Ben Luscombe's. What was the point of that, Juno? He was trespassing. He took cocaine—'

'Like your sister.'

For a moment it was as if I'd struck a match; anger flared in his eyes. Then the flame died down. He smiled, but I could see the muscles in his jaw were tight. 'Emma likes to experiment. She's not an addict.'

'And Jess?'

He bit his lip, furious. 'Jess doesn't take drugs.'

'No? Well, she was snorting something up her nose at Sandy's party.'

He leant forward across the table and spoke softly. 'You'd better be careful what you say.'

'Had I?'

'There's a young boy who keeps flying a drone over our land. I don't suppose you know him?'

I felt a shiver of disquiet but managed a smile. 'Why would I?'

'Just that he was spotted with you in your van.'

'And you would know this, how?'

'We both know how,' he answered steadily. 'Tell your young friend that it's illegal to fly a drone over private property and I'm prepared to take steps to protect my privacy.'

'Is that what you did with Gavin? "Took steps"?'

'The police are satisfied his death was an accident.'

'I'm not.'

'Don't meddle, Juno,' he warned me softly. 'Don't meddle in things that are none of your concern.' He flung a note down on the table to cover the bill, stood, ready to leave.

'You don't think another accident on the Moorworthy estate might arouse suspicion?'

He gripped my wrist suddenly, his face bent close to mine. 'Don't cross me, Juno,' he warned and strode out, letting the door slam behind him.

I watched him go, watched the swagger of his broad shoulders as he set off down the street. I don't like being told what to do, I don't like being threatened. I was glad I'd made him angry.

Late that afternoon, when I was in the shop, I got a distress call from Olly, just back from Honeysuckle Farm. He was crying, almost hysterical. I had to tell him to calm down before I could make sense of what he was saying.

'It's her, next door!' he sobbed.

'Mrs Hardiman?'

'She's coming in. She was round here earlier . . . come to the back door . . . she says, she says . . .'

'Take a breath, Olly,' I recommended. 'Now, what did she say?'

'She says she knows you ain't a social worker. She says something funny's going on . . . And she says, if I don't let her come in and talk to Nan, she'll ring the police—'

'What did you say?'

250

'I told her Nan was asleep, so she said she's coming back at five o'clock and she ain't leaving till she's seen her. What am I going to do?' he cried piteously.

I looked at my watch. It was already nearly four. 'Bake a cake,' I told him.

'What?'

'Bake a cake. Lay the table, nicely, as if we're having guests to tea. Get out your Nan's best cups. I'll be there as soon as I can.'

'But what are we—'

'I'll think of something,' I promised him. 'Don't panic.'

I put the phone down knowing I had an hour to find Olly a great-grandmother. As I ran to the van I was going through my options. Maisie was no good, Olly's neighbour already knew her. Chloe Berkeley-Smythe would have been up for it, would have considered the whole idea of impersonating someone else a hoot, if she'd been persuaded it was a joke; but she was on the high seas, and anyway, no one in their right mind would believe she lived in a council house. I briefly considered Morris in drag, but this was too hideous an idea to contemplate. Anyway, I would have been forced to let him and Ricky into Olly's secret and I had promised him I wouldn't tell.

I was halfway up the road towards Owlacombe Cross when I saw her. She wasn't wearing her blue dressing gown, but beige trousers and a flowery top, and for a moment I didn't recognise her. I pulled up next to her and wound the window down. She peered in at me, giving me a bright but questioning smile.

'Hello, Judith-Marianne!' I leapt out and opened the passenger door.

251

'Are we going out to tea?' she asked as she slid into the seat.

'It's funny you should ask that,' I said, securing her seat belt. 'But we *are* going out to tea. Yes, we are.'

We got Judith-Marianne installed in Nan's chair just a few moments before we heard the determined footsteps of Olly's neighbour marching up to the kitchen door. I welcomed her inside whilst Olly put the kettle on. Two halves of a fragrant Victoria sponge lay on a wire cooling rack, and he had spread one half with jam.

'Now, we must clear up this misunderstanding,' I began, putting on my best smile. 'Do come in . . . er . . .'

'April,' she reminded me, looking around the kitchen as if she expected a gang of terrorists to come leaping out from somewhere. 'April Hardiman.'

Single repetitive notes on the piano drifted through from the living room.

'Let me introduce you to Mrs Knollys.' I guided April into the living room. 'She got up out of bed especially so that she can meet you.'

Judith-Marianne had moved from the chair and seated herself at the piano, where she was prodding each of the keys individually with a forefinger. 'This isn't in tune, you know,' she told us as we came in.

'No, I'm sorry, Nan.' Olly had followed us in, carrying the jam sponge on a plate, its golden top dusted with icing sugar. 'It's been out of tune for quite a while now.'

'This is April,' I said, as she continued to test each note repetitively. 'She lives next door.'

Judith-Marianne did not look up, ignoring April's

proffered hand. 'April, May, June,' she said, as she played each key. She scowled in frustration. 'Out of tune!'

'You play piano, then, Mrs Knollys.' April's face was fixed in a determined smile. 'I'm musical, too. I belong to the Dartmoor Operatic Society.'

There was no response. Judith-Marianne just stared.

'That's right,' I pitched in recklessly. 'April is playing a fairy in their production of *Iolanthe*.'

April then proceeded to warble a snatch of some tune about fairies tripping lightly hither and thither. The effect on Judith-Marianne was extraordinary. It was as if the fog in which she wandered like a lost child miraculously lifted. Suddenly she was with us, present in the moment. She joined in with April's warbling. She knew every note and every word. She had become the person that she used to be. As they chirruped and trilled ecstatically together, Olly rolled his eyes at me in alarm. 'They're getting on too well,' he hissed at me in a whisper. 'She,' he jerked his head in April's direction, 'will want to come back.'

He needn't have worried. Judith-Marianne then tried to accompany them both on the piano, but it was so badly out of tune that after a few faltering notes, she stopped, screaming in vexation and began banging the lid up and down. She burst into tears and April backed away, horrified.

'It's all right, Ju . . . Dolly.' I took her by the shoulders and steered her, still sobbing, from the piano stool to the armchair. 'We're going to have a cup of tea. Look, Olly's made a cake.'

'It's your favourite, Nan,' Olly told her bravely. 'Victoria sponge.'

'Do sit down, April.' I indicated a chair. 'And afterwards,' I promised, 'Olly can play us a tune on his bassoon.'

He began shaking his head.

'Now, don't be shy, Olly.' I directed him a warning glance. 'You know how much your nan loves to hear you play.'

'I'll fetch the teapot,' he muttered furiously and stomped off into the kitchen. By the time he came back, order had been restored. Judith-Marianne was silently contemplating the sponge cake, lost in the fog once again and ignoring April's attempts at making polite conversation. I poured the tea while Olly cut the sponge, handing slices around and for the next few minutes we all nibbled politely.

'Your garden is looking very pretty, Mrs Hardiman,' I commented, by way of filling the void, 'especially for this time of year.'

'Not for much longer,' she sighed. 'The dahlias are almost over now.'

'Bishop of Llandaff,' Judith-Marianne crumbled a morsel of sponge between restless fingers.

'What's that, Nan?' Olly asked apprehensively.

'Bishop of Llandaff,' she repeated, dabbing crumbs from her plate with a wet forefinger.

'It's a variety of dahlia,' I cried, catching on. 'The Bishop of Llandaff is a variety of dahlia. That's right isn't it, Dolly?'

'Would you like to come and see the dahlias in my garden, Mrs Knollys,' April offered politely, 'before the frost gets them?'

Judith-Marianne paused, crumbs on fingers, and scowled at her. 'No! Shut up!' Her moods, it seemed, changed as suddenly as the weather. April's smile had taken on a rigid quality, like the grin on a ventriloquist's dummy.

'I think it might be time for that tune now, Olly,' I said hastily.

'Oh, right!' He opened the case and assembled the instrument from its various compartments. April and I watched him, fascinated. Judith-Marianne took no notice at all and helped herself to more cake.

The bassoon is a very long instrument and the player wears a shoulder strap to help support the weight. Even with this help, Olly had to sit down to play, the end of the bassoon balanced on his shoe. He licked his lips nervously, tried a few experimental notes, fussed with the reed in the mouthpiece, and then played a simple tune.

It was lovely. I didn't recognise it, but Judith-Marianne did. She began to la-la softly in time.

After a few moments, April rashly tried to join in too.

'No! No!' Judith-Marianne threw her plate to the floor, scattering crumbs and icing sugar. 'Not you! Not you!'

'Dolly!' I cried. 'That's not very nice!'

She burst into tears.

'That's quite all right.' April hastily bent to pick up the plate from the carpet. Olly stopped playing, disengaged himself from the bassoon and slightly nervously went to comfort his nan, patting her on the shoulder. April handed the plate back to me. 'Perhaps I should go now,' she whispered. 'It was very nice to meet you, Mrs Knollys.'

'I'll show you out.' I led her down the hall towards the front door. 'I do apologise for Dolly,' I said softly. 'You can see how difficult she is.'

'Oh, I understand,' April assured me, nodding wisely.

'The way she reacts to visitors sometimes . . . well, it just makes life more difficult for Olly.'

She was nodding furiously now, like a toy dog in a car's rear window. 'I think that boy's a marvel!'

'Oh, he is!'

She was hopping from foot to foot, desperate to get away, so I kept her talking another ten minutes. I wanted to be sure she wouldn't come back in a hurry. Every minute or so, Olly appeared in the living room doorway. He seemed to be trying to signal something to me, but I ignored him. 'I apologise again for Dolly.'

'Don't you think,' April suggested tentatively, 'that Oakdene is where she really belongs?'

'Oh, you are so right, April!' I agreed. 'And don't worry, I'm sure she'll be there before much longer.'

We said our goodbyes and I finally closed the door on her. I leant against it, letting out a groan of relief.

'Has she gone?' Olly appeared in the living room doorway.

'She has.' I looked at my watch. 'It's time I got Judith-Marianne back to Oakdene. Is she all right? She's gone very quiet.'

'Of course she has,' Olly answered. It was only then I noticed how pale he was looking, his blue eyes huge with shock. 'She's dead.'

CHAPTER TWENTY-FIVE

'What happened?' I was desperately feeling Judith-Marianne's veined wrist for a pulse. Finding none, I touched her neck.

'I've done all that,' Olly told me, watching my efforts. 'She'd quietened down a bit, so I got the dustpan and brush. I was brushing up the icing sugar,' he pointed to the carpet where she'd thrown the cake, 'and I looked up, and she was sort of slumped over, like she is now. I thought she'd just nodded off. I got a bit worried after a few minutes, and you were still talking . . . so I tried to wake her up.' He watched me as I tried to find her heartbeat.

'She's gone, isn't she?'

'I'm afraid she is.' I sat back on my heels and studied her, eyes closed, her head drooping towards her chest. She looked entirely peaceful. 'Poor old soul.'

'Can't we use her?' he asked suddenly. 'Can't we pretend she's really my nan, get the doctor to come, sign a death certificate—'

'I'm afraid it doesn't work like that. A doctor can only sign a death certificate for a patient he knows, someone he's been treating, otherwise there has to be an autopsy. We couldn't risk it. We don't know who her real doctor is. What if we phoned the surgery and her real doctor turned up and knows she isn't the person we're pretending she is?'

'Well, what are we going to do then?' he demanded, trembling voice rising high in excitement. 'I'm not putting her in with my nan!'

'No, no, I wasn't going to suggest that,' I assured him. 'I've got to get her back to where she belongs . . . Listen, go outside, sneak down the front path and see if April's closed her front curtains.' I hoped she might have done, it was already dark outside. But Olly came back to report the curtains were wide open. He could see April in the light of her television, her gaze fixed upon the screen.

'Well, we'll have to risk it.'

We sneaked down the front path, Judith-Marianne loaded gently into the wheelbarrow. 'It would have helped if you'd got this bloody wheel oiled,' I hissed as it squeaked unrelentingly at every turn. Olly kept looking over his shoulder, making sure April was still transfixed by her television programme. We made it as far as the gate, bumped the wheelbarrow into the road behind the van and round to the passenger door where, with a great deal of difficulty, we loaded our burden carefully into the front seat. I buckled her in.

'Do you want me to come?' Olly asked, obviously praying that I'd say no.

'You stay here. Wash up the tea things and get on with your homework. You know nothing about this, understand? Absolutely nothing!'

'What if you get caught?'

'I won't,' I promised, with a lot more certainty than I felt. 'Now, did you get that phone number?'

He passed me a scrap of paper. 'I looked up their website on the laptop.'

'Good boy.' I took the paper from him. 'And don't worry about April.' I watched her, illuminated by the flickering glow. 'She won't be back in a hurry.' I promised to phone him as soon as I could and buckled myself in the driver's seat. 'Right then, Judith-Marianne,' I said to the silent figure by my side. 'Here we go.'

I drove very slowly and carefully. It was stupid, looking back on it: it didn't matter to poor Judith-Marianne how I drove, but I was trying, in some idiotic way, to drive with reverence. She had done Olly and me a good turn, saved our bacon, and I was determined to treat her with respect. I kept glancing her way, her head nodding gently as we drove along, her eyes closed peacefully, still hoping that she might suddenly stir into wakefulness, into life, even though I knew her poor old heart had given up and she'd never wake again. I slowed the van to a halt on the brow of the hill and pulled out my mobile phone. I dialled the number Olly had found for me and waited for someone to pick up, my eyes still fixed on Judith-Marianne.

'Oakdene,' a crisp voice answered, and I asked if I could speak to Barbara or Camille.

It was dark by the time I drove through the gates. The windows of the care home were lit up and I could see the evening meal taking place in the dining room, residents gathered around the tables. I drove quietly by, around to the tradesman's entrance. As I rounded the corner, I saw Camille hovering nervously by the path, her big forehead pale in the gloom, her hands clutching the handles of a wheelchair. I stopped beside her and wound the window down.

'Pull up by kitchen door,' she instructed softly. 'Is safe. Boss is serving dinner with residents.'

'Where's Barbara?'

'She help boss. But she knows.'

I parked the van as directed and Camille wheeled the chair to the passenger door. Carefully, gently, we loaded Judith-Marianne into it.

'Where you find her?' Camille asked. 'In road again?'

'Yes.' Well, at least that part of it wasn't a lie. 'I was bringing her back and she suddenly passed out. When I realised she was dead I thought I'd better phone and speak to you. I don't want you girls to get in trouble because of her running off again.'

'Thank you,' Camille said devoutly. 'If she found dead in road it would be very bad. We might lose job.'

We wheeled Judith-Marianne into the garden, to a little wooden bench under a cherry tree. 'This her favourite place,' Camille told me as we lifted her onto the seat. 'She often sit here.'

'You won't leave her out here long?' It was dark and getting cold. I didn't like the thought of leaving her there. I wanted to wrap a blanket around her shoulders.

'Soon as you're gone, I run in, tell boss I find her room empty. We will all search. Soon we find her here.'

'You're sure you'll be all right?'

'Yes. Best you go. Quickly.'

I took a last look at the little figure sitting on the seat. I reached out and touched her soft, silver hair. 'Did you know that she could sing?' I asked Camille. 'And play the piano?'

'No,' she answered sadly. 'I never knew that.'

'Thank you, Judith-Marianne,' I whispered and kissed her on her forehead. I hurried back to the van and drove slowly down the path and out through the iron gates.

CHAPTER TWENTY-SIX

No news is good news. At least that was the way I was looking at it. All night I was expecting some feverish call from Barbara or Camille telling me that something had gone wrong, that the doctor had been suspicious about Judith-Marianne's death, that he wanted a post-mortem. But when Barbara finally phoned, late the next morning, it was to tell me that everything had gone according to plan, and the doctor was happy that she had died of natural causes. No post-mortem, no inquest. All was well. I'd relay the good news to Olly later on.

I drove up onto Holne Moor. It was a beautiful day, calm, clear and still, a complete contrast with the wild night when I had last driven up there. I stopped where I had stopped then, searching around for whatever it was that might have hit my wheel, but there was no evidence of any collision with wildlife, no furry corpse, no carrion-pecked offal lying in a heap by the roadside. It remained a mystery.

A bigger mystery was what the hell had happened to Nathan Parr. I was still sore about him standing me up, hoping that it hadn't been part of some plot of Jamie's, that there was some genuine reason why he'd failed to show at the pub and that, sometime, he would get in touch.

I decided not to turn around but to carry on up the road for a few miles. I had an hour free, and the thought of going straight back to the shop was depressing. I would follow the road as it looped around Venford Reservoir and take a look at the water. On my way back, I might grab a quick sandwich in the little cafe in Holne.

A mile further on I slowed to a stop. To the left of the road a ribbon of blue and white police tape was stretched between the gorse bushes, marking off a section of ground that fell away steeply, the short grass scattered with boulders. A metal sign had been set up at the verge, an appeal for witnesses to a fatal road accident that had occurred at this spot on Tuesday evening. A car had come off the road and crashed. It seemed no other vehicles had been involved. Police were appealing for anyone who had been driving this road on Tuesday evening to get in touch.

I got out of the van and a man walking his dog hailed me with a wave. I bent to pat the black and white sheepdog snuffling around my boots. 'Do you know what happened here?'

He pointed to a distant house, just visible through a screen of bare trees. 'I live up there.'

It must feel isolated. No wonder he liked to chat to strangers. 'Someone must have reported it early. I was out walking the dog yesterday morning and the police were already here. They were just taking the car away.'

'And the driver was killed?'

He nodded. 'You can see the tyre tracks. He must have been driving at one hell of a speed to come off the road there. Mind, it was a filthy night. Police think he must have been drunk. He hit those smaller rocks,' he said, pointing, 'the car must have flipped over and slammed into that great lump of granite. He wouldn't have had a chance. The front of that car was mangled—'

A sickening sense of dread was settling inside me. 'Could they identify him?' I asked.

'Not from the body. That had already been taken away when I got here. They were just loading the car onto a lorry. It was a nice little Jag, too. Complete write-off, of course.'

'Of course,' I repeated dumbly.

'Personalised number plate,' he went on. 'It's funny the things that stick in your mind. I suppose it's because I'm a golfer—'

I frowned at him. 'What?'

'The number plate – N12 PAR,' he responded brightly. I must have just stared at him because he felt it necessary to explain. 'Golf, you see? Par?'

'Yes, I understand,' I said. 'I get it.'

I got it. I understood why Nathan hadn't turned up for our meeting at the pub, and that he wouldn't be getting in touch. I understood Jamie's barely concealed laughter when I had told him Nathan had stood me up. He was laughing because he knew that Nathan was already dead; and because he had murdered him.

My first thought was to contact Inspector Ford, tell him everything, beginning with Moss and Pike trying to ram my van with their lorry. For that was what had happened to Nathan, I was sure. They must have lain in wait for him, in that monstrous truck, run him off the road, caused him to crash. And when I'd seen them on Tuesday evening, when I was crouching in the ditch behind the gorse bushes, they were returning from the scene of his murder. But how could I tell the inspector about what had happened without involving Olly? He was the only one who could verify what I said. They might want to speak to him, to his parent or guardian.

Instead, I phoned the police number advertised on the sign at the site of the accident. I explained that I had been driving on the road that night, that I had seen a vehicle coming from that direction, a Moss and Pike lorry being driven very fast and, in my opinion, recklessly. I had been forced to swerve to get out of its way and nearly ended in a ditch. No, I didn't get its registration number. Was it definitely a Moss and Pike lorry? Yes, it was. The officer thanked me very much. They would certainly investigate.

I was late getting back to the shop, and by the time I arrived, Pat was getting fretful.

I apologised and she shot me a sideways glance over her clicking knitting needles. 'Everything all right?' she asked.

'Fine.' I felt spaced out, numbed by Nathan's death. I didn't want company. 'You go on home, Pat.'

'You look awful.' She rolled up her knitting and stabbed her needles into her ball of wool. 'You sure you can cope?'

'I think I just need an early night.'

She didn't look convinced but had to get back to the

animals and so left. I was glad she'd gone. I didn't feel like talking, didn't want to answer questions. I spent all afternoon messing about with my stock. By the time I turned the sign on the shop door to 'Closed' and locked up behind me, the weather had turned dank and dismal. It just about matched my mood. A low mist skulked over the rooftops and the slick cobbles shone with wetness, with drops of moisture too fine to see except where they danced in the haloes of lighted street lamps. I turned up my collar. I needed some cash. I'd have to walk to Ashburton's only cash machine.

Most of the shops were locked and in darkness, their sensible owners having already called it a day. Just one or two antiques dealers, ever hopeful, were bringing in the stock they displayed outside their shops on the pavement. We exchanged goodnights as I went by.

I crossed the road into St Lawrence Lane. The whole town seemed deserted. Perhaps everyone else knew something I didn't. By habit I cast a glance over my shoulder as I fed my card into the cash machine. I caught a flicker of movement at the corner of my vision, a pale shape that was there one moment and not the next. When I swung around for a proper look, the street was empty. But all the time I typed in my pin and waited for my cash I felt a tickle of unease at the back of my neck, a sense of being watched. I stuffed the card and notes straight into my pocket, not bothering to fiddle with the zip of my purse and bag and carried on down St Lawrence Lane.

Someone fell into step behind me. I walked on, past the tower of St Lawrence's Chapel, and then dropped down on one knee, pretending to tie a lace on my trainers. A burly

266

figure yards behind suddenly stopped and peered into the window of a shop. The shop was in blackness, he wouldn't have been able to see much. But I could see him, lamplight shining down on his overhanging belly, his fat face, his green woolly hat. My heart throbbed in panic.

I pretended not to have seen him, stood up and carried on. I quickened my pace and so did he, his heavy footsteps pounding the pavement. As I reached The Silent Whistle I peered in through the lighted windows. This early in the evening no one was inside, no chance of losing him in a packed bar. Instead I crossed the road and walked on past a terrace of houses. At the end of the terrace I had a choice. If I could lose GBH now, just for a few seconds, when he reached the corner, he wouldn't know which direction I had taken. I ran.

I heard a muffled curse behind me. Footsteps broke into a shambling jog. Green Bastard Hat was heavy, but he wasn't fit. He was no runner. I knew I could outrun him. I could veer right, but then I'd have no choice but to fling myself into the traffic of the dual carriageway that bypassed the edge of town. My best chance of losing him lay straight in front of me. I sprinted across the road and headed for Love Lane.

But sometimes, what seems to be the best choice turns out to be the worst. Love Lane is long and straight with just one dog-leg turn towards the end, and so narrow it's possible to touch the stone walls rising on either side without stretching. Like a running track, Love Lane was a place where I could build up speed, leave GBH puffing along behind. Except that a single wet leaf on the ground betrayed me. I skidded, my feet slid from under me and I landed flat on my back, winded, my breath shocked out.

The fat bastard could move faster than I thought. I was still scrabbling to my feet when he grabbed me, his fingers closing over my arm. I turned and punched him hard in his flabby gut. He doubled over, belching like a deflating balloon. But he didn't release his grip. He cursed, grabbed a fistful of my hair and slammed my face into the stone wall.

I felt the force ricochet down my spine. Rough stone scraped against my jaw and cheek.

I tasted blood. He pinned me against the wall, his grip on my hair tightening. He was out of breath, his chest heaving as he pressed his foul body against mine. 'You got to learn to mind your own business,' he rasped into my ear. I slammed backward and downward with my foot, scraping his shin. He swore. He was pulling my hair out by the roots. 'You've been poking your nose where it don't belong. We've had the police round the depot this afternoon, wanting to look at all our trucks. Someone had reported seeing us on the moor the other night. I know that was you, bitch. I got to teach you a lesson.'

I let my body sag, heavy and limp, as if I'd fainted. As he shifted his feet to keep hold of my dead weight, I twisted around, my hand held rigid, fingers poking out straight, and jabbed him in the belly. He yelped and staggered back. I was free, but not for long. He grabbed me clumsily and dragged me onto the floor, rolling his entire grizzly-bear bulk on top of me, crushing my ribcage. His face hung over mine, his bristling double chin like a blancmange rolled in ash, his breath stinking of beer and fags. 'Seeing as you're rather tasty . . .'

One hand slithered between our bodies, groping for his belt. I squirmed, spat in his face and he sat back, knees like boulders pinning my arms to the ground. He raised one mighty fist to swipe me across the face.

The blow never landed. Something parted the air between us. Something that made no noise beyond a soft thunk as it embedded itself in the wall and sent a chip of mortar flying. Instinctively, we knew what it was.

GBH growled. 'What the fuck . . . ?'

'Let her go,' a calm voice commanded.

We stared at the figure illuminated by the solitary street lamp: an elderly woman with a handbag under one arm, a cat tucked under the other and a pistol clutched firmly in her right hand. It was slightly surreal.

'What the fuck . . . ?' he repeated.

'Please don't oblige me to fire this gun again, my cat doesn't like it.' The mystery lady waved the pistol slightly, indicating to GBH that he should back off. The cat wriggled, making an unholy yowling noise as if he was revving up for a fight and she clamped him to her side more firmly.

'Where the bloody hell did you come from, Grandma?' GBH demanded. 'You're not going to shoot me—'

'I won a medal for pistol shooting in my youth,' she informed him coolly. 'It was only a bronze, but you don't want to take any chances, do you?'

He made a move, a slight raising of his hand, and a bullet drilled through his outstretched palm. 'Fuck!' he screamed, clutching his hand and rolling away in agony.

'Your vocabulary is quite limited, isn't it?' My mystery lady kept her sights fixed on him as he staggered to his

269

feet, sobbing and swearing. 'I'd get going if I were you,' she advised. 'I'm a little out of practice, we can't be sure where I might shoot you next.'

'I'll fucking kill you!' he spat, reeling against the wall. 'Both of you!'

'Oh, do get along!' She sounded bored.

GBH shambled off, vowing vengeance. We could still hear him gibbering with pain long after he had disappeared from sight.

'Are you all right, my dear?' my saviour enquired as I staggered to my feet.

'I think so.' The skin on my cheek had been scorched by a blowtorch and my spine ironed flat by tank tracks but otherwise I was fine.

She put the cat down, his lead looped around her wrist and let him wander, sniffing, as she knelt to dig the bullet from the wall with a penknife she produced from her handbag. 'You didn't see where that other shell case landed? I do think it's important to tidy up after oneself, don't you?'

I began to peer vaguely at the ground around me, my feeble brain still trying to process what had just occurred.

'Ah! There it is!' She stooped and picked it up, dropping both cases into her bag and closing it with a soft click.

'Thank you!' I breathed belatedly. 'But how did you . . . um, come to . . . ?'

'I was taking Toby for his evening walk, when I saw you run hell for leather across the street and dive down here, chased by our primitive friend. I thought I'd better investigate.'

'Well, I'm very glad you did. Thanks again.'

'You're welcome . . . er . . . ?' She raised her brows enquiringly.

'Juno.'

'Juno.' She held out a slim hand for me to shake. 'Elizabeth,' she said, and smiled.

CHAPTER TWENTY-SEVEN

'I was married to George for thirty-six years,' Elizabeth began. We were sitting at the kitchen table in *Old Nick's*, each with a mug of coffee, the cat Toby curled up on the seat of the chair next to hers. I was holding a swab of cotton wool, soggy with TCP, gingerly dabbing at my cheek from time to time. 'It's funny,' she sighed, 'how you can live with someone all that time and never really know him. He was in finance, I was a teacher. We lived very comfortably. I knew he gambled of course, but he'd always persuaded me that his losses were small. "My little vice", he used to call it. It was only when we retired that I realised how bad things were, that all of our savings were gone. I had some money, some investments of my own. He begged me to help him, promised me on his life that it would be the last time.' She gave a brief, bitter smile. 'It wasn't, of course.'

She took a sip of coffee. The kitchen was warm and quiet, the only noise a slight hum from the electric heater

I had brought up from the shop and she looked around her pensively. 'You have no idea how lovely this is, sitting in a room instead of in a car with the roof a few inches above my head.'

'We could have gone to my flat. But this was closer.'

'This is fine.' She fondled Toby's ears reflectively and he mewed in his sleep. I wanted her to carry on with her story, and after a few moments, she spoke again, her voice steady and calm.

'In the end, everything went – our weekend cottage, our cars, my jewellery. But it wasn't until George died that I discovered he had remortgaged the house, that the property we had lived in for over thirty years was no longer my home, that I would have to get out. And he still owed money to some very unpleasant people. It didn't matter that he was dead, that the stress of it all had killed him. As far as his creditors were concerned, I was liable. And the money I had in my own name was far from sacrosanct. Their methods were . . .' she paused, a frown puckering her delicate brows, 'intimidating.'

'Didn't you go to the police?'

'I thought about it. But the problem was that, technically, the law was on their side. I soon realised I'd be lucky to be left with the clothes I stood up in. I'd be reduced to living in temporary accommodation on some endless council housing list. At worst, I would be on the streets. Well, I thought, if I'm going to be homeless, let it be on my own terms. I cleared out what was left in my account, and sold everything, all I owned, anything I could turn into cash. It was when I was going through the loft that I found my father's pistol – the old Luger

273

Parabellum.' She smiled. 'I thought it might come in useful one day.'

'It certainly did.'

'I bought the old car and disappeared.' She gave an elegant shrug. 'I simply vanished, left the house empty, dropped the keys into the bank, and left London with no forwarding address. Left all my old life behind. So far, no one has followed me.'

'You had no family? No friends?'

She was quiet for a moment, gone inward. 'No one to speak of,' she said at last.

'And you've been living in the car all this time?'

She smiled. 'Occasionally I treat us to a night in a guest house, but I have to watch the pennies. Of course,' she gave a wry smile, 'I did things all wrong. What I should have done was to have invested in a camper van. But they are rather expensive.'

'What made you come here?'

'George wouldn't countenance the idea of living in Devon, strictly a Home Counties man. But I've always been attracted by the area, so I've been driving around, trying to find the right place for us to settle. I keep being drawn back here for some reason. Ashburton has the right atmosphere.' She smiled again, mocking herself, 'the right *vibe*.'

'You're welcome to sleep on my sofa,' I told her, although I wasn't sure what Toby would make of Bill, and vice versa.

'No, no. The floor here will be fine. I have plenty of bedding in the car.'

'If you're sure? You've got a choice of two rooms. The floors are clean, just recently laid.'

'It will be absolute luxury. I shall be able to spread myself out. What I would love,' she added tentatively, 'is a bath.'

'Help yourself. And don't feel you have to get up early in the morning. I'll leave a note for Sophie and Pat downstairs so that they'll know I have a friend staying. You won't be disturbed.'

'Thank you.' There was a moment's pause. 'Now it's your turn.'

'My turn?'

'To tell your story. All that carrying on in the lane back there, I still don't know what it was about. Please don't tell me that was an angry boyfriend!'

'I'll tell you everything—' I stopped suddenly as a new thought occurred. I glanced at my watch. So much had happened since I left the shop at closing time I couldn't believe it was barely eight o'clock. I looked at Elizabeth. 'How would you feel about a change of plan?' I asked.

'Very well,' she agreed, somewhat doubtfully. 'What?'

'We're going out. There's someone I want you to meet.'

Olly listened with eyes wide, his mouth slightly open, as Elizabeth recounted to him the same story that she had told me.

'So you see, Olly,' I said when she had finished, 'Elizabeth needs a place to stay. And you need a grown-up living here with you – then,' I added quickly as he opened his mouth to object, 'you won't need to worry about your neighbour, your teachers, or anyone else finding out that your nan isn't living here. You can stop worrying about being taken into care.'

275

Olly scowled, jerked his head in Elizabeth's direction. 'What's she know about my nan? You promised you wouldn't tell.'

'I haven't. That story is yours to tell, or not. It's up to you.'

'I know only that your nan isn't here,' Elizabeth said calmly. 'We have to be able to trust each other. If the wrong people found out where I was living, that could be very bad for me. I'm trusting you to keep my secret, and I promise you can trust me to keep yours, whatever it is.'

Olly frowned, unconvinced. 'So, what would happen, then?' he asked, looking from her to me.

'What I suggest, if you're agreeable,' Elizabeth said slowly, 'is that Juno, Toby and I go away now, and then I return in about an hour in my own car. I'll park where we can be sure your neighbour will see me arrive. You can come out and make a great fuss of greeting me, as if you haven't seen me for a long time. In the morning, I will introduce myself to your neighbour, telling her that I'm your aunt, that I've been living abroad, but that now your nan is so ill, I've come back to look after you both . . .'

Olly thought about this for a few seconds. 'What room will you sleep in?'

'Whichever room you'd like me to sleep in. Then, after a little while, preferably on a day when your neighbour has been out, we'll tell her that we've moved your nan into Oakdene.'

Olly considered this plan with a furrowed brow, fidgeting unhappily. 'You're a teacher, ain't you?'

'I was a teacher,' she corrected him.

'What you teach?'

'I taught a variety of subjects, but music primarily.'

His face brightened. 'You play piano?'

'Yes. I hear you're learning the bassoon. Perhaps I could help you, if you want me to.'

At that moment, Toby, who'd been lying in idiotic bliss next to the Rayburn, stretched, flexed his paws and rolled over, displaying his cream-coloured tummy. Olly giggled.

'It looks like Toby's settled in already,' I said.

'You know, Olly, this need be only a temporary arrangement,' Elizabeth assured him. 'You can throw me out, any time you like.'

He slid a glance at me for confirmation. I nodded. 'All right,' he agreed grudgingly. 'We'll give it a go.'

Elizabeth solemnly shook hands with him on the agreement, and then she and I buzzed off, cat under her arm, so that she could return and put her plan into action.

CHAPTER TWENTY-EIGHT

On Friday morning, I went to Ashburton library. I asked the librarian if she had any maps of old tin mines in the area and she came up with an absolute beauty. It showed me the positions of all the known shafts on the Moorworthy estate, including the shaft at Applecote Farm. What it didn't show, unfortunately, were any underground tunnels that might link them. But I got her to photocopy it for me and took away a copy.

I met Elizabeth, as planned, for coffee. She wore a silk scarf at her neck, her face beautifully made-up, hair in an elegant French pleat. She laid leather gloves and handbag on the table as she sat down. Despite being dressed in jeans and sweater, she looked immaculate. I looked like a woman who'd been smashed into a wall. I had a fine black eye, purple with yellow and green around the edges, and my jaw and cheek were freckled with scabs where I'd made contact with granite. I'd had to make up a silly story to explain my appearance to Pat and Sophie. The librarian had looked at me askance and when I told Maisie I had fallen and landed on my face, she just said, 'Bollocks! You've been in a fight!' I was going to have to come up with a more convincing story: I was seeing Ricky and Morris later on.

'How does it feel?'

'Sore.' I asked her how the first night went.

'Oh, fine. Breakfast was a little tense, but Olly was happy to accept a lift up to the animal sanctuary. He hinted I could start running him to school when the half-term holiday is over.'

'Make him walk,' I recommended. 'Where did you sleep?'

'In a room I believe belonged to his grandparents. There's a double bed in there.' She laughed softly. 'The decoration is a bit grim.'

'I'm sorry.'

'I'll survive. And Toby is in seventh heaven. He hasn't stirred from the kitchen range all night.' She sipped her coffee. 'I'm getting the piano tuned, by the way. Oh, I know I'm buying affection,' she added, holding up a slim hand in defence, 'but music is common ground between Olly and me and I want to take advantage of it.'

'Sounds sensible.'

'And I introduced myself to our neighbour as promised. Mrs Hardiman.'

'And?'

'Perfectly charming.'

'You or her?'

Elizabeth gave a low laugh. 'She did take a little winning over, but I got there in the end. She's invited me in for coffee next week.'

'Are you going to be all right living there?' She seemed so elegant, so effortlessly chic. 'Dolly's old house doesn't seem like an appropriate setting for you, somehow.'

She reached across the table and laid a hand on mine. 'My dear, I shall be happy to live there as long as Olly is prepared to put up with me. I have three things I thought I would never have in my life again – a garden, beautiful country surroundings, and a piano. And,' she added wryly, 'the challenge of learning to cook on a range, although Olly has promised to help me with that one.'

'There's just one thing that worries me.' I leant closer to her and lowered my voice, 'The pistol.'

'I'll keep it well hidden. Olly will never know it exists.'

'Actually, that's not what I meant. Jamie Westershall knows about Olly. He made threats. I don't think he knows where Olly lives but it might be wise to keep that pistol handy.'

Elizabeth nodded. 'I will.'

'And I don't want him flying his drone anywhere near Moorworthy House.'

'That boy will come to no harm,' she promised solemnly, 'not while I'm around.'

She sat back and studied me silently. 'But you, you must be careful, my dear. This Westershall man sounds dangerous, don't provoke him. If you don't feel ready to go to the police, please leave well alone.'

It was good advice. I only wished I could have followed it.

I had never seen Ricky angry before. I've seen him throw a prima donna hissy fit hundreds of times, but I'd not seen the cold, quiet anger with which he studied me now, two long fingers pressed against his temple, the cigarette poised between them sending a thin spiral of smoke above his head. He was wearing his specs and the lenses magnified his blue eyes, intensified his gaze. 'So, let's just have a brief resumé, shall we, Princess? The lorry driver in the green hat tried to run your van off the road and you didn't go to the police?'

I nodded.

He continued to glare like an angry hawk. 'Same bloke, same hat, attacks you in Love Lane and you still don't go to the police?'

'I can't prove anything.'

'It's the police's job to prove things, not yours.'

'You had a witness in the van – young Oliver.' At the edge of my vision, seated on my left at the table, Morris was also giving me a disapproving stare.

'I don't want to involve him.'

'You had a witness to the attack,' Ricky insisted, 'the old bird with the cat.'

'I don't want to involve her.'

'You didn't bleedin' want to involve us, did you?' he asked, disgusted.

Morris was silent but shot me a reproachful look over his specs.

I had gone to their place to help them sort out the first of a rash of requests for pantomime costumes, the panto season fast approaching. But so far, we hadn't done any work. My arrival had caused a stir. One look at my damaged face and they had accused me of not trusting them, infuriated by my feeble story of falling over, by my blatant lie. 'D'you think we're idiots?' Ricky had demanded. 'Who did this to you?'

281

In the end, I had told them everything. Well, not quite everything. I left out Olly's illegal burial of his great-grandmother; in fact, I didn't mention that she was dead. But I told them everything else. I had crumpled under the accumulated weight of their hurt feelings. They had been too kind, too generous, too absurdly protective of me over the years for me to keep them out now. And they might gossip about everyone and everything, but when it really mattered, I knew I could trust in their silence.

'Who is this old girl with a cat, anyway?'

Morris shook his head. 'You don't really know anything about her, do you?'

'Only what she's told me,' I admitted.

'She could be a psychopath, for all you know,' Ricky said.

Did I detect a touch of jealousy? Personally, I thought Elizabeth was one of the sanest people I'd ever met, but perhaps it was a good thing I hadn't mentioned her gun. I'd just said that Green Bastard Hat had run off when he'd heard her coming.

'Don't forget this yob in the green hat is still out there,' Ricky reminded me. 'He's still a danger to you. He needs locking up.'

'I think he'll be lying low for a while. In any case, he's working for the Westershalls. It's Jamie who's behind all this.' In my opinion, he was the one who needed locking up, him and his lunatic sister, the dangerous crackhead.

'But what's going on?' Morris asked. 'What's it all about, Juno?'

I wish I knew. 'All I know is that there's something going on at the Moorworthy estate that the Westershalls – and that includes Sandy – don't want anyone finding out about.

282

And maybe it's what got Ben Luscombe and Gavin killed.'

'What about this Moss character?' Ricky asked. 'You said he knew what was going on.'

'He does but he's not going to talk about it, certainly not to the police.'

'This lorry firm,' Morris continued frowning, 'Moss and Pike. Is the firm involved in what's going on, or just the driver?'

'You mean, is he using the firm's vehicle without their knowledge?' Ricky asked.

'I've only seen him hauling bales of silage about,' I admitted. 'There's nothing illegal in that. I've got to find out—'

'Stop right there!' Ricky pointed his fag at me like a smoking gun. 'You are not finding out anything. You're not to go near that place again, understand? It's too dangerous.'

'I don't think I'll be getting an invitation any time soon.'

'Well, we have,' Morris said suddenly. 'Got an invitation,' he added as Ricky and I stared at him. 'Sunday afternoon.'

'My God, our concert!' Ricky suddenly swivelled around in his chair to look at the calendar on the wall. 'Is that this Sunday coming?'

'It is, the day after tomorrow,' Morris responded primly. 'It's a good job one of us pays attention. Why do you think I made us rehearse everything last night?'

'All right, Maurice,' Ricky rolled his eyes, 'don't get a cob on!'

'Listen, Juno, maybe we could find out something,' Morris suggested, glancing sideways at Ricky, 'ask some questions.'

'What kind of questions?' I asked, alarm bells ringing.

Ricky was suddenly enthusiastic. 'There will be drinks and a bunfight after the show. It's going to be a big fundraiser. We'll have a chance to mingle, chat with the guests. If we keep our eyes and ears open, you never know what we might pick up.'

Morris tittered. 'I've always fancied myself as a Poirot.'

Ricky gave a shout of laughter. 'And I could be Miss Marple.'

My heart sank. 'Listen, boys, I really don't think that's a good idea.' I had a vision of disaster looming, of the two of them making pointed and unsubtle remarks that could only lead to trouble. I knew I shouldn't have told them anything.

CHAPTER TWENTY-NINE

On Saturday morning I rose early. I packed the map the librarian had copied, binoculars and all my usual hiking gear, plus a bottle of water, some nutrition bars, a waterproof poncho and spare socks. I was planning to be out most of the day, but home before it got dark. Elizabeth and Olly had invited me to tea. I'd phoned the night before to ask how the rest of Friday had worked out. Elizabeth had laughed. 'I went shopping and shocked Olly because I bought a bottle of gin. He now thinks he's living with an alcoholic. Apparently—'

'Dolly didn't hold with gin.'

'Or spirituous liquors of any kind,' she added.

'Well, you can put me down for one, as soon as I arrive. See you later.'

I drove up to Holne Chase, bumping the van over the gravel and onto the grass, parking so that, from the road, it was almost hidden by gorse. The day was dismal, still, a thin mist malingering above the ground. Trees, bent and twisted by prevailing winds, loomed out of it like skeletons, their boughs bare of leaves. The grass was green underfoot and damp, the rest of the world grey, the air chill on my cheek. Magpies chattered somewhere close, but I couldn't see them. I stuck to pony tracks weaving through the gorse until the rising tumble of rocks where I had sat a couple of weeks ago became dimly visible on my right. There was no need for me to climb it again, but to keep heading on, in as straight a line as I could. If I could have seen more than a few yards ahead of me, this would have been simple, but it's easy to become disorientated in the mist so I kept checking my bearings.

Just a mile or two distant, high on the moor where no trees grew, was a place where the ground never dried out, where peat-black soil held the water like a sponge and what looked smooth and green as a croquet lawn was semi-liquid bog. Unless the sun shone and showed you a glimmer of water lurking amongst the mosses on the surface, you could be boots full of liquid black mud and up to your knees after one mistaken step. Not the place to be walking on your own, to get lost, not in the fog.

Brown ponies, three who had escaped the autumn drift, cantered out of the mist, alarmed by my presence. Snorting, tails flying, they passed so close I could see droplets of mist like pearls on the hairs around their flaring nostrils. Forced to jump back I almost fell over and stood still, heart thumping, until the pounding of their hooves faded into silence.

I came at last to a standing stone, a lump of granite tall as I was, phantom grey, blotched and speckled with lichen.

I'd seen it marked on the map. It meant I was still heading in the right direction. I sensed that the mist was lifting, that I could see further ahead of me now; the day was warming up. As I walked, the sky gradually lightened from grey to gold, low sun filtering through thinning mist.

When I came to the hedge bank I stopped, sat on a rock, drank water, munched a nutty bar and studied the obstacle before me. The foot of the bank was faced with stones, lumps of granite laid centuries ago, half-hidden by cushions of moss and bound together by roots of hawthorn and elder, which scrambled over the top of it and formed a sturdy hedge. Trees grew out of it: holly, blackthorn and mountain ash. The whole structure was roughly ten foot high. I walked beside it for perhaps half a mile before I came to a likely place for climbing up and scrambling through.

A jutting stone gave a step for my boot and ivy stems thick as rope offered handholds to haul myself up the bank. So far so good, but the gap in the hedge was narrow and defended on all sides by vicious spikes of blackthorn. I didn't fancy dragging myself through it, and dropped back down to the ground to look for a bigger breach in the defences.

I found it further on, a handy gap amongst straggling twigs of hazel. I could climb the bank easily enough, grabbing at roots and branches to haul myself up, but it was clear that my rucksack was going to be an encumbrance when it came to squeezing through the tangle. I'd better leave it behind.

At the foot of the bank I inspected the contents. I reckoned I didn't need the Ordnance Survey map any more;

the smaller map from the library was more relevant now I'd reached the farm. It was a dry day and I wouldn't need the waterproofs. I was wearing plenty of layers and my jacket was protection enough. I put my field glasses around my neck, zipping them up inside my jacket. I pocketed my phone, keys, penknife and the folded library map. I placed the rucksack carefully at the foot of the bank where I could retrieve it later, then pulled myself up.

Wriggling through the hedge was an undignified procedure and I was glad there was no one there to see me squeezing my various body parts between twisted branches. As I emerged on the other side, struggling to keep my balance and simultaneously bend aside twigs that threatened to spring back and take my eye out, I noticed thin strips of something grey and white hanging from the twigs like tinsel. I reached out and pulled some off – thin strips of crinkled paper, like the contents of an office shredding machine. As I glanced along the hedge, I could see branches festooned with the stuff.

I dropped down and found more at the foot of the bank, white strips tossed amongst the tide of autumn leaves. I scanned the green expanse of an empty field. There was no sign of any fly-tipping, no telltale trail of refuse littering the grass, but I could only think that this paper had been blown here from some dump site nearby.

I set off, keeping to the concealment of the hedge, walking three sides of a rectangle rather than straight across the field to the gate. I had a few acres to cross before I reached Applecote farmhouse and I didn't want to be spotted and chased off the land by an irate someone with a shotgun before I even got close.

Half an hour later I lay on my front behind a scattering of rocks and looked through my binoculars. I had a clear view of the stone farmhouse, the yard and the sheds beyond, a clear view of the farmhouse door, of the wisp of smoke rising from the chimney. I could smell it, woodsmoke. Someone was burning logs.

The door suddenly opened and Green Bastard Hat filled the doorway, a fag between his lips, a mug in the hand that wasn't bandaged. He stood for a moment, squinting into the sun, before he took a last drag on his cigarette and lobbed the butt on the ground. Two dogs – rangy, lurcher types, one brown, one white – surged out on either side of him, tails wagging.

Damn. I should have thought about dogs. The air was still, no wind to carry my scent to them, but I knew they were aware of me. They stopped, staring in my direction, bristling with alertness. One began to bark. GBH growled at it to stop its row. I didn't dare move, even to duck down out of sight. I stayed so still that a blackbird, foraging amongst the leaf litter, turning leaves over with its beak, hopped close to my arm. The dog barked once, sending the blackbird into the air, chattering in alarm. Its tail wagged uncertainly, and then it was ordered inside and the door shut behind it. I breathed again.

I sprinted across the grass to the corner of the cobbled yard. There was a long cowshed down one side, and I slipped through the open doorway. Inside, the building seemed vast. My footsteps echoed on the concrete floor so that I halted in my stride and tried to tread quietly.

The shed was piled high with rows of silage bales, one black, plastic-coated roll on top of another, as sleek and fat as monstrous sausages. I trailed my hand along the surface of the nearest one. Silage bales are packed tight with chopped grass, the air extruded. They feel solid and smooth, firm to the touch. This one felt as if the material inside was loose. As I prodded with my fingers, I could detect something lumpy, crunchy inside and took out my penknife. The plastic was thick, heavy-duty, intended not to tear. I had to press hard on the point to make a small slit in the surface. Dust drizzled out, dry and grey and I rubbed it between my fingers. This wasn't silage. I opened up the slit some more. Tiny chunks of stone drizzled to the floor. I picked one up. It was concrete or some kind of aggregate, the sort of material you might find on a building site. I moved on to the next bale and made another slit. More gritty dust trickled out, tiny particles glistening, as if within the mixture there were fragments of glass. Further along the row of bales I tried again, thrusting the knife in. When I drew out the blade it was white with a chalky powder. It had a chemical smell. It might have been fertiliser or insecticide; but whatever it was, it wasn't silage.

There was a crunch of wheels in the yard outside, a vehicle drawing up. I took a peek around the bales. Doors slammed. Through the open doorway I watched Jamie climb out of the jeep, followed by Moss, and cross to the farmhouse. Any sensible Capricorn would have beaten a hasty retreat at this point. I ran to the farmhouse, flattened myself against the wall by the window and listened.

'I want that shed cleared.' It was Jamie's voice, loud and angry. 'We've got more lorry loads arriving next week. I don't want us falling behind schedule.'

'I need more help,' Green Bastard Hat whined. 'It's not easy working with one hand. It's all the fault of that red-haired bitch—'

'Yes, and you really fucked that up,' Jamie declared bitterly, 'scared off by some old granny with a gun—'

'She shot me—'

'I'll shoot you if you mess up again. You were supposed to get rid of her!'

I felt sick. I could only think of one red-haired bitch they might want to get rid of and I'm afraid it was me.

'I'll sort her out—'

'Make sure you do. And get those bales dumped.'

Time I made myself scarce. I dared not cross the yard again or walk the open track. I backed off, slipping around the blind side of the building and ran, heading for a thicket of sheltering bushes. I scrambled through a mass of hawthorn, fighting my way through thorns and twigs.

Then suddenly I was rocking back on my heels. I teetered on the edge of a deep, ragged tear in the rock, my boots sending small stones skittering down, bouncing into oblivion. A rocky gorge dropped away beneath my toes: Applecote Pit. I was on the very edge. My senses reeled as if I was balancing on a heaving swell at sea. I stepped back, still clutching at stems I prayed wouldn't break, as the shifting sea settled, the wave of nausea ebbed. I stopped looking down, raised my head to focus on a steady horizon, and across the mouth of the pit to the other edge.

A lorry was parked there, idle, its flatbed raised at an angle, as if its driver's last act before he had abandoned it there had been to tip its load, slide it over the edge into the depths below.

I braved another look down. The pit was deep but I couldn't see the bottom because of what was filling it up from below. Silage bags, burst open like ruptured intestines, spilled their guts into a mass of rubble, broken brick and shattered timber. Pointed metal thrust through in spikes. Oil drums were tossed about like drink cans. And the whole mass was sinking into a slick black fluid that oozed around the edges, only visible here and there, like moorland bog lurking beneath moss and grass. A dry, throat-catching dust hung in the air, but worse than that was the smell, not just of concrete dust, of effluent run-offs and chemicals, but of something putrefying, rotting, something that had once been alive.

I backed away, threading my way out through the tangle of bushes and hit the ground beneath the weight of a charging bull, a ham-like hand smothering my scream.

'Quiet! Quiet!' a voice hissed urgently as I struggled. 'If you scream, they'll hear us and we're both dead. Understand?' I nodded slowly as I recognised the broad and homely features hanging over mine. 'D'you understand, Juno?' He relaxed his grip. 'OK?' he whispered, and took his hand away from my mouth.

'What are you doing here?' I breathed.

'I'm the policeman,' Detective Constable Dean Collins responded, grinning, 'that's my line.'

CHAPTER THIRTY

Spirituous liquor was just what I needed. I handed DC Collins back his hip flask.

'Better?'

I nodded my thanks, wiping my hand across my mouth, feeling a glow of warmth in my throat sliding down into my stomach. We'd retired to a hiding place, an old blowing house abandoned after the collapse of the tin mine, its turf roof long ago disintegrated, its stone walls ruined, the blackened granite furnace the only remains of a place where tin had once been smelted. It was a good place from which to watch the comings and goings at the farmhouse. Dean had been tracking the arrival and departure of the trucks through binoculars but the only visitors to the farm that day had been Jamie Westershall and Moss in the jeep. Together, we watched them depart.

'I thought you were on paternity leave.'

Dean frowned at me, puzzled how I knew. 'I am, in a manner of speaking.'

'So, what are you doing here?'

'You first.' He folded his brawny arms and stared at me. 'You'd better start at the beginning.'

So I did. When I got to the part about Moss and Pike's lorry trying to run my van off the road, he began shaking his head in disbelief. 'You should have called us, Juno.'

It was too late for that. I told him about Sandy's party and Nathan not turning up at the pub, and the conversation I had heard between Jamie and Moss as I hid by the roadside, how Jamie had threatened me next day and GBH had attacked me in the alley. I did not mention anything about boys burying their grandmothers or elderly ladies with guns.

'When I realised that Nathan was dead,' I said finally, 'I wanted to see for myself what's going on here.' I repeated the conversation I'd just heard, lurking outside the farmhouse.

Dean was silent, as if arranging his own thoughts. 'We're both here after the same thing,' he said at last. 'I'd been working with Nathan for some time, on and off. The Environment Agency got in touch with us last year.' He grinned ruefully. 'Waste crime wasn't considered a high priority here at the time, so Nathan got assigned to me. He was convinced something was going on here. When I heard he'd been killed, I knew he must be on to something. Thought it was time I took a look.'

'Please don't tell me that Nathan was murdered just because they're burying rubbish.'

'The illegal dumping of waste,' Dean answered gravely, 'next to people-trafficking and drugs, offers the biggest profits for organised crime.'

'Seriously?'

'We're not talking about fly-tipping,' he said earnestly, 'dumping the odd mattress and a bit of garden rubbish. This is big business. It costs companies hundreds of thousands every year to dispose of their waste legally. And the nastier the waste, the more hazardous the stuff is, the more it costs to dispose of. But if you can pay someone to take it away for you and dispose of it illegally, without all the proper rules and safeguards, it costs a lot less.'

'So, you're saying that all that stuff in the pit, that construction waste, could have come from anywhere in the country?'

'Courtesy of Moss and Pike.'

'Jamie's steward is called Moss.'

'Family firm.' Dean grunted. 'They've been caught more than once for illegal dumping, upcountry. They're just a gang of thugs, the kind of outfit that cruise around in vans, touting for business, looking for someone who's tearing down an old bungalow or ripping out a kitchen. Slip 'em a few quid and they'll cart your rubbish away for you, asbestos included. It won't cost you much and it's a lot less bother than taking it to the tip.'

'But people must know where their rubbish is likely to end up,' I protested. 'Or don't they care if it's spread across some farmer's field?'

He held up a thick forefinger. 'Ah, well that's the good bit! Even if you do care . . . even if you're a law-abiding citizen and you ask the blokes offering to dispose of your rubbish if they can prove they're registered waste carriers – anyone can buy a licence, perfectly legally, on the Internet. You don't even have to prove who you are. I bought one in my little daughter's name,' he added bitterly, 'and she's not a month old.'

'But you said they'd been caught.'

'The fines are small. Prison sentences are rare.' He raised the hip flask in an ironic toast. 'It's worth the risk.'

'And any rubbish can be baled up in plastic,' I said, thinking about it. 'People round here wouldn't take any notice. They'd just think it was hay or silage.'

Dean was nodding. 'That's the beauty of the countryside. You can move stuff around in broad daylight, no problem. And if you happen to know a greedy landowner with old mineshafts on his property who's only too happy to let you pay him to dump the stuff . . .' He shrugged. 'That's where the firm got lucky, when old Moss introduced his cousins to the Westershalls.'

'There's nothing like keeping things in the family.'

'Nathan was at agricultural college with Jamie Westershall. He said he was a bastard, the sort who's always banging on about heritage and tradition but who'd shit in his own nest for money.'

'But if the police know about all this, why the hell haven't you arrested them?'

Dean shot me a fierce look. 'Because there's more to this than a bit of demolition waste or herbicide . . . Look, the problem is, waste crime is usually committed on a small scale, so it gets dealt with by local police forces. To realise the extent of what's going on, nationally, you have to start joining the dots—'

'You need a national agency,' I said, 'like the Environment Agency. Enter Nathan Parr,' I added.

'And exit, unfortunately.'

We were both silent for a moment, lost in gloomy thoughts.

'And Inspector Ford knows all this?' I asked.

'Listen, the boss has got his hands full. He's Head of Serious Crimes for this whole area and with the crisis up at the prison he was happy enough for me to monitor the situation here, but that was all. But Nathan didn't want to prosecute a few thugs for dumping rubbish down a hole. He wanted to catch the people higher up, the people who are producing this waste, the polluters who pay criminals to dump it illegally. He had Westershall in his sights for a long time, ever since the murder of Ben Luscombe—'

'So you know Ben was murdered, then?'

'Let's just say we were suspicious,' Dean admitted, 'but we couldn't prove anything at the time. Nathan knew he'd be putting himself at risk if he approached Westershall openly, but he was convinced that the Moorworthy estate is receiving a big kickback from a major pharmaceutical company—'

'Sandy Westershall was in pharmaceuticals.' I told Dean about the photograph I'd seen on his study wall, of Sandy receiving a business award from some firm whose name I couldn't remember.

'Well, whatever the Westershalls are dumping for them, it's nasty stuff, not the sort of thing they'll risk throwing in an open pit like that building waste. They'll be hiding it somewhere else.'

'I know where it is.' I pulled the folded map from my

pocket and opened it out. 'Moorworthy shaft.' I tapped my finger on the map. 'There. Ben Luscombe reported seeing lights coming from that shaft—'

Dean almost snatched the map from my hands. 'Where d'you get this?'

'Ashburton Library.'

'You're kidding!'

'No, I asked the librarian, she gave it to me.' He gazed at me, astonished. But then, he's a man, he probably doesn't ask for directions either.

'Moorworthy Pit is fenced off, because of the bats, supposedly.'

He frowned. 'Then how do we get into it?'

'We can get there through the adit.'

'Adit?' he repeated.

'This map doesn't show them, but there were tunnels dug so that the miners could get level access to the shafts. I saw some in old engravings up at the house. There's a tunnel connecting the shaft at Applecote with the one at Moorworthy, I'm sure there is.'

'And the entrance to this tunnel is somewhere down in this pit.' He jabbed at the map with his forefinger. 'Do you know where?'

'I didn't see it earlier, but I wasn't looking, I was concentrating on not being swallowed up by all that rubbish.'

'The entrance to this tunnel might be buried under it all,' he pointed out.

'There's only one way to find out.' I looked at my watch. 'It'll be dark in an hour or so.' I realised I probably wasn't going to be sitting down to tea with Olly and Elizabeth. 'We must try and find it now, while we still can.'

298

This time I knew about the pit and we threaded through the hawthorn with more caution. We stopped a few feet away from the edge, lay on our bellies and crawled. There was no one around, no work in progress. Despite Jamie's orders, GBH was not dumping bales today. There was still light draining from the sky, but down in the depths the pit was already deep in shadows. Dean shone his torch, sweeping the beam around its rocky walls. The mine had originally been open-cast; years ago men had dug their way down with shovels, creating ledges and stepping stones that allowed them to cut deeper and deeper into the granite. But there was no sign of a tunnel, no hole in the pit wall.

'Perhaps it's underneath us,' I whispered. 'Perhaps we need to be over there, on the other side, to see it.'

We crawled, keeping back from the rocky edge until we reached the place where the bushes had been cleared away to make open ground for lorries to roll up to the pit edge. It was a relief to stand up, to walk normally for a yard or two. Then we hunkered down again and swept the walls of the pit with the torch beam.

On the other side, the walls were not as clear. Nature had reclaimed crannies in the rock, wind-blown seeds taking root in tiny cracks, growing into straggly bushes. Ivy scrambled over ledges.

'There!' I pointed. 'Just to the right of that metal pole that's sticking up, d'you see?'

The circle of the light swung around the walls crazily as Dean tried to find what I was pointing at. 'Got it!' He lit up a dark rent in the granite, half-hidden by a tangle of dusty creeper straggling down from above.

'Look, we can clamber down to that ledge just above it—' I began.

I heard Dean sigh softly as he turned to look at me. 'Sorry, Juno, but you're not coming. It's too dangerous,' he went on hastily, 'and you're only a civilian. I'm responsible for your safety and I can't allow it. From here on in, I'm on my own.'

I must have gaped at him. 'Are you joking?'

'No. I want you to go back to the blow house, wait for me there—'

'I want to catch these evil bastards just as much as you do!'

'I know.' He laid a consoling hand on my shoulder. 'I know you do.'

I shook him off. The reasonableness of his tone was infuriating.

'Listen, if I'm not back at the blow house in two hours—' he began.

'Forget it, I'm coming with you! I owe it to Gavin,' I added as he tried to interrupt.

'Gavin's death was an accident,' he said quietly.

'I don't care. Maybe someone shoved that sword into him or maybe he did it himself, but the only reason he was in the woods that day was because of what had happened to his friend, to Ben. Accident or murder, his death is directly connected to what's going on here.'

'Juno—'

'You try and leave me behind,' I warned him, 'I'll go straight to Inspector Ford and tell him what you're up to.'

That shut him up. He frowned ominously.

'Because he doesn't know you're here, does he?' I persisted.

'Of course he does.'

I shook my head. 'If this were an official operation, there is no way you'd be here on your own. You'd be working in pairs and there'd be at least one other team on this.' His frown was like thunder, so I knew I was right. 'Detective Inspector Ford believes you're on paternity leave at this moment, isn't that so? And if I tell him what you're really up to, right now, together with what I know, this place will be crawling with coppers in five minutes. And that won't suit you, will it?' I added finally. 'Because you want to be the one to bring Nathan's killers down.'

He seemed lost for words. When he eventually came up with one to describe me it wasn't complimentary.

'Guilty as charged,' I smiled sweetly and waved an arm at the mouth of the tunnel opposite. 'Shall we?'

CHAPTER THIRTY-ONE

Dean couldn't climb with the torch in his hand and clambering down to the mouth of the tunnel was unnerving in the gathering dusk. One missed footing would mean a fall into the pit, floundering amongst filthy rubbish, amongst broken rock, ripped metal and shattered glass or sinking beneath that oily bilge never to surface again.

The ledge we reached was narrow, its rocky edges fallen away. We were forced to crawl on our hands and knees, inch our way forward, dislodging loose chippings and sending them bouncing down the walls into the pit below. Halfway along we stopped for a breather, sitting back on our heels. Dean switched on the torch and shone it along the path to the mouth of the tunnel. 'Just a few more yards, but be careful here.'

Something pale had caught my eye down in the shadows, something like a mask. I pointed. 'What's that?'

Dean shone the torch. I was startled into a gasp and he

swore softly. Staring up from dead eyes was a screaming skull, bone-white and open-mouthed in horror: the face of Ted Croaker, sunk to his neck in an oily swamp, one rigid hand, a black and glistening claw, reaching up in desperation as he had tried to scrabble his way out.

'Do you think he fell or was thrown in?' I asked when I felt able to speak.

'I don't know, but he's been there a few days by the look of him, poor sod. Of course, when they've filled this shaft up, they'll just cap it off with concrete,' he went on. 'A few tons of earth on top of it, turf it over, and no one will know there's anything down here.'

I was still staring into the hollow eyes of Ted Croaker. 'Or anyone,' I added.

It was a relief to drag ourselves in through the mouth of the tunnel, to collapse, to sit there, getting our breath back. We sat for a few moments, our breathing the only sounds in the quiet dark. My stomach rumbled. I thought longingly of the nutty bars I'd left behind in my rucksack. I heard Dean chuckle in the darkness, then a rustle of paper and the unmistakeably attractive snap of a chocolate bar being broken in half. 'Here.'

I'd left my torch behind in my rucksack, so I switched on the light on my phone, its blue glow showing me what he was holding out, and took it thankfully.

'Enjoy it,' he advised with a grim laugh, 'it could be our last meal.'

We munched in silence.

'What's your little daughter's name?' I asked, after a minute.

303

'Alice.' There was love in the darkness, even in that one word. A moment later his features were lit by the colourful glow from his mobile. He scrolled down until he found what he was looking for and then passed it to me.

One bald, pink baby looks much like another to me, but I took it dutifully. I had to admit, Alice was cute. When the photo was taken, she must have been fresh out of the pod, her face red and crumpled, her tiny fist curled tight as a rosebud next to her little mouth, but she already had more hair than her father.

'You should be at home with her, Detective Constable Collins,' I reproved him, 'not sitting here in this dark hole.'

He murmured something unintelligible.

'Does your wife know where you are?'

'Gemma?' He gave a crack of laughter. 'Christ! No.'

'What did you tell her?'

'That they were short-handed at the station and needed me to go in. She knows that uninterrupted paternity leave is a pretty fantastic idea to begin with. She won't fret if I don't turn up till the morning.'

'Did Nathan have a girlfriend . . . ?'

'He'd just been through a divorce . . . Look, while we're asking personal questions, do you have a significant other?' he demanded crossly. 'Because he could do with a bloody good talking-to about the things you get up to.'

'I don't, as it happens.' I could hear an edge in my voice I wished wasn't there. The last time I'd felt attracted to a man, things hadn't worked out well.

'I heard about what happened with the Nickolai murder,' he began.

'Let's just say I'm not actively seeking a significant other at the moment,' I responded before he could get any further.

'Understood.' Dean flicked on the torch and shone it around the walls of the tunnel. Above our heads a cat's cradle of slanting timbers shored up the roof. They were ancient, festooned with cobwebs and some of them looked decidedly dodgy to me. 'It's high enough to stand up in here, thank God. I didn't fancy crawling on our hands and knees.' He rose to his feet and thumped a fist against one of the lower timbers, dislodging a century of dust. 'We'll have to watch our heads, though.' His coughing echoed around the walls.

I got up and fell into step behind him. What little light was coming from the tunnel mouth soon faded. Ahead the blackness was dense, thick, all light blotted out. But in the torchlight the walls around us glistened, tin-bearing ore buried in the rock showing here and there as silver specks and patches.

'I feel as if we're going slightly uphill,' Dean said after a while.

'These tunnels slope up a bit towards the entrance to allow water to run out,' I explained.

'It's quite dry in here.'

'There could be another tunnel beneath this one; the lowest adit was always for drainage.'

'You seem to know a lot about it.'

I only knew what Alec had told me and what I'd read in the library. 'I'm an expert,' I told him. 'I might write a book, *Tin Mining for Dummies*.'

'Well, Miss Expert, do you know how long this tunnel goes on for?'

'It can't be very long, not if it leads us into the Moorworthy shaft.'

'And we're sure about that, are we?'

Why is it that if someone asks if you're sure about something, you're suddenly not sure about it, even if you were perfectly certain about it before they asked? Dean noticed my hesitation and grunted. We carried on in silence.

It got steadily warmer, stuffier, as we went deeper into the rock. I started to find the heat oppressive, thought about shedding my jacket; but then I'd only have to carry it. Around us, the blackness was stifling, closing in around the torch's narrow beam. I'd decided to put my phone away, save it in case Dean's torch failed. The thought of being down here in blind black was too appalling to dwell on. I pitied the poor bloody miners who'd had to spend every day of their working lives down here.

'There's something up ahead,' Dean called out suddenly. He shone the torchlight on a plastic cylinder, white, dustbin size, lying on its side. The lid had rolled away and whatever had been inside it had seeped into the ground beneath our feet, dried into a dark stain.

The lingering smell was acrid, made me want to catch my breath. I pulled my scarf up over my nose. Dean rolled the thing over with one push of his boot to reveal a lot of labelling with some long, chemical-sounding names I did not understand, and a yellow triangle with a black exclamation mark which I did: *hazardous waste*. There was another label to indicate the contents were corrosive and flammable.

'This is what Nathan was on about,' Dean coughed, a hand to his mouth. 'Be careful where you step.' He aimed the torch back, directing the light towards the ground so I could pick my way. This stuff could probably melt boots.

Stack after stack of containers almost blocked the tunnel ahead, all displaying labels with cheery yellow triangles. Dean swore softly. He handed the torch to me, got out his phone and started taking pictures. *Chemical waste, medical waste*, I read as I edged my way past: *explosive*; *toxic*; *reactive.*

'Just small amounts of some of this stuff, if it gets into groundwater . . .'

He didn't need to finish, I got the point. *Acetyl Chloride*, I read, *Chromic Acid*. Chemistry had never been an interest of mine, so I was none the wiser. *Sodium Hypochlorite*, I'd heard of that one. It was not stuff you wanted to breathe in or splash on your skin.

'We need to prove where this stuff has come from.' Dean's camera flashed in the darkness. 'We need to find a company name.'

I wasn't enthusiastic about getting any closer to the containers. The lids all seemed to be safely shut but there must be a leakage somewhere. My eyes were watering, my lips stinging, I was starting to cough. Then, in letters designed for a cockroach to read, I found a printed name. *Dravizax.org*. 'Got it!'

Dean came to look over my shoulder. I pointed the light at the adjacent container and picked it out again. Now that I knew where to look, I could see it written on all of them. 'Dravizax, I remember it now.' Dean leant in close to take pictures. I could sense his mounting excitement. 'Their boss is pictured in a photo with Sandy Westershall,' I told him, my voice rasping. 'I saw it on the wall of his study . . .' My lungs were burning. I was finding it difficult to breathe.

Dean took the torch from me, grabbed my hand. 'Let's get out of here!'

We jogged on. I couldn't count the number of containers we passed, some stained brown at the edges, the plastic being eaten away by whatever was held inside. From somewhere amongst them I could hear an ominous trickling.

We didn't speak, tried not to breathe until we'd left the stacks of plastic drums behind. Ahead of us, tiny dark objects littered the ground like shrivelled leather purses: dead bats. The poor little buggers had flown too deep into the tunnel and been poisoned by the fumes.

Further on the air seemed to be cooling, clearing. At first, I thought we must be nearing the tunnel mouth, but Dean suddenly stopped and shone the torch beam upward over our heads. It was as if we were looking up from the bottom of a well, a stone-lined telescope with a circle of sky way above us. We could see a freckling of stars.

'Ventilation shaft,' I breathed. It would have been sunk when the mine was originally dug, to draw heat and fumes up from the rock face. It was criss-crossed by wooden rafters. Odd little pouches hung here and there, like old leaves clinging to a winter tree; sleeping bats. Disturbed by the torchlight and by our echoing whispers, they stirred and fluttered away.

'They must be the late sleepers-in,' Dean grinned. 'The rest will have gone a-hunting.'

We lingered for a while, breathing in cold, fresh air, gazing up at pinpricks of blessed light far above. Then we moved on, enlivened by the air, buoyed up by the evidence we had of the Westershalls' involvement with Dravizax. Now we just needed to get out.

The tunnel led us straight into Moorworthy shaft. It sloped down to the left, into the furthest reaches of the mine, down to the abandoned rock face. To the right it sloped upward, towards the entrance, to the way out. Our climb upward was made easier by artificially cut levels and pallets laid down to create a wooden walkway. Dean shone his torch over it. 'This looks recent. I bet they laid this down so that they could wheel in all those drums of shit.'

Our boots clumped noisily along it. Ahead of us the blackness was thinning. It might be night outside, but moonlight filtering through the entrance pierced the blanket of a deeper dark. A turned corner brought us our first view of the ragged rent in the rock that was the mouth of Moorworthy Pit.

Excitement and relief drained away. Dean swore fiercely as we stood and stared. A grill blocked the entrance, an iron screen of crossbars, set wide enough apart to allow bats to flutter in and out but not wide enough for anything larger, like us. Dean rattled the grill in vain and shone the torch beam over three separate padlocks. 'I don't suppose you happen to have a set of lock-picks about you?'

'Don't you?'

'Funnily enough, they're frowned upon in the police force.'

'Well, you're allowed to smash down doors. I've seen it on the telly.'

He gave a grim laugh. We were silent then, considering our alternatives. We could go back the way we came, past all the containers, climb back out of Applecote Pit. Or we could scale the ventilation shaft.

We looked at one another. 'Ventilation shaft,' we said as one.

* * * *

Climbing the shaft was just a case of stretching between the uneven rafters that criss-crossed it in a ramshackle ladder. It should not have been difficult, at least not for a long-legged creature like me; anyone shorter would have been stuffed. But the rafters creaked ominously beneath our weight and were slimy with bat shit. It was difficult to find a place for hand or foot to rest without slipping. After a few minutes we were breathless with the effort, and sweating. We rested, clinging onto our respective perches, Dean a few rafters above me.

'Are we getting near the top?' I called up to him. It didn't seem to me we were making any progress at all.

'About halfway,' he called back. He reached up, his hand searching to find a grip on the rafter above him. His fingers locked on, he took the next step up with his boot. There was a sharp crack. I managed to dodge as the splintered halves of a falling beam barely missed my shoulder, tumbled down into the darkness, hitting the ground with a crash. Dean was hanging by his arms from the rafter above him like an ape, his legs swinging.

'You OK?' he yelled down to me.

'I'm fine.'

I heard him straining with effort as he pulled himself up by his arms until he could balance his body over the rafter above him, get a leg over it and sit up.

I wasn't hurt but the fallen rafter had created a gap in the ladder too long for me to bridge. I looked around at the walls of the shaft, wondering if I could edge my way over and climb up the rock instead. But it glistened, oily with bat shit and damp. It didn't look safe.

Dean had both legs locked around the rafter he sat

on. He swung his body down, hanging underneath and stretched his arms towards me. 'I'll have to pull you up. It's the only way.'

'You're kidding.' Like a trapeze artist, he'd have to take the entire weight of my body and I'm substantial to say the least.

'Trust me. I trained in the circus.'

Very funny. But I didn't really have a choice. Muttering darkly about not dropping me, I reached up until his massive paw circled one wrist and then the other. Heaving and groaning, teeth clenched, he pulled me up until I was within clutching distance of the rafter above me, veins standing out on his forehead with the effort. As I grabbed the rafter and hauled myself up, he grasped my belt, helping to heave my body over until I could get my legs round it. I just prayed it would bear the weight of us both.

He sat up, grinning and wiped the sweat from his forehead with his sleeve. The mouth of the shaft was just a few feet above us. Dean climbed until he reached the top and stretched down an arm to haul me out. Solid ground had never felt so good. We lay on our backs in the damp grass, gasping like landed fish, heaving in the fresh air and staring up at a spangled veil of stars. I had lost all sense of time, had no idea how long we had been down in that tunnel, groping our way in the dark. It felt like days.

After the mine and the ventilation shaft, getting over the fence with its razor-wire top seemed easy. We just scaled the nearest tree, shimmied on our bellies along a branch and dropped down on the other side. All we had to do now was to creep quietly down the drive through the grounds to the gate and we'd be out. Safe. Free. Except that I knew we wouldn't. I'd already worked out what was coming next, knew it before Dean opened his mouth.

'Sandy Westershall and the boss of Dravizax,' he said, turning to grin at me. 'I want that photograph.'

CHAPTER THIRTY-TWO

We watched the lights of the house from behind a screen of rhododendron bushes, hoping to see them go out, hoping that the Westershalls might go early to bed. I didn't think it was likely myself, and all hopes were dashed when Emma's open-top car roared up the drive and quenched its tyres noisily in the gravel. Four people climbed out. I recognised Eddie, posh-boy drugs dealer, and Emma of course. I didn't know the other two. All four talked at the top of their voices as they weaved their way into the house and the door slammed shut behind them. A few moments later more lights flicked on downstairs and loud music began to blare from the windows.

Dean groaned. 'It looks like no one will be going to bed for a while.' We decided to work our way around the back of the house in the hope that it might be in darkness. The quickest way was to run across the garden, keeping well away from the windows and anyone who might chance to look out. The lawn was long and wide and running across it felt horribly exposed. 'Watch out for the ha-ha,' I warned Dean in a hoarse whisper as we scurried, almost bent double, across the wet grass.

'The what?'

'It's a hidden drop. Over to our right somewhere.'

We made it across the lawn and into the safety of the shrubbery, crawling in amongst sheltering shrubs. We stayed still for a few moments, watching and waiting. But we'd disturbed nothing except for a hunting owl, which hooted in a tree nearby, its call echoed by another, somewhere in the woods. We crept around the side of the building.

Lights were on at the back of the house and we could hear a radio playing. We sneaked to the kitchen window and peered over the sill. Mrs Johnson was busying herself at a granite worktop, in a vast kitchen that was strangely at odds with the rest of the house: functional and modern, all white walls and stainless steel like an operating theatre. Tray after tray of canapés was lined up on the surface and she was busy covering them with plastic film. At a central island, Moss perched on a stool, reading a newspaper, a mug at his elbow. It didn't look like either of them would be heading for Bedfordshire any time soon either. We hadn't seen any sign of Jamie or Sandy, but presumably they were in the house somewhere.

At Dean's signal we tiptoed away from the window. 'Let's find somewhere to wait until things quieten down.' We slipped down a path. A wooden door led us into a walled vegetable garden, and we crunched down a gravel pathway past serried ranks of cabbages. I could smell sage and fennel as we brushed past a bed of herbs. God, I was starving.

Further on we came to a standpipe with garden hose attached, turned the tap and bathed our hands and faces in the icy gush of water, rinsing lingering traces of contamination from our bare skin and cleansing our hands of bat shit.

We found shelter in a little wooden summer house with garden loungers stored inside; we grabbed the cushions and settled down comfortably on the floor. 'We might as well rest up for an hour or two,' Dean said, 'until they've all gone to bed.'

I awoke in the grey light of morning to the liquid song of a blackbird. For a moment I didn't know where I was. I sat up, staring around, rubbing my stiff neck. Dean was fast asleep on the cushions beside me and I shook him by the shoulder, hissing at him to wake up. He snored, stirred grumpily, blinked at me, uncomprehending for a moment, and then snapped into wakefulness. 'Christ!' he muttered, sitting up. 'That must be the longest I've slept since Alice was born!'

I thought we must have slept away our chance, but he was already staggering to his feet, stiffly stretching. 'C'mon.'

'They'll be getting up again soon,' I warned him as he peered out of the summer house and around the vegetable garden.

'Not if they went to bed late enough.'

The back of the house was still and silent, windows black in the grey gloom. I held my breath as Dean tried the handle of the back door. No luck. A few feet away a pane of frosted glass was set into the wall and the narrow transom window above it was ajar. Dean was considering it, eyes narrowed, calculating its size and I realised, with a sinking in my guts, whose backside would shortly be squirming through.

'I'll give you a leg-up,' he offered graciously.

I snagged my hair in the window-catch as I poked my head through the window, staring down at the windowsill below me, and the toilet beneath it, stretching down to brace my hands upon the sill as I wriggled my bum through the narrow gap. There was a water pipe running down the wall beside me and I transferred one hand onto it, so that I could swivel sideways, get one leg in, stand on the windowsill, then draw the other leg in after me. It was either that or crash headfirst down the loo. I stepped on the cistern, carefully on the rim of the loo seat, and finally, thankfully, stood upon the floor.

I opened the door and peered cautiously down the corridor. The house seemed to be sleeping, all quiet. From where I stood, I could see into the kitchen. I could also see a homely touch that had not been visible through the kitchen window the night before: a dog basket, a very large dog basket. Judging from the snores rumbling from within, it contained a grizzly bear. All I could see was a dark mound, which heaved with each snuffling breath. I crept down the corridor, my heart beating loud enough to wake it up.

As I hesitated in the kitchen doorway, the owner of the basket raised a black, doggy snout about an inch, studied me from a drooping eye and, after considering me for a moment, thumped its plumy tail lazily.

'Hello,' I whispered, in that soppy voice we reserve for dogs and small children. 'There's a good boy.' I crouched carefully, and reached out, praying I wasn't about to get my face ripped off. The dog, a Newfoundland, allowed me to stroke his head and licked my hand in greeting.

Just behind his basket stood an enormous fridge. I swung open the door, bathing myself in icy white light, and gazed upon shelves loaded with trays of canapés. I decided they wouldn't miss a few, peeled back a corner of plastic film, popped a prawn vol-au-vent straight into my gob and gave one to the dog. He sat up, suddenly awake and interested, licking his chops. I grabbed another two and we shared them in the same way. 'Now, you go back to sleep,' I mumbled, mouth full. I crossed the kitchen, shutting the door behind me so that my new friend couldn't follow me out, and drew back the bolts on the back door.

'What the hell have you been doing?' Dean demanded in a fierce whisper.

I swallowed hastily. 'Essential diplomatic negotiations,' I told him.

He frowned. 'Smells fishy to me! Now, which way is it?'

There seemed only one way to go, up a bare flight of servants' stairs with a metal handrail. We tried to tread softly but our boots clumped on the stone steps. We considered taking them off but decided that might hamper a quick getaway and carried on, on tiptoe.

At the top of the servants' stairs we found ourselves at the end of the wide passage that led down the hall to the grand staircase; mercifully, the floor was carpeted, a long Persian runner deadening our noise. The double doors of the ballroom stood open to our left. A grand piano occupied the far end of it, with rows of gilded chairs lined up to face it, ready for a recital.

We crept on until we reached the drawing room. The door was open, and I stifled a quick intake of breath. The four partygoers from last night were crashed out on the sofas, fast asleep. Eddie's cherubic features were squashed against the floral cushions, muffling his snores; Emma's legs, encased in black satin trousers, hung over the edge of another sofa, one silver high-heeled sandal trailing from her toes. The other couple were just a tangled heap on the carpet. Bottles lay scattered around the room and a stale smell of breathed-out booze hung heavy in the air.

We hurried on past, crossing the hall to the door of the study, turning the handle slowly, wincing at the soft click it gave on opening and slipped inside. The heavy brocade curtains were pulled back and the tall windows overlooking the lawn showed us that the sky was swiftly lightening, a faint glow warming the clouds above the horizon. I hoped no one in the house was awake and fancying an early breakfast.

Dean crossed swiftly to the display of framed photos on the wall. In one picture Sandy Westershall was shaking hands with the boss of Dravizax. In another, they were holding a big cheque between them, although it wasn't clear who was giving and who was receiving. Dean couldn't suppress a low chuckle as he framed each one in the lens of his camera and began snapping away. I was feeling jittery. Photographing the pictures was taking too long. It would have been quicker to nick them off the wall. I distracted myself by trying the drawers of the mahogany desk that occupied the centre of the room. I pulled at each of the brass handles, but all the drawers were locked.

'Now can we get out of here?' I hissed, as at last he slid his phone back into his pocket.

He didn't answer. Sitting on the desk was a laptop. He lifted the lid and pressed a button. I groaned as the screen lit up and the blasted machine played a tinkling tune.

'I don't suppose there's a spare memory stick anywhere.' He tried to open the top drawer, then picked up a paperknife. As he bent to insert it in the lock, I heard a click. But it wasn't the desk drawer opening.

Sandy Westershall stood in the doorway, dressed in pyjamas and a silk dressing gown; behind him stood Mrs Johnson, pale and grim in a hastily buttoned housecoat, and Moss, who had completed his rustic ensemble with a shotgun levelled straight at us.

'Johnnie, fetch Master Jamie, will you?' Sandy ordered calmly, without turning his head to look at her. He kept his gaze fixed on us. His skin looked yellowish and blotchy in the early light; he reminded me of a lizard watching its prey. I expected his tongue to flicker from his lips at any moment. He walked into the room; Moss and his shotgun came in after him. Instinctively, Dean and I raised our hands.

'Step away from the desk,' Sandy ordered, and we backed towards the fireplace. He drew a tiny key from his dressing gown pocket, unlocked the top drawer of the desk and brought out a pistol.

'You can lower that shotgun now, Moss. I'd really sooner you didn't fire it in here.' He brandished the pistol in his hand. 'This is far more suited to the purpose. The good old Navy Colt.' He smiled unpleasantly. 'It's amazing the things dear old Barty can lay his hands on if you ask him.' He cocked it, and with an almost casual air, aimed it at my head. 'I'm very disappointed in you, my dear,' he sighed. 'Now, who's your friend?'

Neither of us spoke. Sandy pressed the gun against my temple and ordered Moss to go through our pockets. I could feel the round rim of the barrel digging into my skin. I was fighting to keep still, not to betray the fear I felt by trembling. 'Chuck everything on the desk there. Make sure you get their phones.' Dean must have made a slight move. 'You!' Sandy rapped at him. 'Keep your hands up!' With his free hand he picked up Dean's wallet and opened it. 'Detective Constable Dean Collins,' he read aloud, as Jamie walked in. 'Oh dear, that complicates things rather.'

Jamie took the wallet from him silently and read it for himself. He flicked a glance at Dean, and then at me, his blue eyes cold. 'Juno. I knew I was going to have to do something about you sooner or later.'

'Like you did something about Nathan Parr?' Dean demanded.

Jamie raised his brows. 'And what do you know about Nathan Parr?'

'I know that you killed him, you bastard.'

Jamie picked up Dean's phone from the desk and began scrolling through it. 'I trusted Nathan. I thought he was a friend,' he answered, his gaze fixed on the images on the phone.

'I expected loyalty. I didn't know he was a liar and a spy.' He found the photographs Dean had just taken, of the pictures on the wall, the drums of hazardous waste down in the tunnel. He held up the screen so that Sandy could see. 'I think we'll just erase these.' Our hard-earned evidence vanished with one push of his thumb. 'Parr got what he deserved.'

'And Ted Croaker?'

'He got greedy, thought he could blackmail us.'

'So you threw him in the pit,' I accused him.

'Like the garbage he was,' he responded smoothly.

'You can't expect to get away with this,' Dean warned him.

Jamie just smiled. 'Moss, drive down to the farm, fetch Pike up here, will you?'

'Moss!' I called to him as he turned to go. 'You know this is wrong. You said yourself, too many have died already—'

'I don't know what you're talking about,' he growled, flicking a nervous look in his employer's direction before he hurried from the room.

'How can you do this?' I asked Jamie. 'Three people dead. What gives you the right—'

'Don't you dare lecture me about rights,' he countered, suddenly fierce. 'What do people like you know about running an estate, about heritage and tradition, about keeping farms from going bust and this house from collapsing, about responsibilities towards your tenants, towards the countryside, the land—'

'Which you despoil by polluting it?'

That pulled him up short. He bit his lip, but he didn't want to show that I'd touched him on the raw. He sat back on the edge of the desk and studied the two of us reflectively. 'Now, Detective Constable Collins,' he said after a moment, 'I think it's time we had a conversation about how much you and your superiors know about our little operation here.'

Dean grunted. 'You expect me to tell you?'

'Yes, I do.' Jamie smiled. 'The only question is how much you're prepared to allow the lovely Juno here to suffer before you come to your senses.'

Dean shot me an anguished look.

'Tell him to get stuffed!' I recommended.

'It's easy to sound brave now,' Sandy said sadly. 'You'll feel a little differently, my dear—'

'Mr Jamie, the catering staff will be here soon.' Mrs Johnson spoke with perfect calm, reminding him of an inconvenient fact, unfazed apparently by whatever he and his uncle were proposing to do to us.

Jamie frowned, irritated. 'This early?'

'They've been told to come in early, sir, there's a lot to do before the concert this afternoon.'

Suddenly I realised. The piano in the ballroom, the rows of chairs, the trays of canapés: today was the day of Ricky and Morris's concert. As if on cue, a blue van came trundling down the drive and passed the window, heading around to the back of the house. 'Special Events Catering' was written on the side. The staff were beginning to arrive.

Jamie swore. 'We can't have all these people about. Johnnie, just keep them out of the way, in the kitchen. Offer them breakfast or something.'

She was about to go out when he stopped her. 'Miss Jessica is still tucked up in bed. I don't want her coming downstairs and seeing all this. Take breakfast up to her bedroom, will you?'

'Of course, sir,' she nodded and left.

'What's going on?' a weary voice demanded from the hall. A moment later, Emma stood in the doorway, wobbling unsteadily on her high heels. She was as pale as a corpse and clearly suffering the effects of last night's party. 'You'll wake up the others.'

Jamie swore softly. 'Shit! Emma, are they still here?'

'They slept over,' she responded, gazing around with eyes narrowed against the daylight, her pupils no more

322

than pinpoints. She gestured at me. 'What's she doing here?' She scowled groggily at Dean and tottered into the room. 'Who's he?'

'Never mind, my darling.' Sandy turned towards her and I felt the release of pressure from the pistol as he turned away the gun. I let out a breath. 'They'll soon be gone,' he went on, as if pacifying a spoilt child. 'Now, why don't you go and wake up your friends and tell them it's time they went home?'

'But they might want breakfast,' she objected.

'Emma!' Jamie snapped. 'Just do as you're bloody told! Get rid of them.'

Moss returned at that moment, with Green Bastard Hat, who gave me a foul grin. He was obviously enjoying the prospect of a rematch.

'Perhaps all this had better wait until later, dear boy,' Sandy observed calmly, 'until after the concert. Lock 'em in the wine cellar till then.'

Jamie shook his head, 'Too many people around down here.'

'An attic, then.'

'What happened to Gavin Hall?'

Silence fell, as if they were stunned I had dared to speak. They all turned to look at me. 'What happened to him?' I demanded.

'It was his own fault,' Emma said petulantly.

I gazed at her in astonishment. '*You* killed him?'

She hunched a pettish shoulder. 'Eddie and I went into the woods just to . . . you know, take care of a little business . . . a little exchange.'

'Money for drugs,' I completed for her.

'Well, we didn't know the boy was there. He must have hidden when he saw us coming. He shouldn't have been snooping about.' She smiled. 'He was probably embarrassed about being seen with that stupid sword . . . anyway, he saw us. So what? There was no need for him to have run. We called out after him. I'd have paid the little creep to keep quiet, only . . . he leapt up on that tree trunk and . . .' She shrugged carelessly. 'That was that.'

I couldn't believe how little his death mattered to her. 'Didn't you try to help him?'

'It was obvious he was beyond help. And we didn't want to get too near him, frankly.' She giggled. 'He lost his specs as he was running away. I saw them go flying off. He was blundering about . . . you know, looking back on it, it was really very funny.'

Something exploded in my heart and in my head. I was on top of her, on the carpet, driving my fist into her face, punching her again and again. She tried to fend me off. Enfeebled by her hangover she could do no more than slap and scratch. I just went on punching.

Hands tried to drag me off, to wrench me away. Perhaps Dean used the distraction to make a move. I'm not sure what happened but a shot rang out. I turned to see him falling, heavy and slow until his body hit the carpet and lay still. I struggled against restraining hands to reach him. I realised that someone was screaming. It must have been me.

CHAPTER THIRTY-THREE

I had a vague, half-conscious memory of being dragged upstairs; lots and lots of stairs.

My body felt battered and bruised as if I'd been thumped repeatedly. In a dull, sickening rhythm my aching head throbbed. The taste of blood was in my mouth, I felt around with my tongue. My teeth were all present but my lower lip was split. I was lying on a floor. I felt it hard beneath my body and my exploring fingers touched rough wood planking. I opened my eyes and shut them again, assaulted by bright, grey daylight. There was a strange smell coming from somewhere – earthy, like mushrooms. I pulled myself cautiously up onto my elbows and squinted around the room.

The walls on either side of me slanted steeply towards one end. A small round window was set high into the sloping ceiling, letting in the unforgiving light. I was in an attic, directly beneath the roof. Perhaps a servant had once slept in this room. It was empty except for a metal bed frame, an old chest of drawers and Dean. He was there on the floor beside me. I scuffled across the bare floor towards him. He was lying very still, eyes closed, a deep frown between his brows, both hands clutched to his right side, beneath his ribs. Blood had seeped between his fingers and dried sticky, and run down to stain the wooden floorboards. The sharp tang of his blood filled my nostrils. He was pale, skin clammy, his scalp shining with sweat beneath his stubbly hair. But he was alive, his broad chest heaving painfully at each shallow, ragged breath. I whispered his name.

He opened heavy-lidded eyes and he swallowed. 'Sorry, Juno,' he breathed.

'Let me see.' I moved his hands away gently from his wound and pulled up his sweatshirt. An evil red flower had bloomed across the white T-shirt underneath, dark in its centre. The wound was bleeding, but slowly. I ripped off my jacket and shirt, rolled the shirt into a pad and pressed it against the wound. Then I placed his hands back over it whilst I unknotted my scarf to bind round it and keep it in place. This wasn't easy. I had to slide the scarf beneath his back in order to tie it around him, a manoeuvre that caused him to draw in a sharp breath and swear. The wound began to seep. It was obvious he shouldn't move, couldn't walk.

I bundled up my jacket and slipped it under his head. 'You're going to be all right,' I lied.

I didn't know what was going on inside his body, what organs the bullet might have punctured, what bones fractured, what vital blood vessels severed. But at least the bleeding was slow. Maybe we had some time. 'I'm going to get us out of here,' I promised, touching his hand.

He smiled weakly. 'Green . . . hat . . .' he whispered, '. . . out there . . .'

I pointed questioningly towards the door.

He nodded and winced. 'With . . . gun . . .'

'Don't talk,' I told him. 'Rest.'

'Juno . . .' he began, with what was obviously a great effort, 'if you get out of here . . . tell my wife . . .'

'Don't you dare!' I hissed at him. 'Don't you start all that "tell my wife I love her" shit! We are getting out of here.' I squeezed his hand hard. 'Both of us. Understand?'

He gazed at me sadly. 'Whatever you say . . .'

'Good. Now shut up and let me think. Close your eyes. Concentrate on keeping pressure on this.' I indicated the makeshift dressing over his wound and watched him as he sighed and his lids sank to a close.

I stood up, tiptoed to the door and listened. I could just detect a tiny metallic rhythm, no louder than the ticking of a watch. I recognised that irritating, teensy-weensy, cicada-type sound you hear when someone sitting close to you is listening to music through headphones. Green Bastard Hat was at his post, but only just. Good. I didn't want him to hear me moving about.

I checked the round window. I'd noticed a row of them in the roof on the day I first came to Moorworthy House, squinting up at them from the terrace below. They were set into the tiles, behind a balustrade. They were for show and didn't open. There was certainly no mechanism for opening this one. And it was very high up; all I could see through it was sky, a dull grey blanket of cloud.

I turned to examine the room for anything useful. The bed was no more than an iron frame without a mattress, not even any springs. The chest of drawers was old, probably Victorian, and heavy; two small drawers at the top, four bigger ones underneath, all with round wooden knobs for handles. I pulled out each drawer. Someone had lined them with wallpaper, pale green with cream flowers. But they were empty. Nothing I could use as a weapon or means of escape. No handy implement I could bash Green Bastard Hat over the head with. I stared in desperation around plain, painted walls.

In the corner, where the sloping ceiling almost met the floor, was a door about two feet high, the top edge sloping in line with the wall above it. I hunkered down for a look. Possibly it was the door of a cupboard, but as this was an attic, I thought it more likely that it gave access to the roof space. It could only be a small space, probably big enough to store a trunk or a suitcase or two. The door had no lock, just a plain brass knob. It turned, but whoever had last painted this room had glossed over door and frame together, effectively sealing the door shut. What I needed was something sharp enough to penetrate the coat of paint, and slim enough to slide between the frame and the door. I needed my penknife, which was lying useless on Sandy Westershall's desk.

I glanced over at Dean, watching the shallow rise and fall of his chest. He was still breathing, I didn't know if he was conscious, didn't want to wake him to a world of pain. Anything useful would have been emptied from his pockets downstairs. I wouldn't risk disturbing him. I sat with my back against the wall, thinking.

For the first time I noticed that the chest of drawers was set on wooden feet, only an inch or so high, meaning that there was a narrow space underneath. I lay down and peered under it. Something was lying in the dust, on the bare boards, something tiny but within reach of my fingers. I slid my hand underneath and managed to sweep out whatever it was. I picked it up and blew off the fluff. It was a key – not a door key or a key to the chest of drawers, but the kind of small, flat key that is used to open the locks on luggage, barely an inch long. I tested the end of it with my thumb. It wasn't sharp, but it was metal, and it was hard.

Holding it between my thumb and forefinger, I tried to force the end of the key between the little door and its frame. It wasn't sharp enough to pierce the skin of paint, but the edge was hard enough for me to scrape it away, a centimetre at a time. I began scratching at the paint repeatedly, tiny flakes falling off at first, revealing brown wood underneath. After a few minutes my hand ached from holding the key, from making the same tiny movement over and over. But suddenly the end of the key slid through into space. It was easier then, once I had made a start, scraping the paint off all around as I worked my way along the top of the door to the corner and then down the side. About halfway down I tried the brass knob again, thinking that perhaps I'd freed up enough of the door to make it move. But it wasn't until I had reached the final inch that I was able to yank it open.

The smell knocked me back, earthy like toadstools, the smell of a wet forest floor. It made me cough and raise a hand to shield my mouth and nose. I peered into the small, shallow space under the roof. I was looking up at rafters and the underside of original slates. A bright shaft of light, no bigger than a penny, pierced the dimness, shone through a hole where a slate had slipped to one side. I cast one glance back at Dean and then crawled through the door into the space beyond.

There was no room to stand up. I was on my knees. I poked a finger through the hole made by the slipping slate and managed to push it aside a little more. The circle of light became a triangle, big enough to put my hand through. I felt around, found the edge of the slate, felt the single iron nail that pinned it to the rafter, jiggled it about. It gave slightly but not enough for me to pull it out. I drew my hand back inside.

I was kneeling in what looked like orange-brown dust, the spores of dry rot. I recognised it from Boring Roy's description. The rafters above my head were shrunken and dry, deep crevices in the wood laced with tiny white filaments, delicate as strands of cobweb. Cotton-wool cushions sprouted here and there: the fungus that was gradually eating the timber away, crumbling it to dust.

I put both hands on a rafter and pushed hard. It creaked and rocked. I sat with my back braced against the wall, my hands against the floor. I bent my knees and kicked. The timber groaned. Fragments fell away – not splintering, not cracking loudly, but softly crumbling.

I gave another kick, both boots full on, and heard a tile slide down the roof outside. I paused, ears straining, in case above his music Green Bastard Hat had heard the noise I was making. I peeked back through the little door into the attic, but all was quiet and still – no angry footsteps, no sudden rattle of the key in the lock. Dean lay still as the effigy on a tomb. I didn't want to, but I closed the little door on him, pulling it shut.

Then I began kicking again, hard as I could. With each

kick I felt anger getting stronger within me, pounding inside me with each blow. 'That's for Gavin,' I muttered. 'That's for Ben, that's for Nathan.' I felt as if my thigh bones would break but I could see the rafter sagging beneath my onslaught and I kept going. 'That's for Nathan, that's for Dean—' No, not for Dean, because Detective Constable Dean Collins was not going to die, not if I had anything to do with it. Baby Alice, she of the crumpled red face and tiny pink fists, was going to get her daddy back.

They had taken away my phone and my penknife; they should have taken my boots. I just had time to fling myself to the side as the rafter disintegrated, collapsing in splintered chunks around me, sending up a cloud of thick, powdery dust. A slate, falling inward, caught me a glancing blow on the shoulder. I coughed, retched, struggled onto my knees. Another slate dangled by its nail before my face and I yanked it out. There was a hole in the roof big enough for me to push my head and shoulders through and I stood up. Coughing, eyes watering, I breathed in fresh air. God bless you, Boring Roy.

I saw grey sky and the tops of bare trees. Rooks, like scraps of burnt paper, rose up, calling. In front of me the roof sloped down about four feet towards a narrow gutter strewn with broken slates. In front of that was a stone parapet, about a foot in height, ornamental stone balls along its length. I placed my hands on the slates to either side of me and pushed down, wriggling my hips through the hole, out onto the roof. I sat for a moment, getting my breath. Then I stretched my legs down the slope of the roof and lay back, letting my body slide down, very slowly, until my feet were in the gutter. I bent my knees and lowered myself carefully, turning my body sideways so that I could rest in the gutter on all fours.

I peered cautiously over the parapet. It was a very long way down. Parked cars lined up on the drive looked like toys. The audience for the afternoon concert had already arrived. I crawled along the gutter until I turned the corner of the roof and peered over again. Now I was at the back of the house, looking down at the flagstones of the terrace.

Below me the long windows of the ballroom were open. It was a grey, still day, curiously mild. Perhaps those sitting in the concert felt a need for fresh air, but the open windows allowed the sound of laughter and applause to float up to me. Ricky and Morris were well away. All I had to do was to get down there, where they were. Somehow.

The old wisteria had been climbing the wall for generations, its furthermost tendrils stretched to a third-storey window about ten feet below me. But those delicate stems would not support my weight. I needed to place my feet on stronger boughs, further down. I knew that if I lowered myself over the parapet, even at full stretch, I wasn't going to reach down far enough. I would be a couple of feet short. I needed a rope, and there was no such help to hand.

I sat down in the gutter and unlaced my boots, taking them off and stripping off my socks. They were covered in a thick layer of dust; so were my jeans, which I stripped off next. It was tricky getting out of them; I had to lie down in the gutter to wriggle them over my hips. I sat up and peered over the parapet again. I didn't want to

332

do what I had to do next, but little Alice Collins was depending on me. I wondered whether I should put my boots back on. But for what I had to do next I needed to be able to feel with my toes, I needed the flexibility of a bare foot.

I took a deep breath and crawled up onto the parapet. My arms started to tremble and I felt sick, but I didn't have time for hesitation. Dean didn't have time. If I thought about it too long my nerve would fail. A foot away was a stone ball and I gave it an experimental shove. It didn't budge. I looped my jeans around it and tied them in a knot, like a scarf around the neck of a snowman. Then I wound the denim legs around my wrists. They would give me another two feet or so. I was sweating, though my mouth felt sucked dry.

I stretched one leg over the parapet, feeling for the wall with my foot, bracing my toes against the rough stone. This is the worst bit, I told myself. Remember when you did that charity abseil off Haytor? This is just the same. Except on the abseil, there were proper ropes and a safety harness, and instructors. My life did not depend on a pair of recently purchased, extra-long, pre-loved jeans. I do not pray to any conventional god. If I pray at all, it is to Cordelia. She is the saint who must intercede for me with heaven. I prayed to her now. *Don't let me fall.* And I swung my other leg down over the parapet.

For one horrible moment I dangled, legs flailing, arms at full stretch as I clung desperately to handfuls of blue denim, dreading the sound of tearing fabric, of ripping seams.

Good old Mr Levi. The jeans bore my weight as I clung, toes scrabbling until I found a foothold, a branch sturdy enough to take the weight of my searching foot, a slenderer stem within reach of my hand.

I let go of one denim leg and grabbed. My other foot found a place to rest. For a moment I just stayed there, breathing hard, my heart racing in my chest. Then I let go of my jeans with the other hand and grasped the stem in front of me. Applause floated up from the windows below. 'Thanks,' I muttered. I felt I deserved it.

Wisteria stems, when they are young and green, twine around each other. As they thicken and stiffen with age, the stems become twisted ropes, ideal for climbing. I clung tight with my right hand as I slid my left down as far as I could reach. I didn't want to look down, so my fingers fumbled blindly until they closed around a branch. Then I moved one foot and began to search for a lower foothold. I inched my way downward, hand and foot, hand and foot, placing each carefully, testing whether it would take my weight, before I dared to move on. Below me, I could hear Ricky playing the piano, Morris singing some fast-paced patter song, but I couldn't identify it, couldn't pick out the words.

I stopped to rest for a moment. My arms were shaking, my hands so slippery with sweat I was scared stems might slide through my fingers, leave me clutching at nothing but air. Autumn had stripped the wisteria of its leaves, leaving bare stems. Now and again a blackened, withered seed pod dangled in front of my face like an ancient runner bean. Wisteria seeds are poisonous, I remembered reading somewhere, and should not be ingested. I don't know why this struck me as funny – hysteria, I suppose – but I let out my breath in a silent laugh.

I dared not look down, so I looked up. I was below the windows of the third storey, which meant I must be drawing level with the windows of the second. Making progress, slowly. The fall would still kill me, but I wasn't going to fall. As I clambered down the twisted stems of the wisteria thickened and felt stronger. I dared to move more swiftly. The windows of the second storey were above me now. I risked a peep down, down to the wide-flung French windows immediately below me, down to the stone-flagged terrace just waiting to break my back, to smash my skull. For a moment the world swirled dizzyingly and I clamped my eyes shut. I clung on.

Then I heard a voice, far above.

'Look up, bitch!'

Green Bastard Hat was leaning over the parapet, aiming a shotgun straight at me. I froze, staring up at the barrels. I was a sitting duck. He grinned, his finger on the trigger. Then two things happened at once. He leapt back, swearing, swiping at something in the air that seemed to be buzzing around his head like an angry hornet. And I experienced a sickening sense of movement as the stems that I was clutching began to tear themselves slowly from the wall. I clung on as a hundred years of growth peeled itself away from its moorings. Branches snapped, stems slid through my fingers as the old trunk groaned and the whole plant arched away from the wall, taking me with it, dangling me over the terrace like a fish on a hook. Then the old trunk snapped. I seemed to be surrounded by a moving mesh of branches that landed me in a heap on the terrace and as I let go, slid me bodily through the open windows of the ballroom. Miraculously, I landed on my feet.

I stood there in my T-shirt and knickers, bare-legged as any warrior queen, as two hundred people turned to stare at me. Ricky, hands poised over the keyboard, gaped open-mouthed. In the one still moment before all hell broke loose, Morris, standing before the piano, managed a little smile. 'Hello, Juno,' he said. 'Good of you to drop in.'

CHAPTER THIRTY-FOUR

You can explain away a lot of things. You can, perhaps, explain the unexpected delivery by wisteria of a wild-haired woman in her underwear, covered in blood. But you cannot explain the presence in a locked attic of a police officer suffering from a gunshot wound. More particularly, you cannot explain it to other police officers, who seemed to arrive, as if by magic, moments after I had made my entrance into the ballroom.

Later, when things had calmed down, I asked Inspector Ford how they had arrived so quickly. Apparently, the police had received an anonymous tip-off from someone illegally flying a drone over private property that a woman was clinging on halfway up the wall of Moorworthy House while a man on the roof was pointing a shotgun at her.

By this time, I was decently covered in a coat belonging to Margaret, Wicked Witch of the West, and Dean had been carried off to hospital in a helicopter, which arrived, spectacularly, on the lawn; the Westershalls had been arrested for murder, kidnap and conspiring to kill a police officer and Mrs Johnson and Moss taken away for questioning. The last I saw of Green Bastard Hat was as he was trying to escape across the lawn, pursued by a string of uniforms. Way out in front of the pack, gaining on him fast, was none other than Detective Constable Cruella DeVille. I had to hand it to her, she could leg it.

'Go, girl!' I cheered her silently. But she came to a skidding halt, arms windmilling, struggling to keep her balance on the edge of a precipice as GBH dropped out of sight a few feet before her. Apparently, he broke his pelvis. Ha-ha.

He did nick the next available ambulance, though. And as there was no way that Inspector Ford was allowing me to go home without visiting the local accident and emergency, I was driven to hospital in a police car. As we swept out through the gates of Moorworthy House I spotted a vehicle parked across the road, and standing anxiously on the verge, Elizabeth and Olly. They waved as I swept by. I waved back frantically and cried all the way to hospital.

Most of the blood I was wearing was not my own. It belonged to Dean. I kept asking about him but all anyone could tell me was that he had been flown down to Plymouth for emergency surgery. Inspector Ford promised me an update as soon as he heard anything. And he would take my statement next morning. Meanwhile I had a lot of bruises and scrapes to be attended to. Elbows, knees and knuckles had come off particularly badly. I went through an hour and a half of antiseptic, gauze and wincing before I was finally allowed to go home. The doctor wanted to keep me overnight for observation, but I declined. I asked the nice nurse if she would order me a taxi.

'You won't need one,' she told me as she swept back the plastic curtain of the cubicle I'd been treated in. Ricky and Morris were sitting in the corridor in their dinner jackets and bow ties. 'These two gentlemen have been waiting to drive you home.'

But the wrong man died that day. It should have been wicked Uncle Sandy who made an excuse to go into the study, who put the barrel of the pistol in his mouth and pulled the trigger, but it was Jamie.

'Too proud,' Sandy said sadly, as the police took him away. 'Like his father, always too proud.'

'I didn't know you were watching Moorworthy House,' I said naively to Inspector Ford when he visited me next day.

He responded with the ghost of a smile. 'Just because you have an uncanny, and some might say, unfortunate knack of discovering dead bodies, Miss Browne, does not oblige us to let you in on all of our secrets.'

I felt like a fool. 'No, no,' I mumbled, 'of course not.'

'But I would like to thank you, Juno,' he went on, 'on behalf of Constable Collins and his wife and daughter. What you did was very brave.'

I blushed and came over all unnecessary and mumbled something incoherent. 'And he's going to be all right?' I managed at last.

The inspector smiled. 'He is.'

'So, what happens now, to the Westershalls, I mean?'

'Sandy Westershall will be charged with the murders of Nathan Parr, Ben Luscombe, Ted Croaker and the attempted murder of Dean Collins. In addition, Emma Westershall is facing certain drugs charges. Pike is in hospital under guard and will be charged with your attempted murder. Meanwhile our colleagues in London are interviewing the board members of Dravizax.' I must have looked taken aback at all this because the inspector laughed.

'Mr Moss has been very co-operative – singing like a canary, in fact. His conscience was troubling him. I don't think Mrs Johnson has any trouble with her conscience, but she knows which side her bread is buttered – and your own statement corroborates theirs to an extent. What you and Collins discovered in Applecote Pit and the tunnel leading to the Moorworthy mine is just the tip of the iceberg. Moss and Pike have been dumping hazardous waste for Dravizax in holes all over the country. The Westershalls are not the only landowners receiving a kickback from them – and Dravizax is not the Westershalls' only customer, either.'

I felt sorry for Jess. Her fiancé was dead and her father would be going to prison. And she'd known nothing at all about what was going on.

'And Gavin?' I asked. 'Is anyone going to be charged with his murder?'

The inspector puffed out his cheeks in a sigh. 'If Emma Westershall is to be believed, his death really was an accident. Unfortunately, we have not so far been able to lay hands on Mr Eddie Coates to get his version of events, but we will. Let's just say our investigation into Gavin's death is not yet concluded.'

Poor Gavin. He should have been the hero of this story. He should have been the one to slay the evil giant Dravizax with the Sword of Virangha. I took Olly to meet his parents and we showed them the film taken by the drone, film that showed Gavin waving and looking so happy. Olly sent it to their computer, so that they would have it for ever.

I went down to Plymouth to visit Dean in Derriford Hospital. By then the Environmental Protection Agency had moved into the mines at Moorworthy to begin removing the hazardous waste and decontaminate the site. Alec Pedrick had been taken on as a consultant to advise them about the bats. Apparently, they were due to hibernate very soon and there were great concerns about disturbing their roost.

When I got to the hospital, Dean's wife, Gemma, was by his bedside, along with Alice. I held the baby for a few minutes. She was sleeping soundly, her little pink eyelids tight shut. She didn't wake, but when I moved her rosebud fist away from her mouth, I swear she smiled at me. Dean was going to be fine after a spell in hospital and plenty of TLC.

TLC: tender loving care. It sounds great, doesn't it? I often feel I could do with more of it myself. But after a few days of Ricky and Morris clucking round me like mother hens, during which time Ricky stole my diary and cancelled all my appointments for the week, I decided there's a limit to how much TLC I can take. But we did rescue my van, my rucksack, my phone and, eventually, my jeans. And the Wicked Witch of the West got her coat back.

'We knew something was wrong when you didn't turn up,' Elizabeth told me when I finally made it to tea. 'We knew you wouldn't let us down without contacting us.'

Olly nodded. 'We called you lots of times.'

'I was probably in a tunnel.'

'So we decided to phone your friend Pat at the animal sanctuary—'

'And she was worried an' all,' Olly interrupted, 'because you hadn't turned up in the afternoon for your shift at the shop. And she'd been trying to get hold of you—'

And she phoned Adam and Kate, I said to myself. I'd already heard all this from the various parties concerned, but I didn't want to spoil Olly's story. Kate had insisted on contacting the police, but until I had been missing for twenty-four hours the local station weren't prepared to consider me a missing person. So they phoned them again next morning, when I hadn't come home for breakfast.

'It was Olly's idea to search for you next morning with the drone,' Elizabeth went on. 'He was sure you'd gone to Moorworthy—'

'I had this feeling!' he declared dramatically.

'We thought if we flew it over the Moorworthy estate we might see your van.'

'I'd parked it on Holne Moor.'

Elizabeth smiled. 'I practically drove past it, but Olly spotted it. I thought you might have gone walking and got lost on the moor. But Olly wanted to fly the drone over Moorworthy House one last time – and there you were!'

'I buzzed him, that fat bloke on the roof, the one with the gun, I buzzed him with the drone.' Olly's face was alight, blue eyes brimming with excitement. 'Did you see it?'

'Of course I did,' I told him. 'If you hadn't done what you did, I'd have got my head shot off.'

'We've got it on film. We had to email a copy to the

342

police so they could see it. It's ever so funny, all buzzing round his head. Do you want to see it?'

'Later,' Elizabeth said firmly. 'Let Juno eat her tea.'

She and Olly seemed to be getting on well. The house was more cheerful, somehow. Olly had always kept it tidy, but now it seemed brighter, more polished, as if it had lost its dusty corners, the rooms aired and more lived-in. There was a vase of fresh flowers on the kitchen table, and there were plans afoot to redecorate Elizabeth's bedroom.

I was sure Olly had shot up inches since I last saw him. Free from the fear of discovery, the burden of living on his own, he seemed to be blossoming. I asked Elizabeth how things were, later, whilst he was watching the new widescreen TV that she had bought.

'Bribery and corruption,' she admitted, 'but it works.'

I eyed her doubtfully. 'No teething problems?'

'Of course. But I persuaded Olly that we didn't always have to abide by Dolly's rules, we could make up new ones of our own, as long as we both agreed on them. And so far, it's working. Actually, I believe that he enjoys having someone to boss him a little, he feels more secure.' Toby, who'd been luxuriating in the heat of the Rayburn, decided to stretch his limbs and strolled over, leaping up onto Elizabeth's lap. She stroked his head pensively. 'We're happy here in Ashburton, Toby and me. I've joined the choir at St Andrew's and I plan to find a part-time job.'

'So you're going to stay?'

'There are important things to think about. Olly will have to decide on options for his GCSE exams soon. He wants to go on to A levels and university and the standard of his written English is dreadful. I've told him, it needs a lot of work. And I'd like to buy him a new bassoon. The instrument he has on loan from the youth band is pretty basic. He deserves a better one.'

'You think he has talent?'

'He has an excellent embouchure and, for one so puny, produces a pleasingly deep and mellow tone. The bassoon is not an easy instrument to play, which is why there aren't that many players around. A bassoonist is never out of work.' She laughed. 'Not that Olly is considering music as a career at the moment.'

'He still wants to be a chef?'

'No, at the moment he wants to be a vet. I think it's the effect of working at the animal sanctuary . . . By the way, I must tell you' – she lowered her voice so that Olly wouldn't hear – 'tomorrow, Prudence is coming to tea.'

'Who's Prudence?'

'Well, judging from the picture on Olly's phone, she's a rather scrumptious little thirteen-year-old. She plays the flute in the youth band.' She hesitated a moment, her expression becoming more serious. 'And we have moved Dolly to Oakdene, as far as our next-door neighbour is concerned.'

'So soon?'

'April was away for a few days. It seemed like the ideal opportunity.'

'And she has never questioned your being Olly's aunt?'

'Why would she?' She stroked Toby's head reflectively for a moment before she looked back at me. 'And I don't see any reason why Dolly can't continue to rest in peace beneath the flowers—'

'Ah!' I said, surprised. 'Olly told you about that bit?'

'He did. I was flattered, took it as a sign of trust. When

the time comes . . . which is whenever Olly is ready . . . we simply tell April next door that Dolly has passed away peacefully at Oakdene. Of course, we'll have to kill her off officially in order to stop her pension—'

'What about the death certificate?'

She raised a delicate eyebrow. 'It can't be that difficult to get hold of a death certificate. I'm sure one can be purchased on the Internet if one looks hard enough.'

'You can get copies of existing certificates,' I agreed. 'But the problem is no original exists.'

'I'm sure with a little careful forgery . . .' She shrugged. 'I shall do some research into the subject.'

You know, I like Elizabeth.

After Olly had shown me the film of GBH on the roof five times, including speeded-up and going backwards, he played me a tune, Elizabeth accompanying him on the newly tuned piano. It was a piece they were practising for his music exam. It had taken Elizabeth some time to persuade him that he should enter for it, but she was confident he would pass. As I walked down the path, they were engrossed in going through it again, happily arguing over some minor detail. They didn't even realise I had gone.

'I don't know if I'm ever going to be any good at this antiques business,' I confessed to Ricky and Morris.

Morris looked at me anxiously across a plate of home-made scones. 'Why do you say that, Juno? I thought you enjoyed it.'

'Well, yesterday, I went to the flea market and I picked up a really rare piece of Poole pottery that this lady was selling for a pound. It had been her mother's and she didn't like it. And I knew what it was really worth and how much profit I could make on it and frankly, I felt like a thief.'

'Oh, don't tell me—' Ricky began, rolling his eyeballs.

'So I gave her a fiver and . . .'

He groaned and pretended to bang his head on the kitchen table. 'Look, if the silly cow didn't know what it was worth, that's her fault. She could've looked it up on the Internet, same as you.'

'I know,' I conceded, 'and I know that the whole point of this business is to buy low and sell high and make a profit, but somewhere in the middle is what a thing is actually worth, its true value—'

'Which changes all the bloody time,' Ricky finished for me.

'It's true, Juno,' Morris agreed earnestly. 'Look at my teapots. Some of them are worth far more now than when I bought them, but some of them are worth a lot less. Antiques go in and out of fashion.'

'It's a game, sweetheart!' Ricky cried in exasperation. 'Dealing in antiques is just a bloody game. You take it all too seriously.'

'I suppose.' I wasn't convinced.

'A thing is only worth what someone is prepared to pay for it,' he insisted.

Morris patted my hand. 'Tell you what, there's an auction at Rendells later this week. Why don't we go together, see if they've got anything interesting?'

'Good idea,' Ricky nodded, lighting a cigarette. 'We can keep an eye on your bidding.'

'By the way,' Morris added. 'We need to ask you a favour. We've got a concert coming up in December at

Ashburton Arts Centre. Someone had to drop out, leaving the organisers with a gap in their programme, so they asked us if we would put together a concert, you know, fill in. And we thought the proceeds could go to Honeysuckle Farm, what d'you think?'

'That would be wonderful! Pat will be delighted—'

'Blimey! That's something I'd buy a ticket for,' Ricky exhaled, 'to see Pat looking delighted.'

'Don't be rotten.' I frowned. 'What's the favour?'

'Well, as it will be near Christmas,' Morris rattled on excitedly, 'we thought we'd end the show with our potted pantomime—'

'Oh, great!' I loved their potted pantomime. The two of them played all the different roles and the whole thing lasted just ten minutes.

'So will you help us backstage with the quick changes?' Ricky asked.

'Of course.'

'We thought that we might do it again for our Boxing Day party—'

'You are coming, aren't you?' Ricky interrupted.

Of course I was coming. No one in their right mind would turn down an invitation for their Boxing Day party. The food and entertainment were legendary. 'Can I bring Elizabeth and Olly?'

He waved his fag airily. 'Bring who you want.'

That stopped me for a moment, because the person I would have liked to have brought to their party was Nathan Parr. He had been on his way to meet me on the night that he was murdered. When police dragged his body from the wreck of his car, they'd found a red carnation pinned to his lapel. A thing is only worth what someone is prepared to pay for it and for the things Nathan valued he had paid with his life. I would like to have known him better, sorry that now that could never happen. I would never even see for myself what he looked like without that pirate hat.

My thoughts must have been written on my face because Ricky suddenly reached out a hand to cover mine. 'Don't be sad, sweetheart.'

I smiled at him, at both of them. 'I'm OK.'

'Talking of Christmas,' Ricky went on, in a very obvious attempt to distract me, 'have you thought about what you're doing in the shop? It's November already. You retailers have got to start thinking about these things. You've got to make a bid for the Christmas shoppers, you'll have to put some decorations up.'

'Pat and Sophie have got lots of ideas,' I admitted, sighing, 'but I haven't really thought about Christmas.' The only decision I had made was that I was going to take over Gavin's bookshelves. I was determined to have a bookshop in *Old Nick's*, and if no one else was interested in renting that unit, I would fill it myself.

'Well, we've had a wonderful idea, haven't we, Maurice?'

Alarm bells began ringing. Mentally, I braced myself.

'We can turn your back room into a winter wonderland – Santa's Grotto – bring in the parents with small kids – put on a bit of a show.'

'Well, I really don't think—' I began.

'Maurice will be Santa, won't you?' he rattled on. 'And I can be Professor Yule, in charge of the reindeer—'

'Reindeer?'

'Hasn't Pat got a reindeer?'

'No. She's got a llama . . .'

'Well, that'll do.'

It was only at that moment I realised they were winding me up. I didn't let on that I knew. 'What a wonderful idea,' I agreed. I selected a scone and helped myself to jam and a dollop of cream. I put the cream on first – this is Devon, we do things proper – then the jam. Then I took a big bite, sat back and let them prattle on.

ACKNOWLEDGEMENTS

My thanks go to Jenny Donaldson at Gnash! bookshop in Ashburton, for opening my eyes to the scope and beauty of the graphic novel. I'd also like to thank the Devon Bat Group for their very informative website, and for being there for the bats. I'd get nowhere without my agent, Teresa Chris, the team at Allison & Busby, and my husband, Martin, who locks me in the study and pours tea through the keyhole.

STEPHANIE AUSTIN graduated from Bristol University with a degree in English and Education and has enjoyed a varied career as an artist, astrologer, and trader in antiques and crafts. More respectable professions include teaching and working for Devon Schools Library Service. When not writing, she is involved in local amateur theatre as an actor and director. She lives on the English Riviera in Devon where she attempts to be a competent gardener and cook.

stephanieaustin.co.uk